CONJURE WOMEN

CONJURE WOMEN

A NOVEL

AFIA ATAKORA

THORNDIKE PRESS
A part of Gale, a Cengage Company

GALE
A Cengage Company

Copyright © 2020 by Afia Atakora.
Thorndike Press, a part of Gale, a Cengage Company.

ALL RIGHTS RESERVED
Conjure Women is a work of fiction. Names, characters, places, and incidents are the products of the author's imagination or are used fictitiously. Any resemblance to actual events, locales, or persons, living or dead, is entirely coincidental.
Thorndike Press® Large Print Reviewers' Choice.
The text of this Large Print edition is unabridged.
Other aspects of the book may vary from the original edition.
Set in 16 pt. Plantin.

LIBRARY OF CONGRESS CIP DATA ON FILE.
CATALOGUING IN PUBLICATION FOR THIS BOOK
IS AVAILABLE FROM THE LIBRARY OF CONGRESS

ISBN-13: 978-1-4328-8022-4 (hardcover alk. paper)

Published in 2020 by arrangement with Random House, an imprint and division of Penguin Random House LLC

Printed in Mexico
Print Number: 01   Print Year: 2020

For Mum,
the first storyteller I ever knew

■ ■ ■ ■

PART ONE

■ ■ ■ ■

FREEDOMTIME

1867

The black baby's crying wormed and bloomed. It woke Rue by halves from her sleep so that through the first few strains of the sound she could not be sure when or where she was, but soon the feeble cry strengthened, like a desperate knocking at her front door, and she came all the way awake, and knew that she was needed, again.

She unwound herself from her thin linen sheet. If there were dreams, she'd lost them now that she'd stood up. There was only the crying, not so loud as it was strange, unsettling. She smoothed her nightmare hair and made ready her face. Stepped out from her cabin, barefooted.

At the center of the town, between the gathering of low cabins that sat close and humble, Rue could make out the collection of folks, like herself, who'd been drawn from their sleep by the haunting cry. Anx-

9

ious, bedraggled, they emerged to suppose at that unearthly sound. It was a moonless night, the clouds colluding to block out the stars, and the crowd knitted itself tightly in a weave of black whisperings.

"You hearin' that, Miss Rue?" one of them said when she approached.

What little light there was streamed down from behind the crowd, hiding them, illuminating Rue. She couldn't make out their faces for the darkness but replied just the same. "Can't help but hearin'. That some poor sufferin' somethin'?"

As she walked, already she was holding herself straighter, prouder. It's what they were expecting. No matter how weary she was feeling on the inside, she knew she had to walk easy, like she were floating, same as her mama used to do. Rue's magic ought to be absolute, she knew, not come to them sleepwalking and unsure, or it wasn't magic at all.

"Never heard nothin' come close to that cry."

"Ain't no creature."

"That's one a' Jonah's li'l 'uns."

Rue knew they suspected already what child it was. That wrong child, born backward in a caul, a bath of black.

Jonah himself was opening the front door

of his cabin and stepping out of it, and Rue did hope that Jonah, calm and right-headed, had come to silence the rumors on his child. But there was no denying that beyond him was the origin of the crying. Even his tower-tall presence in the doorway couldn't block out the menacing sound.

"Miss Rue," he called, and his voice was thin like river silt. "You there, Miss Rue?"

Rue did ache for Jonah's predicament. She answered, "I'm here."

"Sarah's thinkin' the baby's took sick. She's wantin' you to look him over."

Rue stepped forward, took her time going up the few sunken-down steps to the little porch. She could feel all them eyes clinging to her back like hooks. At the top step Jonah, dark-skinned and strong and sure, reached down for her and took her elbow in his hand, guiding her. His callused palms were hard against her bared skin, rough the way only a man's hand had cause to be, and as he moved her through the door, he gave the point of her elbow a slow rub, a caress away from their fastened eyes.

"Thank you, Miss Rue," he said and showed her in.

The home was made up of two rooms, more than most folks could boast, though the thatch roof wept from some long-ago

11

storm. Rue followed Jonah to the front room's far corner where Sarah was knee bent, washing the children.

The tub was large enough to fit all three of Sarah and Jonah's little ones, but their elder boy and girl stood outside of it, naked but dry, waiting to be washed. Their faces were damp and ruddy beneath their high-yellow skin, like they'd been crying but had exhausted that sorrow, left it to the baby to do the weeping for them.

Inside the tub the baby was on his back looking like a white island. The steam rose up from his skin in waves. He was crying, Lord, was he crying. Rue heard in it a lost cry, and it was a call she felt compelled to answer, if not with comfort then with a mournful cry of her own. In the water beside the baby a chipped cup bobbed along the ripples created by his movements. It hit the walls of the tub out of time with the high, piercing whine that had snaked its way into Rue's dreaming.

When she leaned forward, the baby stilled his squall. He opened his eyes as if to look upon her, revealed the oil-slick black irises that had heralded his strangeness, that had prompted the name Rue had given him at his birth: Black-Eyed Bean.

Rue said to Sarah of the baby's eyes,

12

"They ain't changed." She spoke it low enough to be out of Jonah's hearing.

"No, they ain't," Sarah said, in just the same whisper. "He ain't changed."

There was no magic in birthing. No conjure, neither. The birth of Black-Eyed Bean had occurred one year back. Had begun no different than any other birth that Rue had known, and she had known many.

Rue just walked the women. That was it. All it took in the birthing room was good sense, the good sense that a thing hanging ought to fall, the way swollen apples brought their branches low before the apples plopped down to the ground. Shouldn't it be the same with a baby? Let them hang low in the mama when it was time to fall, the mama being the branch near snapping.

Since the end of slaverytime, Rue had birthed every last child in that town. She knew their mamas and their daddies, too, for she was allowed into sickbeds for healing and into birthing beds alike, privy to the intimate corners of joy and suffering, and through that incidental intimacy she had come to know every whisper that was born from every lip, passed on to every ear. She knew what folks said about each other, and Lord, she knew what they said about her.

13

What folks said about Sarah, Jonah's wife, Bean's mama, was that she was beautiful, and it was so. She was a fiery woman, petite as an ember but just as dangerous, with skin light as wheat. Sarah was one of those who had sung when she walked the birth walk, had done so the two births before this, sung and moaned and sung right up to the moment that her bigger than big babies came on out to the world. Sarah had sung while she was heavy with Bean, a sonorous song with no words but so much soul. Her one hand gripped on too tight to Rue's while the other hand beat out the tune she was singing against her sweat-slicked thigh. It was when Sarah's squeezing got too tight, the veins standing up like blue rivers in her high-yellow hand, that Rue started her usual worrying.

Truth was Rue didn't want nothing to do with any of that mess, the moan-singing mamas or the anxious daddies — when there were daddies — wringing their hats and their hands outside the door, or the wet and wailing babies, or, worst of all, the babies that came into the world just quiet, gone already before they ever lived, just lost promises with arms and legs and eyes for nothing. Why would she want to meddle in all of that?

As she laid Sarah down Rue had begun to think of how it all could go wrong, and if it did, what was she to do? Because just as easy as folks' praise came, it could turn to hating. Magic and faith were fickle. Life and living were fickle. And didn't Rue know that as well as anyone?

Still, when the time came for bearing down — the women praying with their cussing and cussing with their praying — it was in the way they looked up at her, weepy eyes filled with worship, that kept her door open. Like apples, babies came in seasons, and Rue would always tell herself in the lull, *Not next year. Next year I be done.*

Bean had been born in one such lull, Sarah being the fertile kind. The "Her man gotta do no more than look at her" kind, like Rue's mama used to say of the women who could show up twice in a year with their bellies making tents of their dresses.

It was easy going year after year with Sarah. She was still young, twenty-and-some, and already she'd made two babies who had been born after no more than the usual struggle. Still she stayed smooth and sweet, and her breasts remained like two fat fruits just shy of ripe.

"He's a'comin'," Rue had said, laying her open palm on Sarah's restless belly. How

Rue knew even before the crown of him started pushing through that Bean would be a boy she could not account for, not in words. There was just her knowing.

Rue had rolled her rough-hewn sleeves on up — just about everything she wore and ate and owned was a gift from those mamas who had no other way to pay — and she had knelt the way she had knelt near a hundred times now, though her knees did ache for it despite her youth. Rue was near-abouts twenty also if her old master's accounting was to be believed, not much younger than Sarah, though every day Rue felt more worn, like she were living out each one of her years double, aging out of time.

They'd grown up together, true, through slaverytime, wartime, freedomtime, but Sarah had kept herself young, and even here, at her most vulnerable hour, the sweat sitting on her skin had the audacity to glisten. In every way they were opposites — that was clear enough as Rue laid her thick dark fingers on Sarah's thin thighs and parted them.

"Lord. Miss Rue." Sarah sighed, praying to them both.

Rue had to love and hate equally being called *Miss*. She was every time reminded that she'd earned the title — and the respect

16

of it — only after her own mama's dying.

Rue's mama, called Miss May Belle, had gotten the kind of sickness that could not be seen and for that reason could not be cured. Its origins were in heartache for her man, Rue's daddy, who some said ran himself crazy for lust of a white woman.

Well, let folks have their stories. The only truth was he'd been hanged, strung from a tree just outside the town, his dangling toes making circles in the dirt as his body spun on the rope. And Rue had hardly known him.

She'd been under Miss May Belle's tutelage the whole of her life. From her Rue had learned one true thing, that all birthing was performance. Mamas were made to believe that a bit of pepper by their bed would ward off evil spirits, but it was only meant to cause them to sneeze if what was required was a good last push to get the baby out. Rue learned to tell women to blow into a bottle or to chew on some chicory or to squat over a pot of boiling water to make their babies strong, to make the birthing easy, to protect them in that most crucial hour.

Bean's mama was easy. Birthing came as natural to Sarah as it did to animals who

17

need only to pause and squat and be off again.

Rue knew that she ought to be glad of that, but she wasn't. Sarah was silk, free to slip from one type of wanting to another. Rue was rough, coarse linen, starched in her life. Freedom had come after the war for all black folks. All excepting Rue, she felt, for she was born to healing and stuck to it for life. And stuck to this place. Her own doing that, a secret curse of her own making.

"Lord Jesus," Sarah had crooned as she'd labored. She'd gripped the bedsheets near to ripping. "Get me through this 'un. I swear, Miss Rue, this here's my last."

Rue knew sure as she knew the sun would rise that Sarah would come up pregnant again soon enough. Weren't men drawn to her like flies to shit?

And it was on that thought, potent as a curse, that she realized something between Sarah's legs was going wrong.

Rue nearly drew away in shock. A black mass came out, all in a forceful gush. The coal-dark sack squirmed in Rue's hands. The blood that surrounded it was a red made more ominous by the darkness it covered. Through that black sheath Rue could make out the small surprise of a pale

18

face, the mouth working soundlessly, nothing like suckling but more like an old man chewing on the words of a curse.

It wasn't unusual for babies to come still wearing the veil. "It means good luck," Rue would be quick to tell the mamas when they saw the extra skin wrapped around their baby's heads, looking as final as a shroud. In a moment she could wipe it away, and the healthy wail would fight back the unsaid fright in the mama's eyes that from her womb had come something unexpected, something unnatural.

Bean made Rue's heart jump in absolute horror of him. She felt then that she knew him for what he was, a secret retribution for a long-ago crime, the punishment she had been dreading.

He was fighting, his arms moving inside that black wrapping like he was swimming, or more like drowning. She had never seen a baby so fully encased in the caul.

Rue forced herself to draw up the scissors she'd heated in preparation to cut the cord; she held them near the baby's mouth. Sarah had not moved at all from her position braced against the sheets.

"He come dead?" Sarah said, straining to hear the telltale cry.

Rue might've said yes. The black thing

19

curling and quivering in her palms stayed gasping. It could not break through the veil without her intervention. She might've left it to struggle or smother in its own black sheet.

"Oh, Miss Rue," Sarah started moaning, squinting her eyes hard to get a look at the bundle. "Don't say he dead."

A snip. That's all it took, and Rue did it. A snip beneath the little nose and then slowly, like peeling back the skin of a strange fruit, she shucked Bean of his dark veil and revealed him to the world. He began, finally, to cry.

"He alright," Rue heard herself saying. But was he? Was she?

Divested now of the veil that was like his second skin, his true coloring showed, lighter even than his mama was. There was no warmth to the color, only a pallid white. The baby's skin was peculiar dry too, near scaled, dry as though no loving had ever touched him. Rue had the urge to do more than rub him the way she did to warm life into all the new babies. She had, instead, the urge to scrub the strange skin clean off.

The eyes were the next shock, for when they blinked open they were full black, edged thinly in egg-boil white. The baby's eyes were the same glossy black as the veil-like husk that had held him. He rolled them slow and looked up at Rue as if he could see clearly through to every thought she had in her head.

When she'd sucked the blood from his nose and had him clean as she could get him she tied off the cord. Her practiced hands shook with the force of her nerves as she hurried to lay this strange baby by his mama's side and wipe off the stain he'd left on her hands.

Sarah looked at the child. She did not move to give him her breast. Instead she pulled the dirtied sheets around herself, and when Rue came to press on the stretched skin of her belly to check that nothing had been left in the womb, Sarah would not let her near. She wanted only to stare at her baby, not with that new-mama affection but in the very same way you'd stare at a snake you'd woken up to find coiled beside you in your bed.

"He's a big 'un," Rue said, to say something.

"Them eyes?"

"Like little black-eyed beans, ain't they?" Rue said. She wished she could snap back those words soon as they left her lips. She should have pretended that everything was as it ought to be. Her mama, Miss May

Belle, had she been living, might have had the words of reassurance, might have made the baby a miracle, for she had that way about her that Rue had never learned or inherited.

Sarah still would not take the baby up. His crying grew more shrill in the silence, like an accusation, and Rue felt she had to go on talking.

"Folks says babies born under the veil got the gift a' the Sight," Rue said. It was meant to be a comfort. It came out sounding grim as a burden. Rue found that she pitied that babe if it were true, for here he was not a clock's tick old and already he had to bear the whole knowledge of the world.

Rue had stripped the sheets, stepped out of the cabin without saying any more. There was Jonah, the daddy, waiting. He'd been keeping himself busy chopping more firewood than the hot summer day rightly called for, and when he saw Rue step out, he stopped mid-swing and smiled.

She studied him, taking in his sun-darkened skin and his eyes that were the same easy brown as the bark he was cutting. He bore no resemblance to his son. His son bore no resemblance to any living thing she had ever seen.

When Rue stepped forward, the bloodied

birthing sheets bundled in her arms, Jonah looked up at her with trepidation. He could not lend voice to the question that needed asking.

Rue spoke to spare him the effort: "You got yo'self a thrivin' baby boy."

His sweat-shining face broke out into a grin and before he could ask her anything more, she handed him the bundle of sheets that contained the damning black caul, bloody and shapeless, in its center. She knew even if he got a look at it, he wouldn't understand it. Men could not make sense of women's work.

"What do I do with all a' this?"

"Burn it," she said, telling him what he was needing to hear. "Burn it for luck."

SLAVERYTIME

1854

Miss May Belle had used to turn coin on hoodooing. As a slave woman she'd made her name and her money by crafting curses. More profit to be made in curses than in her work mixing healing tinctures. More praise to be found in revenge than in birthing babies.

In slaverytime a white overseer had his whip and a white patrolman had his hounds and a white speculator had his auction block and your white master had your name on a deed of sale somewhere in his House, or so he claimed. But those things were afflictions for the battered-burnt-bruised body only. Curses were for the sin-sick soul and made most terrifying because of it.

"Hoodoo," Miss May Belle used to say, "is black folks' currency."

She had admitted only once, to Rue, in confidence: "The thing about curses is that you can know who you've wronged the most by who you fear has the notion to curse you."

Black neighbors would whisper against black neighbors, sure, but by and by a white man would come from afar having heard of Miss May Belle's conjure, asking for cure of some affliction set upon him by an insolent slave, or even by his own white wife. Other slavefolk got hired out for their washing, for their carpentering, for their fine greasy cooking. Miss May Belle was hired for her hoodooing.

So it was that Big Sylvia, the cook of the plantation House, came to the slave cabin where Miss May Belle and her daughter lived alone, to ask after a curse.

Rue saw her coming from afar. The diminutive house slave had a crooked walk on bowed little legs, and Rue stood tiptoed in the cabin's one window, watched as the cook came down the dust road at dusk, determination in her little steps but a look like fear on her face, as she headed to the healing woman's house. Beyond Big Sylvia, Rue could see from where she'd come. Marse Charles's white-pillared House blazed big and hazy opposite the setting sun.

"Come away from there, Rue-baby," Miss May Belle said, and Rue obeyed her mama.

"Cook's comin' to ask after hoodoo. Now, you know that ain't nothin' that a child needs to hear 'bout."

How Miss May Belle knew before Big Sylvia's knock what the matter was Rue could not rightly say. But she tucked herself in the corner of their one-room cabin, balled herself small between the stove and the bedpost, and pretended at not listening.

Miss May Belle creaked the door open, allowed their visitor in.

"I ain't been workin' in the kitchen for some months now," Big Sylvia complained. She sat across the supper table from Miss May Belle and held out her right hand. It was bundled up covering a deep cut that some weeks back had near took away her fingers.

Rue's mama undid the bandages, revealed the hideous slash from finger to wrist. It was deep, angry, and oozing. Big Sylvia's dark skin and eyes were shining with a fever she couldn't kick. "It won't never heal 'cause somebody's put a fix on me."

"Who you think done it?"

"Who else? That woman. Airey. She the one that's took up cookin' in my place. She's been schemin' after it for years tryna get herself a place in the House."

Fact was that Airey's mama had been the

26

cook when Marse Charles had been a child, back when the plantation had been all but a few rows of hopeful seedlings. By all accounts Airey's mama hadn't been all that good of a cook neither, but there was no taking a white man from his auntie nostalgia. Airey had believed that because of her mama she was owed the kitchen, with a lineage as good as a lordship, but Big Sylvia had been bought special with commendations for her cooking. Airey had taken after her field-hand daddy instead, a sharp beauty but mule-strong, bred with hands for picking.

"Now I'm left to do the washin', even now I'm one-handed, mind," Big Sylvia said, "and Airey, she at the oven, got Marse Charles smackin' his lips after every meal, thinkin' he gon' get rid a' poor ol' Sylvia, maybe sell me next time the prospector come 'round, keep Airey on."

Miss May Belle tutted. She shut her eyes as if consorting with herself, let Big Sylvia stand there panting for a long while, working herself up into a deeper fury the more she thought on the unfairness.

"You best be sure now," Miss May Belle finally said. She rebandaged Big Sylvia's hand good and tight.

Big Sylvia nodded in earnest. "It was her

27

face I saw when my hand slipped and the knife cut me. Yes, I saw her face plain. She tol' me I was to die. Now I see her in my sleep every night. She set by the foot of my bed with the devil on her left side stabbin' at my hand."

To undo Airey's magicking Rue's mama advised that Big Sylvia circle her own bed with a sprinkle of salt, nightly. This Big Sylvia swore to do.

"But, Miss May Belle, how am I to get my place back?"

"You'll needa take somethin' a' hers. A piece a' her hair like. When you fetch it, come back to me on Friday."

Big Sylvia repeated her thanks over and over. Her rewrapped hand was thick and clumsy with the new bandaging, and she struggled at the pocket of her apron 'til she produced a silver dollar with the promise of more coin to be had come Friday.

"I'd bring you them good ashcakes a' mine too, but I can't cook nothin'."

Rue watched her mama slip the coin easy into her own pocket.

"We'll see to it that you back in yo' rightful place, by the Lord's grace," Miss May Belle promised.

Rue knew that her mama, thin as she was, did have a love for Sylvia's ashcakes.

■ ■ ■ ■

On Sunday her mama picked nits from her daddy's hair and Rue pretended to be asleep. Half days were for praying and for visiting, the one day that Miss May Belle saw her man. He journeyed from the neighboring plantation, a trip that took him 'til nightfall, and Rue would struggle to stay awake to see her daddy arrive in the doorway and greet her mama. From the bed, Rue strained to watch them, but she could see only their shadows twist and join, stretched out black and big on the dirt floor.

Rue fought off sleep but she did every now and again succumb, and their hushed, soothing voices — her daddy's as hard as timber, her mama's as soft as pulp — were sometimes things of her dreams. Her daddy sat on the floor between her mama's bare thighs, his head pushing up her dress, his lips kissing healed-up grazes on her kneecaps, and her mama sat in the chair above, cussing softly at tangles.

When next Rue jerked herself awake, her daddy had the doll baby in his hand. He was turning it around in his thick fingers. He was displeased; she could tell by the lines etching themselves deep in his forehead.

"It look like her," he conceded.

Indeed, the doll baby Miss May Belle had made of blackened oilcloth and stuffed with straw, though crude, resembled Airey completely. She'd embroidered a face even, wide-set eyes and a line of red stitching for Airey's thin, proud mouth. The doll wore spare calico and the type of red kerchief Airey often favored. But the most prominent detail was the mismatched black paint of the legs where Airey was known to have a pattern of birthmarks that freckled in circles black and white up to her thighs, varying smatterings where her skin lacked color, where she seemed almost to be white in unplanned for places great and small. The real live Airey kept the marks hid the great majority of the time, but everybody knew her to be proud on them; she'd hike up her skirt and show them off sometimes in the swirl of her dancing. They were there on the doll hid beneath the blue calico rag dress, beneath the white napkin, an approximation of the kitchen apron Big Sylvia coveted. Miss May Belle had made that miniature live.

"It's a sinful thing to be messin' with," Rue's daddy warned.

Rue watched her mama pause in her brushing. She kissed the very top of her man's head, left her lips there when she answered. "I won't hurt her none."

Rue's daddy set the doll down on the floor gentle, like he feared it might start living.

"What is it you mean to buy with all them silver coins?" she heard him ask.

Rue, dozing, might have dreamed the answer her mama gave her daddy: "You."

Friday came, wicked with rain, and Rue, sent to beg a needle off the seamstress, came back to the cabin wet and cold to find her mama and Big Sylvia, heads bent and conspiring. Beneath the doll's red kerchief Miss May Belle worked in quick, neat stitches to sew down the tuft of thick black hair Big Sylvia had stolen from Airey's comb.

"Didn't hardly think you'd get it," Miss May Belle said of the hair.

"Weren't easy. Had to wait 'til Sunday, 'til she'd gone visitin' that Charlie."

"They still courtin'?" Miss May Belle asked, though she surely knew — didn't she know everything?

"They fixin' to get proper married, iff'n Marse Charles will 'llow for it. And he surely will as he's like to get from 'em good strong babies."

Miss May Belle said nothing. Moved or

31

not by talk of sweethearts, she waited patient as Big Sylvia drew two more silver coins from out of her apron pocket. Only then did Miss May Belle hand her the doll.

Big Sylvia's eyes near gleamed. "What do I do?"

"Scratch off a li'l a' the black paint from the arms of the doll baby every mornin'. Not too much now, but slowly, and by and by you'll get what you're wantin'."

Rue wished for her own magic and, failing that, wished for coin. She had no use for money, had no sense of what she might or might not buy, but she wanted to feel them, as though the action of slipping her hands across the cool, rare bits of silver, carved with regal fine-boned faces, could elicit a kind of magic in and of itself.

She had been spellbound, at that small age, by the curious mystery of white faces. She saw so few, save the master and his sons, more rarely his wife. Rue was acquainted with only one white face in particular — Varina, Marse Charles's red-haired, freckle-spotted daughter.

They were both of them six years old, of an age because the master made it so. Varina's birth was the only clear bright star around which the younger slave children might revolve — you were born after or before the master's daughter, thereabouts. Rue could hitch her birth in the same season as Varina's and so they oft played together, kicking up dust in that one precious hour of their mutual freedom, between dusk and candlelight. Varina wasn't allowed to play at any other time, for the Missus was afeared that her daughter would catch color, spoil away her milk-skim skin.

Rue spent her own days in running favors, not much use in the field or the House and not yet as knowledged as her mama would someday make her. The best use for Rue then was to dash about with a basket, a bucket, or a broom, getting switched on her behind by older folks who complained she was too slow no matter how fast she ran. She was often underfoot. She was often forgotten.

Rue would sometimes look up at the House and spy Varina at the third-story nursery window, knew her for a white figure behind a whiter curtain, looking down. Did she appear wistful? Rue could not truly tell, not from that distance, not with only her hand over her eyes to shade out the midday sun. But it was as though Varina was looking out at her as well, with a sort of wanting, and Rue got to figuring if she ever had magic or money, either, she'd make it so the two of them could play and laugh together in the full sunlight as much as they could stand.

It seemed to Rue that Miss May Belle never had to fetch her coins but could will them into existence, suddenly flipping a flash of silver between her fingers in trade for something or other she was wanting. But where the source was was anybody's imagining.

Rue watched as her mama slipped her daddy one such coin of a Sunday. She slid it clear across the table over knot holes and scratches and set it in front of her man, who did not take it.

"Nah," he said.

Miss May Belle was sore. "Why?"

"That's conjure money."

"Money is money is money," she said and he said nothing and the coin gleamed between them.

"Or is it 'cause it's woman's money?" Miss May Belle took it back and Rue tried to watch where it went but missed that too, an illusionist's trick between her mama's delicate fingers.

Rue looked and looked but she did not find

the coins, not in the way she thought she would at least. One day, after the birth of the Airey doll baby that Big Sylvia had bought, Airey herself came to Miss May Belle to ask after a bit of hoodooing. She came upon them at the river where the water was swelled from a season turned rainy before its time.

Rue's mama said, "I been expecting you to come on round."

Miss May Belle was not the type interested in making enemies. That was the reason she only advised on how to make a trick, but she never did dispel it with her own two hands. She oft said, *The hunter in settin' his own trap'll sometimes spring it on himself,* which was true, of course — they were forever bandaging up men fool enough to go catching rabbits in the dark of night.

Rue looked over their visitor. Airey was truly pretty, made all of thick bones and fine features, such an amalgamation of two kinds of beauty that she could be admired from one direction and feared from another. But now in person it was clear to see just what Miss May Belle's magicking had done: The spangled pattern of white skin that had once been on her legs alone had begun to spread up her arms and to the sides of her neck and along her jaw and nose; a round

35

white swathe sickled around her eye.

If Miss May Belle was shocked by what she'd wrought, she didn't show it, and Airey for her part didn't look vengeful. She came to sit by them at the river's edge, and the reflection of her skin shimmering in the water seemed to make her look like the night sky dotted with stars, beautiful.

"I ill-wished Big Sylvia. I wanted her place in the kitchen," Airey began. "I been up all night with the regret. I had the notion that life would be easier for me in the House, but it ain't easier. No, life just ain't easy nowhere. That's why I come to see you."

Miss May Belle shook her head. "No more conjure," she said. "Y'all settle things between yo'selves. I'll tell Big Sylvia to be rid of the doll and she'll do it if I tell her to."

"Big Sylvia will get her place back I reckon." Airey held up her hands, and Rue saw that the affliction had taken over her wrists and her knuckles. The thumb of one finger looked as though the black had been sucked clean off the skin. "Missus won't let me cook her food no longer, won't let me touch it, thinkin' this is a sign of some cursedness. Marse Charles'll listen to her, just to quit her from her naggin'. He's like to sell me away the next time he's able."

36

"You wantin' a charm to prevent it?" Miss May Belle asked.

"No'm. I'm wanting a charm to help me run away."

Miss May Belle looked to Rue beside her and Rue knew the look, the get-gone look. This she was good at, becoming invisible on her mama's whim. She strode over to where the river started thinning toward the creek and let her mama think that she wasn't listening.

"I can't make you no promises," Miss May Belle said.

"You made this," Airey accused. She held out her arms.

Said Miss May Belle, quietly, "I don't know that I did."

Rue tried to look busy as the women kept on, talking in hushes. They were similar, Rue came to notice, both soft enough to be shaped by life and hardened by it too. She wanted to learn that type of woman magic also, thought she'd find it in the words they traded if she could only pick up on the strands, the half-speak adults often took up when they were aware of a child listening in on them.

"I can't risk it," Miss May Belle was saying. "Iff'n you do get away, but they catch on to it that it was me that helped you . . ."

It was a sentiment not worth finishing.

"Figured you say that, but if you got some charm some somethin', I can pay you for it."

"I'll give you this for free: Stick to the river," Miss May Belle said. "And don't you never look back for nothin'."

"I won't."

"Not even for yo' man? That Charlie?"

"He ain't comin' with me. He think he owe somethin' to these people. And I" — Airey kicked up water with her toes — "I can't be slowed down by nothing. They got all sorts of ways to weigh you down, don't they?"

Rue felt their eyes on her. She pricked up like a rabbit might at some slight, shifting noise, and saw Airey and her mama considering her with their hard, grave expressions, the far-off thinking look of grown folks.

Miss May Belle finally spoke. "You'll wanna rub oak gum on the soles a' yo' feet. Keep to the river, like I say. That'll throw the scent a' the hounds they gon' send. That's all I can give to you 'sides what you already know. An' if you can help it, don't let nothin' or nobody slow you down."

Airey agreed and left then to prepare for it, whatever preparing to leave your life meant. Rue watched her walking away. She was visible for a great distance, her proud back, her speckled legs bared.

By next morning Airey was gone. By late afternoon she was brought back.

They drug her by her arms through the whole of the plantation, her legs kicking, her body twisting and turning over grass and rocks and dirt in a never-ending dust-billowing futility.

The white men she hung between were catchers by trade. Marse Charles paid them handsomely, it was said, heaping handfuls of silver dollars, for the pleasure of having his favorite cook returned to him in a bruised pile. They left her tied up to a horse post out front of the House. Even tied down, Airey bucked and pulled at her bonds, and all the passing black folks watched her do it, watched her scream and piss herself and work one wrist free just far enough to yank at her own thick black hair. They weren't none of them allowed to go near, except at last for Charlie.

Marse Charles gave Charlie Blacksmith the honor of whipping his would-have-been wife, because Marse Charles himself could not be bothered to come out of the House, particularly as the clouds grew dark and it began to rain. He handed Charlie Blacksmith a whip, told him to use all the strength he'd use to forge a horse's shoe, and Marse Charles swore he would know it if he didn't. He'd be checking and expected to see ten good lash marks, drawn blood on Airey's bare back.

Assembled, bade to watch, all the slaves in the plantation came and stood in the yard of the House even as a driving rain fell and slicked down their hair and darkened their clothes and made everything cling.

Marse Charles was somewhere up above and Rue strained to make him out in the windows, not sure what to look for besides a hint of the shape of his darkness behind the billowing white curtains of his daughter's nursery. Or was it Varina herself that Rue spied, looking down on them? Rue searched so hard that after a while she made herself see shadows where there were none.

Whether he was watching or not, Marse Charles surely heard it when the first lick lay into Airey's back; it was that loud.

She hid her breasts the best she could with her arms wrapped around the post she'd been tied to, pushed them up against the raw, splintered wood. She shook with fear as the rain bounced off her, waiting for the fall of a hit she could not see coming, and her heaving panicked lungs rounded out her back just as the whip came down and split clean the skin. Charlie reared his arm just so far back that it looked like there was more force in the action, and the whip whistled through the air and another thwack landed squarely on her spine. Airey hollered and hissed and choked on her sorrow, gurgling out a bit of red-tinged spit. She'd bit her tongue.

"Boy," came Marse Charles up from the window on high. His voice boomed even over the rain, and Rue would have sworn that everybody assembled shook. Up above, Marse Charles was framed in an open second-story window, his arms braced against the sill, the tips of his curly dark brown hair catching the wet. He didn't have to say any more. Charlie brought down the whip harder the next time. Harder still the next.

Rue had to shut her eyes. But there was no blocking that high, fine whistle through the air or the sound of Airey's resistance, quieted from screams now to gut-deep moans then to a silence that seemed altogether worse.

When he was done, Charlie threw down the whip, his one act of defiance, let it sink in a puddle. There they were, the ten strips of open flesh wrought neatly in Airey's back

41

like the lines of crude accounting marks. Already the force of the rain was thinning out the intensity of the blood, and Rue found herself worrying, as the crowd began to murmur and break apart, that if Marse Charles didn't hurry down, he might not see the blood he was after as proof. They might, she feared, have to do it all over again.

Spring came on, like it did, and Rue and her mama stayed busy for seven straight days serving bitters to the slave folks Marse Charles sent through their cabin — a spoonful for each was meant to set his field hands ready for the coming heavy season. By the sixth day Rue was more than tired of looking into the pink expectant quiver of other folks' mouths, of observing their outstretched tongues and the dangling fleshy marble at the back of their throats. Her mama relegated her to filling up the waiting wood spoons, a dull task.

Rue looked up and there was Airey, strange to behold in the sunlight, nothing to her but deep pockets between her bones. Sunken — shoulders and chest and all around her eyes. Her voice came out gritty.

"Thank you," she said, "Miss May Belle."

Rue handed her mama a spoon, and her

mama began to hold out the mixture to Airey's small beak of a mouth, the edges of which were white and dry. At the last minute Miss May Belle pulled the spoon away. The pour puddled down to the floor, wasted.

"Rue-baby," Miss May Belle said. She didn't take her eyes from Airey. "Fetch me a cup instead."

Rue had to dig to come up with a small cup of tinned iron; she handed it to her mama, who filled it high with the bitters. Airey drank it all down at once.

"Meet me Friday night," Miss May Belle said, in a voice hushed and hurried. "If you still wantin' what you wantin'."

Airey nodded once. She gave her cup back to Rue and moved on down the line, her face betraying nothing, no elation and no fear.

The fact was if there was magic — and Rue, as a child, believed earnestly that there was — her mama had not taught it to her, had not wanted to.

On Friday night, Rue lay in their bed with her eyes closed, listened to her mama move about their small cabin. Miss May Belle took her time leaving, as if she sensed that the moment was not quite right or else sensed, in the knowing way of mothers, that her daughter lay tense and restless beneath the thin sheet ready to follow her into the night. They waited each other out.

Rue dozed and found herself dreaming. She was in Marse Charles's House, which could not be so, she was hardly ever allowed in there, yet there she was in a room so white it was as though the very air was ash water, the world all bleached through as though by lye. In the center of the white room was Varina, the master's daughter, waiting on Rue like a prize.

In the dream, Rue took Varina's hand, led her away, took her down the stairs from the nursery and through the House kitchen and there was Big Sylvia, removing ashcakes from her stove. The cook set them by the window to cool. Wriggling free of Rue's hold, Varina aimed to pluck one of them ashcakes from the pile. Rue hissed after Varina, but the cook seemed not to see the little girls. Instead Big Sylvia opened up the fire-spitting mouth of her stove, and now she drew from her pocket the little doll Miss May Belle had made of Airey. Easy as that she tossed it into the waiting fire. The doll made of straw and hair caught instantly in the flames, and Rue woke. She sat up from sleep sweating like she'd been in the oven herself.

The cabin was still. Miss May Belle was gone.

Outside the night was allover chill, the road through the slave quarter empty of souls. Rue steeled her shivering little body and walked through the blue midnight, picking her way to the river by way of recollection rather than by sight.

She found them a ways down the rushing river. Airey had her feet ankle deep in the water, and Miss May Belle had her arm in the knot of a tree. When she pulled her arm slowly out, the silver dollars in her hand glimmered in the moonlight. Miss May Belle had crossed to the river, was speaking in urgent whispers to Airey with all those coins offered in her outstretched hands. But Airey didn't move to take them, and Rue soon saw why. Miss May Belle, one by one, began to drop her silver dollars into the stream at Airey's feet. As she watched them go, Rue had half a mind to jump in after them. They made tinkling little splashes as they hit the surface and sparkled and spun, and then disappeared.

"Travel by night. Follow the shine of 'em coins on the river surface," Miss May Belle told Airey. Suddenly Rue could hear her

45

mama's voice impossibly clear, like it boomed from the river itself. "That shine'll take you where you goin'. All the way to the North."

They embraced there, one woman in the river and one woman out, and Airey who had become so thin looked frail in Rue's mama's arms, she seemed liable to disappear. But when Airey pulled away, her arms flew out with fearsome strength. As Rue watched, Airey seemed to dance, her bones twisting, reshaping beneath her skin; her pouting lips grew sharp and pointed and hardened and, by and by, her back arched and her frame narrowed, and Rue watched as Airey at last sprouted big, thick black wings.

Rue was still breathless in her bed when her mama returned some time later to the cabin. Miss May Belle crawled in quietly beside her, her body radiating warmth like a furnace. Now Rue was sleepless. She lay still the whole night trying to make sense of what she thought she'd seen. A woman become a bird. There was no sense to be made of it. It had to be dreaming.

The very first moment of sunup, Rue stole away, took herself to the river to see if she could make out any bits of silver in its bed.

But the stream was calm and quiet, undisturbed, reflecting the orange haze of the new-day sky. Rue looked upward, like the answer might be there. Her eyes traveled the neighboring trees and there she did glimpse, only in the corner of her sights, a starling — its skin oil black and spotted dazzling white — as it took wing and departed from the ledge of a branch, the starling just then starting to soar.

FREEDOMTIME

Black-Eyed Bean was one year old the night his eerie crying woke the townsfolk, roused them to stir from their beds and whisper their growing suspicions about him aloud in the street. Staring down at the odd little child, Rue was just as staggered by his eyes as she always was, as the folks out there were.

"The water." Beside the bathtub, Sarah spoke it low. "He got a fear a' it."

In the tub Bean thrashed as he'd thrashed beneath the black veil he'd been born in. Now his pumping little legs and arms managed to push round in a swirl the water that surrounded him as he howled.

"He ain't normal," Sarah muttered. "Screamin' like he's bein' killed soon as I lay him down to bath."

Jonah spoke up. "Miss Rue, ain't the water too hot? I keep sayin'. That water be too hot."

"Hush," Sarah said back. "I gotta wash him, don't I?"

Sarah was a sight, her hair in unkempt kinks beneath a roughly cut kerchief. The loose ends of the cotton were streamed through her orange curls like a shredded spider's web. She looked up when Rue stepped forward. Her eyes said something to Rue her mouth couldn't shape.

Rue knew Sarah was waiting for her to get down on her knees beside her and tend to Bean. But Rue couldn't seem to bring herself to it. She felt all at once afraid that if she picked up Bean she'd be accepting some responsibility for him, when all she wanted was to get away from him and his eerie black eyes.

Rue knelt. She dipped her hand into the farthest corner of the tub, keeping clear of where she might touch Bean or the irregular pattern on his skin. "Wet a bit a' cloth, wipe him down good 'til he grow older, 'til he get accustomed to bein' put in the deeper water."

Was it true what folks had been whispering — could Bean be something sinister amongst them, something dark come again? Rue pulled her hand away.

"It's mighty strange," Jonah said. He crossed the room in long strides to help

49

Sarah to her feet, and even when she was steadied he remained, Rue saw, his big hand gentle on the curve of Sarah's hip.

"I done him same as the others," Sarah spoke up. "The other children ain't never cried like that. They ain't never had such a fear of water as this." She shuddered. "Such a cry."

Rue looked at those others, Sarah's daughter and son. Like their brother, Bean, there wasn't much to be found of Jonah in them. They shared their mama's coloring, the orange-brown coils of her thick hair, and the fleshy fullness of her lips, the top slightly plumper than the bottom in them both. *My babies,* Rue's mama would have called them. She'd called all the children hers. Rue couldn't see them that way. When they were born, she handed the babies over to their mamas and she handed them over quick. Rue wanted no babies.

Sarah picked up Bean from the tub with a splash of bathwater. Curled up against his mama's chest, perhaps soothed by having his head near her beating heart, Bean quieted.

"He's surely different. But we all come different," Rue said. "Ain't no accountin' for why we is the way we is."

"That's for God to know," Jonah supplied,

50

but Sarah wore a scowl, like Rue ought to know as well as God did what the matter was with Bean. The skin of his legs bore the faint blue interlocking pattern that was like the scales on the back of a creeping serpent, and from his warm, wet body, steam still rose in coils.

"Awful sorry to call for you in the middle a' the night, Miss Rue," Jonah said.

But it had been Bean that had called for her. Hadn't she been pulled here by his strange cry?

Rue made her goodbyes, walked herself to the door. Stepping out, she fixed her face purposeful-like, ready to meet the waiting crowd, but there was no crowd now, only the dusty road and the moon that had found its way to shining. She felt unsettled in the bottom of her stomach where there began to be a small ache: fear.

She'd already started back for her own cabin when a hard grasp on her shoulder made her spin, but it was only Sarah waiting behind her, her arms free of children, her head now bare.

"Miss Rue, I got somethin' to ask a' you," Sarah said.

She looked unearthly tired. The front of her thin linen nightdress was dark with wet from where she'd held Bean firm to her

51

chest. Through the damp spot, Rue could make out the shadows of Sarah's heavy breasts, still weighted, a year out, with milk.

"Only I was wonderin'," Sarah spoke soft. "If you had somethin' I could use. To keep myself, I mean, to keep from havin' anotha conception. Secret-like."

Rue knew secrets. She knew many a secret stretched out amongst the folks of that little town, some shameful, some devastating, some just too sad to shape into words. Rue kept them all and kept them well and so folks kept giving them to her, their secrets. And never mind that she knew she had some of her own to keep.

"You come and see me tomorrow mornin'," Rue said, "and I'll have what you needin' at hand."

Sarah nodded and turned back to her door, in no hurry to return, it seemed, to what waited for her there. Rue watched her go, watched her slip into her home, haint-silent, like a ghost, and Rue could have gone on and done the same, but there was no man waiting on her and no crying child, or two, or three. So instead, by instinct, she turned the other way, the way of the wilderness, and started walking.

Rue knew that wide road made of dust better than any road in the world. She had walked it so many times she half-expected to see her own footsteps coming and going as she passed, from the slave quarters that were now their cabins, to the field that was now scorched land, to Marse Charles's grand old plantation House, which was now in the final stage of its ruination, and yonder, to the old white church.

The pillar was how she knew she'd reached what was left of the House. Part of the column still stood, as it had stood with its twin years ago, in a stately portico announcing the door to Marse Charles's mighty entranceway. Despite the ash, the pillar was nearly still white, and Rue stopped there as though knocking at the door of an old friend.

The foundation of the House remained enough to mark the ghost of the burned-down rooms and little more. In the very center of the entryway the old staircase made its way up five noble steps toward the sky, then dropped off in a crumble. Rue could, and did, walk straight through the ruin of the House. Her destination was not the House after all but the woods just beyond it.

Trees remember, Rue's mama would say, and so it was. The trees behind the House remembered the war and its bitter end, that southward march of the Yankee soldiers and the destruction that was part of their style of victory.

Folks didn't like to come out this far, not anymore. Cursed, they called it. Word was that Miss May Belle had hoodooed the whole of those woods, laid a curse with the strength of her love for her man and her sorrow at his dying, hanged from these very trees. For wasn't it in those same woods that they'd hanged Miss May Belle's man, lynched him and left him to swing? Miss May Belle's grief had risen there like a flood. Ever since, their used-to-be plantation had existed in isolation, like something locked away and forgotten by time. Nobody came into their town unmolested, folks said, and nobody came out.

If you went looting, you were like to disturb the dead, wake the ghost of Marse Charles, or worse, call up the jealous ghost of Varina, his one redheaded daughter and Rue's old playmate. Beautiful and scorned, they said of Varina, and robbed of her prime, she made a vengeful haint. Rue alone was not afeard — not of Varina, not of her spirit neither.

All that remained was dead earth, then dirt, then wild grass, peeking up from the ground in knots, and it was from this earth

54

that Rue found her plunder, the herbs she used for healing.

She sat down heavy amongst the weeds as though she were one herself. She felt awful weary, but there was solace in the mud, in the dew, in the aroma the earth made when it sighed. Rue made a bowl of her skirt and let the plants she picked puddle in her lap: feverfew for tired blood, stems and leaves and seed of boneset, longwood chips to be mixed with brandy, berries of pokeweed to soothe breasts grown sore and stretched, and the head of a daisy, which she simply found pretty and stuck, on a whim, into the coils of her hair.

There was a clearing where the grass didn't grow, and just past that was the only thing that stood tall in that Eden, save for the trees: a shed that had somehow kept all its four walls and the idea of a roof.

There, sat up with her back against the trunk of a tree, Rue stopped to think about Jonah, particularly his passing touch on her arm. She tried, with some difficulty, to remember the feeling of his fingers when he'd guided her into his house.

They had been rough when they'd closed on her elbow, as rough as the bark of a tree, and Rue loved his callouses, knew they were thick and well-earned. He'd go find work, when he could, on distant coastal islands, unloading at the docks, or handfishing in rivers. He'd be gone for long stretches of months when it was the season for it, and Rue longed after him when he was away, tried to imagine him there, on the banks of some other river, some river she could not know.

Maybe Rue could feel sorry for Jonah, this man with the calloused hands, or maybe she could feel what Sarah felt when he finally came home, for his woman must have felt some relief, and surely some desire. And thinking this, Rue ran her own hand up along the inside of her thigh. Her fingertips were rough from her work, certainly, but not quite so rough as a man's. There was a swell in her of sharper loneliness, but also of satisfaction, because wasn't she in her place, her conquered ground? And as she moved inside herself, all her roots and flowers scattered and fell, for a moment forgotten and reunited with the earth.

SLAVERYTIME

Folks said Rue's mama knew everything the foxes knew. Weren't they her eyes in the woods? Her familiars. How else to explain the uncanny way she figured out everything and everybody's business all about the plantation?

The feral foxes owed their life to Miss May Belle as if she was their own mama, for word was they were not foxes at all but the departed souls of used-to-be human beings, and Miss May Belle had given the dead a kind of immortality by hiding them at the edge of Marse Charles's land. In return they were her sharp eyes, her keen ears. Her survival.

Rue could not have said one way or another how far reaching Miss May Belle's hoodoo reigned. To Rue her mama was always a mystery; in all things great and small, she showed her magic as mamas do, with their knowing. Miss May Belle had a way of anticipating what trouble Rue would find herself in before Rue had even devised the trouble itself.

Trouble usually meant Varina, who often rebelled against her white girlhood and needed always an accomplice to witness her rebellion. That long last summer before the war came upon them, while the white adults fretted and the black adults labored, Varina ran half wild and took Rue running with her.

One particular high noon, they would make their way, without even having to agree upon it aloud, to their usual place by the creek. They ran despite the weight of the heat, trying to catch the wind with their speed; and running behind her on the narrow path, Rue had the pleasure of watching a number of Varina's ribbons come streaming off her curls and getting tangled up in high branches.

Varina reached the shed first and declared herself the winner in a race Rue hadn't known they were having. Then Varina, her cheeks still spotted pink, lay herself down on the grass and in one inelegant swoop divested herself of her calico dress and tugged her lace bloomers down to her ankles so that she sat in only her frilled white chemise, bare-bottomed and unashamed.

She said, "This time you can be Miss May Belle."

They had many fights about this very thing, who got to be the mama and who got to be the healing woman, so that most of their games ended in tears, and for a moment Rue hesitated, wondering what Varina was wanting from her to be so suddenly kind, allowing her to be Miss May Belle.

Before her mind could change, Rue put her hands on Varina's pale legs, examining as she had watched her mama examine, gently parting the skin between Varina's legs, which at first was smooth but prickled up to gooseflesh at her touch. Varina leaned back on her elbows and watched Rue as she did this, not closing her eyes as Rue sometimes did when she was pretending to be the mama. Instead Varina was following Rue's every movement with those blue eyes, which had turned a dull, still-water color in the shade.

"It ain't time yet," Rue said and took her fingers away.

"It is time," Varina spread her legs wider, which was not how the game was meant to be played. The mama was meant to just lie there and wait.

Rue thought about arguing this; she was

the one who had taught Varina the game and so best knew the rules. She was the one whose mama was magic.

"It's time," Rue agreed instead, placing both of her hands on Varina's mound, drawing her open with her thumbs.

"It's a big 'un," Rue proclaimed, imagining a baby with black skin and red, red hair.

"I'm so very happy," said Varina.

"What you gon' name him?"

"It ain't a him." When Varina was the mama all of her babies were girls, and Rue had explained again and again that it was not the mama that got to pick.

"It's a boy," Rue insisted.

Varina growled, or so Rue thought, the sound seemed so loud in her ear. Then she heard grass and twigs crunching underfoot and she pulled away as quick as she could, certain Varina's nurse had come over from the House and was about to catch them at something she would not like to see.

Varina crawled on hands and knees through the grass to reach out for her discarded dress, and so when the fox appeared she froze like that, her hand partway out in front of her as though she might ward him off.

The fox would be the silver of ash forever in Rue's memory, though looking back she figured it had to have been gray. It came all the way out to them, straight into the clearing as though to get a better look at the little girls, one black, one white, playing together in the high grass. Rue could not find her voice to scream, but she didn't need it. The fox stopped only to cock its head at them, then it turned its bushy tail and bounded away into the thick dark of the woods.

Miss May Belle must've gotten her whispers from a fox because come Saturday she beat Rue with the branch of a birch tree.

What Rue remembered more than the pain of the beating was the pain afterward when her mama left her to cry in the dirt of their floor and the pain the next day when they stood in the upper gallery of the church during the service.

The Protestant minister was a white man that Rue had never seen before and could not see now from where she stood amongst the other slaves on the second-story platform in the very back of the church. Rue's view instead was of backs of knees, hems of skirts, peaks of legs stockinged despite the heat to hide fatty veins. Through the gaps of the wooden slats the white folks below were a blur of somber colors made blurrier by the sweat that dripped down Rue's forehead

61

and stung at her already teary eyes, and every time any of the tightly packed black folks around her moved or sighed, itched or coughed, the wooden gallery would moan like it was about to give up.

Any other time to be brought to church would have felt like a treat, to feel the close press of those in the quarter that only ever thought of her as Miss May Belle's girl and to feel like one of them.

She dared to look up every now and then and caught sight of her mama looking tired, restless; she was not listening to that fly-buzz sermon. A sheen of sweat was in the bow of her upper lip, and beneath her one eye was a heavy purple bruise that spread down her cheek and sunk to yellow like the sky of a sunset. Someone had hit Miss May Belle and so Miss May Belle had hit her. That's all Rue believed to be true, but she couldn't think on the meaning of all that.

After the sermon they had to wait for the white folks to leave the church in a slow, repentant tide before it was proper for them to descend from the upper gallery one by one on the narrow stair. Rue and her mama were the last ones down. Miss May Belle pulled her along behind her, her hand holding on so firm that Rue could feel her mama's fingers on the shifting bones of her wrists. That shackling squeeze was as good a way as any for Rue to know that she was still in trouble, though for what she could not figure. Out through the double doors of the dim church they went, where, for a moment, Rue was so dazzled by the sudden bright afternoon that she could sense nothing but the heft of the heat and the sweetness of a voice that was singing.

It was Sarah that was singing. She stood in the very center of everyone, a matchstick of a little girl, small but made large by her inhibition, all eyes on her. The crowd hummed low in their throats for her but Rue could tell Sarah didn't need them, she could have found the tune herself. She was the tune.

"Thank ya', Marse Jesus," Sarah would sing and the crowd would mumble their encouragement, "Yessuh, thank 'im, Lord Jesus."

Rue's mama pulled her away with two hands heavy on her shoulder that set the rawness of her back to screaming.

Miss May Belle turned her around, and when she did Rue saw that her mama's hands were stained bright red.

"You bleedin', Mama," Rue said but her voice was empty of panic. It seemed to come from far away.

"Fool child, you the one bleedin'," Rue's mama said.

She could see Varina coming down from the House to meet them, and in her hands she held new, gleaming marbles. They looked cool, like ice, and Rue longed to touch them, but her mama was pulling her away.

"I wanna play with Miss Varina," Rue heard herself saying over and over. She was crying in her mama's arms, beating at her, kicking at her, sobbing. "I wanna play with Miss Varina."

Rue cried until she couldn't cry anymore and then she slept.

For a while she kept her eyes closed, just to feel. She was awake but not ready to wake up, and the pressure of her mama's hands on her bare back was a wonderful pleasure after all the pain that seemed to have been centered there. The herbs Miss May Belle used were sweet but strong and when she lay them, warm and wet, on the vertical cuts on Rue's back, what ought to have stung felt soothing, the reverse of a lashing.

Rue might have dozed back into sleep. She was thinking of a game of marbles that she was winning when she heard the rumble of her daddy's voice.

"What's all this now?"

Rue felt her mama pull away from her as a vanishing of her warmth. She peeked open one eye. Her father stood in the doorway of the cabin. He held a pass in his hand that was becoming crumpled in the fist he was steadily making. Rue's mama took the paper from him, set it down on a chair. She reached up to kiss him, and he let her for a while before he pushed her firmly away.

He touched the swelling colors on her face. "Who done this?"

Rue's mama touched the scar that showed beneath his collar and wrapped around to the front of his neck. "Who done this?" she said. She touched a scar that worked its way up behind his ear. "Who done this?"

He pushed away her hands.

Rue's mama said, "I caught Missus in a mood and with her ring on, is all. She remindin' me of my place."

"She puttin' you back in yo' place is what she doin'. She fear you know too much."

Rue's mama smiled, her swollen face stretched to a new pattern. "I do know too much."

Her daddy shook his head. "And the girl?"

Here Rue's mama was quiet for a long while. "I did it myself. I'd sooner I do it myself than let anyone else do it. But I gotta

65

make a show of it, don't I, so they know I'm raisin' her up right. It's gotta show."

"Why?"

"She's gettin' to like that Miss Varina too well."

Rue's daddy sat heavy on the end of the bed, and as Rue dipped toward him she closed her eyes down to the tiniest crack. He put his head in his hands, rubbed his fingers along the sharp edges of his hair. They made the sound Rue knew cats' fur made rubbed wrong.

"We some kind of family, ain't we," he said softly. Rue could feel him looking at her, though she'd shut her eyes at the first shocking vibration of his voice. "I guess she mine."

"Ain't no question."

"We got the same birthmark now," he said, touching Rue's back, and Rue near jumped out of herself when she felt his fingers just above the highest of her wounds. But like her mama's healing, his hands didn't hurt her. They were hard but kind, rough but warm.

"Don't you worry, baby girl." He was speaking to her in near a whisper. "I know better'n anybody. These'll harden so's the next time and the next time they beat you it won't hurt quite so bad."

Rue didn't want there to be a next time, but she felt something in his words and in his touch as though he was putting a kinship into her wounds, and a promise.

FREEDOMTIME

There was still the heat of the prior night's impulsiveness coursing through her when Rue forced herself to rise from her bed. Unrest thrummed in her body like drink, and she felt she could still hear the echo of Bean's crying.

She plucked the daisy from her hair, put on her sun hat, gathered a few necessities in a basket, and went calling on Ma Doe.

The day was cool as the night had been cool, and Rue had to keep one hand on the straw brim of her hat so as not to be caught unawares by the sudden whistles of wind. At first, she was not much disturbed when she encountered no one on her walk. It was midday. The men would be out in the fields; the women would be just now preparing their families' suppers.

The old slave quarters had been plotted, boldly, in the shape of a crucifix. Rue's cabin sat at the lowermost point of that cross and so she walked the whole of the empty dirt path, past all the quiet homes. Suddenly, she was struck with the absence of everyone, a swelling goneness.

Ma Doe was there when Rue stomped up to her door, and at her feet were two small children, just past toddling age.

"Afternoon, Miss Rue," Ma Doe said.

Rue drew off her hat and looked around. Long as Rue had known her, Ma Doe's slow gait was trailed by nine or ten children, all of them pickaninnies. In the height of slaverytime Ma Doe had brought up the master's four children too, Marse Charles's three sons and Varina. In rearing them, Ma Doe was known to be twice as fierce as any white governess. Since then she'd become something of a teacher, made a kind of freedfolk school right there in her home where the children scratched their letters into the dirt. Rue knew them to be letters but what they meant she could not say.

"Where's everybody got to?"

"That how you ought to greet me?" Ma Doe said. Rue shushed the woman by kissing her on her leathery cheek.

"What have you got for me, baby?" She locked eyes onto the basket Rue had tucked under her arm.

Rue had known that the charm she'd

brought would offer luck, of a kind. It was a packet of leather tied to the end of a coarse string, and it gave off an awful stink as Rue snaked it from her basket. In the crude pouch she had stuffed asafetida powder, as much as she could manage while holding her breath. Ma Doe had been in the habit of wearing such charms all her life, believing that they could ward off all manner of illness and evilness, and she believed her old age to be testament to that fact, though Rue had her doubts.

She tied the charm onto Ma Doe, who bowed her head to let her do it. The rope disappeared into the rolls of Ma Doe's neck. She tucked the pouch down her shirtfront and it was almost as if she weren't wearing it at all, save the smell.

"Now. You're wonderin' where everyone's taken themselves," Ma Doe said. "They all of 'em hotfooted it out a' here as soon as they caught wind a' the news. I expect they're havin' a fine time down there by the river. For Bruh Abel has come."

Rue startled at the name. She tried not to let her upset show but there was no hiding the quiver of discomfiture that ran quick up her spine like wind up a shivering tree limb.

Bruh Abel. She ought to have foreseen it. It was the season for him after all. He came

70

to preach and to perform miracles. And he came to spread lies, or so Rue believed. How else to make sense of such a rootless man? He traveled everywhere with a Bible in his hand and a too-wide grin on his face. He seemed to want nothing. In Rue's mind folks who didn't say plainly what they wanted harbored the most pernicious type of wanting.

She might have accused him of it if she weren't so guilty of the same. Wasn't last night in the woods evidence of her own reckless wanting?

"D'you plan to go hear him preachin', Miss Rue?" She heard the wistfulness in Ma Doe's voice, like the old woman wished that she could still walk well enough to go with the others to the riverside and see the preacher man too.

Rue closed the top of her basket sharply. "No'm, I'm mighty busy today as it happens."

In truth, she was not busy.

Ma Doe said, "Maybe just as well you stay clear of Bruh Abel."

Rue flushed hot. "Why you say that, Ma?"

Ma Doe shrugged, busied herself observing the letters of her two youngest students, nodding encouragement as they struggled to make meaning out of dirt. Rue doubted

71

the old woman could hardly see anymore with her overcast eyes. But who knew what Ma Doe observed keenly that others could not?

"I only mean that Bruh Abel's so much like your mama was. He's got a nose for secrets," Ma Doe said. "Mind he doesn't catch wind a' yours."

Rue could smell the charm she'd made. A damning stink, it was.

Rue hid herself in the thick of the woods. She simply wanted to know how Bruh Abel did it, how he worked his magic on her people. That was the reason why she was coming round the river from the woods where she could hide in the green and watch him, unobserved.

She feared that once again Bruh Abel had shown up to shake up folks' faith. It would be a fool thing to make an enemy of him. Ma Doe's warning against Bruh Abel's keen sense for secrets clanged in Rue's head. The old woman knew her words, knew to wield them expertly. And these words she had meant to singe in Rue's mind as a brand: "He's got a nose for secrets. Mind he doesn't catch wind a' yours."

But Rue just had to know what sort of healing Bruh Abel had brought with him, what he meant to do to settle folks' fear and gossip about Bean and the clamor of unease and superstition that Bean's strange eyes and cry had raised within the townspeople. The years had passed in peace since the end of the war, yet all of them suspected that peace could not last. They'd listened to cannon fire for so long that the quiet made them anxious, waiting for worse to come. Then a seemingly accursed baby had been born amongst them, suddenly, like a lobbed shell. They had been waiting on reprisal, reprisal for freedom, for the joy of being free, and when that reprisal wasn't fast coming, they'd settled on the notion that that punishment was finally come in the black eyes of a wrong-looking child. Truth was Rue had a share in their suspicions. She had shied away from Bean as they all had. Worse, she'd taken his wrongness as an omen against her and her past sins.

Rue figured it was no coincidence that Bruh Abel had shown up the day after Bean's horrid wailing. Why else had Sarah chosen that night of all nights to try to bathe her youngest child in hot water? Bruh Abel would soon come upon his seasonal visit and set his sights on Bean. He would find the evil in Bean and cure it. Rue felt she could not allow him to be the one to do so.

She came to rest at the seam of the woods and leaned the whole of herself up against the trunk of a tree, peered just around the edge so she could see them all there at the river, but they could not see her.

She hardly needed to hide, for they watched Bruh Abel as though he was the only thing worth seeing, that assembled crowd of poor black folks.

Bruh Abel was a fine-looking man in that same over-big suit, and he carried a Bible though he wasn't ever seen to read from it — likely he couldn't read at all. He didn't need to look at the Bible to do his preaching.

He could pass, that's what folks whispered about him soon as he appeared each year, as if in the time since they'd last seen him he'd grown more fair. He could quite easily pass for white with that light skin and the brown in his slicked hair showing golden in the sun, but sure enough he was colored and he did have a gift for speaking, for lighting up the dullness that had some time ago settled over that town like the dust of the Northern soldiers' retreat.

Bruh Abel spoke with the lilting tongue of some other county, it was there in the spin of his *r*'s and the caper of his *s*'s, a twang like the beginning of a good song. His talk was sweet to listen to and he did talk, not from a pulpit, not even from one place on the sandy edge of the river. Instead he walked back and forth through the crowd. Rue saw the way everybody trained their eyes on him. He'd sometimes walk straight into the river as though he thought he'd float right on top, and he didn't seem one bit bothered by the water that lapped at his ankles.

"Do y'all wanna hear what the Lord say?"

They did.

"He say this: 'It shall be on the last days that I will pour forth my spirit upon all flesh and yo' sons and yo' daughters shall prophesy.'"

Bruh Abel put his hands to his head, shut tight his eyes. "And yo' young men shall see visions. And yo' old men shall dream dreams."

He snapped open his eyes. He looked straight at Rue. Shocked, she didn't move, only dug her fingers deep into the unyielding bark of the tree, went allover still, except for the twist in her stomach, the unrest of her beating heart.

He was not looking at her after all, she realized; he was reading his scripture in the sky.

" 'Even on my bondslaves,' the Lord say,

'I shall pour forth my spirit. And *they* shall prophesy.' "

Bruh Abel walked through the crowd, searching for something. Rue searched with him, trying to see what he saw. There was Sarah standing off to one side, with her three children, Bean sitting on the swell of her bent hip. Rue imagined his sharp black eyes taking in the proceedings. Jonah, Rue noticed, was not with them. Bruh Abel's gaze seemed to linger on the family, on Bean especially, and Rue swore she'd holler, put voice to her panic, if the preacher man so much as picked Bean from his mama's embrace.

But Bruh Abel in an eyeblink passed the baby by. He came instead to Ol' Joel, a man who had always been old in all of Rue's memory. Time had made him stooped, as though he were perpetually bent over in the field. He still worked the land but walked everywhere with the aid of a cane, a fine lacquered wood one that had been given to him by Marse Charles, their former master. Bruh Abel stopped before him.

"You tired, Bruh Joel?" he asked him in the soft, sympathetic cadence of an old friend.

"These ol' bones ain't ne'er too tired to hear 'bout the Lord."

76

Bruh Abel grinned. "Will you pray with me?"

They prayed with their heads together, too quiet for Rue to hear from that distance. She watched as Bruh Abel placed his hands along the old man's back, Joel's crooked spine showing through the thin cotton of his shirt, and when they parted Ol' Joel had tears wetting the creases of his weathered face. He stood at least an inch taller, and with a flourish of strength befitting a man a quarter of his age, he tossed the cane into the river, where it hit the surface and then sank with nary a splash.

Bruh Abel next drew a young girl from the midst of the crowd. She was a wispy thing, maybe fifteen, that Rue had spoken to but once when she'd asked, quite earnestly, poor fool, if there mightn't be something she could take to stop her monthly courses for a turn or two. Now Bruh Abel was leading her into the deepest part of the river.

Rue knew that Bruh Abel had already baptized a number of people in the town, particularly the young women, but she had never seen it done. She watched now and it seemed almost loving, the way he tipped that young girl back. He controlled her fall with one hand on her shoulder, the other spread on her back, and he held her there, as strong as a pillar with the river rushing around his waist. Rue wondered what it must feel like, Lord, to be held down by that man's hand.

He kept her there so long, fully immersed in the name of the Father, the Son, and the Holy Ghost, and finally, when he allowed it, she came up gasping and saved, her hair matted to her forehead, her white dress clinging clear to her little bud-hard chest. He had his arm firmly around her as he helped her step high over rocks and branches. They made their way back to the shore.

Rue wanted to know what he would do next. It seemed impossible that he could perform anymore, dripping as he was, but he shook his hands dry and took up the Bible he'd bade someone hold, and he flipped it open, letting it fall to its natural, spine-worn center.

But the Bible's pages started fluttering in a sudden wind that grew into a gust and before she could reach up and stop it, Rue felt her hat fly straight off her head. It floated down from the woods, clear past the crowd, headed for the river or for Bruh Abel, she could not know, she did not stop to see it land. Rue turned and ran.

Surrender

1865

It had been in the high heat of June, two years back, that black folks had been freed. When the last of the war's rebel fires petered toward Surrender, gossip of that lofty Proclamation had finally come to their isolated corner of torn-up country, the weight of it all winnowed down so that they hardly knew what any of it meant, what good it might do them. Freedom seemed to them to be as useless as the currency of a nation that didn't exist anymore.

Then Bruh Abel had come amongst them for the first time. He appeared one hot day late that June, gusted in as unexpected as cool air off the distant ocean. He'd arrived only days after they'd been told that they, slave folks all of their lives, were free. That nonsense word. He had come and defined it for them, came into their square and showed them just how free could saunter

79

into town and say the most dangerous, daring things.

"This is to be our prosperity," Bruh Abel predicted. "This will be the Promised Time for black folks."

Lofty prophecies. They were wanting to believe him. Couldn't quite yet. Not without proof.

The first time Rue had heard tell of him she was eighteen or so. She had not yet become Miss Rue but was soon enough to be, for her mama, Miss May Belle, had not stirred from her self-made mourning after the death of her man.

It was Sarah who had stood outside of Miss May Belle's cabin door that day, waiting on Rue to come home. Sarah, eighteen too, and pregnant then with her very first child, wide with it, though dignified. With her hands cocked in the small of her back, arms akimbo, stomach jutting, she said, "The preacher man is in there with yo' mama."

"Who?"

There the preacher was, kneeling at Miss May Belle's bedside, a broad-shouldered man, stranger to Rue. His good brown suit was surely borrowed, stolen, or gifted from a white man, and either way Rue didn't trust him on sight. There was something

80

about his goose-greased hair, slicked down to beat back his curls. One stiff brown lock swung free as he bowed his head to whisper some private something in Miss May Belle's ear. Whatever he'd said, it had her lifting her bed-bound head for the first time in a long while. Miss May Belle laughed in that big-mouthed, full-toothed way that recalled the old days so much that Rue ached with envy over their closeness. She stopped in the doorway not knowing what to make of her mama's happiness, but distrustful of it.

"Come on, Rue-baby," her mama croaked. Miss May Belle had been thrifty by then with her words, mean even, saving her speech-making for phrases she deemed of the highest importance. "Come on and meet this Bruh Abel."

Bruh Abel said he was a traveling preacher. Way he told it, he'd got religion from a white master who'd set young Abel and all the other souls he owned to freedom just before the war.

Even back then, Rue had spat at the idea of a story that saccharine being true, but there was no denying that Bruh Abel's presence seemed to soothe Miss May Belle's sadness — a thing that Rue had never been able to do, no matter how badly she wanted to save her mama, not with all the roots and

81

herbs and tinctures in creation.

By that same evening it had been on everybody's lips that the preacher man had laid hands on Miss May Belle, given her a sip of good holy water. Folks said that she had sat up then and spoken clear from her mad stupor for the first time in weeks. They said that this newcomer must be a real man a' Jesus if he could so ease Miss May Belle's pain, a woman who'd eased the pain of so many.

Rue sat with her mama that night, watched her sleeping. Outside she heard them all begin to hum a song of Bruh Abel's. *Lord laid his hands on me.* By the tilt of their voices they were going toward the river, carrying him away amongst them in a swollen tide of worship.

When their voices grew dim and distant enough, Rue had gotten up her courage and stolen through the night. She'd made her way to where Bruh Abel's scrawny mule was hitched up and asleep, left alone to guard a saddlebag filled with the preacher man's belongings.

Suspect, she rooted through his trinkets. There was a knife atop a folded piece of paper, which, held up to Rue's candlelight, bore long-scrawled blue letters through the thin skin of a badly wrinkled envelope.

There was too a pockmarked brass harmonica and a fat button trailing string, but there, beneath that clutter, were three small vials, the exact thing she'd been after. They were markless bottles with cork heads that trapped in them clear liquid. As she wrapped her fingers around them they rolled and clinked together ominously like glasses for a toast. She took one out and put it to her eye to see what it held, and with that done and yielding nothing, she pulled up the stopper and put the liquid to her tongue. It was a mad thing to do. She was killing herself if it was poison that this strange man carried. Still, she did the same with every one of those little bottles, licked the tip of the cork, sipped up the residue on every single one of them, and came quick to realize they held nothing more than a bit of whiskey watered down.

She'd known him for what he was then. His was a clear-water cure sweetened with nothing more than clever words, a con man's type of conjure.

Did Bruh Abel know she'd done all that? There was something in the way he looked at her all the times he came back after, season after season. Like he was itching to accuse her if only he could figure just what she was guilty of. They were suspect of each other, she and him, from the very start of their acquaintance, and the askance Bruh Abel sent her way only got weightier after Miss May Belle passed. Rue had not been near to comfort her mama when she finally went to her rest — but Bruh Abel had been. They said he'd been right beside Miss May Belle, praying and holding her hand.

Miss May Belle's final curse would go on and outlive her. It was said that she laid it in her grief after her man had been strung up, lynched for lusting after a white woman, or so the story went. Miss May Belle cast her agony over the whole of Marse Charles's burnt-down plantation, folks said, and over the wilderness just beyond.

After the war came Surrender and in that time of flux, of fortune and misfortune, of raised white flags and dead white folks, Miss May Belle had believed, or so it was told, that the only way to keep their isolated plantation and the colored people in it free was to keep them chained up, to make for them a master out of the invisible white of the river fog.

This master was not a fat-bellied cotton king in a big white House — was not, as it was told, a master at all but was in fact a conjure come to form as a haint. A ghost was said to weave in and out of the woods surrounding their town on gray nights, was said to wail and to howl, to rule the packs of rabid foxes that overran the unkempt wilderness. The haint she'd made, they believed, lamented the lost war and the Lost Cause. Was said to be so greedy over the land as to keep away all the other whites who might covet their little lost country.

But nothing comes free. It was a tale oft told that Miss May Belle had made her curse like as if she was sat at a blacksmith's wheel, so expert had she honed her hoodooing, as though to make a double-edge sword, for hadn't all their white folks died as she had foretold? Dead but not gone. Three years after the war, still among them, their white masters were ruling over them as ghosts. Haints in the woods. Haunting.

After Miss May Belle died, they said the river swelled up fit to weep for her. It occluded the roads and the old byways; it ruined the roots of the trees. Living water, it swallowed up the old, proud stalks of cotton, and still the river rose. And Miss Rue, the only one left to sustain her mama's curse, found herself afeared of what the river water might dredge up, secret things better left hidden that haunted her, a curse that might rise to the surface.

In that same season of Rue's fear, Black-Eyed Bean was born, as though he were the new leaving of an old black tide.

FREEDOMTIME

One night, just after Bruh Abel's arrival, the plantation's old corpse bell snuck its way into Rue's dreaming. She was shocked awake, halfway out of bed and partways dressed when she put it together that what she heard was the ringing of that church bell that had no earthly business being rung.

The evening was a perfect mirror of the night that Bean had cried and unsettled the whole of the town. Rue could see it on folks' faces that they were thinking the same. They stood in the road, hesitated on their porch steps.

The bell stilled to silence, and there was Sarah with proof that Bean was not the cause of the disturbance, for she had come amongst the crowd with the baby asleep and silent on her shoulder.

And there was Bruh Abel too, pristine in his good pressed suit.

"What's the cause a' all that commotion?" he said.

Didn't the man ever sleep? For he looked always ready to come amongst them. Rue squinted to see which house he had come from, where he had been fed and bedded for the night. There was always some or another of the womenfolk after having him stay with her family, taste this and that bit of cooking.

"The bell," folks were telling him now. "Ain't heard it ring in an age."

It had rung harshly only once and then again weakly like somebody, or something, had only the strength or the daring to ring it but the one time and no strength to stop the clapper from coming round the second time and giving out one more hollow knell.

Bruh Abel looked at Rue. His expression was one of benevolent amusement, like he'd figured out the lesson but was ready to let them struggle over learning it.

"What y'all think that clanging was, Sister Rue? You know this here town better'n I."

Rue kept her face hard. "There's an old fall-down church way out what used to belong to our marse."

"Is that right?" Bruh Abel said. "Maybe I oughta take up preachin' there?"

"You wouldn't want to," Rue said in a

rush. "The ol' church just about come to its collapse durin' the war. More like than not that sound we heard was the old bell fallin' over, breathin' its last."

"Just as well," Bruh Abel said. Did he wink or was it a sparkle of starlight? "Me myself, I prefer to pray with nothin' but sky between me and the Almighty."

He shepherded the townsfolk over to their homes, easing their worries. Rue didn't follow after but kept her sights on the east horizon where she knew the white church stood just as strong and sure as it ever had. She feared the ringing would sound again. But all was as silent as silent got.

When all the good folks of the world were sleeping, Rue crept out of her cabin. She had not been out in the woods for some days. She'd stayed away too long. Now she felt she'd grown arrogant in things kept hidden, grown too proud and sure. Bruh Abel's coming had stoked a fear in her. Ma Doe's warning about secrets clanged. She had let him catch wind a' her alright. But she wouldn't allow him to discover the precious thing she kept hid.

She had feared she'd become lax on her sojourns, forgot to make certain that no one saw her coming and no one saw her going when she made these clandestine trips of miles to the old white folks' church with a brimming basket of secret provisions in tow.

In slaverytime, the black folks had been taken to that church like a marching army, driven there by their Missus especially, who seemed to think on it as her Lord-ordained duty to save her black folks' souls on the one day a week her husband wasn't breaking their bodies.

There was a rectory there meant to house a minister Marse Charles had never been able to entice to stay, no sir, not out there in the heat and the solitude of their vast land, not amongst his slaves, who outnumbered his white family something like one hundred to one. Marse Charles had ousted all his white neighbors over time, bought up their land, and made himself an island in the center of a wilderness sea so impenetrable few would brave it, even, or especially, a man of God. Marse Charles hadn't cared much for religion anyhow except to pay a minister every now and then to make the trip out of a Sunday to say, "Slaves, obey your earthly masters with fear and trembling," and then be gone again. Eventually, the South had fallen in surrender and all those white folks were busied with a different manner of praying.

Now Rue's lone penance was an irregular one, and it had naught to do with God. But times like these when the townsfolk got to gossiping, when an unrest settled around Rue skin-close as clinging vine, she had to go and look at the church, even if she couldn't always bring herself to go all the way inside. It was enough to know that the woods and the church were undisturbed, the double doors still shut like she'd left them last. Rue would set down the burden of her basket, stand on the steps, and breathe in the still of the wood and know that all was calm and right, and then she would journey back to the town.

It was Ol' Joel who caught Rue this night as she made her way back home. He grabbed her at the last half mile where the trees grouped so thick that even the river lost its way. He seized her by the arm and squeezed, his grip surprisingly sure. He squinted at her as the crickets chirped their alarm. There was a sour smell about him stronger than his usual rotgut stink.

She took in his shriveled frame, the way his body seemed to tremor with impatience beneath his nightclothes, a thin shirt with the buttons mismatched in their holes. And he was leaning again, on that old lacquer cane. Had the river brought it back? Spat it up like something distasteful? Or had the whole scene been bunkum, with Bruh Abel brandishing a smartly painted stick?

Rue loosed herself from Ol' Joel's hold.

"Miss May Belle, where you think you comin' from at this hour?"

"It's Rue," she corrected.

Ol' Joel waved that fact away. "You best stay clear a' patrolmen. It's after curfew."

"No, suh." Rue spoke in slow, gentle rolls like she was calming a spooked horse. "Ain't no curfew no more. Remember? Ain't no slavery no more. War's been over and we been freed."

Ol' Joel scratched at his hair, a meager snowcap that looked alarmingly bright next to his blue-black skin. He was old, folks said, so old he dreamed of Africa, woke some nights and thought that he was there again. Was this one of them nights? Rue took him by the elbow and tried to guide him home with her. In the morning he'd be back to himself, sharp-minded as a laid trap and just as likely to bite. But the sun would dip low again and so would his senses. It was a madness that reminded Rue so much of her mama's final demise that she could hardly wait to be away from him.

"I know what you been doin', May Belle. Don't you deny it."

Rue patted his elbow and sighed. "Been doin'?"

"I seen you with her."

"With who?"

"That haint in the woods."

Rue halted at the gravel road, stopped at the head of the cross that started the old slave quarters that were slave quarters no more. She could turn around now. No one would have seen her with him. She could lead the old fool back into the tangle of woods. Turn him round 'til he worked himself lost. She could make the trees swallow him up if she needed to.

"Ain't no haint in no woods," Rue spat.

"I seen you with her." Ol' Joel tried to free his arm from the crook of her elbow. She wouldn't let him. She had a hold of him and he was curling in on himself, his lips flapping, his voice rising near to a holler. "I seen you walkin' through the trees with her, visiting her, whispering with her. I seen you summoning her. The haint. The ghost."

"Stop that. You ain't talkin' sense." Or he was talking too much sense for her to stomach.

"You a witch, same like yo' mama was," he said, and Rue did not know if he was accusing her mama or her grandmama. He'd got his generations, his healing women, all tangled.

"Y'all alright? I heard hollerin'."

Rue was more relieved to see Jonah then than she could say. He came up the path to them quickly, threw her a knowing look as he steadied Ol' Joel. Jonah's broad, sure frame towered over Rue and the sunken old man both.

"Marse Charles'll hear of it," Ol' Joel kept on. "Just you wait, now, Marse Charles'll see to ya."

Rue looked to Jonah but it seemed neither of them would correct Ol' Joel, would tell him that Marse Charles was long dead. If Ol' Joel could not recollect his own liberation then he was locked in a different kind of hell from which there was no emancipation. Rue would pity him if he hadn't made her so afraid with his accusations.

"I'll take him home, Miss Rue," Jonah said. "Thank you fo' findin' him."

Rue nodded, tried to come up with more, some easy explanation should Jonah ask just how Rue had found him so far from her own home, so very late at night. But Jonah was preoccupied with the care of Ol' Joel, who struggled against him too — whose hoarse voice took up a cry again: "She turnt yo' baby evil, Jonah. He a devil, ain't no flesh a' yours. She made him in the woods

94

from river water, from clay. I seen her."

Bean. He was speaking on Bean.

"I seen her."

But Jonah shushed him, led him away, and still the old man raved 'til he got so far out of earshot that Rue couldn't make out what he was muttering, couldn't account for which things were lies and which things were truths so that all of it began to feel, not like words, but like a danger rising up all around her.

SLAVERYTIME

May 1861

Miss May Belle says: Marse Charles comes to me talking about War.

He don't knock. He walks straight into my cabin in the very middle of the day, something he ain't ever hardly do no more. I'm warned of his coming before I even see him 'cause outside the slave quarter goes allover hush except for the trumpeted-up sounds of slaves attending to hard work. The repeated greeting comes out like blackstrap molasses, bitter as it is sweet, "Good afternoon, Marse Charles," and it ripples all the way to my doorstep. But the wave of fawning gives me time to sugar up my countenance so I'm smiling like I ain't got a thing to hide when my marse comes charging into my cabin.

He sits hisself right down in the center of my bed, says, "It's to be war, May Belle. Do you know what that means?"

I ain't say nothing, ain't know what to say. I'm sweating. It's one of them blazes-hot days that drag long, never-ending, what with tending to my work round the plantation. The sick and the soul tired, the overworked and the underfed. *War,* my marse is saying, and nervous sweat drips down my spine like lazy sap off a sycamore. Is he asking if I know the meaning of the word?

"Where's that girl a' yours?" Marse Charles looks round my little home like the cramp of it displeases him. I smile so that he keeps his eyes on me instead of picking out anything that might be amiss. But I don't like him asking after Rue and I know I can't answer the truth, which is that my Rue's like as not off mischiefing with Varina, his white daughter.

"Rue ain't here, suh," I tell him. "I sent her to look over Homer."

"Who?"

"Field hand what fell over in the heat yesterday."

"He malingerin'?"

"No, suh," I say. "Homer done fell over onto his threshin' knife."

Marse Charles grunts. "You teachin' yo' girl yo' knowledge?"

"Sure am," I say, and that much is the truth. Ain't that the deal I have with my marse? He keeps my child in his ownership and I make her worth the owning. Marse Charles has far sights. Already he's thinking when I'm dead and gone he'd like to have another healing woman trained up. I can't fault him that, or fault Rue neither. Ain't every woman's daughter made from the death of the mama, somehow or another?

"War," Marse Charles mutters.

So we back on that? I shift from foot to foot impatient to have him outta here but not fool enough to let him know it. I do not wish Rue to be witness to this visit. My child may be knowledged in healing, but she don't know nothing of the ills of the world, and I intend to keep it that way long as I'm alive and able.

Marse Charles unbuttons his shirtsleeves at the wrists, rolls the cuffs up; he's mad enough to near rip the good fabric.

"This bastard Lincoln, he's took the reins and now he's smartin' at the loss of us Southern states," he says. "As well he might, seein' as we make all a' America's worth on our goddamned backs. Now we Southerners are seein' our own way, son of a bitch won't let us go free."

Marse Charles leans his big body back. My thin mattress in its creaky wood frame shifts noisily beneath him. He works at the worn leather of his belt, struggles to reach the buckle under the paunch of his belly. When we was both of us young and his stake was new, Marse Charles was lean, strong. Ambitious. Now he's the most prosperous landowner for miles and miles. His fields spread; his body do too.

"It's an ungodly business, Belle. I've just had a letter from an associate who witnessed the siege. He's thinkin' on sellin' his slaves all away. Better that, he's sayin', than the Northern hounds descendin' to take his property away by brute force. Cussed coward." Marse Charles punches his meaty fist into his empty hand. "I sure ain't of the same mind."

I'm glad to hear it. Every soul sold away feels to me like flayed skin ripped off the flesh. I keep my face peaceable.

"But if it is to be war," Marse Charles goes on, "changes gotta be made round here."

"How you mean, suh?" I don't much care at all about his gossip of war. Ain't I fighting little battles every day just keepin' his slaves alive on his behalf?

But I gotta keep talking. Keep his attention on me and no place else.

"You let me know who ain't pullin' his weight, May Belle. If there's a hunkerin' down to be done, that'll be where I start sellin', you hear?"

"Yes, suh," I say. It's a sick power, but it's a power, ain't it? Who stays? Who goes? Keep his eyes on me.

Now that Marse Charles has mastered his belt buckle, he shucks off his pants. Leaves them to fall in the shape of him on my floor.

"Come here, May Belle," he say.

I kneel between his legs, keep my eyes on him, only on him. Can he tell I'm afraid? Scent my fear?

He partway lowers his drawers, just enough so that they choke at his thighs, and I can't say if the flush that flames his cheek is from bashfulness or exertion. Or shame.

Two weeks back a canker bloomed up like fire, red and angry, on the tip of his prick. Now it's given over to a blotchy red rash, like I told him it would. Marse Charles come to me too late with the symptoms of this sickness to nip it early. He delayed over the choice: me or the white doctor a county over. But the white doctor's a relation of Missus's. And Marse Charles told me that he could not live with the guilt if his wife was to hear of his ailment. More like, he can't live with her exiling him from her bed once and for all.

"The rash is clearin' up some," I tell him, and it is too. It ain't too proud to say the truth. I do good work.

"I've heard passin' talk 'bout the mercury cure," Marse Charles says. "Men say after a few rounds, this dang sickness gets all the way cleared."

I suck wind through my teeth. "Sure, suh. Can't be sick if the cure done killed you."

He chuckles, rubs my head like I'm his best dog. I help to get him back into his pants so he don't go bending over. Eyes on me. Only on me.

"You stay takin' the rabbit root," I tell him. I've got his cure ground down to a fine powder and always at the ready, thank the Lord, so it's enough to give him a pouch with one hand and guide him out the door with the other.

"Y'all will keep all I've said to yo'self, Belle?" He says it to me sweetly, as if I'm a good friend doing him an easy favor, instead of a bit of good property without even the right to say no when it comes to touching his pockmarked pricker.

" 'Course I'll keep it hush," I say, and it's a lie. There's a number of his favorite house girls that I've already warned after. Little use a warning is. I keep the rabbit root at the ready for them also.

But it ain't his sores he's speaking on.

"No sense worryin' the lot of 'em with

101

talk a' battles and warrin'." Marse Charles inclines his head in the general direction of his fields, like to encompass the whole of his three-hundred-odd slaves. "They'll be afeared over nothin', get wrong ideas in their heads. They can't understand, they're like children. Not you though, Belle," he says fondly. "You about the smartest nigra I ever did meet."

He bangs out of my cabin, satisfied. I stand alone, shaking for long minutes, 'til I'm sure he ain't comin' back.

"He gone," I say at the bed. "You can come on out now."

My man slides his body out from beneath the wooden bed frame in slow inches 'til he's all the way clear. I try to help him up, but he refuses my hand. It's afternoon and he's meant to be in his own marse's field, working to death and whistling with the glee of it. And I've kept him too long already. But at least I kept him safe.

"You hear what my marse say?" I try to put some cheer to it. "War. The Northern hounds is comin' for the Southern foxes."

My man shrugs off dirt and dust, says, "Iff'n the hounds do come, May, you best be sure you ain't turnt to a fox yo'self by then."

"What's that s'posed to mean?" I bark.

102

But I know exactly what he means. He's told me and told me, my man has, that he won't abide my spying on Marse Charles's behalf. But how else am I to keep the things I love protected? I reach out to kiss him, but he slams out the door too, albeit a sight quieter than Marse Charles just done.

Now I'm truly alone, but I don't suffer for it. My Rue-baby'll be back any minute now. Safe. Near me another day. Marse Charles won't cross me. And that makes anything I see or say or sell well worth the loss.

You can lose a hundred battles, 'long as you stay winning the war.

FREEDOMTIME

Rue saw Bruh Abel for what he was, a thief in the night. The thing he meant to use to snare folks was Black-Eyed Bean, the child that many had begun to whisper was the herald of some dark despair. Bruh Abel promised to baptize Bean before everybody and in the eyes of the Lord. To save him. A spectacle.

The baptism would mark the culmination of Bruh Abel's seasonal appearance in the town, and amongst folks it held a rising anticipation like the peak festivity of a fervent holiday. It was all anybody wanted to talk about. The baptism of Black-Eyed Bean. The day he would be washed clean. Saved.

Throughout the former slave quarters, Rue saw the baptism clothes folks planned to wear hung like white flags of surrender, flapping from washing lines, billowing in the wind so that from afar it seemed as though souls hung in them, too, writhing. Rue had never quite understood it, the airing of one's belongings on lines for everybody to see. Neither had her mama. When Miss May Belle was living, she'd hung their clothes indoors, never mind that it took longer for their clothing to dry in the close warmth of their cabin. Just one more intimacy they kept close.

But the white clothes did make a lovely sight from afar, Rue had to admit, strewn like decorations from house to house, all through the old quarter.

Rue troubled on the problem of Bean alone and came over and over again to the same dissatisfying conclusion: Miss May Belle would've known what to do about Bean. Rue herself did not.

Dinah, a slight mulatto woman who was known to mend clothes, ran to catch up with Rue. As much as she was pretty, she was talented, and Rue liked her fine for this, thought on her something like a friend, if she were to allow herself to indulge in friendships.

"Y'alright, Dinah?"

Dinah's tiredness showed in the squint to her light-colored eyes. She'd wrapped her little baby to her back to make her arms free, a little girl whose name Rue couldn't quite recollect.

"She's caught a chill, I'm thinkin'." Dinah tilted her back and arched up her behind so Rue could look at the child up close.

Rue tucked the wayward arm of the sleeping baby into the fabric belted at the small of Dinah's back. Without waking, the baby girl sucked appreciatively at her thumb. Her skin was warm but not alarmingly so.

"She'll come right," Rue said, and Dinah beamed, took her word on it that easy. "Feverfew. I'll bring some over to y'all presently."

"Y'all goin' to see Bean be washed?" Dinah asked.

Rue shrugged like she'd shrugged every time somebody had asked after Bean. "Surely," she said, "this town got more pressin' matters than the baptism of one li'l boy."

The room they'd put the struggling baby Si's crib in might as well've been in the ground already, so dark was it and so chill. It was an old mud-made room that had belonged to Marse Charles's kitchen, meant for storing things that couldn't last long in heat, and the clay walls made the outside world's sounds come together muffled and wrong. It was a rough quarantine but a necessary one, she'd thought, to keep little Si from suffering the heavy air of the late summer heat, to keep him away from his brothers and sisters. Si was only three days old; still his heartbeat had that telltale tripping of a drumbeat out of time. Rue had heard its like before; she knew well what it meant. Stillborn babies happened more than she liked to think on, but the ones born alive who did not thrive were a more weighty kind of tragedy. It was the waiting for the next breath and the next and the last. It made her sick and sleepless every time, that helpless waiting.

Rue jumped as Si's daddy came into the room. The sound of his steps had been swallowed up by the clay floor and her own overthinking. And now he stood close behind her. She felt him, watching her watching his son.

"It's a hard thing, Miss Rue."

"It is." What else was there to give than that?

"Heard other babies round here been fallin' sick also," Si's daddy said. The words sounded ominous and cruel and he'd meant for them to, laid out in the room, a threat against her healing power, and an implication.

His voice seemed too harsh to Rue, what

with his sickly boy near. She didn't much like the man. He was one of those come lately after the war from yonder knows where, dragging along his freedom in search of some woman he'd been separated from years back. Well, he'd found her, Si's mama, and gave her four other healthy babies before this weak, wanting child had come. Now he stood with his whole weight blocking the doorway, and he seemed more put out than grieving. He seemed to be watching Rue, or so she thought. He was baiting her like she were an unruly creature. He said, "All these babies fallin' ill. What you make of that, huh, Miss Rue? Is there a sickness come onto us?"

"Nothin' of it to make," Rue said. "Cooler seasons coming on is all."

"Heard newborn children ain't hardly thrivin' this whole year. Not since you birthed that Bean."

Suddenly Rue was full aware of just how large Si's daddy was in the doorway, overflowing the close room with accusations against her, against Bean. She came aware of how fully Si's daddy blocked her one escape from the room, standing squarely in the outside light.

She thought on Ol' Joel's wild accusation declaring that she herself had made Bean as

108

a haint and a blight against them. Ol' Joel had found willing ears for his conspiracy, and who better to fill up with lies than a daddy made empty by the shame of his weak son.

"And this one here, he won't latch on the teat." Si's daddy had clearly decided Rue was guilty of every one of those wicked rumors.

"He needs rest," she managed.

Si's daddy shook his head. "We mean to see him baptized by Bruh Abel."

Si gave off a cough then. Rue leaned over the child, cooing nonsense words as much to quiet him as to get out from under his daddy's stare. The baby struggled to open his eyes, gave up on it, returned to uneasy sleep.

"I don't think it's wise to put him to the water," Rue made herself say.

"Weren't askin' you if it were wise."

Rue pulled back from the crib like it'd burnt her. No one had ever before turned away her healing.

Si's daddy kept watching her and did not stop watching her as she moved around him toward the door.

"Keep him restin'," she said. "It's good to speak to him. Even a voice can soothe. I'll be back in the evenin' time." She couldn't keep away, not with a sickly child involved, and she hoped that later it would be the mama she'd find tending the boy — someone softer, sympathetic. Women tended to look more kindly on her, Rue knew. They understood the necessity of her work better than the daddies did.

She'd hoped to return to her own cabin and collect her troubled thoughts, but there, just past the doorway, was Bruh Abel. The good book was gripped in his right hand, like at any moment he'd be called to fight something off with its heavy binding, its flock of pages.

He smiled when she neared. Did he smile that bright trickster smile for everybody? Why was it that no one else seemed able to figure him for what he was?

"Sister Rue," he said. She balked. She was nobody's sister, and if she had a quicker wit or a whittled tongue she would have said so.

"Miss Rue," she corrected.

He barreled on forward like she hadn't spoke, said, "I was hopin' I'd cross yo' way."

Rue was aware that from a distance folks were watching them. She didn't have to turn this time to sense Si's daddy's approach from behind. He didn't bother to invent a pretense to look on this moment — when the healing woman and the preacher man were stood toe to toe.

Rue had to make herself speak up. "If it's about li'l Si, I tol' his daddy already. Y'all will only make him weaker if you take him to the water."

Bruh Abel's smile widened. His face was near pretty, up close, she had to admit. He had a spray of freckles on his nose from the sun, and even the way he looked down on her had an air of respectability for all that it made Rue wary. She squared her shoulders. He was a foot taller than her, easy, but not so broad as Si's daddy, and even if he was laughing at her she felt she'd sparked something in him that wasn't all the way saintly.

"Now, you may know better than I, Miss Rue. After all, the gift of healin' was put in yo' hands." If Bruh Abel was bothered by the gathering audience he didn't show it. He kept his focus on Rue. "But I'm only lookin' to ease the way for our li'l Si should the Lord see right to recall him to heaven."

"Our Si?" She was surprised by the bitter flavor of her own venom. "It's my thinkin' that our Si ought to have the easiest path to heaven, seein' as he's nary a week old. Baptism? Ain't no sense in it."

"Ain't no sense in salvation?"

Rue managed to still her tongue before she said more. Here she was, handing him the rope to hang her, with everybody looking on. She took a step back. "I only mean that I hope to give Si every chance at seein' another day, good Lord willin'."

Seemed Bruh Abel could use patience like a weapon. He paused to mull over what she'd said in what looked like pious consideration.

He spoke at last. "Lord willin' an' if the creek don't rise, we'll all see another day, Miss Rue."

She shook at the old nonsense saying, took it as her leave to go. It had been a favorite of Miss May Belle's when she'd been alive, and Bruh Abel surely knew it. The two had talked together, right up 'til the very end.

"Oh, Miss Rue," Bruh Abel called after her. His voice was teasing, lilting. "I ain't even get round to sayin' why I'd been lookin' to speak with you."

She'd made a mistake by walking away from him; now he had to yell to her to carry across the distance. Surely everybody for miles was listening. She turned to him, and her face felt hot.

"Only I was wantin' to ask you formally to come down from outta the woods and join our worship, Sister Rue."

So he had seen her that day at the river-bank. And he'd waited 'til now to slip the knot. She walked on, feeling dismissed and not liking it the least bit, not with all those folks watching and counting it as a retreat.

Rue returned that night to see Si as she promised she would, found his mama and daddy both in the chill room hovering over their sleeping baby like new parents over any ordinary newborn. But in his crib Si was still, his face almost waxen in its serenity.

"How he doin'?" Rue stepped forward but their eyes on her felt as cool as the room did.

"He'll be baptized, and in the care a' Jesus, soon enough." That was the mama, voice hitching. She was slight and soft-spoken, barely old enough to be called a woman, let alone a mama. She moved toward Rue, as if to block her from Si, and the light made visible a bruise at her jaw so garish Rue let out a hiss. Purple as bloomed larkspur the bruise ran down her neck, perfect in the shape of a handprint.

"What happened?" Rue asked, though wasn't it clear? Si's mama said nothing, and behind her her man towered. He picked up his dying son. Si was so little he took up

113

not much more than the wide stretch of his daddy's open palm.

"We mean to have the boy baptized," Si's daddy said.

Rue appealed to the mama. "I come to tell you again that you ought not to."

"Ain't it the Lord's plan?" The bruise stretched with her speaking. Rue tried to catch her eye, to will some honesty between them, but the mama didn't want to receive it. Rue pushed round her to look over Si.

She meant only to feel the baby's forehead for fever, but Si's daddy caught her by her outstretched wrist. He squeezed that wrist so hard Rue felt the burn of her skin splitting.

"Woman," the daddy spat the word as a curse. "We don't want none a yo' devilment near our boy," and threw Rue toward the door by her arm.

She caught herself, only just, on the edge of the crib with the same outstretched arm he'd mangled. There was a loud pop in her wrist, not so much heard as felt, and Rue curled around the throbbing pain. It shot through her arm like a lightning bolt and stayed throbbing, but she held her face and looked to Si's mama.

Rue spoke with her jaw clenched like to crack her teeth. "Si needs lookin' after."

"Not by you," the mama said in her soft nothing voice.

Rue turned her back on them, on Si, stumbled for the door, and as she fled, she thought she heard, though she could not be certain, Si's daddy hock and spit in the path of her retreat, that old true method for dispelling a witch.

Rue put her broken wrist in the river and howled. The water was inky and cold and it eased the damaged limb as much as it pained her. Like a whetstone, the rushing current honed her senses to a wicked sharpness. She might have done better to go on home, to calm the swelling with a poultice of comfrey and to soothe her upset with a draught of brandy.

Instead, at the riverside Rue set her wrist with one slow, agonizing twist, tasted blood in her mouth but kept her eyes on her destination. In the distance over the treetops she could just see the bell tower of the old white church.

"It's Rue," her voice echoed. "You listenin'?"

She did not make her entrance quiet. What was there to fear? She walked down the center aisle, knowing she had an audience even if she couldn't make out any movement in the shadowed corners of the church's vaulted second story.

"That was a fool trick you done with the bell," Rue called up to the haint. But she felt a certain guilt as well, as good as if she'd rung the bell her own damn self. Because she'd stayed away too long. Let this whole fool thing go on too long. But she had to go on with it, particularly now with Bean's eyes on the back of her mind.

So Rue thought on what her mama might have done. What a haint might do. She cradled her aching wrist near her body, spun to see all the shadowed corners of the old church at once.

"I need you to go out there."

That night everybody in the town said they heard it clear, the screaming in the woods. It was a sharp, suffering scream, high-pitched and awful, roiling louder and then cut off abruptly. In the morning they saw what it had done. Strewn out on the mud-died ground were all their baptismal whites in piles on the ground, muddied and ruined.

Already by midafternoon folks had built stories on top of other stories about the haint, so that in a matter of hours it was no longer a faceless spirit but one jealous of

116

their glory, come to tear down the marks of their freedom-worship.

When anybody asked her straight out what it might have been that night in the woods, Rue put it to foxes. Their wilderness had a long history of foxes who were vicious, fearless, who came into town looking to tear up chicken pens and rabbit holes, just because they could. Foxes had that sort of cry that sounded like a woman in terror and, heard in echo, it could come out all wrong. But when folks started saying for themselves it was the haint, the drifting ghost some had half-seen in the woods, Rue did not immediately dispel them of the notion. A haint was an affliction she could deal with, or appear to leastwise. Something she could care to that Bruh Abel and his Bible could not.

Rue again met the preacher man in the square. This time he was on hands and knees alongside his flock, helping to pick up the ripped-down white clothing. She joined him in his stooping, though it vexed her to do so. Better, she figured, to seem to be just another knee-bent sinner in his estimation. Together they shook out a dusty bed cloth, held out opposite ends, and met at corners to fold it and fold it again. Bruh Abel set the neatly folded sheet down at the bottom step of somebody's porch, then took a

117

handkerchief to his forehead like he'd done a whole day's labor.

"Thank you, Sister Rue." His eyes flashed warily at her bound-up wrist. She'd fashioned a splint of tree limbs and twine, the loose ends of which rattled when she moved. "I can't seem to disabuse yo' people of their backwards superstitions. Tell me, why is that?"

Rue shrugged. "You newly come to these parts. We got a long history that ain't easily laid to rest."

"Even so," Bruh Abel said, "the baptism of the baby Si will renew their faith."

Rue frowned. It was not altogether what she had expected to hear. "You mean to go on with it after all this carryin' on?" She gestured round the square where even now folks were discovering their washing in far-flung places. The white clothes had settled everywhere like an early frost foretelling winter.

Bruh Abel stood, brought himself up to his full height. Rue took a step back and cussed herself for it. Her wrist throbbed and maybe Bruh Abel sensed that, as any animal might sense another's weak spot and prey upon it. He took her bandaged hand and held it gently between his larger, lighter two

118

hands, as though he meant to pray the break away.

"Tomorrow mornin' will see Si baptized," Bruh Abel promised her.

"It ain't right," Rue said.

"It's what the folks are needin'." He turned over her hand, gently. "You can't change faith, Sister Rue. And a haint can't neither."

In the end, neither Rue nor Bruh Abel was proved right. Si died that night. His body met the grave unwashed, unbaptized. Unsaved.

SLAVERYTIME

How long could a white girl keep sucking at her thumb? It was the year that Little Miss Varina would turn seven years old, and everywhere through the quarter the slaves gossiped on her outside of their master's hearing. They had it in whispers she still behaved like a small child with a small child's desperate habits. Yeah, they'd laughed about her, wondered at what it was that had made her so strange, and they came down on the fact that it had to be because her mama, the Missus, didn't ever love her, not even for a minute.

"You don't love on a baby enough they come up wrongly," Miss May Belle told folks who'd asked for her wisdom on the matter. "It's the same as lettin' 'em to starve."

They'd been corn shucking and they'd been singing. Seemed that they were surrounded on all sides by pale yellow kernels and the fresh green shed skin of corn that'd already been shucked and the darker green husks of those still wanting shucking. Everywhere were the white silky strings, which had gone all up in their hair, rendered them cobwebby and wild. Rue sat near her mama's feet, letting Miss May Belle drop husks into her lap.

Up above, Miss May Belle sat on a stool someone had brought out. She was winding her toes around the legs of the stool, and Rue knew she was anxious about something, though her mouth smiled as she gossiped and her fingers flew as she tugged and plucked.

The mismatching collection of benches and stools and house chairs dragged outside made the square in the quarter look like a parlor room had bloomed from the center of the earth. The corn they worked was piled high, a proud mountain of bounty. Above, the sun was dipping down in the sky, shining its last rays on them sweetly, and Marse Charles had seen fit to give them a few jugs of whiskey, which they were allowed to pass amongst themselves as long as their hands didn't stop moving longer than it took to sip. The world had gone all golden, and their tongues were loosed.

"Don't think that Missus picked up that

child but the one time," Fannie the house-maid was saying with a glob of tobacco thickening her lip.

"And when was that?"

"To hand her over to Ma Doe, 'course."

Ma Doe for her part huffed and said no more. Her arthritic fingers worked slow at peeling back the corn skin, and every now and then she'd set her work down and sigh. Those times Rue would see Miss May Belle reach out to the woman and rub at her fingers and then Ma Doe would begin again.

It was well known that Ma Doe had seen to the rearing of all of Marse Charles's children, his three sons and his one daughter. To Rue, Marse Charles's eldest were as solid as suggestions. The three boys had come to him by his first wife, a woman Rue had never known alive, though she'd heard of her from her own mama, who looked on the dead woman with a sort of reverent respect.

"She had too much beauty, that 'un," Miss May Belle would sometimes say, and the saying of it would come out of nowhere, as though Mistress Violet, for that had been the first wife's name, had just then left the room, her ever-present scent of peppermint oil left to linger.

"Was my mama what commended it to

her, that oil she got to love so well," Miss May Belle would say, proud. "And she knew there was stock in it. Mistress Vi, she believed."

Mistress Violet in stories was pale, thin, her wrist and temples always wet with the anointing of oil. But the sons she made in quick succession were strong and overconfident in their own strength. The coming war would take them quickly in the order Mistress Violet had brought them into the world. But that was not to be for a while yet.

"You think he'll send Varina away? Make a belle a' her?" asked Big Sylvia, who had little patience for Miss Varina. The girl was forever in her kitchen stealing away with the ashcakes left cooling on the windowsill.

"Varina's not going anywhere for a long while," Ma Doe said. She divested a thick piece of corn of its covering in one irate tug. "Ain't that so, Miss May Belle?"

Rue's mama had that far-off thoughtful look on her face. She was looking into the woods, which just then echoed with a chittering of unseen animals. That wilderness seemed louder even than their singing, than the soulful plunking that came from across the high piles of corn where one of the drunker hands was entertaining himself by

123

picking at a fiddle.

The high, woman-like scream of a fox cut through the newly fallen night, and one of the house girls leaned in and hiccupped and said gaily, "Now, Miss May Belle, ain't that yo' babies callin' to ya?"

The other women laughed but Ma Doe didn't and Miss May Belle didn't. Sitting skin close to her mama's leg, Rue felt her mama go rigid like she was holding on to something tightly.

Playing along, Miss May Belle said, "I'll see to 'em presently," but there wasn't any playfulness in her voice despite the good, hard work of the night, despite the harvest, green and yellow and white all around them.

Rue came home alone one afternoon to find their cabin door was slight-ways open. It didn't lock like the doors in Marse Charles's House did, with their heavy brass knobs and heavy brass keys, but it was a rule between Rue and her mama that their front door be kept firmly closed whether they were in or out. Miss May Belle said it was to ward off creatures, spirits, and bad air.

Could a creature have gotten in now? A spirit? A type of badness? Rue knew she'd closed the door firmly when she'd gone out. She always did everything her mama said to; her voice was always in her ear.

"You want me weepin'?" her mama would always say when Rue put herself into some childish danger, went picking flowers too close to where the patrolmen snatched up runaways, or climbed up a tree she couldn't climb down from, or waded into the river past where her toes could feel the bank. Never you mind the pain of death or injury; the worst pain was to make your mama cry.

Rue pushed open the door of the cabin anyway, thinking herself brave. She still jumped when she saw Varina. The white girl was sitting up on their dinner table, her dress spread out around her like a tablecloth, her legs back and forth dangling, her thumb, as always, in her mouth.

"What you doin' here?" Rue asked. She knew she wasn't meant to speak to Varina that way — was meant to call her Miss Varina, give her all the respect a white girl was deserving of. "And why you all pink?"

Varina's face up close was mottled with blushing. Snot glowed from the hollow beneath her left nostril, and before she answered Rue, she took the time to rub furiously at her puffy eyes with both fists.

"Mother slapped me for sucking my thumb. She said she 'shamed of me."

It was unlike Varina's mama to say anything to her, kind, cruel, or otherwise, but it was well known to everybody — to the black folks at least — that the master's second wife was not much proud of what she'd produced, her one child, his only daughter. And Lord that red, red hair.

"I'm lookin' for the healing woman. May Belle," Varina said.

"That's my mama. What you want with her?"

"I want to be cured."

Rue crawled up onto the table beside Varina before she could think better of it. She half-expected that the master's daughter might push her away, but instead Varina made room for Rue on the table's surface, scuttling unladylike, baring white frilled bloomers that Rue decided were the prettiest things she had ever seen.

Varina wiped up snot with her forearm. "Will she help me, you think?"

"She surely will," Rue said.

Up close Varina had only her daddy's face and none of her mama's. Marse Charles's severity, his thin pink lips, the small ears with the heavy loose lobes and hair in dark, curling barbs. But where had that red color sprouted from? It came up from her head in corkscrews.

Rue let Varina rest her head on her shoul-

126

der. After a while she looped her arm around her waist, and that seemed to quiet Varina's sniffles. Miss May Belle would have words here, but Rue had none except "Mama will know what to do."

When Miss May Belle came in, she did not look surprised at all to see the two girls on her supper table. She only looked weary and stopped to pull off her hat. "Afternoon, Miss Varina," she murmured.

Miss May Belle set down her basket, sat on the bed for a spell, and gave her left arch a forceful rub like she could squeeze out her foot pains. Only then did she say, "A'ight, what's the trouble?" as if trouble was a constant, and not particularly urgent, part of every day.

The question set Varina off weeping again. She told it between hiccups, that her mama had come into the nursery and seen her at her studies. Varina was tasked with copying a page of the Bible as a means to perfect her crooked script. She did so every noontime, for she wasn't allowed to go out when the sun was high and like to spoil her skin with freckles.

"I was making the most lovely *V*'s," Varina said, and she did one there in the air to show them, her wrist flicking about the invisible flourishes. There weren't, she despaired, enough letter *V*'s in the Bible.

Ma Doe had stepped out to see Big Sylvia down in the kitchen about their luncheon and Varina had been there alone thinking very hard on her lessons and her piety, she swore. Well, everybody knew when Miss Varina got to thinking hard she was liable to suck her thumb with a distinct abandon, and that is when her mama had come in and seen what she was about.

"She smacked my hand from my mouth. She called me dirty as a nigra and sent me out the House saying I belonged out in the slave quarter. So," Varina sobbed, "here I am."

"Oh, Jesus," said Miss May Belle, and that made Varina cry harder. "S'alright now, Miss Varina. But we just gotta try to heal you off the habit."

Varina looked at her thumb. Rue looked down at her own thumbs, trying to figure what the pleasure in sucking them might be. Her hands were work-worn, the nail cut down to the quick. Rue's hands were too busy to spend time in her mouth. Now that, she thought, was where Varina's trouble was.

"What if I tell you a story to ease yo' mind from it?" Miss May Belle said.

Varina sniffled. "Yes, please."

"Now, lessee," Miss May Belle began from

her seat on the bed.

It went like this, that Bruh Rabbit was going all throughout the wilderness, bragging on himself, saying how smart he was, smarter than any animal in the wood.

Well, Bruh Fox, who had declared himself the master of that wilderness, did not like hearing Bruh Rabbit's claims, and he set out to prove Bruh Rabbit wasn't so smart after all.

" 'Good gracious. Who he think he is anyhow?' " Miss May Belle mimicked Bruh Fox and the girls laughed. She was a good mimic, gave the fox the type of high-minded tongue of a fine, white gentleman. Bruh Fox's companion, the Snake, she made slither out his words like any upstart overseer.

Bruh Fox, just to put Bruh Rabbit in his right place, set him a task, gave him a haversack and told him to bring him something back in it.

"Somethin' like what?" Varina asked gamely.

Miss May Belle wagged her finger. Bruh Fox wasn't about to tell Bruh Rabbit what he ought to bring. If Bruh Rabbit was so smart he'd surely figure it out. But Bruh Rabbit stayed puzzled. He got to talking to the birds — maybe they had an idea how to oblige Bruh Fox? They just shrugged their feathered shoulders.

"By and by, an idea come into Bruh Rabbit's head. He asked them birds if he might beg a feather off a' each a' them."

From beneath their bed Miss May Belle began to pull up lengths of fabric scrap cut to long, spooling ribbons of the type she'd use to tie up newborn baby cords.

"Bruh Rabbit stuck all 'em feathers to himself and soon he had, there gathered, enough feathers to fly over to the Big House where Bruh Fox lived."

Miss May Belle tied neat fast knots of ribbon all the way up Varina's arms, a prism's worth of color, and bade her flap her new wings. Varina did so, stuck her arms out stiff and let her ribbons stream with her flapping. Rue, beside her, had no ribbons. She felt earthbound and ordinary.

In the story, Bruh Rabbit perched himself on a tree outside of Bruh Fox's house. There he spied Bruh Fox chatting with his old friend Snake.

"What kind a' bird is that?" Bruh Fox asked, squinting at the creature dressed in the strange mix of colors, like nothing he'd ever encountered. Snake could not say, and suggested that they might go down and ask Bruh Rabbit, since it was true he was mighty clever.

"Y'all won't find him," Bruh Fox declared. "I sent him on a task he won't figure. He don't know that he's 'posed to fetch me the Moon, and the Sun, and the Darkness."

"Once he overheard that, Bruh Rabbit flew away," Miss May Belle said. One by one she untied the ribbons from Varina's arms. Before Varina could complain, she left two ribbons behind, one on either arm, red strings knotted around the hitch of Varina's elbows.

Meanwhile, Bruh Rabbit went around creation. He snatched the Sun from the east and the Moon from the west. He snatched the Darkness out of night itself. He put them in the sack and lugged them up to Bruh Fox's Big House, where all the animals were gathered, waiting.

" 'Lessee how you done, Bruh Rabbit,' " Miss May Belle quipped as Bruh Fox. Enthralled, Varina went to raise her thumb to her mouth, but the ribbons hitched around her elbows made the movement clumsy. She put her hand down, leaned closer instead, better to hear the end of the tale.

First Bruh Rabbit brought out the Darkness. The assembled creatures screamed and shivered in the total dark. Then Bruh Rabbit brought out the Moon, and they were calmed by the low light. Lastly Bruh Rabbit tugged the Sun out from his sack, but it was so brilliant and bright that it burned at the animals' eyes.

"And that," Miss May Belle finished, "is how Bruh Rabbit brung a sometimes blindness into the world. Because he may be smart. But ain't no one smarter than God. And sooner or later they gon' learn it."

■ ■ ■ ■

PART TWO

■ ■ ■ ■

FREEDOMTIME

1868

The men began to spit wherever Rue walked. They did not do it in her sight. They were not so bold as that. Not yet. But they saved up their spittle behind their lips like cud, spittle being the best defense to ward off what they'd decided must be the cursing of a witch.

Rue felt it, and she felt the men watching her as she walked through the center square of the cabins. They still nodded greetings, tipped their hats. But when Rue went round the corner she knew that behind her back they were hocking up their hate, swirling it in their mouths. Spitting that hate in the path she'd just walked through like she'd left a bad taste on their tongue they could not wait to be rid of.

Rue had thought of running away long before the spit began to fly. In the years after Miss May Belle's passing, the urge would

135

sometimes come upon Rue in the middle of some effort. Say she had to reach up on a high shelf for a vial of medicine, say she was walking clear across the town on a rain-blustering day. Now, after baby Si's passing, all the mamas were watching her like she had the dust of his death caught under her fingernails. And all the while, Bean, the strange child, thrived.

After they'd laid Si to rest, Rue resolved to work harder. She paid no mind to the spittle or the suspicion that trailed her like runoff of some venomous sea. She looked in on the sick folks and the elderly and the new mamas like she was dim to their whispers and accusing stares. There were things she'd been neglecting. Things that wanted seeing to. It was the opposite of running. A digging in.

She was isolated, estranged, but hadn't she always been? Perhaps from the very moment she'd been born, if memory could take her back that far, for from the start Rue had ever been Miss May Belle's daughter, her destiny marked because of it.

Rue knew there was only one other baby born as she had been with distrust heaped upon him, as soon as he blinked open his bean-black eyes. The more alone the towns-folk made her feel, the more she felt a pull toward Bean. The more she felt for him, the more she feared for him.

Folks did not like what they could not put an explanation to. All she could think, over and over, was that she had not been able to save Si from the affliction he was born with. She would not let Bean fall too, to add to that number of perished children whose births had not saved them from death. Her fear of the dead clawed at her, buried secrets that might surface from her dreams into the waking world. Didn't everything over and over surface and come again?

And so, one cool evening, Rue came into Bean's family's cabin, unannounced. She had been looking for Sarah, had gathered up all her courage to ask after Bean. The grim fact was that where Rue's name was whispered, Bean's was often liable to follow. They could hurt Rue with their tongue wagging and their cussing, but Bean was just a baby still, and it made Rue's freshly healed wrist ache anew to think what way they might devise to hurt a child like Bean if words were not enough.

Rue was looking for Bean's mama but she found his daddy instead, and she paused on the threshold unsure if she ought to turn and go before Jonah saw her. She couldn't help watching him, unobserved, a part of her thrilled. Jonah was head bent at the family supper table shifting grain into a haversack, a strangely womanly task that endeared him to her, for he seemed to be practiced in it. She watched as he took a well-measured cupful from the larger barrel and transferred it to the sack, keeping a count of what he was about with a silent movement of his lips.

Behind him a suppertime fire was burning itself down. There was Bean on the floor, braced on his hands and knees, his black eyes staring into the fireplace, unblinking. He was still and silent, focused wholly on the dying flame.

"C'mon in, Miss Rue," Jonah startled Rue by saying. She hadn't thought he'd noticed her there half in his doorway.

"Night's unseasonably cool, ain't it?" he said. "Come in an' warm yo'self."

She knelt beside Bean, who looked up at her. She sat herself down heedless of the ash near the stove and pulled Bean into the cradle of her lap. He was small for his age, and she could feel his little jutting ribs beneath his shirt. He did not start up his crying, even as Rue held him at his wriggling waist, but seemed content to be held by her.

"He likes to sit there 'cause it's warm," said Jonah. "He won't go near the fire."

"How you know?"

"Sarah teaches 'em young how to stay outta the flame. She make sure they know well enough that it hurts."

Rue did not make it her place to tell folks how to rear their children. But she did wonder what Jonah, placid as he was, thought of Sarah and her ways. They were both of them orphans — Sarah after her mama's passing, Jonah sold to Marse Charles in an ill-assorted lot of slaves. They had chosen each other, Sarah and Jonah had. After Marse Charles, after the war, after freedom, they had chosen each other in that hazy time when everybody was pure drunk on choosing. Made a home in this cabin, and a baby, and another, and then this third child that wriggled now warm in Rue's lap, still mesmerized by the fire and sucking at his thumb. The low flames were reflected in the flat black of Bean's eyes, and Rue felt Jonah as a safe presence behind her.

Her skin just about buzzed when Jonah leaned in toward her, though he hadn't touched her. He said, "You here after Sarah, I expect? Women's work?"

Rue had near forgot why she'd come. It

was comfortable by the fire and in Jonah's company. Bean eased himself into her arms, dozing.

"Yes, I'm lookin' to speak with Sarah. She here?"

"She down at the river. Bruh Abel got most of the womenfolk out there prayin', showin' they thankful as we got such a good harvest this year."

It had in fact been a miraculous harvest, and Bruh Abel had appeared right in the heart of it. Rue wondered if that was no simple coincidence but a type of divining. Had the preacher known that it would be the best moment to descend upon them, what with full stores and satisfied bodies?

"You eat yet?" Jonah shifted the full sack of grain from the table to the ground, proceeded to fill another.

Rue had not. She often found her meals here and there, a collection of benevolences from the mamas that she looked after, as were her clothing and her other little comforts, and a fair stack of coins that she hid in a distant knothole as Miss May Belle had done. Just in case. But there was no denying that lately Rue had found those favors harder to come by.

Rue grinned up at Jonah's work. "You look like you fixin' to cook a feast."

140

"No, ma'am, I'm tithin'," he said.

"Tithin'? To that preacher man?"

Jonah nodded. He did not look up from the careful transfer of the next cupful. They had not fed her like this. Never tithed to her, nor had she expected it.

Rue set Bean down, back farther from the fire than he had been, and she stood, the better to look at the grain Jonah was giving to Bruh Abel as it moved from the depleted barrel to the fat haversack. They had used to give Marse Charles a portion of what they'd been allowed to grow for themselves in the piteous gardens in front of the slave cabins. Those growings made up their only food aside from the slave portions. Jonah's tithing now made Rue envious. It smacked to her of that time before the war that she had thought was safely in their past. But here it was again, taking on another type of robbery: no Big House, but now a fair-skinned black man who'd set himself up above them on little more than his talent for telling tales down by the riverbank.

"Bruh Abel ain't ask for it, mind," Jonah was saying, perhaps guessing at Rue's unease, hedging it like a wildfire before it could get blazing. "Folks spoke on it and decided amongst themselves that they ought to offer him somethin' regular-like. In hopes

141

that he might deign to stay on out here, where he's needed, rather than move on to some big city."

"Where he's needed?" Rue felt she'd be wiser to hold her tongue. She did not like to show to Jonah especially that bitter side of herself that felt so quick to turn to distrust and envy. But she could not overlook those nettles of fear, the clinging notion that something dark was rising up higher and higher against her. Turning her over like loose sand in this town where she had thought she could stand forever surefooted, respected.

Jonah spoke on the many wonders that had come to pass now that the town was turning more solidly toward its own faith, not the one pressed into their backs by Marse. The good crops and fair weather, the wind blowing and the moonglow shining and the sun rising and setting as it was supposed to, seemed all of it was down to the faith they'd found. The faith Bruh Abel was guiding them in.

"And Bean," Jonah added.

"What about him?"

"He ain't made that awful cry, not one night since Bruh Abel come and start prayin' over him. Seems to me we can't go on like we have been," Jonah said. He'd set

142

down the measuring cup, came toward her empty-handed. "We was froze up. All of us been waitin' on the future to reveal itself. Waitin' on what freedom means. Bruh Abel say we don't gotta wait no more. We can just go 'head and put aside the old ways."

Rue felt it in her bones: She was the old ways to which Jonah was referring. Her and her mama and her grandmama. Made for a world that wasn't anymore, that had been shook off like fetters. But Rue was still bound, to this place, to these ways.

"What if it's nonsense?" Rue said. "What if it's all empty air what Bruh Abel speaks on and seems to do?"

Jonah shrugged. "Seems to me if faith was tangible it wouldn't be faith, would it?" He surprised Rue, reached out and touched her cheek like he was soaking up a tear that wasn't there. His touch was so gentle it startled her.

"What he makes folks feel is real, ain't it? You'd know that, if you went to pray with us."

Rue turned her head away from Jonah's palm, buried her face in Bean's soft brown hair so she wouldn't have to look at Jonah and show him her hurt, or her wanting.

" 'llow me to fix you supper," he said.

Jonah served up dried fish stew on a tin

143

plate. The food was still warm from when Sarah had made it earlier. Rue wondered if Jonah had caught the fish himself out there on one of his working trips on the docks of white men's boats, reeling in catches for them. Rue liked to think that he had. She motioned for him to eat along with her, both of them head bent over the steaming plate.

Bean grew restless in Rue's lap, leaned across the table, curious of the food. She pulled him close to her chest, fed him fingerfuls of corn mush off her plate. Bean gnawed at her fingers, sweet as any teething child. Why were folks so quick to heap their fear and foreboding upon him?

"I'd like to see after him, your Bean," she said, "to make sure he come up right." She did not know why she said it, only that she felt worry for the boy as much as she felt a kinship for him. It seemed right to promise it there in the quiet still of Jonah's home, her belly filling up warm with his easy kindness. What else could she give Jonah but that? Women's work, he'd called it. Rue wanted to prove herself worth much more.

She could smell Jonah this close. Scented of malt and of hay. He laid a hand atop hers, seemed to study her awhile. He nodded, maybe in acceptance of what she'd offered, but when he finally spoke he said, "Bean's to be baptized soon. Bruh Abel promised."

She thought again of the weak baby Si who had lived and died before Bruh Abel could make a spectacle of him. She had to wonder, if Si had lived would Bean now be saved from all this high-mindedness? Wasn't he just a child? He felt like one. Safe in her arms, he was banging at the supper table, amusing himself like any baby would with the discovery of his growing strength. But his arms did bare that strange hexagonal pattern, like the surface of a bee's hive, and that skin all over was sickly pale. And the eyes. Rue looked from Bean to Jonah.

Jonah spoke softly, so soft Rue had to lean in to hear. He said, "I want Bean to be saved."

"Yes." Rue was watching Jonah's lips. "So do I."

The sound of the front door hitting the clapboard startled them apart. Three sharp footfalls and there was Sarah in the doorway. Long and thin, willow reed in coloring and in ease, Sarah seemed to mold herself to the doorjamb. She looked at Rue and Jonah and Bean through slant eyes, like there was something about them to see if only she could squint harder.

Rue stood from the table, jarring Bean

suddenly. He let out a low of displeasure. She clutched him closer, like a thief hiding behind the very thing they meant to steal.

"Sarah. We was waitin' on you," Jonah said. "Rue wished to speak to you on some matter."

"Evenin', Sarah."

"Miss Rue." Perhaps the address galled Sarah, for she said it in a bite. After all, they were near the same age and yet so different.

"I'll let you two get on." Jonah took Bean from Rue's hands, but Bean struggled to stay with her. He cried out to her like to break her heart. Jonah took him into the next room, deeper into the dark of the house.

"If we talkin' let's do it outside," Sarah said. "It's too hot in here."

Rue followed Sarah out onto the narrow porch. They both leaned on the slanted railing, uncomfortably close in the thin space. It was too dark to make out Sarah's expression but there was the quirking open of her mouth, the baring of teeth as she said, "Hope my cookin' was to yo' likin', Miss Rue."

"Yes," Rue said baldly. "It was. But that wasn't why I come callin'."

Rue shuffled in her pockets, her hand grasping around a vial. It was warmed from

146

where it had stayed pressed against her body and Bean's. She pulled it out and showed it to Sarah, who made no motion to grab for it.

"Some time ago you asked me after a protection for yo'self. You said you did not wish to have more babies. I ain't want you to think I had forgot. Or maybe, it was more you didn't feel quite comfortable askin' again."

It was a delicate business, Rue knew. It was a secret thing that Rue and before her Miss May Belle would spirit to women who could only hint at wanting it, fearful of either their man's hearing or their master's. Sarah, brave as she was, had said the words in a stutter after Bean, who she had devised to keep hid, caught the town's tainted attention. But she never had come back for the cure. Now Rue turned the vial in her hands so it glistened in a twinge of moonglow.

"I ain't want it no more," said Sarah.

"No?"

"No."

The bottom of Sarah's dress, Rue noticed, was shadowed in wet, damp all the way up her legs from kneeling at the river. Bean wasn't yet two and Sarah had regained her thin frame, her small sharp breasts, her

147

sweet girlish shape, like Bean had never been part of her body at all. Rue found she hated her for that, the way she'd shrugged Bean off.

"I don't wish to stop havin' babies." Sarah sounded sure of herself. "It ain't a godly thing to do."

"Who tol' you that?" But Rue knew who.

"Please," Sarah said, turning her back toward Rue, retreating to her cabin. "Don't worry after me or my family no more."

SLAVERYTIME

"The water ain't worth more than the bucket."

If it were a song, her mama would have sung it as gospel 'til her throat ran hoarse, and after her mama was dead and gone, Rue had a habit of saying it to herself, below her breath, as a kind of prayer.

Miss May Belle had spoken many things before she passed on and most of them Rue had let the years take away, had let erode on purpose, but there were some she held on to fast and kept whole.

"Scrub," Rue's mama had said, so that the whole of Rue's first memory of Miss May Belle was the smell of lye soap and the sensation of her skin prickling as the water dripped down her elbows.

"You clean?" her mama would always ask.

"Yes'm."

"What you do next?"

"Don't touch nothin'."

149

"That's right, don't touch nothin'."

For sure it seemed always to be in the middle of the night, what her mama called the witch's hour, that they'd find themselves yanked from floating dreams and the freedom of sleep, to stumble half-blind to some woman's bedside with her particular howling filling up the whole of the plantation, and Rue, herself half-asleep and waiting with her little sleeves rolled up her little arms and her arms held out in front of her, wet but drying, and her jaw clenching with the urge to catch a yawn in her palm but with the instructions *Don't touch nothin'* steadily knocking around in her head as good as law, 'cause if she touched something the baby might die.

"Thank the Lord, you come just in time, Miss May Belle," the man might say when they'd first arrive. His face would be twitching restless with the desire to look brave. It seemed to Rue that the men were always trying to look brave when really what they wanted was to leave Miss May Belle to it.

Rue's mama kept her dark face hard and neutral, for she believed excitement or fear, love or loathing, could spread through the touch with the ease of pestilence, and the last thing you wanted was an excited mama too near her time. Miss May Belle was known to look bored, as if the making of life, the creation of a whole person, was simple and ordinary, and to her it was.

"Brought my own baby out on my lonesome," she liked to tell folks.

Miss May Belle was something else, a soul come again, people said, born and born, with the knowledge of some other place.

And if Miss May Belle insisted on a thing, she'd have it, as good as willing it into existence. She found fire to warm up babies born too soon, and old sheets to keep down the dust from the floors, and soap, soap in frothing handfuls, and because she kept their property from dying, white folks let her have it. They let her have her own way, and the other black folks looked on in just as much awe as envy at how she lived like a white woman amongst them.

She'd show up moments before a miracle, wash up, flick her wet hands, first the left then the right, always the left then the right, and the excess water would arc off her and sparkle by the light of the candle she alone was allowed to have, and that meant it was time to settle in.

"Oh, we got a while yet," she'd say, and she'd shoo the man off with the reasoning that men were bad luck around birthing. Truth was they just ran her nerves.

"Now, who you think help Eve push out Cain and Abel?" Miss May Belle was heard to say, loud and often. "Surely wasn't no Adam."

And folks got to saying that Miss May Belle hated men though that was not true — "I wouldn't have no work if there weren't men to keep women bothered" — because by and by she did let herself get bothered by a man, and that man was Rue's daddy.

Rue couldn't know if what all she knew of her daddy was from real knowing or if it was from hearing the same story over and over 'til the story became as good or better than remembering.

What she did know was this: what the network of raised scars looked like on the bare skin of his back, the puckered flesh ridged in ruined pink, and how the pattern of the long, thick lines had always made her think of the pattern in the palm of a hand. How the line that was the longest wormed its way from the bowl of his neck and traveled around to his back and down his spine. The ugliness of it never scared her before she understood that they were the lines from a long history of whippings and how that was what she could make out the most in the moonlight on those nights when he'd

152

crawl up the bed on hands and knees, like some pleading nighttime creature, to bother Rue's mama.

"I didn't have any wanting for him at the start," Miss May Belle would say. But in Rue's memory her mama always seemed to want him as if she was half a woman without him, would wait and wait for Sundays when visiting was allowed with the kind of shrugged-off longing kept by someone who near believed Sunday wouldn't be coming that week.

And in those Sunday nights Miss May Belle showed her wanting. Rue would wake to her little breath-catching sounds, like the reverse of weeping. Rue's daddy crouched down over Rue's mama, and on the fullest of full moon nights Rue could see the arc of her against him as if she were floating up off the bed into his body, and Rue could see the tense fist of his left hand baring all his weight against the mattress and the softness of his right hand as it went off by itself and burrowed in the cotton of Rue's mama's hair, or drifted down her cheek to rest a thumb in the dimple of her lip, or disappeared completely downward to fill up the little space left between them. And Rue could see the muscles shifting beneath the damaged skin of his back, like clouds stirring in the night sky, until she lost herself in sleep again.

When Rue's daddy died, Rue's mama died, though his death was a grim and sudden surprise and hers was a slow consumption by way of vengeance, spread out one long year after her man's death, easy as decaying.

"You clean?" Rue's mama was forever asking.

"Yes'm," Rue would say and shake dry her left hand and then the right.

When Rue's daddy died Miss May Belle stopped wanting to touch the mamas, maybe suspicious of the warmth of their flesh or the roundness of their baby joy. Whichever it was, she certainly had a distrust for them, which started up one day from a bad taste she found in her mouth.

"A curse been put onto me," Rue's mama said and she spat on the dusty ground, not even caring they were right outside of Marse Charles's House. Rue looked down at the pink tinge to the white foam of her mama's spittle and wondered if it were so.

In the cabin they shared alone, a privilege to be sure, Rue's mama began hanging fruit from the wood beams of the ceiling, any fruit she could get hands on, mainly apples,

154

cut in half, their black seeds gleaming like eyes in their white flesh. Even mealy, even molded, they spun in lazy circles and drew lazy flies. And Rue could not know if her mama had run to her madness or if she was warding off something she didn't want to name. The redder Miss May Belle's spit got, the more fruit she'd find to let swing.

If her mama was mad then Rue was mad too, at least in the eyes of other slavefolk. The rotting fruit smell clung to them both, trailing them, persistent as haints. It was beneath her mama's fingernails, which she had let grow long as creature claws, for she would not cut them, afeared that somebody would gather up the nail clippings to use against her in conjure. Rue, herself, washed and washed, trying to get the smell out from under her own skin. Now they'd kneel down at the birthings together, but it was Rue who touched the mamas, who tugged the babies into being. Her mama's guidance was as good as if Miss May Belle had her hand atop Rue's, as if their touch was one touch.

There came a day that Miss May Belle and Rue returned from a birthing of twins, an all-night and all-day affair, as if the twins had not wanted to come on out to the world but had preferred to stay curled together

155

with just themselves for company. Rue and her mama returned to find that all the fruit in their cabin had dropped to the ground, lay in blackened, defeated piles, on the chairs, on the stove pot, in the rut of the bed, and the once-languid flies had lifted and made a frenzy in the air like they'd lost their sense of meaning. But Miss May Belle didn't weep like a more earthly woman might. She walked around stooping, collecting the bits of skin and pulp and seed that near turned to nothing at her touch, and it was because of this quiet triumph against ruin that Rue couldn't bring herself to say, and never would, that she had been the one to pull the fruit down in a sudden fit of rage against her mama's rising madness. Hoodoo would not bring Miss May Belle's strength back, nor her man back. But neither would Rue's bitterness.

Miss May Belle pounded what was left of the fruit. She sat up in bed, for six days and six nights, from can-see to can't-see, a crude mortar in one hand, a rock for a pestle in the other. It was on the seventh day, when she'd become like a ghost in her own imprint in the mattress made of straw and pine tags, that they were told they were free.

Rue carried the message on to her mama, the words sitting like tar on her tongue, for it was something they'd so long wanted and now had but couldn't figure the use of.

"Free." Rue's mama said the word and then lay back down in her own hollowed-out shape in the bed. She let the mortar fall sideways and moved only to give herself room to spit a glob of red onto the blackened pile of mashed fruit, done with it at last. And Rue knew at least some part of Miss May Belle's sickness was healed, though it felt like a cure come too late to save her.

Even when Miss May Belle stopped going out, the women stayed coming to her. It was the end of secession, the end of the war and the beginning of that thing, freedom, that idea that had been bandied about for four long years and more, lobbed like cannonballs by the North into fine Southern houses. The smoke cleared and freedom stood. But freedom hadn't changed things much, not in their isolated country, down in the quarter, where women still had the same aches and pains, the same swelling and suffering, the same look of pure dumb wonder when Miss May Belle let them put their newborn to the safety of their chest. Maybe now they needed her even more because freedom was a word with weights.

It meant deciding — to stay or to go. To have or not to have. It was a heady change — becoming the master of one's own self.

"Not all women is intended for mamas," Rue's mama liked to say, lying on her back in bed looking up like she was looking for stars on the inside of her eyelids.

Even with her eyes shut Miss May Belle could direct Rue to this or that sachet or herb or salve, and it didn't take long 'til Rue knew what to fetch her before she even asked it. And then she knew what to fetch before the women finished describing what it was that they were needing. Soon enough Rue could just tell by looking at the expressions on some of the women's faces that they had come for that particular type of magic that Rue's mama kept hid.

The water Miss May Belle gave them was so clear it felt harmless enough, though what it tasted like Rue could not say. She only knew from watching what they experienced, and it looked to her no worse than the agonies of birth, only what they were pushing out was nothing but blood, not much heavier than what came month to month. Still, sometimes they'd cry and cry and always it amazed Rue, and still did, how hard it was to keep a baby and how hard it was to be rid of one.

■ ■ ■ ■

"You clean?"

"Yes, Mama," Rue'd say, only sometimes they weren't doing anything at all; sometimes they were doing little more than sitting around staring at each other on a Sunday, the day of rest, waiting for the next time they were needed, because they were bound up together by blood but also by the way folks had of keeping their distance. Inside of her on-and-on sleep, Rue's mama was beginning to get muddled; for her the present was the past come again.

They could just about hear the singing from outside if they felt like reaching out their ears to where the whole of the town was gathered in the church down the way, singing up to the Lord, thanking him for the day he'd made. And to Rue the sound of their voices was so absolutely lovely, like a thing she could hold in her hands, like a faith she could touch.

"Don't touch nothin'," her mama would say. A bad touch was all it took. A bad touch could kill.

The first time Rue pulled a dead baby from its mama, she felt that she had killed it herself. It was a baby boy, or would have been, sweet and black and small, a perfect fit for Rue's two cupped hands. He was still caught up in the cord he'd come out with, a constricting braid of blue and red, that wrapped too tight around his neck.

It had been a rough time from the very start. The mama was mostly a child herself with her eyes turning big and red and watery as the heat of her flesh rose. Her husband was an old man — his eyes were filmy and white — and he'd taken the young girl up because she had no people left of her own and he'd molded her into a wife.

There'd been a choice.

"Freedom," as Rue's mama liked to say, "be all about choices."

And so Rue had put the question to the man: his little woman's life or his little child's.

"Well now, Miss Rue," he said, his white eyes roving around lost and looking for somewhere to settle. "You know better than I do."

But how could she?

"The water ain't worth more than the bucket," Miss May Belle had said, not aloud in that moment, but loud in Rue's memory, as she'd said it so many times before.

No, Rue's mama was at that moment in

her bed, in the cabin she'd had built especially for her, far away from everybody else, for a healing woman had to live her life separate and die that way also. There Miss May Belle lay with the spit frothing red at her lips, the black cotton hair her man had loved so much in tangles, and the things she said choked by nonsense so that her very last words received and relayed by a lone traveling preacher had meant nothing. Rue had had to replace them in her memory with better words, with ones she wanted to keep: The water ain't worth more than the bucket.

Rue sent the old man away from the birthing — men, after all, were bad luck — and alone she spoke in a soft voice to the young mama, trying to give her comfort. For childbed fever there was black snakeroot, for grief, a few soft-spoken words.

"You gon' be alright," Rue told the young woman. "You gon' live to love lots more babies."

Miss Rue chose the bucket then as she would over and over and over again. She let the water slip right through her fingers.

FREEDOMTIME

More and more children were falling sick. There was no denying it or ignoring it or quieting it neither. It was most apparent in Ma Doe's schoolroom, where every other seat sat empty, words not written, lessons not learned. The illness had come on sudden and at a speed that shook Rue, coredeep. Out loud she blamed it on the cool weather, on those childhood ailments that came and went. But this sickness was clinging on in a way that worried her. Maybe Rue was glad then of the draw of Bruh Abel. At least it took folks' minds away from their suspicions about her. Still, the illness was unnatural, they were saying, an ill punishment brought on by the few sinners left in their midst. For Bruh Abel had baptized just about every willing sinner he could find, excepting Bean. And Rue.

And *that* woman. That woman — her name was Opal, and everybody knew her, biblically, as Rue's mama would have said. She'd lived on the only other plantation neighbor to theirs, the smaller settlement where Rue's daddy had lived. It was owned by Marse John, a piteous white man always in Marse Charles's shadow and in his debt. Opal had been Marse John's favorite right up 'til the day he died, *the damned apple,* Marse John had used to say, *of his god-damned eye.*

The rumor of it was that her master had died in bed with her, in fact, deep inside of her, his foul mouth running the whole time, until it wasn't.

"Goddammit goddammit goddammit god—" Those had been his last words if the things folks said could be believed, which in Rue's estimation, they usually couldn't.

Whatever the truth was, Opal had rolled right out from under him and made a life for herself the only way she could after that, which was by offering what she had to offer, on roadsides, in outhouses, more than once in the chicken coop, and Rue had had to treat the cuts from the chicken wire that made dizzy patterns on Opal's back. And Opal seemed alright with it, sure enough, there wasn't a bit of shame on her, *not enough shame to sew a stitch,* was how Miss May Belle might have said it, and Rue liked that about Opal, the way she owned her place and lived it, whisperings be damned. 'til Bruh Abel set on her.

When Bruh Abel came into town he took up quarters where he could, expecting a bed and finding a different one weekly or even nightly in the houses of the most devout. Opal kept him for three days, and on the third day she shrugged off her wickedness and was reborn.

"I'm just tired," Opal had said and maybe that wouldn't have been enough repentance for most preachers for a lifetime of wild lusting, but it was enough for Bruh Abel.

He did it in the square, in the center of the cross that was their town. Someone had brought out a stool, so Opal sat with her feet hovering over the bucket, her toes twitching above the water in spasms of virgin hesitation.

"Like this?" she asked, but already Bruh Abel was rolling up his sleeves.

Rue wouldn't have watched except that she was already at Ma Doe's, bringing a new pouch of herbs to wrap around the superstitious old woman's neck.

"All of this carryin' on. I liked the old prayin'," Ma Doe had said. " 'twas quiet."

But same as everyone Ma Doe went out to her porch to have a look at Bruh Abel, whose preaching she didn't often get to witness, the river being too far for her rheumatic knees to take her. Today Bruh Abel had brought the river to them, by the sloshing bucketful, and had placed it at Opal's feet.

Easing herself down into her rocking chair, Ma Doe nodded appreciatively. "He is fine lookin'," she said to Rue. "Who on earth wants an ugly preacher?"

This day Bruh Abel's expression was closed off and serious as though there was great focus required in washing a whore's feet. Opal had her skirt tucked up beneath her knees. Bruh Abel knelt before her and took both of her arches in his two hands and lowered her feet into the bucket. He had a small chipped cup that he dipped into the water between her legs, and he drew up a cupful and poured it onto one foot. Bruh Abel switched to the other foot, again pouring a stream of water as he held on to her heel, leaned forward, and placed a kiss between her biggest toe and its smaller partner. He held his lips there for a long reverent while.

Ma Doe drew Rue into her empty cabin with no more than a sly cant of her head.

No children in there. Rue flinched away

165

her foreboding.

"I've had news from up north," Ma Doe said.

She settled herself down behind the desk that had used to belong to Marse Charles. They'd only just rescued it from the fire that had destroyed the House. Now it dominated Ma Doe's schoolroom, a burnt-out treasure chest that held their secrets. Ma Doe's arthritic fingers turned the brass key and from one locked drawer she pulled out a letter, still in its envelope, and held it up to Rue. "Do you know what it says?"

No, Rue did not know, not by reading, but she recognized the big scrawling letter *V* that named the intended recipient of the correspondence, Varina, and from that she could easily imagine the rest. Ma Doe had read to her every one of those Northern letters which so rarely said anything new.

"The lady writes to her dear niece with concern for her niece's health," Ma Doe read. "Asks Varina, once again, to join the family in Boston. Says Christmastime is a most lovely occasion for the blessed reunion of estranged relations."

Rue tutted, "Ain't any time a lovely occasion for the reunion of relations?"

Ma Doe ignored her, went on, unspooling the letter to reveal its second page. "The

166

lady asks that her beloved niece think again on the proposition of finally selling her stakes of this ruined Southern land altogether. She writes that she understands the reluctance to give up one's childhood home and its fond memories, but mightn't Varina, her dear niece and the last of her brother's living children, come up to Boston to live permanently where she will be lovingly received?"

Ma Doe set the letter down on the top of the blackened desk. The fat, looping words of the letter written by Marse Charles's sister meant nothing to Rue, never had, not in their individual meaning, nor in each single character crowded on the page. But the piling-up pieces of paper, which Ma Doe had hoarded in the desk these three years — which formed an organized stack in that selfsame desk — the mere existence of those letters meant everything to Rue, for they meant that their secret conjure held, hers and Ma Doe's. The aunt did not suspect the hoax.

It was necessary that somebody out there where it mattered in the white world of records believed that the blacks of Marse Charles's former land were still owned — yet in the new way they were now meant to be owned, as devoted sharecroppers working the land for love of their stalwart white mistress, Miss Varina.

"What you gon' write back?" Rue asked.

Ma Doe worried the string of the good-luck charm around her neck. Said nothing.

"You gotta write back, Ma." They'd had this conversation before. Likely would have it again. It wearied Rue's soul but not her resolve. That correspondence, those bits of paper and their pen marks, they were more powerful a protection of the town's isolated existence than any curse that Miss May Belle had ever laid. Rue was proud on that fact, for it was an act of power better than conjure, the only real shield over their people being discovered by the type of whites who did not think much of government-given freedom.

" 'Thank you kindly, Aunt,' " Ma Doe said. Her wrinkled hand shook only slightly as she mimicked deft pen strokes in the air. "We'll say, 'Your concern as always is a great comfort to me. But I am most happy here and intend to stay on as long as I am able.' "

" 'God willin',' " Rue added.

Over some eighteen months of deception, Rue and Ma Doe had sent such fantastic tales up north they had a quilt's worth of stories about Miss Varina. To respond to the Northern relation, they'd given Varina

Christian faith and a penchant for acts of charity. They'd given her a keen knowledge of the harvests on her profitable property. They'd invented for her good white neighbors and the earnest interest of a fitting suitor, a kindly widower who was winningly cautious in his courtship, and finally a husband so that Varina's aunt might believe there was a good Christian man to manage Miss Varina's property and her prosperity. This loving Northern auntie had not once met the Southern relation she wrote to, didn't know the willful child or the sick woman Varina had grown up to become. It was easy for Rue to dictate a Varina of invention and easier still for Ma Doe to sign Varina's name. After all, Varina had learned her penmanship by tracing her black nurse's hand.

"Are we wrong for carryin' on this deception, Miss Rue?" Ma Doe asked. She was looking out the window, watching the folks out there enraptured in their praying. The sunlight played tricks on her face, showed wrinkles like valleys.

Rue figured Ma Doe was not looking for her to answer. Wrong or right was of little use to Rue now. Better she stay keen to the greater danger she sensed building in the air about her. Rue was troubled over the

169

babies and the young children who were falling sick with winter's maladies much too early this year. She troubled over the ire with which her name was spoken in the town. She troubled most especially over Bean, who so far had escaped the illness that had laid low the other children. She knew the strange little boy was soon to be Bruh Abel's next target. Rue was surrounded on all sides by more immediate fears and so she could only leave it down to trust that Ma Doe would go on writing the letters they agreed to, send each letter off by way of one of her students — one of the ones too slow to read it and make meaning of what the schoolteacher and the healing woman were keeping hidden between them.

Rue drew a newly made hoodoo charm from her pocket. Its wretched stink of crushed carrion flowers and asafetida powder was enough to ease the worry lines from Ma Doe's forehead. Rue untied the string of the worn-out good-luck charm Ma Doe had been wearing and replaced it with the new one. Knotting the string at the back of the ancient woman's neck, she came around her and settled the low-hanging pouch, making sure to tuck it neatly in the collar of Ma Doe's dress.

There, no one would see the conjure

trinket Ma Doe kept near her heart, nor the thick strand of Varina's curly red hair that Rue had worked artfully into the knot — a lock that held their tenuous magic all together.

The townsfolk hesitated to hang out their white baptismal clothing again, even as the promised Sunday of Bean's baptism drew nearer. They reckoned that to do so would be to tempt the return of the haint that had come to tear down their faith before, along with their white washing on the occasion of Si's death. Yet they were afraid of Bean and demanded to see him saved, for their own sake.

"It'll be alright," Rue told them, and it would.

Rue took the climb to her mama's grave on the hilltop cemetery slowly. She felt she was dragging along all her fear behind her like a yoke. Fear for the sick children, fear of Bruh Abel, fear for Bean.

Folks believed they'd found in Bean the evil that needed washing away: Bean, a baby boy born with hideous black eyes like he'd come up from a coffin, rather than from a womb. Now they demanded to flush the evil out, through baptism.

As she walked, Rue came upon the new-

171

est graves first, closest to the town by planning. The white family's graves were as large as monuments — cherubs and weeping women and ornate crosses all.

When she and Varina were children they'd often played in the solitude of this cemetery. Varina had read aloud the headstones on one such visit. They had loved always to play the type of games that contained secrets, Rue and Varina had, loved even more the forbidden thing that was their friendship.

Beyond the white graves, where the former slaves were laid to rest, there were no headstones. There were, instead, bits of wood and pretty glass and here and there a natural stone, renewed each season like a clearing of harvest and a sowing of new seeds.

After Surrender, after the war and the fire that ate up the House, after the Northern army had marched through, plundered what they liked, and moved on to the next place they could pick at as any scavenger would, after all of that and after freedom, the black folks had made their way up onto this hill and begun calling out the names of their lost dead, names for bodies they couldn't bring home or bury.

Ma Doe, ancient as she was, learned her letters in a time when there weren't yet laws against slave-learning, and when the laws did come it was too late; they could not take the knowing away from her. On the plantation there were a few other former slaves who had also learned their writing and reading, in secret, all of them having done so despite threat of death or worse if they were caught at knowing. But just like that, the threat was lifted, knowledge emancipated. And so in the graveyard Ma Doe and the other learned black folks etched into crude planks the names of the lost dead. Everybody had promised that if by some miracle lost bodies came walking back from the far-off places they'd been sold to, then they'd pluck the crosses right up, but few of the lost had ever returned.

Folks had made a grave for Varina, after she'd been burnt up in the fire that took the House. Even though their young Missus was not their black kin she was still *theirs,* and lost, and they figured she needed remembering also. Remembering for good or remembering for ill — well, that was a private matter.

Rue touched the crooked cross she knew spelled out Varina's name, touched the first letter, which Rue knew was called *V* only because Varina had taught her that letter over and over in their girlhood.

173

In front of the little cross Rue bent her head and mumbled words like prayer, and anybody that might've spied her at it would think she was caught up in sorrow.

Rue moved on to sit at her mama's grave. Miss May Belle's body had been laid down in a most mighty plot, because Miss May Belle had dictated what it ought to look like. The planning of it was the only thing that had made her smile from deep inside the swamp of her sickbed. She'd chosen for herself pot marigolds in the yellow and orange of a slow-burning fire, and now, two years since she'd been gone, the things grew wild, threatened to spill over onto other graves, eat up the white folks' monolith headstones. For certain she'd meant it that way, and it fell to Rue to beat the plants back.

Rue pulled up an armful of her mama's weeds before they could come to seed. She swam in the musky scent. Whatever else her mama had intended, the marigold plant made for a fine base for a number of tinctures, a thousand kinds of healing. Might they be the first ingredient in a cure to heal the town's sick children?

It was only on her way out that Rue allowed herself to look at the newest grave, freshly dug, a small plot suited for an infant child: Baby Si.

Though she knew who was laid in that child grave, strangely she thought first of Bean and shivered. But that was wrong, and foolish besides; this grave was not his. She would not believe that Bean was some omen, nor some dead child come again. Rue was determined not to believe it. How else to go on and convince the town of the same, before their hate of Bean turned to some desperate, dangerous action against him?

Rue finally drew the strength to go back into the town proper, and even there she slowed to force a smile and talk a little with folks. Yet now they hurried past her, as though afraid to linger in her company, and the little children she came upon at the roadside declined the posy of marigold she offered them like she held out a bloom of poison.

Bruh Abel passed her, aloud wished her blessings, and whispered in her ear. "Soothe them away from this foolishness about the haint. They'll listen to you, Sister Rue. In matters of superstition," the preacher man said, "yours is the voice they hear."

Rue soothed them by bidding them to take a broom about with them to sweep away footsteps they left in their wake, so that the haint could not follow them home.

"You can be known by a footprint as sure as a face," she told Dinah, who began to sweep her pathway in earnest, her baby on her back. Dinah had got to feeling particularly fixed upon, seeing as she'd seamstressed so many of those fine white clothes that had been torn down.

"Will that haint try an' take out my eyes, Miss Rue?" Dinah asked as she moved the dust in swirls behind her. On her back her baby still looked sickly. Looked worse. "I can't see my stitches. My eyes, they burn in my head."

"How long this been going on?"

"Well, now. Started up round the time folks started wanting to see Bean washed."

"Boil some mullein leaves in whiskey," Rue said, unsettled. "And rub it on the back a' yo' neck and the soles a' yo' feet, and any spirit will lose the scent a' you. Do it every morning, every night. Do it three mornings, three nights."

Dinah said that she would, and she would too, Rue reckoned. The cure would do nothing for a haunting, but it would keep Dinah off her sewing for a time and the smell of the leaves might cut through her baby's sniffling.

Sometimes Rue dreamed of Miss May

Belle, and she dreamed of her on that next night before she got herself out of bed at the hour of the midnight moon.

Rue had nightmared a memory: Miss May Belle standing before her with a bloodied sheet bundled in her arms.

"Mama? Is it Varina?" Rue asked her dream-mama. "Is she alright?"

Miss May Belle wouldn't answer, only held out the black bundle.

"The shame," her mama called it. She said, "Bury the shame in the river and let us be rid a' it."

But there was no sure way to be rid of shame, no conjure to be rid of guilt. Even if the bundle never rose again it still flooded around Rue, the shame did. It rose in the mind, in her dreams and then in her waking, and in the face of every slowly sickening child she could not save.

She woke feeling as though Miss May Belle were truly there, standing over her. There was nothing for it but to get up and out of the cabin. She gulped the cool night air to clear her nightmare, like clarity was breath. She had to think. She had to act to save herself.

While others slept Rue walked a long lone circle round the plantation to weave a protection spell. A sprinkling of black

177

pepper here and there on the long, sweeping trails folks had left with their brooms to dispel the hungry foxes that were said to be Miss May Belle's familiars — her eyes where her eyes could not see. Rue did not wish to be seen.

Then Rue went way out past the burnt-up edges of the plantation where most folks were afeared to go, on to the old church, a basket filled with fruit and biscuits and a bloom of fiery marigolds tucked under her arm.

The double doors of the church were shut against the night, but there was a slight, silent rocking up there at the top of the small bell tower. Its rope swung with a motion more forceful than could be accounted for by the wind alone. At the doorstep she laid down the basket and left, returned to her cabin, careful to see that she had not been followed or observed. There she waited, sleepless, for morning.

It was the day that Bean was to be baptized and so folks hardly paid much mind to the other news: Dinah's baby girl had died in the night.

"I called for you," Dinah said when Rue came to confirm what was already cold and clear. The little baby's body was wrapped

178

up in the fine linen Dinah had seamstressed herself. "You wasn't home."

Rue had missed the knock at her door. It had come when she'd been out, tending to haints, and in that little time Dinah's baby had sickened and died.

In folks' fervent enthusiasm for Bruh Abel they did not pay much mind to one more quiet tragedy that had moved through the town while they slept. But Rue was altogether haunted by this new-come illness, by its stealth and its power.

Bean was to be washed in the eyes of the Lord at midday.

The townsfolk passed by Rue's cabin on the way to the river, and inside Rue pretended at grinding pokeweed berries for longer than was needed. She burst the black skin of the berries in her agitation, freed the red juice and still continued to pound and pound. Errant flecks of red stained the front of her dress and still she pounded as though she could work herself to the kind of exhaustion they'd all felt in slavery times, a complete utter exhaustion too great to leave room for rage. She felt rage at herself for allowing Bean to dredge up that old secret shame inside of her. The past was made up of bloody losses she could not change, while

179

here, now, real living babies might suffer and die.

Yet Rue's rage grew, not only at herself but also at Bruh Abel and his false spectacle 'til finally she marched on out to the bright morning. Still she took the long way round, came upon them at the river from the height of the trees.

They were all in white. Bean, Jonah, and Sarah with their elder boy and their only girl. Someone had made them all little white caps that gave them the closest approximation they had ever had to a unified family resemblance. Bruh Abel, for his part, was not in his usual suit but was instead dressed in white too, in a robe that showed his audacity as the length of it caught and rippled on the water's surface.

Rue took careful steps on the slope that led down to the riverbank, and many times her feet failed to find a grasp on the shifting silt and rock, but she didn't look down; she kept her eyes on the curious scene, on Bruh Abel, who was leading the family one by one into the river. She kept right on watching them as she reached the edge of the crowd, where a few people murmured or nodded to her, said in greeting, "Miss Rue." They couldn't hardly pull themselves away from the show to look at her; they were

180

transfixed, all of them, and singing.

Rue did not know the words to their song. She could not join them but she could listen, and she picked out the words on which their voices lingered: *Jesus* and *Jordan* and *river*. The refrain was something heavy with wanting, and she liked the part they kept repeating about going home, going on home.

Out in the water they had formed a snaking chain, Bruh Abel at its head, then came Sarah holding Bean, then the boy and the girl and last Jonah. He made them form a half circle, so that the two older children stood in the shallowest part of the river where the water lapped up against their chests, and Jonah and Sarah beside them looked as small as the children because of the way the bank dipped down. Bruh Abel stood just beyond them and took Bean from Sarah's arms.

Bean was in Bruh Abel's hands when the first splash of water reared up against his skin and there it was, his horrid cry. It pierced their ears as Bruh Abel tried to cross the boy's pale arms against his chest. Everyone hushed their singing, waited for Bruh Abel to set things right, to stop the awful child with his awful crying. If only he could catch Bean's flailing fists, could halt that otherworldly wailing.

Bean's family stood in the water beside him and seemed shamed, like they wanted to look away but couldn't. You could not draw away from such painful screaming.

Rue didn't know she was moving. It was not until she felt the shock of cold water at her thighs — each step was a struggle of pride, a struggle just to push her legs against the water. Her last thought before she reached for Bean was that there could be no worse death than this, being pulled down by a river. But that was a pure fool thought as well, because there were so many worse ways to die — hadn't she seen some of them?

Her foot hit a loose stone that spun and bobbed away from the riverbed and she was falling sideways. Rue saw Jonah's shocked face first and then Sarah's blank one, then she saw nothing but the expanse of the river's underside, which was black and black. There was no bottom and no top to swim to, and all the while she heard Bean's crying and yearned to comfort him the way she yearned after air.

Bruh Abel caught her and pulled her up and set her on her feet again with one hand, Bean clutched in the other. Water ran down her face into her mouth. Jonah and Sarah had not moved to help her. Already Bruh Abel was placing Bean into Rue's arms. The baby reached out to her. His crying stopped and she held him tight.

Around her Rue heard voices begin to pray. *Lord trouble the water.*

In her arms Bean had quieted. She didn't know what it was about her that soothed him, and he her. Maybe it was that he remembered her, the first person that had held him. Or maybe it was that he remembered her, from before even that.

Rue felt Bruh Abel's hand squeeze the nape of her neck, felt his other hand rest on her waist a moment before he tipped her backward.

When she felt the water again it was a shock, like she was falling in a dream when she hadn't yet figured out that she was sleeping. She held fast to Bean. His head on her breasts positioned him just high enough that he was not all the way submerged beneath the water. He was halfway in; she was the one who was submerged, who was drowning. She was the island he clung to.

Bruh Abel put his hand on her stomach, his thumb in the dent of her navel, and he kept her down, pushed her down even as she struggled to rise. She saw the flush of bubbles leave her nostrils and rush to the surface. Held just above the water, Bean was a weight on her chest and there was Bruh Abel's hand below her belly, pushing down into a place she'd never felt any hand pushing but her own.

Then that cold upward rush and Rue knew she was standing again only because she heard his voice, hard and brassy, confident: "As Jesus died and was reborn, so Rue and Bean, you have both died and been reborn."

Surely, they had died. With Bean in her arms Rue was shivering cold like they were still down there, stuck together in the watery grave of their shared baptism waiting to rise, waiting on a rebirth she did not believe in.

It was just after Bruh Abel left town that the sickness began to pull down more children. It had taken away Dinah's baby girl, but soon enough death rode boldly through the town, made itself well known in every home. The men plowed graves and laid the lost children in them, and Rue stood behind in the furrowed field, unable to offer any help or any explanation. Faced with the blooming grief of the mamas and daddies, she did not know what to think, nor what to do.

When Bruh Abel had been in town they'd

all still been hopeful, basking in their fall of plenty. But as he did every year, Bruh Abel followed the warmth, descending south. The season turned quick to winter. An unusual cold glazed the grass in rare stiff white as more of the children began to burn with fever, to writhe in their beds, to moan and cry out and fight, and then to die.

Dinah's girl might have been the first, but gradually it took hold from all directions and before long there was at least one suffering child in each home with children. For the first three nights of the thick of it Rue did not sleep but drifted from door to door facing folks who wanted healing but didn't trust her to deliver it. Rue did not trust herself. *What would Miss May Belle have done?* they started asking, and she didn't have an answer there either. Folks blamed Bean and Rue. She knew that all round town they told and retold the story of Bean's baptism so that it had become more legend than memory in the retelling.

One truth was repeated over and over: Bean had not been fully submerged, nor fully baptized. For Miss Rue, the witch, had held Bean half aloft.

Rue did not have an answer for all the illness, but she did have a rule, one she had not learned from her mama, but one she'd

185

come, in that grim time, to form for herself. That rule was to wait. It was only the difference of a moment, a hair's breadth of time between when the knowledge of a death came to her and when the grave words came out. But there was power in that moment of stillness, power in waiting before telling a mama her baby was dead, and Rue held tight to that power.

She told herself it was a kindness, the waiting, because a mama might know it already, holding her baby as a stiffened bit of flesh in their arms. Only moments ago, that same baby would have been writhing fever-hot. Now they were still.

The desperate mama had to know it, but 'til Rue said it, it was as if they could convince themselves it wasn't so, as if Rue might have a cure-all with which to raise the dead. She did not. What she did have was the power of pronouncement, the power to delay absolute sorrow for a few long, weighty seconds.

Dinah's girl and Beulah's boy were the first of them to die, though after those deaths many turned to saying it had all begun even before, when Bean's cry had yielded Si's death all them months back. Si had never been baptized and now look here, all these little children, dying, before they

186

could properly get saved. Rue told them it was only a grim coincidence. After all, the sickness had taken Beulah's boy suddenly, in the space of a single evening.

"He was playin' just this morning," Beulah had said the night she'd roused Rue from her cabin to come have a look at her sick little child. When the fever started rising, Beulah had braided her son's Red Indian hair into a silken rope, perhaps to keep him cool. It lay beside him on the bed, that braid, and it was intricate and lovely, made of four wound strands that snaked in and out of each other, that held without the aid of a ribbon or a pin. Rue counted the knots with her eyes while she waited.

"I'm sorry," she said and she was, but more so, she was frightened.

Li'l Sylvia had five children and each of them caught the sickness, and each of them died of it, one by one. She took to her kitchen in her inconsolable grief, cooked ashcake after ashcake, good as her mama Big Sylvia used to make for the master in slaverytime. Li'l Sylvia set all of them ashcakes down on her supper table, a place laid out for each of her little ones, and waited and waited like she hoped they'd come back from the grave with a hunger.

Three of Ma Doe's orphans came down with it next. Two lived, one died, and though the one who died had no people alive to mourn him, the whole town took up the job of steady grieving. The sorrow was in everything they did, the sorrow and the fear.

When it got to be at its worst, Rue heard, though no one would tell her straight, that they had sent Charlie Blacksmith to get the white doctor down the way. Down the way was a journey of two days' walking, less if Charlie could beg a ride along the big road someplace, and at the end lived the Quaker doctor who was known to show a kindness to black folks provided they could pay. They'd sent Charlie with a purse of money, an appropriately enticing offering, and they had set aside another amount waiting for the doctor to arrive, which he never did. When it had gone a week with no sign of Charlie Blacksmith, Rue knew that they had all given up, though they hadn't said so. She could see it in the slack set to their faces that they had come to believe that what they were needing was not a healing woman, or a white doctor, after all, but a preacher man.

Ol' Joel was the first of the old folks to get it and to die of it. He went to bed in the afternoon and didn't get up after. Rue knew it was the same sickness. Folks said he'd been complaining all day of the heat though the day was mighty cold. The townsfolk sent Rue after him and she found him that evening, cocooned in his sheets like he was a body already bound for the coffin maker. When Rue neared his bedside he began thrashing, fighting like he had as a boy when the slavers had plucked him out of the jungle in Africa.

"There's a witch," the old man insisted. "She setting on my chest."

"Hush now," Rue said, glad no one else was there to hear. To accuse.

She was afraid to leave him lest somebody else were to take up the vigil and hear the madness that was frothing up like the spittle in the corners of his toothless mouth.

"Witch done made that boy-child outta river clay," Ol' Joel railed.

Bean. Rue wouldn't say his name, like to bring mention of him into this sick room was to curse him. But it was on her tongue. She knew he was the boy-child Ol' Joel was speaking on.

"Witch gave him air from her own mouth an' fire from her own belly. Marse Charles'll know of it."

Or was he speaking on the hidden shame?

How could he know?

Rue stood up so fast the chair she'd perched in crashed to the ground.

"Marse Charles ain't know nothin' but what the inside of a grave look like," she said. "And you gon' know the same, soon enough."

Ol' Joel's cheeks went hollow as he gasped out his shock, like the sunken-down face of a skull. Rue stepped back from his bedside and righted the chair and tried to right her breathing but there was nothing for it.

"I ain't mean to say that," Rue said. "I'm sorry."

Ol' Joel's expression turned gleeful. He clapped his hands together like a child at play, spoke singsong as he made mud pies in the air. "I know about Bean."

"Hush," Rue said. If she could only soothe him. Get him to rest.

"Miss May Belle tol' it to me."

But Miss May Belle had not lived long enough to see Bean born. "Tol' you what?"

"She say Bean's eyes is the hole you dug to bury the baby in."

Rue had never left a dying man or woman or child, not ever, not even when she herself was a child, kneeling beside deathbeds. She'd listened to every rasp and rattle and final godforsaken wheeze. But she could not listen to this. She fled.

Come the morning, Ol' Joel was dead. She returned to his bedside at sun-up to find him still, silenced. Rue took up the chair she'd toppled over when she'd run. She sat herself down and let folks think she'd been sitting there all night.

Then Bean's brother and sister both caught the sickness. The skin of their high-yellow cheeks became dotted with twin flushes of red.

Rue, afraid for Bean, afraid for them all, was sleepless. She spent most of her evenings visiting the sick — children and the elderly came down with it the quickest and fared the worst — and even when she was not needed she'd wake suddenly in the middle of the night, imagining that somebody had been pounding at her door, though nobody had.

Sarah had the same harried look as all the mamas in the town, a kind of sickness in itself, that worry, but at the mention of Bean a line creased deeply between her brows.

"Bean, he's the onlyest one the sickness ain't touched," she said. And the suspicion was there in her voice. "These 'uns need you, now."

Rue looked over the brother and sister

who lay together in the same bed, fighting against each other in helpless writhes against the heat, but at least they were fighting. The boy's ways for breathing seemed clear but the girl's nose was blocked up; it dripped in a sad puddle onto her upper lip.

Rue drew out her pipette. It was only a bit of tin that she'd found and rolled and smoothed so it had no rough edges, and ever so gently she placed it into the girl's one nostril and then the other, drawing the plugged-up business out of her with a careful inhale. The trick was to get it just far enough up the pipe to give the child ease of breath but not to draw so far as to have the snot end in her own mouth. It had happened once or twice, the sickness sitting thick on Rue's tongue. It had so worried her each time that she'd taken to her roots and plants 'til she was dizzy with it, unsure if she was suffering more from the sickness or the cure.

The trick with the pipette was more a balm for the mamas' nerves. They were given to panic when their babies gulped open-mouthed for air. The only cure she knew of was time. Either the babies would die or they wouldn't, but that's not what anybody wanted to hear, and so Rue knew better than to say so.

Rue insisted on looking over Bean before she left. She found him with Jonah behind the house. He was at the age of walking now, and he stood wobbly and watched with those wide black eyes of his as his daddy worked. Jonah was carving up the carcass of a wild pig for their supper. He had it hoisted up on a wood frame, swinging by its neck, tongue out and listless.

She observed them for a while, daddy and son, recollecting two years back. After Bean's birth she had spied Jonah cutting firewood, wet with sweat as he was now. Then she had shoved into Jonah's arms the black caul from which Bean had slithered and told Jonah to burn the sheets. For luck, she'd said. Now the whole of the town stunk of burning sheets, and behind each house great plumes of dark smoke would rise like a silent signal for a grief that had gotten so bad that they no longer had the words for it. The thinking was to get rid of the sheets as marks of their dead, but the sickness, Rue feared, was well beyond being burnt up.

Jonah put a long, neat slit down the belly of the barrow hog he'd strung up. He began to peel back the skin, buried his hands deep into its belly to tug away its innards.

"It's a bad year, sho' 'nuff." He spoke round a grunt of effort. The pig's intestines slopped downward. "Folks is down on they knees, prayin'. We needin' you to help us, Miss Rue."

Bean reached for her. "Up," he was saying. "Up, up." He raised his arms in that easy gesture of children, and Rue wanted to hold him as much as he wanted to be held. When she hefted him up, he was a nice weight in her arms, and that close he smelled sweet to her, healthy, even over the sickly smell of the hog Jonah was butchering.

"I can't answer all a' them prayers," Rue said.

" 'Course not," Jonah said.

Rue wanted to thank him for that, his comforting lie. She knew what folks were saying. They'd lost faith in her, even feared her, some of them. She juggled Bean in her arms and reached out, touched the swell of Jonah's upper arm, the only place the pig blood hadn't reached. It was supposed to be a loving gesture, but she pulled sharply away before she could give it. She hardly had to get near him to realize: His skin was near to burning.

It would pass in him, wouldn't it? It had to, a man so strong and grown. Even if he had the sickness it would not ravage him like it might his children, but something

194

about the power of it, to weaken even Jonah, made Rue feel weak herself. She told Jonah he better lay himself down for a rest, and she pulled Bean tight into her arms and hid her face in the softness of his baby hairs to rest there awhile herself.

Beulah, who had been among the first to lose her baby, was the worst.

"He gone," Rue told her. The woman had begun to wail as if the scream had been building and building in her, saved 'til just this moment.

Beulah collapsed like her legs were of no use and Rue went down with her as an instinct, afraid she'd smack her head against the ground. Beulah did the opposite. She reared her head back as she screamed those two words: *Your fault.* She smashed forward, catching the edge of Rue's jaw. Rue felt her mouth filling up with a rush of blood — she didn't have a second to worry or to spit — because Beulah was hitting her with her fists now, punching at her shoulders in time with the repeated hollow syllables of her son's name. She was saying it over and over, and saying, "You done this! You and that Bean. This y'all curse."

Beulah's man came out of nowhere to pull Beulah away. He did it easily, put his arms around her waist and picked her up like she was a child, and she weakened and wept against him, the whole shape of her fitting to his chest.

Rue heard it all over then in every corner of the used-to-be plantation, what folks were saying. They wanted help. But not from her. *Bruh Abel. Send someone to find him, to fetch him. Give him word. Bring him to pray over us. For Bruh Abel is,* they were saying, *the only hope we got* as more children sickened daily. It seemed to be passing through all of them in no sort of order, only weakening some, but snatching away others. It was Ma Doe's health that Rue feared after especially, though to say so was an ugly thing. If Ma Doe died all those orphans would be orphaned again, but most importantly, if Ma Doe died the spell of protection Rue had created with her over the town would be broken. Without Ma there was nobody Rue trusted with the secret, nobody to send correspondence north, nobody to pose as their white mistress behind the looping lines of oak gall ink. And if there were no letters to the Northern auntie it would only be a matter of time before some white official came along wondering after their white mistress and her untouched acres. Freedom wasn't free.

On this day Ma Doe was teaching in the usual way. She held up letters that she'd written big and bold, each one existing solitary on either side of thirteen sheets of yellowy paper. She made the sounds and the children made them back, a call and response that Rue found soothing. Sometimes she mouthed the sounds with them, though she did not add her voice to theirs. From Ma Doe's side she looked them over, the children, checking for sweat sitting on the skin of the darker ones, red blooming on the cheeks of the lighter, or for a pair of shiny, unfocused eyes struggling to make sense of their mud-made letters.

Rue hoped each day would be the day when they'd finally be free of the spreading fever. Winter would soon be giving way to spring, and everything, as her mama would have said, good or bad, had an end.

When Rue arrived this morning, Ma Doe dismissed the children in a hurry. The younger ones were pardoned to go play then return for a lesson in figures; the older went off for the work waiting on them at the side of their mamas and daddies. Rue found herself sorrowing after it, those blind simple days when she herself had been a child.

"How you doin', Ma Doe?" she asked. She took Ma Doe's hand in hers in greeting, believing that whatever the old woman said, she'd find the true answer in the heat of her palm. The skin was warm but dry, and Rue held on long to a callous that rose up when Ma Doe had been writing.

"Well, you know what folks are sayin'," Ma Doe said. She culled gossip from her children who were in the habit of repeating, with some authority, the things their daddies and mamas said in private. "They're all of 'em mistrustful of you and your Bean."

Now when had Bean become hers? Ma Doe was slowly retracting her one hand from between Rue's two.

"And what they sayin'?"

"He isn't sick. He hasn't been sick. So people are thinkin' he isn't goin' to be sick. Of all the children, seems he's the only one that's kept his health."

Rue frowned. "Say it plain, Ma."

"Some folks think you're the one keepin' him healthy. And some folks think you pullin' vitality from the other little ones to do it. Usin' that contraption you've got."

"Contraption?" Rue stumbled on the word.

"Your tool for suckin'. It isn't natural.

Like root magic, they're sayin'. Like witch-craft."

"Where this come from?" But Rue, as soon as she asked it, knew where it had come from. It was inevitable, like birth and death and birth, like smoke rising toward the sky, it was just the way things went. Folks were scared. They needed their finger-pointing for succor.

"They talk of little Si," Ma Doe continued. Rue thought on Si often, thought on how he'd lived three days and died before they could put him to the water. They'd wanted him baptized but she'd wanted him to live.

"Folks say you went to see him and tracked graveyard dirt by his sleeping face. They don't want you near their children, Miss Rue," Ma Doe said. Her voice held that steely finality she used to end her lessons. "They've asked me to not allow you in here any longer whilst the children are near."

"You tol' 'em I could help their babies, ain't you?" Her voice was rising. "You tol' 'em that ain't none a' that foolishness is true?"

Ma Doe shrugged. "I felt I hadn't the right to tell them anythin'." She touched a hand to the pouch of asafetida that she wore just under her collar, perhaps without even

199

realizing. "I find in my old age I haven't got any more strength for lyin'."

Rue felt something awful building up inside of her chest, something like a sob. "It ain't a lie."

Ma Doe's nimble fingers were unsteady as she pulled a key from a chain of many at her waist. She put it to the desk drawer, turned the key in the lock with a sharp *clink* that sounded loud in the empty schoolroom, like bullet to chamber. "I haven't yet sent a reply to our Northern relation. I don't know that I will."

"Why not?"

"Nigh on two years we've been tellin' lies about Miss Varina. One lie to the auntie, another to the townspeople. Our own people." Ma Doe bowed her head as if it was too heavy suddenly for her to hold on her neck.

"Ain't nobody the wiser," Rue said.

"Don't you sometimes think, Miss Rue, that the Lord has been takin' his good time to punish us? That the best contrived punishment is the one that you near forgot you deserved?"

"This ain't to do with us, Ma, or with Varina neither," Rue said, and she gestured at the empty air like their haint was right there with them. "It's a simple sickness. It'll pass. You best send that letter."

Ma Doe relented. But Rue couldn't help it: She thought of Bean and the day he was born, the moment she first saw him swathed in a caul as black as a blood-soaked blanket, like something she'd seen before. Another ill omen. A wrong come again. Rue knew why she had thought about killing Bean in that moment. But she had not. The past was the past.

Now she wanted Bean to live. Jonah already seemed stronger than he had on the night she'd touched his skin. Sarah had complained of a sudden bout of sweating, but there was little that could put her down, and anyway the sickness seemed to flutter more easily past grown folks and instead settled its grip on children.

But soon there was only Bean, untouched.

That night Rue didn't sleep. She felt she ought to be crying. But she could not make tears or didn't trust herself to. At any moment she feared she'd have to get up and answer another accusation. The pounding of death again at her door.

The longer the night stretched the longer her fear did. She thought on Bean, on the sideways glances folks would give him when they saw him playing in Sarah's yard. He

201

played alone. Rolling a ball or a hoop from one end of the narrow garden to the other, then rolling it back again in the same little rut. He'd always been a solitary sort of child, but now the other mamas wouldn't let their babies play anywhere near him. Like he was the pestilence himself. It ought to have been the other way around. Their children carried the sickness; he thrived. And because he did thrive and showed no signs of sickening, Rue figured they were both of them in an even worse kind of danger.

Rue tried to clear her head, to think on how to avert their envy of Bean's vitality, all their loathing after his very life. She couldn't count on Sarah to protect Bean, even if he was her child. She had two other children to worry about after all. Would Sarah sacrifice the one to shield the two? Rue didn't know. She was not a mama herself.

What she was was a healing woman, and she found herself thinking on how to heal Bean from an affliction he did not have.

What would Miss May Belle do? It was a question that had been posed to Rue throughout the town as though they half-expected her to go on to the cemetery, to pull up her dead mama's body and ask her for a cure.

Rue paced the little length of the cabin. The room had seemed so much bigger when she was a child. She'd lived there all her life with her mama, but now, empty, it felt more like a cage than it had ever done. In her pacing she felt like Miss May Belle was there, sitting on the end of her bed like she'd just come in from a long day of hoodooing and healing to toss her basket down and throw off her hat and to look at her child with that certain furrowing of the lines of her forehead like she couldn't remember why she'd allowed herself a daughter in the first place if that daughter was going to go ahead and be so foolish.

"Rue-baby," Miss May Belle would've said, "there ain't no easier lie to tell folks than the one they wanna believe."

Miss May Belle had always spoke in loops and swirls that may as well've been written down for all the use Rue could find in interpreting them. But this bit of recollected wisdom Rue let latch on and suck at her 'til it became fully grown. Soon she had an idea.

SLAVERYTIME

1855

Miss May Belle had made another doll baby. Rue had found it hid amongst her mama's healing things and knew right away that it did not belong there standing behind the tinctures. Surely, the doll baby was meant for Rue, was to be a gift for her seventh birthday, the first birthday gift she was ever going to get. It looked like Rue. Had her flat nose and dark skin. It had her hair done up in black corkscrews, a bramble that stood up straight no matter how it was brushed. The doll baby had Rue's thick red lips, painted in a bow, and black beads sewn on for glistening walnut eyes. It wore a green dress, which was the color Rue most preferred because it reminded her of the woods, flush in springtime.

Miss May Belle had her ways. Healing herbs were in one place and cursing roots in another, and not a thing was ever mislaid or misplaced. Lord forbid she ever get the two things mixed up.

Rue found the doll baby half-made. Its fabric face was unstuffed, its sack arms dangled with unfinished thread. Beneath its green skirt the black body dropped off, all hollow inside as a tree trunk.

Rue was not supposed to be looking where she was looking. She was not allowed to get at Miss May Belle's medicinals when her mama wasn't at home to advise at them — and even then her mama hovered. But Rue liked to look on the liquid cures and poultices of dried herbs that sat up there on the high shelf. She wanted to ruminate on their ingredients, to memorize the plants from which they took their origin. Better than magic, that.

The doll was sat on the back of a high shelf in their cabin, behind a jar full of jimson weed tea, a place that a doll did not belong — and a thing in a place where it did not belong was oft there for secret reasons, Rue knew.

Rue figured she was about to turn seven years old that spring because Varina was about to turn seven. At about-to-be seven years old Rue's favorite thing was secrets, and she had become quite good at gathering them, the way she was good at gathering leaves and seeds and flower heads; *my li'l rabbit,* her mama called her.

With both seeds and secrets the approach was quite the same — go where other folks don't. The path between the House and the slave quarter, for instance, was over-trod, with the coming and going of hurrying black folks who woke at cock's crow and were off, to serve Marse Charles in his home or in his field depending on his pleasure. Rue found the best plants for her mama in far-off places, less traveled. At the wide part of the river or in a thicket beyond the hen house, or down at the edge of Marse Charles's land, the very edge of creation as far as she knew it — that was where the best wildflowers grew.

Secrets were the same. Rue heard them in isolated corners, and because she was slight and dark and quiet and because she was often dismissed as the strange healing woman's shy daughter, she could go where others could not and hide in sight of folks and not be seen at all.

At first, Rue gave Miss May Belle all her gathered secrets, same as any yielded crop. Say that Rue crept by the outhouse, overheard the house girls talking that Marse Charles had made a visit to their rooms, *chose a mulatta like he choosin' a horse from his stables for a day's ride out.* Rue might not know the meaning of the secrets, but she could repeat them fine enough, pass them on to her mama, and sure enough Miss May Belle would slip a cure to the mulatta in passing — a pouch cupped in a handshake — that would set the girl to rights before she would ever have to utter her shame.

Rue heard the secrets of white folks too, and that's how she first heard tell of the war, from Missus and a visitor of hers, a translucent pale woman in a big blue hat that highlighted the frosty color of her eyes and the veins beneath her pale skin. Rue had had the misfortune of walking past when the visitor had come calling. Perhaps Rue hadn't looked busy enough, being on her way to bring water to the hands in the field. Missus had bidden Rue to put down her bucket, picked her out to come and fan them with a fat palmetto leaf while Missus and the visitor took iced tea on the veranda. In sight of her guest, Missus rubbed Rue's head adoringly as a beloved pet, "for luck," she said and chuckled.

Rue spent hours there working the fan, listening to the women jaw on and on. The ice cubes in their glasses glinted like diamonds before they dissipated into filmy sugar water with the midday heat, and not a drop of it for Rue the whole long afternoon. The white women started to swim in her vision, hazy, and still she fanned.

"They talked and talked and talked like I was deaf and dumb besides," Rue complained to her mama that night. Her arms still ached, felt to her like they were still in motion, up, down, up, down to the rhythm of the white women's chatter.

Miss May Belle shrugged. She had her own hurts from a long day and evening and night of seeing to the hurts of others.

At the supper table, Miss May Belle shut her eyes. She did this sometimes, like to shut out the world, the eyeballs spinning clear beneath the lids like she was searching. Folks saw it and thought it was how Miss May Belle got her knowledge on what hoodoo to wield or what salve to soothe a pain with, but Rue knew the secret of it. It was her mama's way of snatching at a little bit of quiet, and Rue knew better than to talk when Miss May Belle was about her eye-shutting.

Unobserved, Rue let her sights drift up to the shelf where she knew the doll baby was hidden, wondered when her mama might give it to her. Perhaps her birthday, though she didn't know quite when that was. Varina got presents for her birthdays, pretty wrapped packages done up with bows. Rue wasn't for all of that wrapper fuss, but she wouldn't have minded just the present-getting. Maybe this year.

"What else did Missus have to say?" Miss May Belle had come back to herself.

Rue picked up the story of that afternoon's secret-getting. She told her mama all about the white women's terror, which was that their sons, their husbands, their menfolk all, would stomp off to war to defend King Cotton.

"Who's that, Mama?" Rue envisioned a white-haired master with a crown of thorny cotton bolls. Miss May Belle waved Rue's tale on.

Rue told of how the women spoke on the impetuous nature of men, always hungry after bloodshed to prove themselves. Miss May Belle grunted her agreement. Rue told her of how the women feared they'd be left alone if their men up and left — how they feared it and longed for it. They spoke on how the plight of the darkies shadowed all other concerns. *What of temperance? What of suffrage?* Rue worked the fan over the white woman words.

"They said if all the males is gone it ain't safe for the children, what with all the niggers growing bold with all of Lincoln's ideas," Rue repeated, proud she'd remembered the way the blue-veined lady had put it.

Rue soon came to the part of the telling that she deemed most important. "Mama," she said. "Missus say she thinkin' on sendin' Varina away to Northern relations for what she call 'refinement.' Said if the world's goin' overall upside down she want her daughter to come out on top."

Rue told the secret to Miss May Belle and next morning Miss May Belle told the secret to Ma Doe who, once she heard of Varina's leaving, turned gray as a dropped stone.

"It ain't happenin' yet," Miss May Belle said. "You know Missus ain't got no say in it. She just like to think she do."

Ma Doe's face wrinkled down to a frown even as she set out one of Varina's cranberry red dresses for washing. You would've thought the little white girl was in it, the way the old woman laid it down lovingly, smoothing all the frilly edges.

"I don't wish to see her go," Ma Doe said.

On her knees at the wash basin Miss May Belle laughed in a way that Rue, listening from behind the washboard, thought

210

sounded almost cruel. "Don't you got better things to wish after than one li'l white girl's comfort?"

Ma Doe didn't answer, only picked up the dress and shook it and laid it down again as if this time she might lay it neater.

"What you askin' for, Ma?" Miss May Belle said, gentler, though Ma Doe was not her mama any more than she was anyone else's. All of Ma Doe's sons had been sold away young, but that was the type of secret that everybody knew but didn't ever speak on. "You wantin' me to fix it so she stay?"

"No!" Ma Doe seemed to startle even herself with her vehemence. "No, none of your root work, Miss May Belle, none of your trinkets or devilment. I don't want any of that superstitious nonsense near Varina."

Miss May Belle met eyes with Ma Doe over the washboard. "I hear you, Ma," she said, and a solemn look passed between them, an agreement, fast as a whipcrack. Rue saw the truth and then it was gone again and they were just two slave women busy at the washing.

"You know I don't care one wit for conjuration," Ma Doe said even as she worried at the string of the new asafetida pouch Miss May Belle had only just gifted her that morning. She had it tucked under her stiff

211

collar where it was hidden. It was well known that Missus expressly forbade any sign of hoodooing in the House.

"Why don't you just go 'head and speak to Marse Charles if it bother you so. Tell him you'll see to Varina's 'refining' just fine. He soft on you," Miss May Belle tutted to her. "He still think he in the nursery nuzzling at yo' teat."

Ma Doe swatted at Miss May Belle's upraised behind, same as she would any of her misbehaving children.

"Ain't nothin' to be promised for those boys, though," Miss May Belle said, serious all of a sudden. "But maybe if you do speak to Marse Charles about 'em?"

Ma Doe was quiet as she tied up all those little white ribbons on Varina's dress. For a while the music of Rue scrubbing a shirt along the boards was the only sound amongst the three of them. Her knuckles rapped rhythmically on the wood of the washboard as the water sloshed.

Finally, Ma Doe spoke slow, like the words were being pulled up from inside her body. Said, "Last time I spoke out of turn to Marse Charles on the rearing of his sons he drove a fountain pen through my palm."

Rue stopped scrubbing.

"You ain't never tell me that," Miss May

Belle said.

Ma Doe sighed down at the red dress, worshipfully. "You can't know everything, May Belle," she said.

What Miss May Belle couldn't know she sent Rue to hear and see and gather, up through the winding back hallways of the Big House. She sent Rue to the nursery to gather up a lock of Varina's red hair in Ma Doe's stead.

Miss May Belle, for all of Rue's life, had been banned from venturing into the House — ever since the birth of Varina, in fact, as though the disappointment of Missus's worm pink daughter wriggling out of her instead of a son of a type her predecessor had produced for Marse Charles had solidified Missus's distaste for all black healing. Indeed, Miss May Belle might've saved Missus's life during Varina's breached birth by tending to the emergency before the white doctor could even arrive, but the healing woman hadn't helped her where it counted — raising Missus's esteem in her husband's eyes required a son.

Folks said Missus was barren after the birth of her daughter and because of it had told Marse Charles that it was ungodly to take pleasure in her. It was a nasty secret,

213

Miss May Belle said, and one Rue ought not repeat unless she wanted her skin whipped clean off her back. But the ugly bit of gossip was likely the truth, or close to it, and everybody knew Marse Charles took his fancies elsewhere.

Rue troubled her way in through the back door of the House, simply waited on it to swing open when the cook, Big Sylvia, bustled out of the kitchen heading to the storeroom set out in the yard. Rue slipped in the gap just as the door creaked shut and thankfully found the kitchen empty. It was easy then to steal up the service stairs.

Now Varina would be in the ladies' parlor, Rue knew, all the way on the opposite side of the vast House, in the middle of one of her daily lessons in needlework with Missus. The lessons always left Varina pinpricked and ornery even when she was finally set free to play with Rue and the slave children in the cool of the evening. Despite the good distance of a whole grand wing stretched between them, Rue still chilled at entering the nursery without permission. But she'd promised Miss May Belle that lock of red hair and there was no better place to snatch it but from one of the bone brushes Ma Doe used to rake at Varina's thick fall of curls.

Cursing, conjuring, Miss May Belle claimed, was easy enough done with any old bit of bodily property — a toenail, or a loosed tooth. Urine or blood or even tears. But a conjure that was meant to bind was something else, much like a love spell, Rue's mama had explained. It called for the deeper essence of the person the fix was to be put upon, and hair was most preferred. Hair tells, Miss May Belle often said, hair tells health and hereditary both. You and the roots of you.

The nursery was done up in white frilly lace that had aged to yellow in places over time. Rue knew it had been Varina's half brothers' nursery once and Marse Charles's before that. Varina often complained of the drab white and the stale air and the fact that the baseboards were all carved up, pockmarked in places where her half brothers had etched their initials, claiming everything long before Varina was even born.

The only thing not white was the crib, which was a solid red oak. Varina had outgrown it long ago in favor of the wide white canopied bed across the room, but the crib was still there and in it sat Varina's collection of blond-haired china dolls, which seemed to wink at Rue when she rounded the corner and came face-to-face

215

with them.

There were a dozen at least, sat in the crib, arranged in a row like an audience, and Rue nearly fled from the room altogether when she met their glazed porcelain eyes gazing out at her from between the bars of the crib.

Shook up by the dolls, Rue crept past them quick as she could. The floorboards creaked wickedly with her every step. Across the room she could make out what she was after: All the combs and pins and brushes were laid out neatly in a row on the vanity, doubled in the mirror. Rue made her footfalls high and careful, tested each floorboard before she came to rest on it. Marooned halfway across the room on an especially whining plank, Rue leaned forward, reached out her arm. She snatched up the first comb she could lay hands on, plucked a clump of orange hair, and quickly replaced the comb next to the others. Now that she had the tuft of hair, she didn't know quite where to put it. She could hardly walk out of the house with a handful of Varina's hair. Rue settled on stuffing it into the lining of her dress and turned herself around, traced her laborious route back to the door.

She stopped again at the dolls, like to see if they had observed what she'd done. They

216

hadn't moved from their faithful vigil, staring blind and straight out at the dust motes Rue'd unsettled.

"You're not so pretty," Rue whispered at them. "My mama's gon' make me a doll baby. One that smiles. Black. Sweet as can be."

Rue dared to reach her arm out to touch one and found it cold, as far from a baby as a rock at the river's edge was. None of them looked like Rue but none of them looked much like Varina neither, with their impossibly white skin and painted-on pink cheeks. The bodies of the dolls jutted out at hard edges beneath a rainbow parade of pretty dresses made of nicer fabrics than any Rue had ever owned. Rue's first thought was to grab the nearest doll and shuck off the dress to see if the white shining skin continued downward, smooth as a dinner plate.

"Are you meant to be here?"

Rue spun at the voice. It was a white boy, almost a man, behind her, one of Marse Charles's sons. Rue looked down before she could see which. She knew she was not ever allowed to meet their eyes.

He came into the nursery from the hall. Rue watched his black boots stomp up to her. He made the floorboards moan as loud as he wanted, didn't care. About him she

217

could smell a heavy stink she knew to be liquor coming up out of his sweat. It was like a cloud he carried. He kneeled before Rue. Grabbed her chin in his rough, dry hand and pulled her face near to his. There was nowhere else to look then.

Rue recognized it was Marse Peter who held her only because he was the youngest of the three brothers. He tilted back Rue's head roughly, and for a terrible moment they breathed the same air. She tried to figure what he was after by the tick in his jaw, the pulse of a vein in his temple. He had Varina's tight lips and round blue eyes. But his hair was a murky brown, and above his lip an equally dark mustache was pushing its way through. It looked like a smudge of dirt on his mouth.

He squeezed her jaw. "What you about, huh? Answer me, girl."

"Miss Varina sent me, suh," Rue stuttered out. Her mouth was near clinched shut in his grip. He shoved her off, and her teeth clicked together so hard she feared they'd shatter.

"I don't think you're tellin' me the truth," he said. "I think you're up here stealin' my sister's belongin's."

Rue cringed away and feared she would be hit for it. "No."

"No? I saw you. At my baby sister's hair things first and then at the dolls. Shall I tell my father that he's got a li'l thief in his house?"

"No, suh, no."

"Perhaps if you ask me kindly I'll keep it from Father. Rather I see to the punishment myself?"

Marse Peter grabbed the pull of her apron strings. The knot came undone easy, fell away to swing at Rue's bare legs.

There was a high-sharp giggle at the doorway, no humor in it.

"There you are, Rue." Varina bounded into the nursery, skipping, laughing again that high false laugh. Her face was over-bright and flushed, her curls undone in the heat.

Marse Peter slid his eyes to his half sister, just rolled them like marbles in his head without even turning his neck.

Rue tried to catch Varina's gaze and plead, but Varina was grinning gap-toothed at her brother.

"We was playin' hide-and-go-seek, weren't we, Rue?"

They were doing no such thing. Rue didn't know whether Varina wanted her to speak the lie or if she'd be punished for it.

"Peter, do you want to join our game?"

Marse Peter spat. Right there on the nursery floor, a gleaming glob flecked black with old tobacco tar. "Shit no, I don't. That's children's stuff."

"I'll tell Daddy you were cussin'."

Marse Peter whirled on Varina. He grabbed his half sister's wrist as she let out a cry, seemed to crumple to her knees in pain.

"Peter, you're hurtin' me!"

"Aw, hell," he said. But he let her go.

He thrust his hands deep into his pocket and turned his back on them. He began to whistle, a jaunty manic tune, and he kept on whistling walking out of the nursery. They heard him descend the main staircase in great thudding stomps, whistling the whole while, so that they weren't sure he was gone 'til they couldn't hear him any longer. Only then did Varina rise from the floor.

"Y'alright, Miss Varina?" Rue's voice shook. "Let me look on yo' wrist."

"Oh, it don't hurt none," Varina said, waving the arm that Marse Peter had grasped. The expression of screwed-up pain she'd shown her brother was gone. She had a big pleased grin on her face. She'd played him like a song and now she looked about her room with her hands fisted on her hips, like

220

she was figuring what she could conquer next. "Rue, shall we play a game?"

Rue kept it a secret. She couldn't say why precisely, only that she felt ashamed of the way Marse Peter had leered at her, of the way she'd stuttered, of how her apron had come untied like it meant to betray her too. She kept the secret even from her mama — whereas before she had told her everything — because Miss May Belle didn't lately listen well to her daughter's hurts.

"Ain't we all of us hurtin'?" she'd say, if Rue uttered any complaints.

Miss May Belle was making a doll baby at the supper table. A white one, with a face made from an old handkerchief, blue corn seeds for eyes, lips painted on red, thin as a wound. The hair was of straw, stewed to bright orange in calendula and carrot juice, save for a sprig of Varina's real hair in the very center. The twisting real strand was hid in plain sight, where you'd have to know to look for it to find it. That secret lock was where the magic lived that bound up Varina's fate to her home.

The doll baby was Varina all over, right down to the cranberry red dress, a scrap of fabric cut from a dress she'd fast outgrown.

"Why couldn't Ma Doe just've asked after

the conjure straight?" Rue wanted to know. It hurt her somehow to see her mama put so much love and care into a thing that was not for Rue herself.

"She know the cost's too high for her, if she had a hand in it," said Miss May Belle. She didn't raise her head from her sewing to say it.

Seemed to cost Miss May Belle nothing to sit there and sew, humming to herself a little. Seemed it had cost Rue too high to do what Ma Doe wouldn't, to snatch Varina's hair for the conjure. But Rue thought on Airey, and the way she'd been whipped raw in the yard of the House at Marse Charles's whim. Was that the cost? Rue couldn't imagine Ma Doe treated that way. Ma Doe was everybody's mama, white folks' too, even if she was colored, and who could dare hurt their own mama?

"You thinkin' too hard, Rue-baby, I can see it." Miss May Belle clicked her tongue. "Lord, you just like yo' daddy, ain't you? Come on over here."

Rue crossed the cabin to sit on the floor at her mama's feet. She was about-to-be seven — she was no baby, and Miss May Belle was never oversentimental, said she didn't have the time for petting. It was rare and wonderful for Rue to rest her head in her mama's lap, to feel her mama's long, thin fingers drift lovingly through the tangles of her tight head hair.

"Mama?"

"Yes, Rue-baby?"

Rue wanted then to tell her more than anything, about the hunger she'd seen in Marse Peter's eyes that had made her stomach curdle. But she didn't know quite how to begin it, and perhaps it was as Ma Doe had said. Miss May Belle didn't know everything, or need to neither.

"Nothin'," Rue said.

She let her mama's threading fingers on her scalp lull her into an almost sleep and she did not wake, even when she felt one sharp twang at the very center of her head.

Varina ripped through paper, through ribbon and lace. The box opened up, and from its innards she drew out a little model carriage pulled by a little white horse.

"How lovely," Varina cooed from up above. The rocking chair she sat in creaked with her delight.

Curled up at Varina's feet with the other black children, Rue bit back a yawn. It had been a treat at first, to be picked with Sarah and Beulah and Li'l Sylvia to make an oohing-and-aahing audience as Varina opened her birthday presents. But now the floor of the veranda was littered with ribbons and bows, with shreds of paper, with piles of toys and books, knitting needles and sewing sets, dresses and hats and hairpins, and Varina placed the pale horse burdened with its white carriage on the very top of that mess of gifts where it threatened to fall over but did not. Rue oohed and aahed with the rest of them.

"I painted it myself," Marse Peter boasted. He leaned on one white pillar of the veranda, watching at a distance, smoking from his daddy's pipe.

"Why, thank you, Peter," Varina said, but she was already on to the next gift. A simple box of brown paper and twine. "No name on it. Now who could this be from?"

Varina didn't wait on an answer but began working furiously at the knot of the twine. Rue peeked behind her to look at the white family. It was rare to see them all assembled, Marse Charles and his three sons, the elder two dressed in new, stiff military uniforms, and Missus there too, complaining of the early spring heat in little mumbles that no one was paying any mind.

Rue couldn't know it then, but it would be the last time she would see them all gathered, the last time she'd see the elder two sons at all. They'd joined up, to defend King Cotton and the honor of their women-folk, showing allegiance to the very cause their step-mama was afeared of, to be called Rebels and worse. Marse Peter would follow not too far behind his brothers. He'd live two more years, dead before he was eighteen — or presumed so leastwise — on a battlefield, in the midst of a Northern ice storm. Varina would read aloud the letter that made it so, with her remaining slaves gathered around her, just like this, like children primed for a bedtime story, Rue amongst them, and Varina would not even weep on the words that presumed her last living brother gone to meet his maker. She had never liked him much and anyway with the last of her daddy's sons dead she would finally be the sole mistress of her daddy's land, which would soon be only vast ashes.

Varina would never leave that place and Rue wouldn't neither — but they couldn't know that then, couldn't know how well Miss May Belle's conjure would take. Today Rue was seven years old because Varina was, and even that she couldn't know for sure.

"How lovely!" Varina said. She'd managed to work the box of her last gift open and she'd pulled out the prize. Rue turned back around to see it emerge, though she knew already that it would be the little redheaded doll baby her mama had fixed to conjure for Ma Doe to keep Varina tied to the land. Perched in her lap it really was a perfect double of Varina. And Rue knew the girl would love it for that.

"Well, ain't this darlin'," Varina said, inspecting the doll.

"Isn't it darling," Missus corrected.

Varina ignored her mama. Instead she turned the doll over and lifted up its skirts, and for a moment, stunned, Rue thought she meant to strip the baby nude right there, before her brothers and her daddy.

But Varina flipped the doll baby on its head and pulled down the bright red dress over the white face. Sewn on the opposite side was another dress, a bold green one, as bright as the trees in springtime, and there where the white doll's legs ought to have been was another head, this one black with fat red lips and brown eyes and hair wild like bramble.

"It's a topsy-turvy doll! How clever!" Varina said. She hugged the black side close. "Look! A li'l nigra."

Rue ached in secret where only she could know. Was this the gift that Miss May Belle had all along meant for Rue to receive? Not a present but an emptiness where a present

226

might be? Rue at seven realized then what she ought to have known all along — that she, and even her own doll baby, a thing made in her own image, would belong always to Miss Varina.

FREEDOMTIME

What would Miss May Belle have done? Rue had only the memory of her dead mama to put the question to. But the dead did sometimes answer, in their way, and Miss May Belle answered Rue now with a way to save Bean.

All at once that mind-apparition of Miss May Belle turned back to the empty dust-dark corners of the one-room cabin, and Rue might have felt lonely if not for the fact that she knew the spirit of her mama was upon her, that spirit being conjure.

She left her cabin almost in a run, her skirts fisted up in sweating palms so she could hit a full fast stride. If she was going to do it, if she was going to find the cure for Bean's vitality, she'd have to do it quick.

The skeleton of the House loomed, the black remains of Marse Charles's mansion, its charred stairs leading nowhere. Rue rubbed her hand against the white pillar at

228

the entryway as she always did when she passed, but she couldn't stop there. She made her way into the clearing beyond. She knew at once which plant she needed but it was a struggle to find it in the little moonlight, and it had to be right.

It was a pattern to the leaf — Rue knew to look for black backward raindrops, and, true, she'd need only the barest hint of it, a handful, no more, crushed down into a dust, into a powder; it would be so easy to go into Sarah's house and put it on the tip of Bean's tongue. He trusted her now. If she timed it rightly the swirls of red would rise up on his pale skin as brightly as it had risen in his sister and brother, and a fever was bound to take hold. If taken by mouth, there might be vomiting, a flux — not quite the symptoms the other children had, though it would not be so different as to raise doubt, and it was all good toward the growing curse and toward the show. If Rue timed it rightly and gave Bean just enough, the sickness would overtake him in the evening, so that Sarah would have to knock at her door, would have to ask for her help plainly where everyone could see, and by the morning the artificial sickness would pass, as though Rue had healed him, and likewise the pestilence of suspicion would

229

pass, and pass by Bean and Rue with it.

But with her face so close to the ground that the grass tickled her ears she felt suddenly ashamed. Maybe she was ill herself to dream such a wild thing. Was this the madness of fear, or a fever coming on? Or worse, was this the way her mama had felt in that final year of her hate-filled grief, hanging fruit that spun from the eaves? Rue sat upright to catch her breath, to feel the cool earth against her hands, which she had planted firm against the ground. She was not Miss May Belle. She did not rush headfirst into madness, sorrow, or wanting. She did not spit curses. She had to think. She waited.

The woods were almost quiet as she listened to the beating of her own heart and tried to breathe away that coil of fear. In the distance she saw the trees and heard something give a mournful hoot from high amongst the leaves but that something did not show itself. The creek beat quiet against the pebbles of the bank, rushing down a ways to the place it opened to the river and then, she supposed, somewhere beyond that, to the sea.

She stood and approached the cabin by the creek. Heard from within it the telltale sounds of a scurrying animal. A fox?

The door to the shed almost didn't move. The bottoms of the wood had burrowed themselves deep in the mud, and Rue put all her strength into one forceful tug.

Inside she found him, not a fox but a man. She near toppled over at the sight of him. He lay on his back fully on the ground, his legs splayed unnaturally, his fingers laced over his chest in the way she'd lately been arranging the dead. She would have thought him dead if not for the slight rising and falling of those pale fingers with his chest, and then he confirmed himself alive by giving off a grunt of a snore.

He was white. Had to be — the pale hands, the ease with which he slept out in the open. And what she could make out of his face in the shadow was the sandy color of wheat. She had not seen a white man in years. Not since the war, at its fiery end. If she stepped away slowly she would not wake him, but already her hand on the door was rattling with fear and if she had to walk backward the way she had come, she was certain she would fall.

Then Rue saw that his face was not his face but was a hat made of straw, one she'd lost, she realized, some months back. The clothes he wore were in the shape of a crumpled suit separated from its jacket.

Then a flood of knowing came on to her so fiercely that she cried out. It was Bruh Abel. Come back.

His whole body jerked at the sound as though his sleeping had been only surface deep and he sat up without pulling away the hat, which tumbled into his lap. Bruh Abel's gray eyes quirked into a squint and he looked right at Rue in bafflement.

Was he ill? He had that glassy gaze in the brief blinking open of his eyes that she had seen over and over in the town. He leaned all the way forward, his head rolling in a tilt on his chest.

Rue crept closer. After some unsureness she picked a safe place on the inside of his wrist. His body felt warm beneath her hand and there was a slickness to his skin made of clammy sweat.

"Rue," he said in a husky hiccup and she knew then, from the smell that wafted out with her name, that he was not sick. He was drunk. She dropped his hand.

She didn't like the strength of the liquor smell that was suddenly all around her. It smelled to her of danger.

He said, "Don't go, Rue." It was the lack of "Sister" before it that made her stop a moment, one leg over him, the other still trapped against the shed wall.

"If ya go I might die."

Rue had heard of a man that had died that way, a white man who had drunk himself quite on purpose to his death when the Yankees took his little mulatto children away to freedom.

"Gimme a cure," Bruh Abel said and stuck his arms straight up. Rue feared he was grabbing at her, but as she stumbled back she saw he was not grabbing but pointing, pointing upward with both hands at a bottle that sat above them on the curve of a collapsing shelf.

"Oh, you don't need no more of that damned mess," Rue said and surprised herself. She sounded like her mama. "What's the matter with you? All them folks in town is waitin' on you and this is what you doin'?"

Bruh Abel swatted at her. He rolled over on his side, showed his back to her now. She grabbed his shoulder and rolled him back over, so he could be looking at her for what she had to say to him.

"You a shame," Rue said. "They need you."

She was upset with herself most of all because in that first moment when she had seen him and when she had recognized him, she had felt relief. A hope down in the warm of her belly. She could hear the voices of the townsfolk in the back of her head. *Bruh Abel has come. Bruh Abel will know what to do.*

But now, that hope had dispersed in her like so much smoke. He didn't know any more than she did. He wasn't a savior any more than she was. He was just a man, fallible as she was. More so.

Bruh Abel took her hand, squeezed it weakly the way any invalid might. He was lucky he hadn't froze to death, sleeping in this fall-down shed, gaps in the wood and sharp cutting drafts, and she found she wasn't mad enough to wish that he *had* froze.

"That's exactly what I'm afeared of. They need me." His words scuttled around on a slur but he seemed to want to make himself understood. "This winter I was down almost to the gulf, got me a good setup down there, ministerin' to dockmen and to the women that work the wharfs when the sailors come in. They got them a lot of sins, them women, and they cook mighty good too. I'm thinkin' to myself I could stay down there the whole length of the winter season. Maybe into spring too. But one fine day a rider comes up say he's been lookin' for me all over. Red-haired mulatto?"

"That'd be Red Jack."

Bruh Abel grunted, went on. "Red Jack say that he's ridden down the whole length of the coast lookin' for me. There's a terrible sickness, the Ravagin' he call it, in one of the out-of-the-way towns in which I sometimes stop. He say, 'We need you,' and I say, 'I shall pray for you,' and he say, 'Come on back to town with me,' and I say, 'No.'"

"They believe in you," she said. But then, they had used to believe in her and look all the good that had done them, or her, or anybody.

"Yo' Red Jack took himself away and I stayed down there in the gulf. But I found that it didn't sit right with my soul, thinkin' on all 'em children, children I baptized. Just dead.

"I gathered my courage and I wound my way back up here and it wasn't 'til I was half a day's walk away that I realized I come empty-handed. I ain't got nothin' to give y'all. They need me? I can't save nobody." He stopped himself with a hiccup. "Thought I'd buy myself some thinkin' time when I bought myself some whiskey at a stand along the road. But it ain't make the thinkin' any easier."

Rue stood up. "It seldom does."

235

She stepped over his body, clutching her dress tight to her legs for the long leap over his torso so he couldn't see up her skirt. He was only a man, after all.

"Why'd you tell me all that?" Rue half-expected him not to answer, expected he'd fallen back into the pit of his drunken sleep.

"You understand." He slurred. "Don't ya, *Miss* Rue?"

She did understand. What it meant to be praised and praised and then suddenly tumble from grace. It was a long, lonesome way down.

Rue left him lying there, and he let her go this time with only a mewl of regret. She didn't go far. What she could assemble would be crude, only the plants that thrived in the wet that could live in the ever-present shade cast by the shed. But they were there to be found and she picked them.

Back in the shed Bruh Abel's gaze followed her as she moved about. Rue stood on the tips of her toes to examine the shelves that hung by halves on the wall. Feeling in the darkness, Rue found his Bible and beside it the bottle of liquor with nothing but a puddle left at the bottom. She pulled it down. It would have to do.

"You lookin' like Miss May Belle," Bruh Abel said. "I used to pray with her, you know, before she passed."

Rue knelt on the ground. "She was foolish for believin' in you too."

She bashed the bottom of the bottle against the thistle she had collected. The poison she'd gathered for Bean was still in her basket, waiting. She thought about it and beat harder. She kept bashing 'til the job was done.

"Hey now, with that racket."

"See these here thorns?" she held up the battered stems to him. "They set out to prick you. Y'all can swallow 'em whole if you like, and bleed. Or y'all can do it my way. I'm curin' you like you was askin'. Unless you was hopin' to wake up with the devil on yo' back in the mornin'."

Bruh Abel smirked. "And look, here I ain't got nothin' to pay you with."

Rue said, "Don't come into town tomorrow."

He looked away, perhaps ashamed as he should be. He swirled the handful of seeds she had given him. They were smooth and as black as Bean's eyes, and free of nettles.

"But iff'n you do come," Rue went on, "then come as their preacher man. Don't show them yo' doubt or yo' fear neither; they got enough a' their own. You can't save them babies what's meant to die. And I

237

can't neither."

Rue thought of her mama, saw her there, same as she had in the shadows of the cabin. Bruh Abel's kind of faith hadn't kept Miss May Belle from dying any more than Rue's healing had. But it had made the difference in her last few hours that he'd sat at her bedside. He had made her dying easier. Rue had never thanked him for that.

"If you gon' be a liar, Bruh Abel," Rue said, "then be a useful one."

When Rue walked back home she was looking for the sunrise but there was none to be had, only the gradual receding of the black night in favor of the hard glow of day. The morning was gray all over with a fog that came up heavy from the river and hung low, made it hard to see anything clearly through the thick of the woods and made her think of Bruh Abel's eyes, that same kind of unknowable gray.

She was nearly halfway up her own porch when she saw the billow of smoke, moving only the way smoke can move, distinguishing itself from the sedentary thick of the fog to say *Someone has died here.*

It came from the house nearest to hers where a family of three was living, a mama and her two boys, the daddy long ago gone, took up his freedom and left with it. Had one of them boys died? Rue changed course. In the pocket of her dress she held her pipette and she pulled it out, something like a talisman, hoping there was a child left alive that might need her. But when she came upon the house, there, blocking her way, were Red Jack and Jonah and Si's daddy and Beulah's man, their arms full of kindling to stoke the fire of the sickbed sheets.

"Both boys?" Rue asked it to Jonah but he didn't answer.

"The eldest passed," said Red Jack. "The younger one's caught it. He sweatin' fierce."

Rue meant to pass them, but they did not move for her. Those four men held bundles of wood in their arms and their eyes moved near as one to look her up and down. She'd forgotten where she'd come from and how she must look, her skin flush, her dress dotted with nighttime mud and stains of grass. Madness, that's what they were seeing. Her gone mad. The witch they had been whispering after.

Rue tried to smile at Jonah but he wouldn't let her. His face was set.

He asked, "Where you come from?"

Rue didn't know what to say. "I was out there," she answered as if she'd descended

239

with the fog.

Behind Jonah, Beulah's man made a noise of disgust in his throat, shared a glance with Si's daddy, who nodded at some unsaid thing. Rue wanted to smack the cradled wood from out of their hands. "It's true then," Si's daddy muttered.

"What's true?"

But they would not say more.

"Jonah. What's true?" Rue stepped forward that she might speak to only him but in the same moment he backed away, evading, as if to be touched by her was to know some plague.

"What Ol' Joel said before he passed." Jonah hesitated. "That you out conjurin' with somebody in them woods."

"You know ain't none of it true," Rue said. But she herself did not know it to be fully a lie. "Let me by now, let me see to the sick child."

Before her the four men were a barricade, and at any moment they could turn against her. In her eyes the sticks they bore were no longer kindling but menacing switches. She felt herself shrinking.

"Please let me by."

"We takin' care of him. He'll survive it," Red Jack said with finality. He stuck a bit of tobacco in his mouth, gnashed at it with a purpose.

Rue took a step back.

"Go on then," she said. "Don't waste yo' precious time threatenin' me. Go see to the sick boy."

They went. They moved toward the cabin that plumed still more black smoke. She knew that they thought they could do what she could not, those men with bundles of sticks cradled in their arms thinking the work of carrying kindling was as precious as carrying a newborn.

"Jonah, wait," she said. She feared he would ignore her.

Yet, he stopped on the porch and waved the others on into the cabin before he turned back toward her. His expression seemed as shut to her as a locked door.

"Jonah, what's happened?" She meant to ask *What's changed?* but couldn't. It cut too close to what she was feeling. "Is somethin' the matter with yo' li'l 'uns? Is Bean took sick?"

It was the wrong thing to ask. "Why you worryin' so much after Bean?"

"I tol' you I'd take care of him," Rue said and tried not to think of her deception, or her plan of false poison, lest it show on her face.

"Folks keep tryna tell me you workin'

devilment." He looked about like he feared he would be heard. Or worse, like he feared he would be seen with her. "They wanna run you outta town. They say Bean's the only one that ain't took sick. That it must be your doin'. If you don't loose yo' hold over Bean they plan to leave him out in the woods for the foxes to eat."

To hear it said pained her, but she'd known all along that that's what this all was tipping toward. Ma Doe had warned her of it; even Bruh Abel in his way had suggested trouble would come from Bean. And to Bean also.

"Bean's just a child," Rue spat. "Yo' child."

Jonah flinched. She'd struck where she'd meant to.

He led her away from the main road, closer to the edge of the woods where no one was likely to pass and hear them.

"Sarah say he was born dead but that you brung him back from the dead. Is that true, Miss Rue?"

"He was born different," she said slowly, as if she were trying to remember. But of course she had never stopped fearing that exact thing, that Bean was a curse come back from the past, to be visited upon her alone. A shame she could not escape.

Rue said, "Bean was born with a caul. A veil like. Heard tell it's lucky, means he got the Sight."

"Sarah say you jealous a' her," Jonah went on. "That you made Bean as a curse on her. That you was gon' give her a poison to stop havin' more babies."

Rue felt horror stab through her, sharp as a dagger.

"Sarah say maybe you put somethin' evil in Bean when he was born. That you hid evidence of it. Somethin' sinister."

"I didn't."

Jonah looked ill. "I burnt them sheets he was born in like you said. Was it conjure, Miss Rue, what you tol' me to do?"

"No, no. It was only what Miss May Belle used to do."

"Folks seen you go out into the woods at night. They say you go to practice yo' witchery." Jonah was looking at her like he was afraid of her. She could not bear it.

"What about that night I saw you with Ol' Joel?" Jonah said. "Did he have it figured? Is that why he died?

"Where'd you go last night, Miss Rue?" He asked it like he was desperate for her to come up with a good lie, an explanation that would make the danger pass. But she didn't have one ready. Her head was full of secrets.

Her basket was full of poison.

"Folks say you nigh on twenty but you won't take no man. Is it true you got a lover in the woods?" Jonah asked it like it was the worst of her sins. "That you conceived Bean there to lay in Sarah's stomach? Is that the truth of his black eyes? Why he don't cry when you hold him?"

By now Jonah's chest was heaving with the tumble of accusations, more passion than Rue had ever seen from him in all the years she'd known him, and suddenly she resented it, her anger coming on her like a hot brand, the realization that'd he'd never looked on her 'til now and that this was how it was going to be.

" 'Folks say,' " she mimicked. "What do you say, Jonah? You believe it? If I am a witch maybe you ought not to cross me."

Jonah took a reeling step back, good as if she'd slapped him. "I don't want no harm to come to the children."

"Neither do I," said Miss Rue. "You go on and tell folks I never did none of those things they say. I ain't much more than a woman that knows some things, things anybody could know if they wanted to. Ain't no devil in the woods, Jonah. Ain't no lover."

When Bruh Abel came amongst them, she

heard it: the simple commotion of him, that thing she'd told him to stir up. Hope. By the way folks were carrying on, you would have thought Jesus had finally come, that or the white doctor with his shining black bag of medicine vials, but it was just Bruh Abel and his prayers, as though hope was better than healing. They were all of them out of their houses — the healthy, the living, the left behind — and then they were praying and then they were singing something mournful.

She tried to picture Bruh Abel coming out from the accursed woods, his timing perfect. They could have no sense of how he'd spent his night, or his months away from the town. He existed to them only when he came down from the trees, as seasonal as falling fruit. But she knew.

Rue was bent at the table with pestle, with mortar, grinding down the green leaves with their little black raindrop pattern, a sign she'd learned to avoid, a sign for poison. She ground the leaves down as fine as she could and finer still and swore to herself it was the right thing to do to save Bean and herself. Never mind the right thing to do, it was the only thing, and that mattered more. She would make him sick for a short time. A spell.

PART THREE

PART THREE

The Ravaging

Folks would not trust the healing woman to heal. All her days, Rue had been a healing woman, and that meant waiting her whole life on sickness. On some calamity to befall others so that she could come in and stop it. But for all the calamity amongst the children, Black-Eyed Bean had shown no signs of sickening.

Rue could not wait any longer for Bean to prove that he was an ordinary boy capable of ordinary illness. It might never happen. All the while other children would fall sick around them, fall sicker, die.

Rue was resolved to go on with her scheme. She had set aside her hesitation over serving Bean a treatment of poison. No power in hesitation — Miss May Belle had taught Rue that in her every action.

Rue commenced to cook the sickness up in her kitchen. She had no food to prepare there anyhow. The goodwill of the townsfolk had fed her before but that goodwill was gone, dwindling with every child she hadn't saved, with every whisper made against her that the pestilence that had befallen their babies was because of her and Bean.

Stooped at her fireplace, Rue tended to a swinging pot filled with the black dotted leaves she'd gathered and their rolling seeds. Poison. She refused to call it otherwise. She had to have a clear mind on what she was doing, on why she was doing it. No sugar, no dose of molasses syrup to ease the going. Poison, plain, simple. If Bean showed the same sickness as the other children for a spell — and Rue could make it so — then no one could think him special. Nobody could think him favored as some witch's creation, or by some conjure of protection that she had given him, nor could they go on believing that he was leeching away the vitality of the other children for his own benefit.

She'd fallen asleep with Jonah's threats inside her head and she woke that morning terrified. At her front door there came a scratching.

They come to burn me up, Rue feared.

She pulled the pot from where it hung; the metal handle burned her skin. Still she clutched tight to it. They couldn't find her out. She had to get rid of the poison before she was caught at doing precisely what they'd accused her of all along. Cooking up sickness. They'd kill her for it.

Rue tossed the simmering poison to the ground, stashed the heated pot amongst cool ones on a high shelf just as Bruh Abel barreled through, rocked the door on its hinges. He held in his arms bundles of vegetables. He wasn't in his suit but a pair of overalls too large and clean for working in, the shirt too small. Looking at her from the doorway he sucked wind through his teeth the way her mama might've if she weren't so long ago dead, so long past drawing breath, angry or otherwise.

No time to hesitate. Rue ground away her secret, crushed the leaves away with her boot heel.

"Why you here?"

"Christian charity," he said.

He set down the food on the table, and the spread rolled out wide enough to make Rue's stomach growl. She didn't move out from her corner, hid her burnt hand behind her back.

"Unless, you already got supper goin'." He glanced at her spitting fire and above it the empty place her cooking pot was meant to hang.

"No," she said too loud.

"Figured that." Bruh Abel looked down like he was embarrassed, or pretending to be leastwise. "Folks loaded me up with all they had when they saw me. In thanks for my comin' and all. You was right. It brightened 'em to see me come."

"I knew it would." She wasn't going to let herself get jealous for it, not now. She realized that Bruh Abel had the power to ease the suspicion amongst the townspeople. But he could just as easily stoke it if he had a mind to.

It came to Rue then that folks all had been waiting on his healing, same as they had once waited on her, and on Miss May Belle before her. Likewise they would wait on his assessment of the state of things. If he pronounced she was accursed, then she was accursed and Bean along with her. What would it take, she wondered, for him to pronounce them otherwise?

Rue crossed the room, blowing at her burnt hand. She tried to lead Bruh Abel to the door, but he stood still in the middle of her home.

"It was good a' you to come," she finally said.

"I ain't leavin'," he said. "I'm stayin' here."

"What you mean you stayin'?"

"You one a' my flock now," he told her. "I stay amongst my own and administer after they needs. There's somethin' asunder in yo' home, Miss Rue. Right here is where I'm needed. So right here is where I'm stayin'."

The air all around them smelled sweet with the poison she'd been cooking. No way he couldn't smell it.

"I'm to watch," Bruh Abel said, walking the length of her supper table. He began sorting through the food, busying his hands on leeks and squashes and sweet potatoes. "Three days. On the third day I ought to know the truth a' the matter."

"So you set yo'self up as the judge and the jury a' my trial?" And the executioner, Rue thought, and she clipped her mouth shut, suddenly afraid. "Is that why you come?"

"If I ain't come, they aimed to run you off, or worse." Bruh Abel's expression was more honest than she'd ever seen it. "They tol' me to come to you, the townsfolk did. They begged it. Do you know what they sayin' 'bout you, Miss Rue?"

She hadn't for one moment stopped thinking on Jonah's accusations. Knowing him like she did she didn't doubt that Jonah had softened the threat, only repeated half

253

the hateful accusations he'd heard, too cowardly or too cautious to give voice to the worst of it.

"I ain't come to hurt you," Bruh Abel said. "I mean only to bring reason to the matter. I come to settle things before it's all gone too far. They all of 'em convinced that Bean's yo' familiar. That he's workin' as yo' spirit to steal life from the li'l 'uns. They say it must be that Bean come from the Devil. What kinda preacher would I be if I ain't confront the Devil?"

"You ain't no real kinda preacher."

Rue's venom seemed to surprise him. Well, she had surprised her own self. She sat down heavy on her bed, her face hid in her hands, her poison crushed up in the dirt under her feet.

"Last night you saw my weakness for drink, it's true," Bruh Abel said after a time. "Just 'cause I'm a preacher man don't mean I can't sometimes lose faith. Just 'cause you a healin' woman don't mean you can't sometimes fall ill."

He came round the table to her and Rue did not back down. He laid his hand on her head like he was feeling for fever.

"Are you sufferin' some sickness, Miss Rue? I mean to find it and flush it out."

■ ■ ■ ■

They passed the evening and late into the night like two strangers, man and woman in too small of a home.

Despite his swagger before a crowd, Bruh Abel was not altogether comfortable in the presence of one person, that one person being Rue, who was watching him from the corner of her home, distrustful.

Seemed Bruh Abel didn't want to be hated. He kept trying to talk at her. All the while her mind stayed hopping about, figuring at some way out. She'd play along at sweetness if she had to. For Bean's sake. And her own.

It brought Rue to mind of slaverytime when Marse Charles had took it upon himself to pick a man slave and woman slave to couple together for no other reason than that he liked the look of them and figured them for good stock. Sometimes they wouldn't hardly have the hour to get acquainted before Miss May Belle was sent in to scent the sheets, check between the woman slave's legs for blood if she were a virgin, leastwise for slick if she was not. As a child Rue had always figured if she were to ever get a man, that would be how it went.

Hadn't that been how her mama had got her daddy after all, that first time? And Rue had followed some nine months after, just a tick mark on Marse Charles's accounting book.

Freedom turned everything all over. Now a man was something you took because you wanted him. A baby something you might have for the sake of loving it.

Maybe Rue had let some of her confusion snake onto her face because Bruh Abel asked, "What you thinkin' on?"

Rue could not say what she was thinkin', which was how to be rid a' you, so she answered instead, "Bean."

Bruh Abel perked up. "You layin' some kinda conjure? Is that how it works? By thinkin' on him?"

She cussed. "I'm worryin' 'bout him."

Bruh Abel settled himself down. "I heard you the one that named him."

Rue shrugged. "I ain't mean to. Just somethin' I said, and Sarah repeated it to Jonah maybe and Jonah repeated it to somebody and it just got goin' like that and there he was, Black-Eyed Bean."

"Black-eyed peas what my mama called 'em where she from. Ain't that somethin'?"

Rue had not altogether thought that Bruh Abel had a mama. Thought maybe he

sprung up like some weed of his own voli-
tion.

"We come from the same people," he went
on, "but we come up with all different ways
a' sayin' the same thing."

He said it like they were sharing a joke. It
lighted the dimple on his cheek. Rue
shrugged, decided it was better to not look
at him at all if he was going to try to be
friendly. She suspected his friendliness for a
trap.

Having him there in her cabin reminded
Rue of the first time she'd seen him at the
side of Miss May Belle's bed, ministering.

He'd been there when Rue had not been.
How much did he know of Miss May Belle?
Of the townsfolk? Of Rue herself? Were
there secrets Rue's mama might have told
him? Confessions of her deathbed? Fact was
at her end Miss May Belle had trusted in
him, and in his vials of holy water. He had
that way about him, to get everybody's
trust. Whether he served poison or snake oil
or whiskey water, why was it that they all of
them were so ready to drink it up?

"You gon' save Bean, won't you?" It was
the first thing she'd said without his prompt-
ing, and it got his attention right off.

He looked at her, somber. "I meant what
I said. No harm is to come to him."

"Then do somethin'."

"That's my intention. I'll save yo' soul and I'll save him, also."

Rue meant to save herself and might have said as much. But an idea flitted through her head, small at first, on moth wings, then larger still.

"Minister to Bean, Bruh Abel," she said, "same as you did my mama. I ain't never rightly thanked you for that. But when you came to her, folks saw that she was healed."

Bruh Abel nodded like it was all his idea. "I mean to do the very same."

Rue smiled at him and her smile was all poison.

The second day he made a soup, he told her a tale, and Rue devised a way to get herself out.

She set down a bottle of good strong brandy on the table between them, the kind she saved for sicknesses, and she put beside it a crystal glass, a pretty one, one she'd saved from her white folks' house before the fire.

Didn't matter, she knew, if a fish saw the hook so long as the bait was something they couldn't help but hunger after.

"Go 'head, Bruh Abel."

Rue tried to make herself sweet, the least

like a witch that she could be, and she filled the glass up high and set it before him glinting amber in the firelight. She knew men had a myriad of weaknesses, but she only trusted herself to seduce him with the one.

He pushed the glass over to her. "For you, Rue."

Then he took up the bottle itself, winked at her, and drank from it straight. Bottle in hand, he went on cooking.

Bruh Abel cooked with the same flare with which he preached. He alternated between a whistle and a hum as he chopped up vegetables at her small table, made a broth in her only pot, rolled dough in the bowl she usually used to make a draught for colic.

Sitting on the sharp edge of her bed, Rue watched him, sipped at the glass she'd poured. She aimed to keep her wits about her as his slipped from him. Then when he was fast asleep she could steal into the woods. Fetch more poison leaves for Bean. Finish finally the idea she'd started.

Bruh Abel came over to her with the soup and coaxed her to taste his concoction, proffering an outstretched spoonful. She looked into his heavy-lidded eyes and smiled, took the spoon for herself, and tasted. It was hot, it was good.

"Where'd you learn all that?"

259

"From Queenie, where else? My mama."

He told Rue about Queenie in a heavy slur. He called her Queenie 'cause everybody called her Queenie and everybody called her Queenie, he supposed, because she was the queen of her kitchen. Her master was a sea captain, though Bruh Abel in his overflowing enthusiasm made him sound something more like a pirate — thickly bearded, full gray eyes — and that sea captain had loved Queenie so much he'd had her likeness etched into the figurehead of his boat, down to every last quirk and birthmark. He'd made her a mermaid. The snaking curve of her back jutted her out over the sea, and the sea captain even had them sculpt in the two dimples on her back where her ass spread wide and became the scaled pattern of the bow. That ten-foot Queenie was made all of mahogany picked for its perfect match, the exact color of her skin.

"He weren't a superstitious man and he'dda had her on the ship with him if he could, but his men weren't gonna have none of that," Bruh Abel told Rue in a hiccup. "Women on ships is sour luck."

Rue had to wonder why the wood figure of a woman on a ship was good when a real, flesh woman on a ship was bad but she didn't ask, just watched Bruh Abel tip back the bottle.

Queenie lived on the quay, Bruh Abel explained as he ladled out a bowl of soup, in a sea-battered cottage with her baker's dozen of children, who had a way of being born nine months or thereabouts after the captain's ship left her port. Bruh Abel had been the youngest of those and the petted favorite. Her boys she offered to the sea, her girls to other folks' kitchens, but Bruh Abel, being her littlest, she kept close. He'd learned her cooking looking up from under her skirts.

Bruh Abel made his way to where Rue sat on the edge of the bed. He tasted his soup, made a noise of satisfaction, and tasted it again. He sat himself down on the bed too, his legs tangled in her sheet. Rue had to push up against the headboard to give his tall angular body room.

"The sea captain loved her and her way with food so much he done declared that when he died he'd free her and all us li'l 'uns with her. He died inside a year a' writing the words. Folks says she killed him on purpose."

Rue frowned. "Did she?"

Bruh Abel laughed so hard he spit out some of his soup. "Nah, just he loved her

261

cookin' so much he got to weighin' half a ton and died from the strain of it."

He handed her the bowl and Rue ate from it, sharply hungry and hungrier still with each bite. The salty broth floated with greens and sweet potatoes that must have come from Ma Doe's garden, and a dark meat so smooth she could swallow it whole.

"Don't you want any?" she asked him.

"Nah," he said, smiling dreamily, "I got all I need right here." He patted the brown bottle like a lover. Rue felt almost sorry for him.

Bruh Abel didn't stir from where she'd left him, blanketless on her bed. She'd watched him sleeping for a while, perhaps longer than she should have, listening to his easy snore and wondering if she ought not stay and pray with him after all.

In the end she snatched up her basket, her mortar, and her pestle and left, stepped out into the wilderness with only a dim lantern as a beacon, so determined to go through with her plan that she could hardly wait out the inky dark to conceal her. She walked to the little bed of green leaves she'd come to two nights before. Their dotted surface glistened with the start of dew drops as if to greet her. With sure fingers she

262

plucked them from the ground.

This time, though, she did not return home, turned instead to that old fall-down church, the only place she knew for certain she'd go unseen.

After the war, folks had forgotten the white folks' church, shunned it as a hated place, a place they'd been taught to submit, to bow down in the Lord's name. To hush and to surrender. Bruh Abel's church was water and sky, his Bible was a hymn and a battle cry. What use did they have for the grim gray four walls of the old Protestant church? They'd shiver just to go into it, to feel encased all in brick. They'd sooner let it crumble, but they'd never tear it down. The Northern army, too, had stopped their hellfire short of burning it — as Rue had bet they would — just as superstitious in the end as they accused black folks of be-ing. They feared the ill luck that destroying a sacred place would bring, and who could blame them? Whatever folks believed or didn't believe there was no sense fueling the wrath of things not seen.

Now Rue came to the pews and set down her bowl and began to grind down the leaves by lantern light. A fine powder, finer than fine. She didn't dare hesitate. When she was finished she stowed the poison in a little vial and hid it in the folds of her dress.

Above her the roof creaked sharply. She glanced upward.

Up, where the slaves, when there had been slaves, had listened to those sermons, had had obedience whupped into their minds with words as sharp as any cat-o'-nine. The boards groaned again with the noise of someone shifting their weight, unsure, and from the corner of her eye Rue caught the movement of a woman's white night shift rippling back into the shadows.

"Varina," Rue said.

The woman rippled out again at the sound of her name.

"S'alright, Varina," Rue said. "You might as well come on."

Varina took the steps down from the loft slowly, taking care to step where she knew the old boards would still hold her. She creaked all the way down and then crossed the church slow, too, trailing her long white nightgown through dust, came like a reluctant child about to be scolded though she was a woman grown, and a used-to-be mistress. "Is it safe?"

"Safe as it ever is," Rue said. She put down the bowl and pestle, made room for Varina beside her on the bench. The white woman sat down next to her, so close their

264

two dresses touched.

Varina petted Rue's hand like she wanted to make sure Rue was altogether real. She looked sallow in the lantern light, and there were black rings beneath her eyes.

"You've been gone away too long," Varina complained. She always complained no matter if it was a day or a month since Rue had last been to see her in her hiding place.

"I'm sorry, Miss Varina. I met with a bit a' trouble in town. Nothin' to worry after. Cure's in hand." Rue patted her pocket where she'd kept the poison for Bean.

"Is it Ma? She unwell?"

Rue shook her head. "No, no, ain't nothin' like that. Ma Doe's well as ever. She asks after you."

Varina looked up at the broken rafters. "May I come out soon, Rue? I'd so like to."

"Soon," Rue lied. "When all is well and settled."

Rue could go on and on putting off Varina's demands, could keep on telling the woman that it was not safe for her to venture beyond the confines of the old church. But she looked at Varina now and there was some of that old defiance starting to crackle on Varina's face, there and gone, fast like lightning.

In their hide-and-seek game, Varina kept

herself well hid in the distant church, far off from the plantation. The old routes to the church had been cut off by a particularly bad swell of the river that made the woods look all turned around if a body wasn't over-familiar with traversing them.

Varina made her home in the rectory. On braver days she ghosted through the empty church aisles or up in the vaulted second story where the corpse bell swung through dust and gleaming spider webs.

Those first hard months after the fire destroyed her home, Miss Varina had near wasted away in her bedroll, her mind gone, fogged over with fear and sorrow and shame. Every shadow was sin or a Northern soldier in a war she didn't know was ending. Without Rue, Varina might have died, or lost her senses altogether. Might have hurt herself, in some final brutal way, just to be free of the torment of her own memories.

But Varina had gradually healed. And Rue knew that one of these days she was going to reclaim that old hunger. Then she wasn't going to stay satisfied eating up the simple lies that Rue kept on feeding her.

Rue's ears pricked up to some sound outside. Was that the crack of twigs beneath a quick approach? She stood from the bench. Tried to listen. There again, motion. Varina stilled. "Rue?"

"Go." Rue took up her lantern, moved as swiftly as she could, and slipped her way out through the double doors. Shut them behind her, hard.

Bruh Abel was there in the field of the church. His eyes were arrowhead sharp in the rocking light of her lantern.

"There you are, Miss Rue." His breath smelled of brandy, but his voice was steady when he spoke. Exacting. Sober.

"You ain't drunk," Rue said.

"I poured out the brandy, boiled it up into the stew, while you wasn't lookin'." He seemed pleased with himself. "I wanted to know what it is you hide in these woods. What you ain't want me to see."

Rue glanced behind her, tried to make it look like she wasn't looking for anything. But she was looking, up at the high windows of the church and into the bellhouse, but there was no movement there, just the chill of a disused building, frozen in time.

Bruh Abel was wanting an answer. She had to give him something, she thought, one secret to keep another.

"Go on and look then."

He stepped through the doorway of the church. He took Rue's lantern from her, held it high and set it to swinging, and the shadow his body cast stretched out long and sinister over the empty room.

Rue followed close behind him, struggling in his wake to see over his shoulder. She tried to see it through his eyes, the cracked church pews and the broke-down altar and the second story that looked about ready to collapse. She tried to read the shadows for a hint of white movement.

Where had Varina hid herself?

"What is this place?" he asked. It was like his preacher voice knew it was a church house and felt at home — it echoed sharply taking up the whole of the room, made Rue's heart scud in terror.

"Nothin' but where we used to get made to worship," she told him. "Forced to worship."

"And you stay comin' here?" Bruh Abel illuminated one sharp corner. In it was a rocking chair. There was a handkerchief draped across the seat with a half-finished bit of embroidery, lily of the valley, in neat green stitch, the flowers not bloomed in yet.

"Folks don't come here no more. Can't, I s'pose," Rue said quick. "But I do. For quiet-like."

Bruh Abel tipped back the chair, set it to rocking, but it didn't rock right and as he moved, dragging the lantern light over the stores of dry food by the altar, the chair kept rocking. Its crooked pace fell in time with Rue's wracking heartbeat.

"And this?" He'd turned his light into the farthest room of the rectory proper. Past the stove and water basin was a little back room with a bedroll on the floor, the scant covers neatly tucked.

Rue hurried in after him. The back room was all empty too, but he'd lighted on something tucked into the bed. He picked it up and turned it in his hands, studied it closely. A little black doll baby in a green dress, a crude likeness of Rue but a likeness all the same. May Belle's creation had held up all these years. Threadbare, but it had held, and if he flipped the doll over he'd see the face of the white doll hid beneath her skirts. He did not flip it over but tossed it on the sleeping mat.

There was the one small back door. It took Bruh Abel out into the night again and Rue after him. There was no grass beyond the church but an area of hard-packed mud that looked red in the moonlight. Carved out in its center was a neat square door made of heavy wood, an entrance to a slave jail in the earth.

Bruh Abel seemed to know what it was

from the moment he saw it. He recoiled from the spot, yet the circle of lantern light settled on the thick metal padlock that sat atop the door. The lock was open, Rue saw, and the chains had been disrupted, left a track in the mud from where they used to be to where they'd just been moved. Varina.

He reached down, as if he meant to pull open the heavy door.

"Don't."

Bruh Abel swung the light up at Rue, near blinding her with the sudden motion. She covered her face, spoke through her hands.

"Miss May Belle," Rue said. "Marse Charles locked her down there once. For three days. Punishment."

She let her whole body shudder with the memory of it as though it were a fresh hurt and she were overcome.

She heard the lantern clatter to the ground. Bruh Abel pulled her into a fierce embrace. Her head at his chest, Rue listened to the pounding of his heartbeat, fast as hers, like a drum on her ear.

"You punishin' yo'self by comin' here, Miss Rue," Bruh Abel said. "It ain't right. This ain't the right way to make peace."

"It's like you say," Rue spoke into his chest. "I can't seem to let go a' the old ways."

"We can set this to rights."

"Please," Rue said. "Help me."

SLAVERYTIME

1860

Before the war, they found a dead man in the woods. They'd found him on the edge of the thick trees, at the crest of a small hill, as if he'd used the last thrust of his life to get up it and had succeeded in that at least. And all the folks agreed that the rusted iron collar locked around his throat looked like a crown of thorns fit for Jesus himself.

It was the little pickaninny boy, Red Jack, that found the dead man, a mercy that, folks said, for what if it had been one of the girl children who'd come across him? You see, the dead man was full naked, stark as the day he was born, save for his collar of rusted iron.

Still Red Jack, too, was only ten years old if he was a day, and it was often said that he did not have enough wits to rub together for a fire, so when he stumbled into the thick of the wood to relieve himself and saw

272

the dead man there, facedown in moss, Red Jack shrugged and shook dry and went to Ma Doe, who was the only thing like a mama he'd ever known, and said to her, "Ma Doe, there's a dead man in the wood."

Well, Ma Doe, who minded the children — the master's and the slave ones and the ones who didn't or couldn't know their mamas — well, she'd heard all nature of things in her long life and she thought she had heard every last thing there was to hear 'til she heard that.

"Who is he?"

"Don't know."

"How'd you know he's dead?"

"He ain't movin' none."

"How long's he been there?"

" 'least as long as right now."

Ma Doe had a baby on either hip and one swathed up on her back, and she was in no type of place to go running off into the wood on Red Jack's half-clear declaration, but she had a sense that something dread had come to them and she knew Red Jack didn't have it in him to lie. If he said there was a dead man in the wood, then there was.

She sent Red Jack to fetch Charlie and Ol' Joel and take them to the place where the dead man lay. He did just that, and the two men and one boy came back to her, hats in hand.

"Sure 'nough he is a dead man," said Ol' Joel.

"Can't make no sense a' who he is or where he come from," said Charlie.

"Runaway," said Ma Doe, who had wisdom of such things.

Ol' Joel was for telling Marse Charles, as he always was for telling Marse Charles. Charlie, who thought himself wise because he'd been allowed to apprentice at the side of a white blacksmith, commented on the iron collar. One of the long, cruel bars was bent enough to allow the man to lie, his head propped up awkward as if on a pillow of air. But at a touch the whole thing was rusted, weak. Perhaps he'd come up through the water, from the river, risen.

It was Red Jack that came to the solution, which was as simple as saying, "Miss May Belle oughta know."

Ma Doe sent Charlie and Ol' Joel to fetch the dead man. Standing in the doorway, draped in her orphan babies, she watched as they carried him through the crossways center of the plantation. Ol' Joel with his bad knees took the legs, Charlie held the head and shoulders, and as they passed her by Ma Doe couldn't help but to say how young the dead man was, how he was surely just fresh from his first shave and how sad, how very very sad, was the world.

Rue was not there when they brought the dead man into their home. Ma Doe had had the sense to tell Red Jack to run ahead, to warn Miss May Belle of what was coming her way, and in turn Miss May Belle had sent Rue on a fool's errand — go pick some sassafras from down the road a ways, as if there wasn't sassafras sprouting up all over the place, but Rue went.

Sassafras, Rue knew, liked gaps, dwelled in drops of light where the soil was moist but not too wet, and like all good things, it came wrapped in bad. It had a way of tangling itself with poison vines, trying to hide. But Rue's hands were small and already well practiced, and she picked the two apart and came back to her mama with only the good, a whole mess of sassafras sprouting out from her arms like she was herself a garden.

They'd put the dead man on the table, drawn the curtains, hid the sun. His raised head was turned at attention, like he'd been startled by the opening door, and though his eyes were half-closed, his blue-lined lips were partways open as if he was making ready a greeting.

"Who's that, Mama?"

"Nobody know."

Nobody did know. His yellow-brown skin could have been anybody's yellow-brown skin, as could his shorn black hair, as could his broad nose, his calloused fingers, his flat, bloodied feet. He was young enough to be any mama's son and old enough to be any baby's daddy. The lash marks on his shoulders could come from any overseer's licks, and it was only the iron around his neck that made him the least bit remarkable. Sure as a brand, it meant he was trouble. It meant he had run away and been brought back and made an example and shackled. Then he had run again.

There was a quilt for his nakedness, though it seemed small on him and only covered his lower half: his raw knees to the crescent of his belly button, shrouded. Rue looked long at the quilt then up to her mama, who stood behind the stretch of the dead man the way other mamas might stand behind a supper they'd cooked.

"He ain't died of no pestilence, leastwise. Wouldn't let them have brung him here if he had. Nah, body's strong, wiry-like, sure, but strong."

Miss May Belle touched the taut skin over his calves, thick as tree trunks. She moved to the top of the body, past various scars and scratches, a short life's worth of hurts and healing. His eyes, not all closed, were hooded, so she opened one of his lids all the way for him and looked in.

"No yellowin'. No cloudin'. Nah. He just die scared." She let the eye slip back to half-shut. "See how he look afraid?"

Rue could not tell what afraid looked like on a dead man. What did he have left to fear for?

"But, Mama," she said. She was still frozen in the doorway with all her flowers. "Who is he?"

"Nobody know," said Miss May Belle, but that didn't stop folks from trying to figure it. They came through the cabin one after another to look at him, the dead man, to confirm his strangeness and to make hollow suggestions about from where he'd come.

"Young buck," said Ol' Joel. "They like 'em like that down south way. Strong, they is, but got no sense. Disobedience is his name if it's anything."

"He got some Injun in him," said Beulah, who'd seen Indian in her red-skinned daddy and so saw it everywhere. The dead man's ears, she said, were like arrowheads; he could hear danger and that's how he'd run so far, for so long.

277

Opal, who knew a whole mess of men, was known to know them intimately, could not make sense of him.

"I ain't never come 'cross him," she said, as if she'd come across every man since Adam. She swept her hand over the peak of his pointed cheekbone. "Woulda like to known him, though. Face like that, surely he was somethin' good to somebody."

Seemed the dead man was something to everybody. They kept coming to look him over, though it was clear no one could name him. Even folks from the neighboring plantation came by if they could get the leave, not even to speak, just to stare. They put the pennies on his eyes after a while, to respectfully weigh down the lids. They all agreed there was something shiver-stirring in the pureness of those half-mooned whites. White as they knew cotton to be, white as they'd heard snow could be.

"It's foul luck to spend the pennies off a' dead folks' eyes," Miss May Belle warned the children that came to peek, "so don't you dare go an' think it."

Rue did not think of it. What she did think was how strange his stillness was, this dead man, with his muscles still poised as if at any moment were he to hear the hounds barking or the guns firing or the footsteps of white men's boots on wooded ground, he could take off. He could run again. Rue sensed it in him, and it sent a sort of thrill through her she as yet had never known. She had never before been so close to a man, dead or alive, and it was his potential to run that thrilled her. Women, she realized then, were not built that way. Women were for crouching, for becoming heavy-bellied, for bearing down and pushing close to the earth, that different sort of running, that sedentary sort of endurance.

They all of them conspired to keep the dead man hid from Marse Charles. It was a dangerous folly, they knew, but a risk worth taking to bear the dead man home. He had the look of every runaway sketch hanging from any tree in the county, but still someone might come to claim him if they knew where to look. There was profit in runaway corpses. Even dead, his white folks might string him up in the center of their cotton field as a warning to the others, a scarecrow to watch rot while they worked. His white folks might conspire to have him cut up, each limb and ligament worth a silver dollar from some white doctor curious on how a black body differed from his own.

The dead man, therefore, had to be prepared, and quickly, for the homegoing. Charlie Blacksmith came through to Miss May Belle's cabin. He sent a storm of sparks into the air, but he did it — the collar and its serpentine spikes fell away, and beneath it the dead man's neck appeared, seeming small and vulnerable. When they pulled it away, the collar, once sinister, fell to pieces like so many petals. What power it had had was gone from it now, left to bits of rust and iron.

Rue and Miss May Belle had to sleep with the man; there was no better place to put him than where he already was, stretched out on their supper table. The proposition didn't seem to bother Miss May Belle much, who long ago had lost her discomfort with life and death, with other folks' bodies, if she'd ever had any discomfort to begin with. She slept deeply through the night that he was with them. Rue lay awake beside her mama in fear and in wonder both. Across the room she could not see the dead man clearly, but she could make out his bulk and the shape of him, and beneath the lighter color of the quilt, she could make out perfectly the pale white bottoms of his feet, which caught the moonlight.

Miss May Belle was as boisterous sleeping

as she was awake. Her breath came in gusting stutters, a force, for certain, but so rhythmic that Rue most often found it soothing. But there was no comfort this night, and so awake, Rue listened and counted each of her mama's breaths as a way to keep time 'til it felt safe to move, whenever that might be. When she did get up she did so without telling herself she would. She was just suddenly in motion, quick but quiet to sit up and sweep the sheet from her legs and then stand so that the bed would shift slowly with her spare weight and not disturb her mama, who stayed snoring.

Rue crept across the room. She ghosted her way across the wooden floor until she reached him. The dead man waited, his head tilted toward her.

She held her hand to his open mouth, not so close as to touch his lips, but close enough to feel air. There was none to be felt and, emboldened, she hovered her hand down lower and lower still. The quilt was thin, a pattern of interlocking scenes, each block bearing little stitches of activity. Faceless black men and women — made women by the bell of their skirts — danced here and tended harvest there and bore black wings up to white misshaped stars. Rue

281

dared. She pulled back the thickly bordered corner of the quilt and followed the taut V of the dead man's waist. She saw the dark coiled hairs surrounding the mass of flesh there, long but unmenacing. It was what made him a man, she knew; it stuck close to his left thigh, dead too. A wrongness roiled in the pit of her belly. Rue dropped the quilt back down.

Across the room Miss May Belle's breathing came steady, slower than the rhythm of Rue's nervous heartbeat. Rue slipped one foot toward the bed, another, another. She froze when she saw them, the knowing bare whites of her mama's eyes. Watching.

"You done, girl?"

Rue could scarcely remember how to nod.

"A'ight. Come on back to bed now."

Rue did as her mama said.

The suit they found him the next morning fit as best it could, being something borrowed and not meant to be returned. It was a dusky gray, and folks said he looked ready for his wedding day. Wed to death, some of the older women were saying, wed to Jesus. But no one could spare him shoes, shoes being so rare to begin with. "Where he goin'," they assured themselves desperately, "he ain't gon' need 'em."

Still, the pale white bottoms of his feet seemed accusatory in their bareness, even after they had washed the worst of the blood from between his toes and from beneath his splintered toenails. That task, too, fell to Miss May Belle, who had the most knowledge, it seemed, of what was needed to make ready the dead. She surrounded him with flowers to keep him sweet smelling and cleaned his skin, gentle, as though he were her own son. The feet she saved for last, and Rue watched as the cleaning made her strong mama finally weep.

"He look like yo' daddy," she was saying under her sorrow.

Rue nodded, but he did not. Her daddy was stronger, older, darker. Alive.

How beautiful they'd made him when it was time for him to go on. Rue knew they'd cinched the suit in the back, so it pulled about his shoulders in the right way, and she knew the coffin was nothing much more than spare bits of wood left from the repair of other things: chicken coop stake, cracked church pew, things worked together and hastily painted one hue, as if that made for belonging.

They held the funeral at night after the work was done, and though they were tired they danced and though they had sorrow they sang. They made themselves a slow procession going by him in a manner strangely similar to when he'd first appeared to them. The dead man's head was pillowed by flowers, by quilted bits of pretty fabric, the finest anybody could spare. In death he looked himself like a celebration, though surely his life had never been. But here it was, close up, freedom. He'd reached finally what he'd been running toward.

Rue lingered back with the other children, all of them giddy like it was Christmastime and overtired besides. They did their best imitation of their mourning daddies and mamas, bowed their heads when bowing was necessary, keened when others keened. So, this was grieving. Rue followed last in the line that visited the dead man's motley coffin. She was not sure what she was meant to think or feel when she touched the splintery surface as others before her had done — what message she was supposed to be imparting through her fingers. Goodbye? Sleep well?

She looked out into the wood, focused on fixing her face in solemn dignity, for the sake of others if not for the sake of the dead man — and that's when she first saw them, there amongst the dark of the trees, looming white faces watching from afar. Had the dead man's white folks come for him after all? They weren't advancing to pay their respects, only looking on, eerie-still in comparison to the commotion of all the black folks' mourning. Rue took her hand from the box, moved on. Surely she was not the only one who had seen them. For certain everyone felt their presence. Their eyes, watching.

The movement of mourning had turned to a tight circle around the coffin. The four strongest men lifted the coffin up high onto their shoulders. Rue's daddy made up the back left corner and she watched closely as he and the other men bent as one, like something they'd practiced, to heave the dead man forward. They made the lifting of it look easy, and for sure it was compared to the back-breaking labor to which those sun-blackened field hands were accustomed. It was an honor to lift this burden and so the burden was light.

They processed through the wood and someone far back kept time with just the clap of their two hands in lieu of a drum, which was surely a devilish instrument to hear white folks tell it, but those two hands were as good as one drum, thundering off the trees so that it was joined up a hundredfold in furious echo. Rue kept an eye to the white faces, tried to keep solemn sight of them. They kept an equal distance from the black mourners, but they did follow, all the way up through the trees and there they stayed as the casket borne by the black men crested up the graveyard hill, illuminated full for their audience in the big moonlight.

They laid him down in his plot slow. At the head of the grave they were meant to place his belongings so he wouldn't come out again, a hungry spirit jealous after their own belongings. But he'd come to them with nothing but the twisted collar on his neck, and so that's what they left there to mark his rest. It bloomed from the ground, rusted and bent and broken, as good as any bit of stone bearing words could be. Better.

They formed up in a final circle for him and took up singing. Rue felt strange to be part of it, to hook her arms in with folks who'd paid her little mind before. But there was a warmth there that she liked and the song they gave was easy to learn, looping through them as it did, the words simple and sharp and real. Rue thought even that the white faces could learn the song if they chose to journey up the hill, but they didn't join and they didn't sing, only watched from the black shadow of the trees as on the graveyard hill the singing rose and rose.

"Wonder where is my brother gone?" a voice would lament.

And then another would come from the night. "He is gone to the wilderness," and another would join: "He ain't comin' no more."

"Where is my brother gone?"

"He gone to wilderness, ain't comin' no more."

"Wonder where will I lie down?" Rue asked when the circle of the song came round on her. Her voice felt thin but she made it hold. "Wonder where will I lie down?"

THE RAVAGING

On the third day of Bruh Abel's watch, he took Rue walking. They moved through the town square on a gray rain-slicked afternoon, and though no one came out of doors, Rue knew that all of them were watching through windows as the preacher man and healing woman passed.

"They ready to forgive you," Bruh Abel said.

"Are they?"

"They will want to witness yo' redemption." Already he was planning it, like a show. "You need only to admit yo' wrongdoing."

Rue did not feel like she had committed wrongdoing that needed admitting, not yet anyway, but she walked beside Bruh Abel just the same, going where he led her, up the steep hill to where the town cemetery sat veiled in mist.

At the peak of the hill, they stopped to

look down on the town below. They watched as a line of black smoke plumed from behind a cabin. The sickness wasn't gone.

"You broke my mama's spell," Rue told him.

He looked at her confused.

"Folks say before she died she laid a curse on the town, made it so's no one could come in an' no one could come out. But you come in and you come out easy. How's that?"

"Maybe I'm magic too," Bruh Abel said, "and don't even know it myself."

He spoke of magic with that amused expression that lit up his crooked dimple.

"C'mon," he said, and he took her over to her mama's grave. He knelt beside it. "She was a good 'un, yo' Miss May Belle. Glad I knew her the time I did."

Rue stayed standing, didn't speak. At the end she'd felt her mama hadn't been really happy with her. She'd always felt that, throughout her life, she'd gone up and down on the bobbing tide of Miss May Belle's esteem. That last year her mama hadn't been proud of her for choosing to hide away Varina. Wanted no part in it. Cussed Rue for a fool and worse.

It was like Bruh Abel was picking thoughts from her mind when he said, "My mama wasn't so kind always."

"Yo' Queenie?" Rue had rather liked the fanciful tales Bruh Abel had told of his mama, though she didn't half-believe them. "Thought that you was her favorite."

Bruh Abel rocked on his haunches. "Favorites come and go," he said. "First thing she did when the captain gave us our freedom? She turnt round and sold me right back to bondage."

Rue took a step back from him. Recoiled at the very idea of it. "Y'own mama? Sold you?"

"Sho' 'nuff. She had other mouths that were wantin' to be fed, how she told it. Her older sons were grown by then, no property of hers. She weren't like to sell off her daughters neither. Men do nasty stuff when they buy up pretty mulattas, she tol' me, but I was a boy, and sons is meant to leave, that was her thinkin'. Or leastwise what she said aloud. When I recollect it all now, though, I suspect it was more the eyes."

Bruh Abel tilted his head all the way back. He opened his eyes wide for Rue so that she could examine them for herself.

"Like the captain's," he explained.

Rue looked hard. He was kneeling below her still, the same height as the lesser gravestones all around him, and in the bright of high noon his eyes were the same swampy mixed-up gray of those rocks. His whites were red-rimmed, like he'd lost as much sleep as she had been losing. He blinked hard and carried on. "I was the only one that got 'em. Ain't it funny what we pass down? Her man was dead but she always said I had a haint in my eyes. Now, how could she be free with a white man looking on her from beyond?"

Rue said nothing, had nothing to say to something so hard.

"Ain't no one reason for anybody doin' anythin', is there?" Bruh Abel said. "Like as not it was just as much that I was what my new marse was lookin' for to buy. Boy, young enough to still be molded. He used to be a breaker before he got religion. Don't think they have a word for what he become."

Breakers. Rue had heard of such men. In slaverytime Marse Charles would threaten to send his more discourteous slaves to a famed breaker a few counties over, though he never had done it, perhaps more because of the prohibitive cost than the cruelty of the breaker's methods. But the threat still rang in their heads, which was just as good to keep them in line and cheaper besides, a fear on the inside of their backs, always rolling up their spines, the knowledge that they could be sent away to a place whose whole function was to leech you of your spirit, to send you back home hollowed and broken and thankful for it.

Bruh Abel pulled Rue close to him and leaned his head on the soft bottom of her stomach, buried his nose briefly in her belly button like it was meant to fit there naturally. Rue had a sudden moment of sorrow, and of wanting. A flash thought that she ought not go forward with her poison scheme. But just like that it passed in her. She did not pull away from him, not even when his grip on her hips tightened, each finger digging in with individual need.

"I ain't mad at what my mama done or what the breaker done," Bruh Abel said. "The scripture teaches forgiveness and the scripture is what my marse branded into me without even lifting a hand. There's other ways to make a boy the man you want him to be, and that's what he was after. To prove it could be done another way. Through the spirit, he said."

Bruh Abel went on, and said, "It started off as a drunken parlor bet. Can you teach a bird, teach a monkey, teach a black man how to worship so good he draws in a white crowd? Funny thing is, he never did collect on that bet, my marse. Man he laid the bet with said in the end it didn't count, didn't prove nothin' seein' as my ability might've come from my half-white side. Well, my marse, bein' white and smart hisself, he recoup in another fashion. He took me all round. To every state and out on the ocean, in trains and steamboats, and out west to wildernesses not even yet staked or named, all so that folks could look on me as an example. Of all the things a black man could and could not be. That's the part I ain't forgive, Miss Rue, that he aimed to diminish other black folk through use a' me."

Bruh Abel pulled himself up by her hips. Rue bristled but did not pull away. His truth had his body shivering, nothing eloquent about him now. Just another mama-less child.

"I've been wantin' you to know that," he said. "Didn't know how to tell it but in a story. Figure you'd understand. I don't care for what folks are expectin' a' Bean, lookin' the way he does. Layin' they burdens at his feet. Seems to me they should 'llow him to be a boy, not just an evil or a spectacle."

"You mean to go to him now?" Rue asked. "To pray over him the way you done my mama?"

"Just this minute," Bruh Abel said.

"Before all to see?" Rue pressed.

"I swear it."

Rue kissed Bruh Abel. A brief pressing of her lips to his in which neither of them moved or even breathed, the better to feel. She wound her hands down his body and lingered at his taut chest, and then at the waist of his belt, and then at his pocket, where she swapped the vial of holy water he kept there for her own plugged-up vial of poison.

When she pulled back, she was almost reluctant to leave him. It was like peeling away from a place that she belonged.

"Go on then, Bruh Abel," she said. "With my blessin'."

He moved her hair and kissed her again, easy, like he'd always had the right.

Rue waited and imagined. She was not to be seen when Bruh Abel led Bean out amongst the townspeople to be healed through prayer and singing and drinking holy water. So she had to picture it, and sit and wait, alone.

Her cabin seemed overlarge now that it was hers alone again and empty of Bruh Abel. His watch was over. He had the truth of her, or so he thought. He'd gotten the witch to promise that she would admit before everybody her misdeeds. It was to be

294

done in the harsh light of the next day's dawn. Now he was free to minister to her changeling, to free Bean of her hold.

Bruh Abel had no sense of how well his freeing would go. He didn't know that his praying was laced, that by daybreak Bean would have the froth and the fever that had wracked the other children. Just enough sickness to silence all suspicions.

Rue had to imagine too, Varina in the old white church, imagine how she must have sat for hours in the prison she had put herself in, 'til she could be certain it was safe to return to the rectory. Rue had cautioned Varina over and over that she must never be seen, and if she were to be seen she must do everything she rightly could to appear like she was dead, only an apparition in the eyeblink of any superstitious gaze. Seemed Varina had took Rue's warnings to heart.

So Rue kept on, waiting, sat by the warm of her fire as the things she had laid unfurled. She pulled from her pocket the bottle of holy water she had stolen from Bruh Abel, replaced with her own more potent liquid. Rue pulled up the cork stopper and at the fireplace she overturned the vial and let the whiskey-water out. It hissed and sizzled where it met the heat but the fire kept on burning.

When the sickness came, they needed her, Jonah and Sarah did. They had to believe Rue had been absolved by Bruh Abel's word, because he said so. She was the only one with enough knowledge to tell them what had befallen their youngest son. They sent Bruh Abel to fetch her and he led her to their door, hovering behind her, like he was still suspect of her power for all that he had vouchsafed her coming redemption.

The poison had worked quicker even than Rue had figured. In his bed, Bean twisted and sweated against an inferno fever. They had called on her for help though they had not trusted her. What else could they do?

"Don't touch nothin'," Bruh Abel told her, and Rue did as she was told.

Rue stood beside him as he looked over the sick boy.

"He's sweatin' out somethin' awful," Bruh Abel said. Rue could see that. Could see the way the boy was succumbing to the fever. Like he was being cooked alive.

"Y'all need to cool him." Rue turned to the mama and daddy. Jonah eyed her with suspicion but seemed to be thinking on the whole situation, deciding. Sarah's expression was drawn, like she'd gone away and left her body behind.

In the bed Bean reared up. The black in his eyes seemed to have spread. He spoke. Not sentences, not even words, just the harsh sounds of a muddy guttural language, hard tongue pangs on the back of his teeth.

"Take him to the river," Rue said.

Sarah and Rue followed behind the men as they went ahead. Bean, slung over Bruh Abel's shoulder, was a limp weight in his arms, looking back at them through half lids, an uncanny stare like an accusation.

"The cold water outta help cool his burnin'," Rue told them.

"You know he afraid a' the water," Sarah said.

Bean fought them. As Bruh Abel and Jonah both walked into the deep of the river, the little boy between them thrashed and hollered. They had to hold him in it, beneath the water made icy with night. But he did soon calm, maybe shocked by it into an eerie still. On the bank, Rue's heart ached for what she'd done to him. But she'd had to. Every wrong she'd ever done, she'd done to protect others. Bean. Varina. The whole of the town and every soul in it.

"Folks won't come after him no more at least. They can't say he ain't suffered." Sarah spoke the words of the thing that Rue

297

had been hoping after, but to see it there before them enacted, it seemed a cruel means, hardly worth its end.

"I love him," Sarah said. They watched Bruh Abel and Jonah drag themselves out of the river, Bean hanging limp between them. "You may not think it, but I do. I love him the way anyone loves any child, because they a child. It's not like he mine. It's like he came outta me but he ain't hardly touched me."

In the silver of the light Sarah looked pale, resigned, like the haint of someone Rue used to know. "You'll know when you got one a yo' own what it's like," Sarah said. "That Bean, he don't belong to me. I can't say who he was meant for."

They took the boy back home, dripping, to shiver in his bed.

WARTIME

1861

Varina never did bleed. Varina had been their pacer for all those years, the girl and then the woman by whom they, her black servants, might set the clocks of their own bodies, for they had no better way of knowing their own age besides looking and guessing at their reflections in the glass they were scrubbing or in the water pails they were fetching. Then all at once Varina, who was always first, fell behind, came up dry.

Sarah bled, and then Beulah that same spring that they counted as their thirteenth year. Then Rue bled in the rainy season, the last of a crop of girls turned to women in the course of one evening, now elevated in value by the promise of their multitudes.

Varina came to Miss May Belle's cabin each time she heard that one of the black girls had become a woman. She pestered, sniffed it out of them, like a beast for the blood, and when she caught the scent she'd come knocking at Miss May Belle's door.

"Girl, ain't nothin' wrong with you," Miss May Belle would say. "It'll happen when it has cause to happen."

It was Rue that set Varina on wanting to bleed. They were where they should not have been, up in the lofted gallery of the little church, which, every Sunday, creaked and buckled under the weight of the black congregation. It seemed so much smaller, Rue realized, absent of that press of bodies. Rue and Varina lay together on their backs, the way they might've in their field. Outside the sky flashed and rocked with thunder and lightning, working itself up to a downpour.

The little church was much farther down the path outside the plantation than either of them had the right to go, but Varina had urged them one step farther and one step farther still.

"If we come across someone I'll say you mine." Varina had it all figured. "I'll tell 'em I brought you out here to give you some religion." But they did not meet anyone as they picked their way east through the wood and there was no religion to be found in the building — only below them the simple pulpit and the empty pews, important to no one on a black-cloud afternoon, for the minister lived in the next county, which was by horse hooves still a day's trip.

Still, Varina said it was better to stay hidden in the church's second story than to be caught out by the pews should anyone wander in. But they had trouble lying still on the wood floor, and Rue felt that they were only doing a gimcrack imitation of their younger selves, those carefree children who could lay about, mindless and gathering grass stains.

The passing of time was most obvious in Varina, whose round, full face had grown pointed, whose freckles had faded altogether. In Rue's memory was Varina as she'd always been, fat and thumb-sucking, defiant in a calico dress bearing patterned flowers. Now Varina was growing round-chested, requiring new sets of lacy frocks and fresh fine-boned corsets seemingly every fortnight.

Rue had hardly grown. She still wore an apron of her mama's, so long it had to be hemmed. But beneath her thin, easy muslin skirt she had a secret.

"Touch here," she said, and she guided Varina's hand to her waist and moved her fingers for her as though they were her own, letting Varina feel the smooth round shape of each bead on the ribbon hid beneath the

301

rough fabric.

"Show me," Varina demanded.

It didn't feel as easy now to show Varina her body as it had been when they were young, back when the only real obvious difference between them was the light and dark of their skin.

On the roof, the first fat raindrops fell and sounded like knocking. Finally, Rue untied her apron, pulled up her skirt.

The beads fit close to her skin just as her mama had tied them the night prior, a pattern of red and orange and brown stones that reminded her of the earth lit up by the sun. The string of beads crossed under her belly button like a horizon. They *clicked* quietly when she moved; she'd heard that *clicking* all day.

Varina was just as drawn to the beads as she was to the red strip of fabric they held up. The strip disappeared beneath Rue's white skirt, secure between her legs. Rue tucked the skirt back into place before Varina could be bold enough to follow the bit of red fabric with her creeping, greedy fingers.

"What is that?" Varina could make even a question sound like a commandment.

"My mama gave it to me. Last night I bled."

Varina's eyes rounded. "Why?"

"What you mean, why?"

Before then it had not occurred to Rue that Varina didn't know about blood the way she did. She herself could not remember the first time she'd understood that being a woman meant being bloodied, but then she could not remember the first word she spoke, or the first time she knew herself for herself — some knowing just felt like it had always been.

"Ain't yo' mama tell you 'bout it?" Rue knew it for a foolish question as soon as it left her lips. Varina's mama, who folks knew to be as brash-mouthed as a clarion in the keeping of her household, was as mute as a fish when it came to her only trueborn child, as though the girl was nothing more than a spare room that a housemaid sometimes neglected to dust. The rearing of Varina fell most to Ma Doe, who could command the girl in schooling and dress, but lately was losing her authority in even that. But in the manners of a white woman and the matters of her body? Rue imagined Ma Doe — who easily was the most proper woman she'd ever known, slave or not — making up Varina's bed each morning, relieved to find those soft white sheets unstained another day.

It took Rue what felt like hours to set the girl right. Varina's ideas were all muddled. She supposed that the bleeding happened only when the woman went to relieve herself. She supposed it was an unusual, unending affliction. She supposed there was shame in it.

"It's natural, my mama said," Rue explained. "There's no shame. It's beautiful. That's why my mama made me the beads to hold up the cloth."

Miss May Belle didn't believe in shame, or so she'd tell anyone who'd stop long enough to listen.

"What's the use for it?" she'd often say.

Rue knew it was no good to be ashamed when she'd had to wake her mama in the middle of the night. She knew she had to look brave holding out the front of her white sleeping gown, pointing out the bloodstain she'd left there long enough that it had dried to brown. But she was scared. "Look, Mama."

Her mama stirred from her sleep. There was no surprise in her when she saw the blood, and Rue was used to that. Miss May Belle smiled. She knew girls and women before they even knew themselves. Her mama crouched down beneath the bed frame to a basket of spare things she kept there: bits of fabric, tore-up trinkets, and dried posies of no particular use but to be pretty to look at. She pulled the length of beads out inch by inch, like a garden snake. She wrapped the beads around her neck to free her hands 'til she worked the end out at last.

"Do you hurt, baby?"

Rue shook her head. She couldn't feel a thing but a warm damp. It was like a new-sprung well. A thing happening without her say-so.

"Sometimes you will and sometimes you won't," her mama explained. Rue knew this already. There were folks who suffered with it, she knew, women who came to them once a month or more, wanting something to fight away their aches.

Rue had seen Miss May Belle take care of women her whole life, had done so at her side, at her command. But now, bound by the papery warm feel of her mama's work-roughened fingers, she felt something she had not known she had wanted so badly.

"These beads is special." Miss May Belle held out the belt to its full length, the whole stretch of her arms. The red rag hung in the middle like the flag of some proud country. She shook the string so that the beads *click-*

clacked together loudly. "Iff'n you ever forget yo'self, let that sound be what reminds you."

She drew the beads up along Rue's body with her hands splayed, and Rue felt the thrilling spin of them all the way up her hips. Her mama pulled the ends of the string tidy so they'd lay flat beneath even something as flimsy as her nightdress.

"A man come and bother you, he can make you a mama. Now that's a good thing sometimes and a bad thing another. Depends."

Rue knew this too. She had seen new mamas collapse in their crying, brought down by all manner of tears, overjoyed or sorrowed.

Miss May Belle laid a palm on the flat of Rue's belly. "When the beads start to pull too tight, well that'll be one of yo' first signs that somethin's changin'."

Then Miss May Belle did something Rue wasn't at all expecting, something she never did with the other women who came to see her with all their needs and all their wanting. She pulled Rue close and wrapped her arms around her, spoke quiet words with her lips in her hair.

"I'm proud a' you."

Rue did not know what she had done that

306

deserved pride but anyway she was glad she had done it.

Outside the rain had soothed itself down to beat but a few half-hearted patterings on the roof of the church.

"We ought to get back 'fore they know we gone," Rue said.

Varina was quiet as they descended the church steps. She walked down slow, over-careful in her hoop skirt, and Rue coming down behind her was impatient. Outside, steam curled up from the ground drawn out from the heat. Already the sun was returning and Rue felt very tired thinking on the work her mama would surely have waiting for her.

"Make one for me." Varina's demand came out of nothing and nowhere. She ghosted her hand over Rue's hip, where she knew the beads were hidden.

"What you need it for? You ain't bleed yet."

"But when I do. I'll for certain need one when I do."

Irritation rose in Rue the same as the tendrils of mist that came up off the rainwater. She wanted then so suddenly to slap Varina it was like a sting she already felt in her palm. Varina had pearls and brooches, bows and combs; Rue could have no one thing of her own.

Varina made her separate way up the road to the House. Rue watched her go, watched her skip round puddles and pockets of mud, her pale hand shading her pale face, her hair glowing like a beacon fire in the growing strands of sunlight. Rue watched Varina all the way until she disappeared into the House, and then she turned and walked home herself, her beads going *click-clack-click*.

In their cabin Miss May Belle was working nutmeg, grounding it down to a fine powder. It raised up in a spicy earth smell, Rue's favorite scent.

"Where you got to?" Miss May Belle didn't need to look up to ask it.

Rue watched her mama's elbow go up and down with her grinding, and she knew she was in some kind of trouble.

"Fetched the skullcap like you asked." Rue set down the basket of damp purple flowers and knew it for a meager offering.

"Now, wasn't that near an hour ago?" It wasn't a question.

Rue picked up the flowers from the basket one by one at the stems the same way she'd picked them from the thicket. She drew the dew off the leaves and tried to look busy

308

doing it.

"You and that Varina, y'all got different lives to live," Miss May Belle said. It wasn't the first time she'd warned it, but Rue had to be impressed at the uncanny way her mama had of knowing what was what. "You listenin'?"

"Yes, Mama."

Rue bound the skullcap stems with twine and hung the bundled posy up by the window. There were a mess of other herbs up there, waiting with their bottoms up, their stems to the sky as they dried. Rue tiptoed and stretched and added her new pickings to the others, choosing a spot where they could get the full of the heat without getting the full of the sun. The skullcaps hung awkward. To Rue it looked as if their drooping violet heads were straining to stay upright.

"You got to obey her, fine, but you don't got to follow her," Miss May Belle said. Rue was uncertain of the distinction. She wished her mama would leave off the topic. A low twisting pain had started in her stomach, not a stabbing but an ache, and she knew she had to bear it. Miss May Belle of all people wouldn't have sympathy for woman pains.

Her mama passed her the ground-up

nutmeg without a word, but Rue didn't need telling. In a large jar on the shelf was where they kept the mama's milk, an extra bit of help for mamas too thin or too sickly, too overworked or just not at all able to call up any milk of their own. Rue poured out a splash from the jar and stirred in the nutmeg before it could drink up all the milk. The trick of it was to add just the right amount, make a paste not a soup, and Rue had the knack for these kinds of mixings, better, she thought, than even her own mama had.

Still, Miss May Belle kept up her faultfinding. "You takin' too long with that. It ain't Sunday supper."

Rue was bleeding. She was tired. She was thirteen, thereabouts, and a woman, thereabouts. But all her mama wanted to talk about was how she ought to stay clear of Varina.

"You ain't," Miss May Belle finally said, "friends."

The ache in Rue's stomach grew to a spasm of pain. She set the bowl down suddenly on the table like she'd lost the strength even to stir. Rue heard Miss May Belle *click* her tongue at her, presumably in disapproval. It was that small noise, that lifelong *cluck* of her mama's correction, that sparked her ire. Rue drew back her hand

310

and slapped the bowl from the table.

The mixture of mama's milk and soothing nutmeg splattered, sent a streak across the floor and dashed along the skirt of both of their dresses. The bowl clattered and spun so long it was almost comedy, before Miss May Belle raised her foot and stepped on it to clap the bowl down into silence. She stood there like that with the bowl under-foot, like a turtle subdued, its head and limbs pulled in in fear.

Rue wanted to run. She'd done a horrible thing, she could feel it in her stomach, a pooling of shame.

"Good," said Miss May Belle in a nasty bite. "Good, you go ahead an' get it all out, girl. But don't you go an' forget it. You not a child now, so you best hear it from me an' remember it well. You can sass all you want in here. But out there" — she pointed hard in the direction of the House — "you never say no more'n, 'Yes, Miss Varina.' You hear?"

"Yes, Mama."

Miss May Belle stepped over the bowl in coming closer, stepped through the mess of their ruined tincture. She took Rue hard by the shoulders, something desperate in her grasp.

"That girl ain't yo' friend."

The slap Miss May Belle gave Rue was

hard, shocking. The pain of it resonated long after, tremulous on Rue's skin like the reverberation on a drum. But it was what Miss May Belle said that was slapped into Rue's memory and stung just the same, years after: "Varina ain't yo' friend. An' I ain't either."

Rue made Varina a belt. In rare moments of baby-less, mama-less, blessed quiet, Rue drove holes through pieces of nutmeg. She'd stolen the knitting needle, just the one, straight out of Ma Doe's basket on a hot afternoon when they'd both been tasked with watching Varina dance.

It was in a back room of the House, a forgotten parlor, disused and dust-ridden, and it was its emptiness that Varina had taken a liking to when she'd developed all sorts of peculiar wants and fancies shaped by the perceived tastes of other white girls. To Rue those girls were real as haints, which was to say not real at all, and she held ghostly impressions of these playmates of Varina's, with whom Miss Varina was sent to sometimes take luncheons, a mission for her propriety, endeavored with all the purposefulness of a war campaign.

Varina was all glory on those visiting days. With her frizzed hair brushed out to an

312

obedient shine, she'd sit beside Red Jack as he drove her to her visits like a queen on her throne. Red Jack for sure was thrilled to have the permission and the pass to leave the plantation. He had a natural way with horses, something holy in the way he yelled "Hey now," that made him safe to drive the cart that bore the master's daughter. He had a natural way with a simpleton's smile that made him safe to come back with her by nightfall.

Varina would return from these visits with, as Miss May Belle would put it, "some fool idea rattling like beans in her empty head." The white girl would make herself half-sick with wanting until she got what some other white girl possessed or something better still.

Now Christmastime was coming on and the cool season and the good harvest and the bounty of babies was making everything languid and slow, and Varina had seen to it that her Christmas present came early, a book of dancing steps that she'd ordered, come all the way from the North. She'd spied an advertisement and sent away for it and some months later the thick tome was there, spread on Ma Doe's knee. Rue could only pick at certain letters but she liked well the drawings. They were mostly intricate footprints going this way and that, trailed by dashes to mark from where they'd come to where they had to go. The gentleman's footprints were always the larger, the lady's daintily following in his wake.

"You gotta be the man," Varina had said but Rue had already figured that. She was clumsy at it, trying to lead as the book suggested, but Varina, who squirmed in her arms, wouldn't let her do the leading, and all they had for music was Ma Doe reluctantly smacking the base of her chair with the heel of her shoe, and she wasn't very good at that neither.

"No, no, no, it's all of it wrong." Varina stopped Rue right in the midst of a turn. She tugged at her curls, let them spring back to her head to mark her agony.

"Now, Miss Varina," Ma Doe petted, "you needn't learn all this foolishness to be well-liked. You have any number of fine virtues. You'd do well to remember that."

It was on Christmas Day that Varina remembered her finest virtue, and that was her wiliness. She knocked on their cabin door just after supper and grinned up at Miss May Belle.

"Fannie's took ill at the house. She's needing someone to nurse her."

Miss May Belle was not a fool. She squinted down at the white girl.

"And they sent you all the way down here, Miss?"

Varina grinned demurely. "I volunteered."

"Then I'll be up presently."

"Oh, you needn't trouble, Belle. Rue'll do just fine." Varina leaned in conspiratorially. "I suspect it's only a block of the bowels that's botherin' Fannie. Mother quite spoils her with sweets."

Rue came out sleepily, armed with a sloshing gourd of palma christi oil to soothe Fannie's complaint. She followed awhile in silence before Varina made an abrupt turn away from the House through a thin path in the woods.

"Dump that someplace." Varina waved away the oil.

"Where we goin'?"

Rue kept the gourd hugged close to her. They stepped through uneven craggy ground, over bent weeds and barren land. They walked for some time, Varina just ahead, Rue struggling behind.

"What about Fannie's bowels?"

"Don't be foolish, Rue. Ain't nothin' the matter with Fannie's bowels. Come on now, keep up."

Where they were going there was music.

315

It snaked out at them through the trees a little at a time 'til Rue could put it together whole as a song, and closer, as someone picking a banjo, and closer, as folks keeping time with their foot stomping. Closer too there were the words, easy to pick up in their repetition, saying, "I got a right, y'all got a right, I got a right to the Tree of Life."

Red Jack had guard of the place. He was crouched atop a log like a frog, his hands hanging between his legs, and he shook his head at Varina like he'd been expecting her and was disappointed to see her all the same. Still, he gave them leave to pass. Inside the singing grew forceful. "You may hinder me here but you cannot hinder me there. God in heaven's gon' answer my prayer."

Varina and Rue came up to the weathered cabin, stood at either side of the doorway, and listened. They said nothing but watched each other's faces in the flicker of warm light leaking out. Varina smiled her thumbworn gap-toothed smile. "Let's join 'em."

Rue followed behind Varina. She thought that the silence that hit the inside of the little cabin was for her, but of course not; it was for the white girl who'd entered, for the master's daughter, and it wasn't a whole silence at all but a hiccup, a dampening not

316

of the sound but of the exuberance, of the joy. Black folks turned from what they were doing and faced them.

There was the seamstress Dinah, and Big and Li'l Sylvia both; there was Charlie Blacksmith and Ol' Joel, grinning toothless, with Opal and her sweet bottom sat on his lap. There was Fannie even, who should have been asleep at her mistress's feet or else straining in some outbuilding somewhere else. Anna's daddy twanged at the banjo and Sarah sang prettily but loudest, and beyond that was folks from Marse John's plantation, and Coffey and Homer and Mary John besides, and folks Rue could not name but whose drawn faces looked familiar. And beyond all of them was Rue's own daddy.

She caught eyes with him from across the room. He didn't say anything but shook his head the way Red Jack had shook his head when they'd arrived.

Rue's daddy was playing spoons, a trick she'd never known he had, and he did not stop playing when she stood dumbstruck in the doorway watching the metal flash in his hand like the anxious metallic heartbeat of the whole of them.

"S'alright," Varina said at last over the hushed music. "Y'all carry on. We not here

317

to stop you."

Someone provided the white girl a stool, wiped off the dust from the seat, and bade her sit a spell. Rue settled in by Varina's feet, which tapped along feverishly with the music. Sarah was singing again, joined in a lilting harmony by others.

Red Jack came in next, trading his post with one of the other young fine-armed boys. They didn't need to speak to swap the sentinel but passed a jug of something swishing clear between their two hands. Red Jack leaned his head back and drank and then passed the bottle to Ol' Joel, who thanked him with a wink of one of his clouded eyes. He released Opal, giving her three rhythmic taps on her bottom along to the music, which was fine with her. She swished her way over to the center of the cabin floor where the dancing was.

"We shouldn't be here," Rue said.

Varina said, "Huh," and continued her foot tapping.

Across the room, Rue's own daddy rested down his spoons. He took up the floor to where they danced a breakdown, their legs sawing to the beat like it was a job of work. Their whoops of laughter started out for Varina's benefit, but surely they grew genuine as the beat deepened. Rue felt it too —

there was no earthly way to deny a good beat.

Marse Charles did not altogether frown at his slaves dancing. He'd been known, especially at Christmastimes, or after a particularly bountiful harvest, to encourage it, to bring certain visiting guests of his to look upon the boundless happiness of his slaves, to even clap with them if he felt so moved by their native kind of frivolity. But it seemed different when he wasn't there looking on. Like as if their amusement, for its own sake, was a waste. Now Varina clapped like her daddy might have clapped as the dance floor grew crowded.

Red Jack slid up to them. The close room was overwarm with so much activity, and a fine sheen of sweat was shining up his face. His eyes glittered too, and someone had passed him back the jug and this time the smell of whiskey wisped clear out when he swallowed. He smiled toothily and began to pass it back on down the line.

"Now wait." Miss Varina snaked out her arm and took the jug from him. He didn't resist, couldn't really. Varina took a dainty sip, grimaced, but tipped back some more. "Go on," she said and held it out to Rue.

Rue still held in her lap her bottle of unneeded castor oil and she hugged at it with

319

one arm while she reached out for the proffered jug. Varina would not hand it over but motioned that Rue should tip back her head. Now Rue did so and Varina spilled into her a burning mouthful. Rue's tongue floated, her lips burned. A trickle escaped down her cheek as she swallowed thickly. Varina returned the jug to Red Jack, and between them they seemed to share an easy amusement that made Rue's stomach roil.

"Take a turn, Rue." Varina didn't take her eyes off Red Jack. "Rue's the finest dancer."

Red Jack raised his brows, feigning at being impressed. "That so?"

"Show him." At Varina's urgings Rue got to her feet, feeling the slosh of the whiskey and the slide of the earth as she did so.

Red Jack led her out with the briefest tap on the small of her back. The music was already at its swell and, bidding her to watch him, Red Jack strutted to the foot-stomping rhythm that was taking up the whole of the cabin. Feeling loose, she rocked with him, then bent her knees and hopped from foot to foot as he did. Their arms wheeled in large, free circles in the air like they might any minute take off into flight. They caught elbows and spun past each other, not certain where they'd end up.

Rue laughed breathlessly as Red Jack

aimed to outdo her with his own enthusiasm, throwing back his elbows, launching himself forward in wild skillful imitation of a hot-footing chicken. Rue found herself clapping, dancing in improvised whirls 'til she couldn't draw a blessed bit of breath and had to break free of Red Jack and sit herself back down. She fanned herself at Varina's feet and caught her daddy smiling at her from his own side of the dance floor.

"Really such fun." Varina clapped gaily but she didn't seem to mean it. She kept her eyes on Red Jack pivoting and twirling in the midst of all the others, light as air, his two feet gifted with springs on the bottoms.

"We best get back before you missed, Miss Varina," Rue said.

Varina got reluctantly to her feet, made her way around the dancing to the door. "G'night, Miss Varina," folks were saying with ingratiating smiles stretching their faces, and they looked more than glad to see the back of her as Varina and Rue went out into the night. "An' Merry Christmas."

Full-on dark seemed to have taken over the evening. Rue could have cussed with the trouble they'd be in if anyone noted that Varina'd been gone so long.

"Oh, Jack."

Rue jumped. She hadn't known Red Jack

321

had followed but there he was, slinking behind them. "Mightn't you escort us back?"

The boy could not be so foolish as to keep getting close to this girl so near to being a woman, and a white woman at that. Rue answered for him. "We be alright. We know the way."

Red Jack echoed her. "You be alright, Miss Varina. It ain't so far."

"Yes, if you say so," Varina said. "G'night then."

"A Happy Christmas to ya."

"And say g'night to your sweetheart."

Rue balked. Whose sweetheart?

"G'night, Rue," he obeyed.

"It's alright," Varina said. She bared her teeth. "You may kiss Rue if you like. I won't tell."

Red Jack leaned in. Rue didn't know whether she could pull away. In her face his whiskey breath was a visceral thing; it had manifested itself in the cold night air and clung between them, as good a barrier as any cloud was, 'til Red Jack got up his courage and kissed Rue through it, leading, lizard-like, with his tongue. When he pulled back, it was not to check on Rue's pleasure but on Varina's.

"Good night," their mistress said again.

"And a very Merry Christmas."

Rue's lips felt wetter for the cold. She wondered then if Red Jack was so dull after all, or if he'd just devised a way early on to seem to dance to the white folks' tempo.

Varina and Rue walked side by side back to the House. Rue aimed to put the kiss far from her mind, found she was thinking instead of her daddy and the easy way he'd rattled those spoons.

"Have you ever kissed anybody before, Rue?"

"No'm." She hadn't and had never found that she'd particularly wanted to.

"I have," Varina said, dreamily.

Rue reckoned she ought to ask who but she wasn't sure she really wanted to know the answer. They were coming up onto the House, preparing to part ways.

Ahead of them came the noise of crunching footsteps on frost-hardened grass.

Illuminated by the lantern she carried, Miss May Belle was coming around the corner like a bad omen borne of light. The shadows that skittered across her face told of her displeasure better than the frown on her lips or the hardness of her words ever could. The lantern in and of itself was a bad sign. It came from the House, a place Miss May Belle never had cause to go except in the case of some unusual trouble.

"She been callin' for you, Miss Varina," Miss May Belle said. Varina stopped just behind Rue as if knowing she'd be in need of a shield. Their shoulders overlapped. Rue could feel Varina's body shiver.

"Who is?"

"Missus took ill in the night. Ain't you heard?" Miss May Belle knew full well they hadn't heard. She must've been smelling the corn whiskey on them heated up by their sweat. Rue, self-conscious, wiped at her lips, fearful they were glistening still.

"What's the matter with Mother?" Varina sounded troubled.

"Can't say. But they done called for the county doctor. They say he on his way." That was a journey of miles.

"Why won't you help her?" Varina stomped her foot same as she had when she was a child, a child still in so many ways.

"It ain't won't, Miss Varina." Miss May Belle held higher her head and her lamp. "It's can't. She won't 'llow me or anyone else to see her. Cusses and spits and foams when we get near. But she been askin' fo' you."

"For me?" said Varina. "What can I do?"

"Set with her, I s'pose. Just be with her."

Varina paled. She did not argue but followed last in line behind Miss May Belle and Rue as they hurried to the House, came out into the clearing together, purposeful, like nocturnal creatures starting their day. Varina went up to the porch. The lanterns were all lit in the windows, despite the late hour, further signaling that all was amiss. Only in the circle of their light could Rue see that it had begun to snow, white bits of nothing-ice were hanging in the air, melting before they ever hit the ground. From the depths of the House there came a high, sharp woman scream. Rue already knew death by the turn of a scream the way she knew when babies were hungry or wanting to be held by the turn of their cry. She thought, the white doctor won't come in time.

In the doorway Varina stalled at the sound her mama was making. Miss May Belle nodded her on, and the girl disappeared all the way in.

Now alone with her own mama, Rue feared a scolding but all Miss May Belle said was, "Ain't nothin' we can do here now. Best we get us some rest. Long days ahead."

Her mama reached out to her then and put her palm on Rue's cheek, a gesture that felt loving. Rue smiled, and her mama looked in her eyes. Miss May Belle licked the end of her thumb, and Rue saw there the sparkle of a silver ring that she had never seen before. It belonged to Missus. Or used to. Miss May Belle wiped the wet thumb across Rue's cheek, cleaning away something only a mama could see.

"Ain't nothin' we can do," she said.

Missus's funeral fell in the cradle between Christmas and New Year. She'd put it in her will that her slaves ought not to mourn too heavily for her and should not be expected to cease in their work at all. Bless her heart, the black folks said, for even in death she could give them the gift of toil. They did not have the day off to attend her burial, and those of the House were put to work double, preparing for the elaborate stages of weighty mourning, black ribbons and black crepe veils, black door pulls and flowers blackened for wreaths. Black makes you blameless, folks said, makes death look the other way when it's deciding on who to chomp at next.

They'd all know the moment she was put into the ground when they'd hear the church bells ringing out her years.

"Forty?" Red Jack had asked, wide-eyed.

"Yea, forty," Ma Doe had told him, exasperated, and then she'd had to call on Rue, who wasn't strong enough to pull on the bell's thick cord to set it ringing — but she was good at keeping count. Rue had never had cause for reading, but she'd learned her figures, had to learn them well when keeping labor time for the mamas.

Rue and Red Jack crawled up in the church bell tower like thieving mice, unseen by the mourners just then pouring out from the lower levels behind the fine, heavy coffin. Red Jack was fast and agile with his climbing. Rue was slow and clumsy and had to be helped up the last few rungs. She brushed away his helping hands when she got to the top and tucked herself in the farthest corner from him.

From above they could see clearly the white mourners retreat up to the graveyard, trailing behind the coffin like black ants bearing a prize back to their hill. Rue was nervous. If they timed the bells wrong they'd surely be whupped. You didn't get between folks and their mourning. She told Red Jack as much, but he just shrugged.

"I been whupped before," he said, which was surely true and maybe explained why he was so damned slow. He seemed excited by the pull cord for the heavy brass bell. He kept running his hands over the knots in anticipation.

"Why'd you do what you done on Christmas night?" she asked. She'd never quite shook off the taste of that whiskey kiss. For days after it had come to her, swirled into her nose like it was fresh, a kiss just laid.

Red Jack shrugged again. Rue hoped his head would fall plum off with the movement. "Miss Varina said to, ain't she?"

"That all?" Rue didn't want her voice to give out or to give away her true feelings. He'd only been obeying Varina.

"Sure, I thought it might be nice to kiss you." He let go of the cord. Crossed over to her, hopping the dangerous place where the floor of the tower was opened for the ladder.

"You alright, Rue," he said. "When you ain't frownin' at every damned thing."

He kissed her again. She tried to decide if she liked it at all. It was warm and strange. Her teeth got in the way.

She let his lips go. The mourners were all on the hill.

"One," she said and Red Jack leaped back to his position and began to toll. "Two," she said.

Forty years resounded off the corpse bell loud enough to give Rue a headache. She watched Red Jack, who partway through the counting had felt it necessary to undo his shirt. His back muscles worked as he pulled, and when he was done he used his bundled shirt to wipe the sweat from his brow and then from each tuft in the red-brown coils of hair in his armpits.

"Forty," Rue said and then, "Don't never kiss me again. Iff'n you do I'll put a goopher on you, fix it so yo' lips turn black-blue and fall right off one night in yo' sleep."

Red Jack let her precede him down the ladder and through the empty church where the bell's last echoes still pealed. He held the double doors open for her and let her leave before him down the way.

He said, "Uh, thank you, Rue. For the countin'," and he didn't say one more word to her for years after that but hello and goodbye and ain't the weather fine.

The belt for Varina was done. It clicked nutmeg shells when Rue gave it over to her. Still swathed deep black in heavy mourning, Varina looked pale and suspect but she took it anyway.

"I ain't yet bled, Rue," she said. She held the belt with its dark seeds and bright red ribbon around the tapered black waist of her mourning gown.

"I know, but I wanted to give you somethin'. Figure you still a woman bein'

329

that you turnin' fourteen years."

There were no invitations, no letters to mark the occasion of this birthday. Varina, who had so longed for visitors, could receive none, then, or for a full year after her mama's death. In that season there was only brittle frost on trees and crepe black sheets over mirrors in the parlor, crippling Varina's vanity. The white doctor had come too late and said after that it was the flu that took Missus. They'd sealed up her room right off just as tight as if it were the tomb in which she'd been interred. Afterward, the house girls gossiped, said Varina sometimes walked the hallways at night to stand in front of the door like she was still waiting on her mama to summon her in.

Marse Charles wore his grief as a tight black armband and nothing more. Folks said all his widower thoughts were of expansion. The whispers of the war coming to their doorstep might've had others making themselves smaller, less vulnerable to change, but that was not Marse Charles's way, never had been. He was wanting more, another acre, another wife. He'd had made a mourning locket for Varina, woven gold from her mama's brown hair, and Rue was yet to see her wear it.

Now Varina pulled back her skirts and her

petticoats, which had been all hemmed black lest anyone spy her underthings and think her lost-mama grief was not full. She held her skirts close to her skin. Beneath the flurry of fabric Rue helped her secure the belt above her small freckled hips. The bloom of color looked like a scandal and Varina laughed in giddy delight, despite her mourning, as she smoothed down the many layers of black.

THE RAVAGING

"Now, Sister Rue, in Jesus's name," Bruh Abel said, "renounce the Devil."

Rue's redemption, when it came, didn't feel the way she thought it might. She hadn't pictured the way that folks wouldn't look at her. They stared. They stared so hard she felt she could hear it, like a low contemptuous buzz, but when she picked out eyes from among the crowd at the river, they shifted and skittered away. They thought Bruh Abel safe to look at, it seemed — when they caught his eye, they smiled.

Rue pictured Bean, hoped thinking on him would give her strength. Bean was likely home with Jonah still boiling up with a fever, not made by nature or the displeasure of God but out of her own benevolence. She would not be ashamed of that, whatever this day brought.

Ma Doe was absent from the crowd also, though Rue hadn't truly thought the old woman would be there. Sarah had come, bringing only her eldest boy, not Bean, with her. The boy stood between his mama's legs and twisted his face into her skirts when Rue passed by, like he was scared of her, she who he had known his whole little life, she who had twisted his head and tugged him out on the end of Sarah's meager, singing thrust. There were only a handful of other children there. Most were still weakened, she knew, from the sickness she was said to have cursed them with.

As she made the long, slow walk toward Bruh Abel, he looked at her with a certainty. He strutted forward, and the crowd parted for him as he approached Rue head-on.

"Renounce the Devil," he said again.

"I do," she said loud. Murmurs shivered up from the crowd. "I wish him gone. I do."

Bruh Abel put his hand heavy on her head, as though it were an effort to do so, and he pushed her down, down, down 'til her knees and her legs and her hands were all in the dirt. Still she kept her eyes turned up to him.

"You only need tell him, 'Leave me.'"

"Leave me," she repeated.

"Louder."

"Leave me." Her voice cracked. "Leave."

"Louder for all to hear, Sister Rue."

She felt a monstrous sorrow rise up in her like a swell. She looked away from Bruh Abel, down at her hands spread out in the dirt, and she began to sob. Tears dripped clean from her face to darken the ground beneath her in fat circles that made strange patterns as they wetted the dirt — looked like stars set out on a sky below, and all the while she ground out the words, "Leave me."

The ground shook when folks started up their foot stomping to the rhythm of Bruh Abel's words raining down: "Cast off your wicked ways. Don't let them demons have no more hold on you."

She wanted it, salvation, not in the sense she'd always known — as a promise of hereafter eternity. Instead, she wanted salvation in the here and the now, for herself and for Bean, or a glimpse of it at least, a place she might feel safe and rest her head at last. Bruh Abel was beside her, his warm hand on her face.

"Out. Anything not of You," he said, "out."

In the far-off distance she felt her throat constrict and release and cry out. Her tongue flickered out words of no clear form, desperate sounds articulating something kin to wanting, kin to ravening. She seemed able to observe her own body in its flawed entirety from afar.

Then all at once the euphoria left her — a sudden depletion, like the moment after a passing gust of wind when still air seems strange and inexplicable. Someone lifted her at her armpits and set her on her feet. She swayed but stayed standing.

"Was it the spirit a' Jesus what come to you?"

"Yes," she said. "The Holy Ghost entered me."

All around her people were staring and murmuring, holding out their hands to touch her. She turned to Bruh Abel, who was now some distance away from her, though he hadn't moved at all. It was the crowd that had rushed in. Over their heads he was puzzling her out again, a slow eyeing from top to bottom and back up.

"Tongues is a sign for unbelievers." If he was speaking for the crowd or just for her she couldn't figure, but either way it sounded like something he'd snatched whole cloth from some other preacher's mouth. "Prophecy is for believers."

"In Jesus's name," she mumbled. That was what folks kept saying, wasn't it?

"What He say, Miss Rue?"

"He say, I be His. I be healed."

■ ■ ■ ■

After, Rue took herself over to the old church. She walked the long way to be certain she was not followed, stood outside in the well-trod path, that rut made over time from years on top of years of folks going back and forth in search of worship. For Rue, faith had always flickered in and out of her consciousness like a flame on a candlewick, sometimes resilient against wind, other times extinguished easy in a sibilant hiss. She could not account for what she had felt that afternoon in the town center, any more than she could account for why Bean hadn't caught the ailing naturally while others had.

After the walk of several miles Rue was glad to push through the double doors and shut them tight behind her. The air was heavy with dancing dust motes like loosed cotton bolls. Rue sat herself down in the front row of the church where she had not been allowed to sit. It still felt wrong, after all those years, to break the white man's nonsense rules. Up above, the floorboards creaked.

"You listenin'?" she asked, staring straight at the pulpit. If anyone else were to come across her they would have thought she was arguing with God. Either way there was no answer.

"Varina," Rue called out, and her voice bounced through the vaulted ceiling and seemed to return to her tenfold.

There, a groan of wood, and summoned, Varina came out of her hiding place, behind the rectory door. She looked wan, skeletal.

"You didn't come back," Varina said.

Rue sighed. "I'm sorry, Miss Varina."

"You ought not leave me for so long." Her voice came at a warble, and Rue looked at her proper and saw fear there. "You really ought not leave me."

"Ain't I always come back?" It was like speaking to a child, but that's just what Varina looked like now, one startled from a nightmare, looking for any comfort. But there was only Rue to give it to her, and it was the threadbare sort. Varina had been raised to have a hundred black souls at her call. Rue alone must have felt like a pathetic disservice.

"That white man you came in here with. Was he a soldier?"

So Varina had seen. "Bruh Abel? He weren't white. He's colored, Miss Varina. Just real pale."

Varina rocked on the heels of her bare feet

337

like she wished to run but had no place to go. Rue hadn't seen her mistress so agitated in an age, not since the early months of her hiding. Then Varina had prowled the rectory, fitful and crying, or euphoric in turns, and there had been only the one way to soothe her then, one awful way. Rue had made the white doctor's medicine last as long as she could. It was all she'd thought to grab from the house before it burned, a small supply, and she mixed it with wine or thinned it with water to ration it and still Varina had screamed in her agony that she was dying.

Those draughts of laudanum had run dry finally and Rue could not get hold of more. She had broke Varina of the awful addiction the long, hard way, like breaking down a wild stallion by receiving a hundred kicks to the face. The hundred and first time Varina came away clean; the only stain the poppy had left on her were the dreams. The nightmares.

"I can't sleep, Rue," Varina said now, recalling an old complaint. "I see the soldiers comin' for me."

"Ain't I say I'd keep you safe, Miss Varina?"

But her mistress seemed not to hear her, was trapped in a danger of her own imagin-

338

ing, and in her mind that danger was still marching toward her, as it had been three years past. Rue let her keep her nightmares. Let her think they were still real.

"When will this goddamn war be at an end?" Varina moaned.

"By God's grace, any day now."

Rue held her body still when she heard the knock at her cabin door, though she'd heard so many knocks before and more urgent ones to be sure. This one, if she could presume so much from simple knocking, sounded resigned. Rue took her time crossing the small room and opening the door. Took her time in saying, "Sarah. What's the trouble?" because she knew what the trouble was.

Sarah was weary-looking, likely from taking care of her family in the way all the women in town had grown tired on their kinfolks' behalf. If there was a sickness in the town, every woman was made weak by it, whether she had the symptoms or not. Worrying was a disease for women, and it came as a chronic ailment. By the time Rue opened the door to her, Sarah had rested her arm up on the doorway, her head cradled weak on her forearm.

"Bean," she said, lifting her eyes but not

her head. "He's sicker now."

They walked in the same purposeful stride, matching their steps unconsciously, side by side. Rue had the sense they were in some kind of race where the winner had to be the first to arrive and the last to lose their composure.

The night long ago that Bean's strange crying had come to her bloomed in Rue's mind. She recollected how the sound, the peculiarity of it, had yanked her from a sleep with no dreams. Rue had forgotten the exact quality of the sound. She could recall only how horrifying it was, how it had set Bean apart before this trouble had even begun. She could recall only wanting to keep him quiet, like the cry would speak something she didn't want heard.

Rue let Sarah lead her inside. Jonah was there, sitting on the floor of the front room with the little girl in his lap, the little boy around his shoulders. They looked healthy, and Rue was glad to see it. They played on him like he was a tree, and Jonah was just as immobile as one, to be sure. He watched her cross the room behind Sarah, not saying a thing, and all that silence led Rue to believe that something had passed between them, some sort of dispute. He'd been the loser, Rue figured, and then Sarah had come to find her.

Rue knew what to expect from Bean, but she was still shocked to see it. The froth and fever, when she'd sought out the right mixture to fix the symptoms, had sounded in her head as ordinary. To her, sickness — death and birth — did have the habit of growing ordinary over the seasons, until one case cropped up to shock her. And this was it and, worse, it was of her own making.

Bean's breathing came in wet shards, a wretched sound like someone drowning. He was not fighting but lying still, as if weighted down by something only he could make sense of. He locked eyes with it, this oppression in the air, and did not stop staring it down, even when Rue and Sarah drew near.

Rue rested her palm on his forehead. She felt exactly what she knew she'd feel. Fire. She couldn't keep up the pretense long and drew her hand away, hid it in the apron of her dress as though it had been branded to tell of her guilt.

Rue slipped from the room. There was only so much she could do, and she'd done too much already.

In the outer room she found Jonah risen from the floor. He'd put the children in a rocking chair in the corner. They huddled

341

together in the seat, fighting a doze and losing.

She could sense his distrust from across the room, as thick as though it were a thing he could hold in his hand. A stone to throw. Jonah did not like her looking at his children. Rue looked dead at him, feeling suddenly bold. *I am still your witch,* she was about to say. *So you best be scared of me.*

Rue opened her mouth to speak, to cuss, but it was Sarah's wailing that came, mournful and absolute from the other room. Rue rushed back, but Jonah was quicker, and she followed after him as close as she dared. He stopped himself in the doorframe with his hands braced against each wall. Rue had to slip beneath his arms to get past him. She near had to climb over Sarah crouched at the foot of the bed. Bean's strange eyes, Rue saw, had shut.

"What's the matter?" Jonah was asking. His voice was urgent and aggressive, like he was ready to fight with the truth if it came to it.

Rue put her hand to Bean's mouth and felt no breath. She put her hand to his neck and felt no rushing blood. She put her head to his chest, hoping, hoping to hear a distant pounding there, but there was nothing to hear and no way to hear it besides. All Rue could hear was the sound she knew well, Sarah's howl, the desperate sorrow of a mama who already knows.

Still, it fell to Rue to pronounce it like it always did. Like it always would. "Bean," she said. "He dead."

WARTIME

There is a new fox in the wood. Miss May Belle jokes that she's gonna go out and skin it, wear it for a coat when the season gets chill.

It's a woman. Ma Doe says the right word for a woman fox is a *vixen.* It's brown and bold, been seen prowling round the House like it thinks it belongs there, pawing at the front door trying to get an invitation in.

Miss May Belle got herself a new ring that don't belong to her, come off a bigger hand, it only fits on her thumb. Word is it used to belong to Missus, who isn't even yet cold in the ground. Did Miss May Belle thieve it? Did Marse Charles gift it?

Lord, but that Miss May Belle is uppity.

Who can say — except that a thief would never be so proud. The only time Miss May Belle's seen to take off that ring is when she's birthing. Says it's bad luck, she does.

The fox prowls. Missus's grave chills. The

South divorces the North, wanting its freedom.

Mary John, the kitchen girl, her new baby comes too early, comes out feetfirst, comes out still. Makes sense, the world turned upside down the way it is. Miss May Belle and Rue see to Mary John, who's burning up, sparked with the birthbed fever.

Heard Marse Charles is looking for a new wife, a third. If you listen hard in the wood you can hear them two foxes fighting, the old one and the new, two vixens baring teeth, going at each other's throats. That's how all women are, Miss May Belle says. Territorial. Soon the woods will be flooded with foxes, before the coming war is done. Those foxes won't let black folks alone. They'll run in packs. An *earth of foxes,* that's what that's called.

Marse Charles's sons look mighty fine in them tintypes sent home. Proud with their new uniforms: epaulets, scabbard and sword, gleaming new buckles, yet untouched by dust or dirt or by blood. The House flies a proud new battle flag. They're calling it the *Stainless Banner.*

Miss May Belle finally oversteps herself. She asks for too much. Soap and candles in war times? That's one thing. Now she's begging after medicine for Mary John. Real medicine. What comes in glass vials. The birthbed fever burns, inferno.

Miss May Belle begs. Says she'll do anything. *Anything.* She pleads after Mary John's life. Marse Charles says, "What, now you niggers too good for grass?"

Varina's needing a husband. She ain't never bled yet. She's the missus now her mama's gone. The tousling foxes sound like women screaming through the night. Screaming 'cause their sons are returned to them dead, if they're lucky, or else not returned at all, left wounded and trampled on and ground up in some Northern dirt. Morning come, there's blood in the grass. Blame them foxes. The South renames their flag the *Bloodstained Banner.* Whose blood? Red-backed and blue-crossed, stars along the middle, corner to corner for every Southern state that says hell no.

Marse Charles said no, but Miss May Belle's got ahold of the medicine some other way. Mary John comes back to life like the last few mighty embers of a fire you think been full stomped out. She'll live to love lots more babies.

Now, what is that screaming? Ain't no fox. Out of the door and into the night. In the square and Marse Charles got Miss May

346

Belle by the hair of her head. He's saying how dare you? How dare you disobey me? His strong white fist is squeezing out her curls like to make them straight. He's dragging her out and into the night, and as he goes her body spins on the end of his fist, on the twirl of her hair, over the rocks and mud and grass. She's fighting hard, yelling words that ain't even words no more. Maybe she learned them things from her African mama. Savage promises of violence. Her face is bloodied, red on her like tears.

Lord Jesus.

When Marse Charles gets tired of dragging, he throws her over his shoulder like a sack of grain. They go clear out of the plantation. It's a bleach-white moon-filled night. You can see where he's taking her to. Right off in the distance, the church looms.

Where's her girl? That Rue. Found her hid under the bed. Yes, it was Rue, not the fox, doing the screaming.

White folks planning for themselves a jubilee. Let the shooting stop for a while. Let the sons come home. Let the fox go shrill in the field. Why doesn't Marse Charles just go out and kill those foxes? Folks says he hasn't got the heart. When mourning for Missus is done in three months' time, Marse

Charles says, we'll have ourselves a fete.

Three days now Miss May Belle's gone. That jail beneath the white folks' church? You ever seen it? You ever been sent to it? That's where he's locked her up, ain't it? There beneath the ground. On the inside it's five steps this way and five steps that way. No sun, no moon. All dark. All black. They say the water seeps up, down there, when the river swells. Water how high? Not high enough as you'd be hoping, by day three. Not high enough to drown you or them rats neither.

Ain't no one deserve that. Not for trying to save a dying mama's life. Not even Miss May Belle.

Do you think Miss May Belle killed Missus? Killed the first wife too? Conjuring them into foxes to haunt them woods?

Marse Charles let her out, finally. He let her keep his dead wife's ring. Miss May Belle come out from the jail afraid of the sky. North of here them Yankees win another battle. Ain't this war ever going to end? Miss May Belle come out afraid of the light.

Folks said, should we go and see to her? Nah, she'll be alright. She's a tough 'un, that Miss May Belle. Let them alone. Let her daughter see to her wounds. In the woods two foxes stay prowling.

349

THE RAVAGING

Rue was trapped. Living in the syrup slow motion of a dream, words wading their way out of her mouth thick and strange. She gave the town the words and they repeated them, and even when she heard them echoed back, still they did not feel like sense: "Black-Eyed Bean is dead."

Ma Doe's home was a natural place to end up, but Rue came to realize that only when she was standing in front of it. She shied at the door, sat instead in the rocking chair and brought her knees to her chest. She closed her eyes and tried to think of Bean. Bean as he was and Bean as he would be. Now she'd have to see him buried and know she'd done it, completed the circle she'd hesitated at on the day of his birth with her scissors raised high. Did he know it then? she wondered. Folks do say babies born with their caul got the Sight.

"Rue-baby." It was what her mama had

called her. Ma Doe knew that. She was being kind, calling her in. Rue went into Ma Doe's cabin glad to see there weren't any children there. Ma Doe sat alone, her legs raised up, her feet resting on an overturned bucket bearing her thick, dark calves, pockmarked and black bruised in places after a whole lifetime of standing on the behalf of other folks, nursing at their children in the middle of the night, rocking them to sleep.

"Come here now." Rue was not expecting Ma Doe to hug her, to kiss her on the cheek like someone's mama might, to hold her at the end of her arms and look her over and say, "Shall we pray?"

They bowed their heads as close as conspirators, the mess of their hair mixing together at the end of their spirals as though that were the way secrets were passed.

"Almighty Lord." Ma Doe had her hands on Rue's shoulders, was holding herself heavy on them, weighing Rue down. "Be with Brother Jonah and Sister Sarah, for the loss of their child must sorrow them."

Rue felt she was holding them both up, like if she backed away she'd send their two bodies tumbling down.

"And, Lord, keep Miss Rue." She shuddered at hearing her own name. "She's done the best she could by you, for she is your instrument. And Bean's death —"

Ma Doe's face fell then, sunk down on the left side like a razed tower. Her eyes got wide and fearful. She began to hum a continuation of her prayer as if she'd suddenly run short of words.

"Ma?" Rue clutched her close.

Ma Doe nodded, working her lips like chewing. "Alright," she managed.

Rue had forgotten. Ma Doe was everybody's mama and she was nobody's. Her boys had all been stripped from her, easy, like petals off a stem. Same age as Bean was, when each of them were sold.

"I'm alright," Ma Doe said, but she seemed to struggle to say more.

Rue led her back to her seat and helped her settle down. Ma Doe leaned back, looking hollowed. She nodded her head and it reminded Rue of the mindless way Varina had used to suck her thumb. Like Ma Doe had, in all her grief, been dumbstruck and turned into a child.

Rue's fault also. She didn't know that she was weeping. Not 'til the tears were at her neck, wetting her collar. She sat herself on the ground by Ma Doe's raised feet, buried her face in that ancient knee, and let the weeping take her.

Miss May Belle wouldn't have prayed and she'd suffer only so much weeping. When Rue would come to her as a child, snot-nosed and guilty, she would say only, "That's enough now. Fix what you've done. Or live with it quiet."

Still, Rue wept.

WARTIME

Their plantation held a ball. Marse Charles demanded it for himself, said he deserved a jubilee. Missus had been dead a year by then and he'd grown restless with grieving, bored already with playing the widower. Every day there was news of young Rebs fighting battles and winning to fight another. Or losing and dying of it. Marse Charles had sent his sons to those battlefields, but he was impatient on their glory. He wanted his own safe sort of victory and decided not to wait to celebrate a Northern defeat. But the black folks were whispering behind their hands calling it a Dead Man's Jubilee.

The House was made to gleam, a shining beacon of sophistication that had many of the indoor slaves' hands rubbed raw from keeping those parts of the House that were well-trod from looking like they were ever lived in at all. Even Rue and her mama had to work in a way they'd never been expected

354

to before. Miss May Belle had for so long got by on being too busy with birthing, on giving the plantation its robust number of babies and maintaining the bodies of others. She'd been so important in that above all else, that it was almost like her own body was free. But now she scrubbed with the rest of them, tasked at cleaning the tall white pillars that wrapped around the House's porch, and it was a lofty type of falling from grace, as she was made to climb up high to remove years of dust and dirt and errant grime between each ridge, approaching immaculate.

If Rue were to keep an image of her mama in her mind it might be that: Miss May Belle on the top of a rickety stepping stool, the legs of it lodged deep in dirt to keep it steady because it was a waste of a worker to have someone hold it there, even a child.

Each day of that long, tedious week of preparation, Rue passed by her mama outside on the porch on her step stool, scrubbing. Varina had asked for Rue in the same way she'd asked for a new frock — a heavy blue gown of a certain fabric she'd seen on a rare trip to the nearest town three months prior, on a bolt that had already been sold and made into something for somebody else. Because the dress she got

355

was not the exact shade of blue that she'd been wanting, she felt she could ask for shoes to match it. She asked for Sarah and got her too.

Rue and Sarah found themselves draping behind Varina like the two ends of a veil. She wanted to practice at being a lady and that in itself was a masque in need of spectators.

Varina's preoccupation was her red hair. It had always vexed her, made her look strange and bright and not as demure as she might have wished, what with carrying brimming locks of hellfire everywhere she went. But that had been when she was young and small and a thumb-sucker on Ma Doe's lap. Now, despite the continued arid nature of her monthly visitor, she'd decided to count herself a proper woman and, in her mind, proper women did not go about having the red cherubic hair of little children.

"We ought to darken it." This she said to Sarah, who stood stock-still and held up for her the glass so that Varina might better see herself at all angles.

It was a thin, garish space, Varina's bedroom, a place Rue did not often find herself and did not like when she did. Varina had long since moved out of the nursery in favor of one of the disused guest rooms. Her wide bed with its thick posts like tree stumps took up more of the room than made sense to Rue, and up above it a canopy hung in thick drapes that made her hot just looking at them. With three bodies and all their warm, restless breathing, the room was particularly stifling, and Rue relegated herself to the cool varnished wood of the floor, which she was tasked to scrub from end to end. It would have been an alright place to make herself invisible if not for the fact that this position, on hands and knees, put her eyeball to eyeball with the dust-mottled collection of Varina's ceramic dolls heaped all in one corner. Rue sweated under their staring, and the white gleam off their porcelain skin was like to make her blind. All the dolls were a striking straw-headed blond, unlike their owner.

Varina and Sarah were already stepping in the part of the floor Rue had just washed. Sarah's bare feet left little gray imprints of themselves, and Varina's impatient foot tapped dirt from her small dagger-hilt heel. Sarah fussed, brushing out Varina's hair. Rue could have screamed as the red spirals drifted out and down to the floor. She'd have to sweep it again when they were all through.

"Darken it like how, Miss?" Sarah, with her sweet voice, was being just as doting as Rue had ever seen her and Rue had a good sense of why. It was no secret to them that as much as the world seemed to be changing it was not changing so much, so quick. Varina would be needing to become a lady — a lady in pursuit of a husband — and a lady in pursuit of a husband would like as not be in need of her own nigra housemaid.

Fannie had been the Missus's girl for all of their lives. A perfect petted favorite, she'd oft be seen to flit all around the House in the Missus's old clothes, reminding other folks of her favored place, putting them down in theirs.

Rue watched Varina and Sarah in the mirror, didn't like how easy they were with one another, how close. They'd just together drew the black crepe off Varina's large wall mirror and found that, beneath, the glass had been streaked black by the press of the fabric over those long months of mourning. Their doubled reflection was marred, lines over their faces like trenches through mud, and Rue just knew Varina was waiting to tell her to clean off the mirror soon as she finished the floor.

It made sense that Sarah would be chosen. That Sarah would go to the fete that night and serve drinks to fancily dressed white folks, that she'd follow behind Varina and make sure that her skirt wasn't dragging in anything dusty. It had never been said, not out loud, but it had always been meant to be Sarah, anybody with eyes could see that. She'd never had a place in the field, not with her skin smooth and light.

"Miss May Belle's likely got somethin' I can use for yo' hair. What you think, Rue?" They were both looking at Rue, their heads turned just sideways. Their mouths and noses and eyelashes in profile were strange and synchronous, and Rue could not deny that she felt a burst of foreknowledge.

She was invigorated with envy also when she stood and glanced at her own figure in the glass Sarah still held. She was small and dark-skinned and, in that moment, just as ugly-feeling as they must have imagined her, raisin black between them.

"I'll run on out and ask Mama."

Miss May Belle had not been the same after that time spent locked up in the jail hold of the church. Starvation and silence, three days of it, for disobedience, the simple sin of getting a mama some medicine.

"I done so many worse things than that," Rue's mama had said when she'd first come back, like she'd been thinking on all of those things she had done during her time locked away.

Rue didn't know what to make of her mama, come back the way she had, with nothing on her to heal. Her body had taken care of itself, the way a body can, eaten up the stored-up flesh so she was just left to sharp, angular bone. Sealed up cuts and scabbed over hurts. There was a chipped tooth far enough back in her mouth to not change her smile, unless she smiled real wide. All of it superficial, save the patch of her scalp where Marse Charles had pulled the hair clear out of her head. It was tiny, barely even there, Rue had assured her mama. It was star-shaped. Fist-shaped, Rue realized after. It didn't grow back, never would, but it was easily brushed over.

Why couldn't she magic her way out of that jail was what Rue kept wondering. A deep resentful hurt centered in her like a pit in fruit. If Miss May Belle was as powerful as folks would have you think, so mysterious, so feared, couldn't she free herself, or feed herself, turn the ground seepage in that dank cell, water to wine, hoodoo herself into one of them little fleas that had left hard red welt bites on her skin and hop on out?

Miss May Belle was still scrubbing at the

balustrade when Rue came out from the House, and Rue felt her mama tracking her from deep within sunken eyes as she went past. If Marse Charles's punishment had been meant to make the slave woman obedient, then it had failed. Instead she was all the more outcast, all the more feral. And Rue always became what her mama was.

Rue had never had any intention of asking Miss May Belle after a way to darken Varina's hair. It was just that Varina could not be pleased. First Rue returned with a poultice of nettle and sage, and Varina did not fancy the color the leaf skins would make. Next Rue returned with tea, steeped to black as ink, but Varina had turned up her nose at the smell. The cure Rue returned with last was a pleasing amber-brown liquid she knew that Varina would take to, the darkness in it likely to bring out her light.

"There isn't very much," Varina complained when Rue showed the small bowl to her. "Do you think it's enough?"

Rue could see in Sarah's eyes that she recognized the stuff where Varina didn't. There was a hard-questioning look to Sarah's face, but she stayed stiff-lipped and mute. Who knew? Maybe Sarah was feeling just as vengeful against Varina as Rue was.

Perhaps they could be vengeful together. Rue turned the bowl, roiling the liquid enticingly so it would not begin to settle.

"It's enough to work," Rue said. "Color's like to bring out your eyes."

"Alright then," said Varina, ever easy and trusting.

It wasn't that Rue blamed Varina for what her daddy had done to Miss May Belle. Rue didn't believe hating was transferable. But it awed her that Varina had never in her life had any reason to be distrustful of anything handed to her, even by Miss May Belle or Rue. Never thought that she could be hated for no reason, or for the simple reason of existing. The sweet smell of the gummy resin wafted up between them. Varina had not a clue and Sarah said not a word. Rue kept on turning the bowl in her hands, roiling the brown liquid. Soon it would start to set, harden; it would give the trick away.

Varina sat on her stool inspecting her hair, her nose almost up to the glass, curling a strand and uncurling it around her finger like something were going to change if she kept doing so.

"Try it on her first," Varina said, gesturing at Sarah.

Sarah and Rue looked at each other. Open-mouthed.

"Ain't enough for both," Rue said.

"So y'all will go out and fetch more. But I'd like to see how it's lookin'. We got close kinds a' hair."

It was true. Varina and Sarah were similar, especially sitting together like that in front of Rue. Both thin and drawn and pretty, pug-nosed and curly-headed; the only difference in them was a matter of wording. Varina's ringlets were red. Sarah's nappy curls were rust. Sarah, there holding the little mirror, was holding a different version of herself in the glass, or so it seemed to Rue, a different kind of life Sarah could have had.

Rue struggled to come up with a lie, an excuse that might prevent her being whupped for daring to play such a trick. But Sarah was resigned. Without a word they'd been caught out in their trick before it ever began, and now they had to see it through. Varina and Sarah traded places. Sarah took the vanity stool and Varina held the mirror, playing at being a servant. Rue raised the slow-dripping syrup to Sarah's waiting head where it would settle and harden, thick as tar.

"What were you thinkin' of?" On Miss May Belle's cabin floor Sarah's cut-off hair lay

363

left behind, hardened like petrified bugs in amber, though Sarah herself had long since gone, sent to bed shorn and weeping. Hair grew back, Miss May Belle had assured her, saying nothing of her own hidden star-shaped scar.

"I wanted to get her back," Rue said. "Make Varina feel somethin' for what Marse Charles done to you."

That was the simple answer, the answer that Rue figured her mama, who was always juggling a hundred schemes herself, would be proud to hear. Truth was, Rue could not put simple words to her anger, just that it was anger. She'd wanted to hurt Varina for love of her and did not so much mind hurting Sarah in Varina's place.

"And see yourself whipped for it?" Miss May Belle moved about the cabin in her distress like she mistrusted the distance between walls. Even as she raved she walked up and down, smacked at one far wall then crossed the length of the room to smack at the other. "You lucky Miss Varina ain't catch on to what you was about. You wanna see yo'self hanged? Or worse, sent where they sent me? You couldn't never survive that place."

It was the only time Miss May Belle ever alluded to the three days she had been buried alive in the church's jail. Rue took her mama's scolding with her face set sullen.

"Stupid girl. Ain't you know it ain't worth it? Don't you know there's no way round it? Aiming to curse white folks is like tryna slap at a fly sittin' on yo' wound. It's never gon' do you no good. You only gon' smack yo'self, and that fly gon' go off laughin'."

Rue felt defiant. "Varina say I could go to the party tomorrow in place a' Sarah."

Marse Charles was never gonna let a bald-headed slave girl into the House, not while there were guests there, chittering on in the face of the North-brought war about the fine way they treated their slaves. Like family, they'd lie. Like beloved children needing a stern hand to be raised right.

"It's my own fault. I kept you shielded." Miss May Belle ricocheted off the far wall and sat down hard on the dirty hair-covered floor, drew her knees up to her chest. Curled in on herself. Rue didn't know what to do. "Go on then. Let Miss Varina take you."

"Take me where?" The party was being held up at the House, only a stone's throw.

"Let her take you away and show you how the world is."

Rue's mama had told her once that Cain and Abel were not brothers, not twins. They were, Miss May Belle said, two sides of the same person, good and evil warring against its own inclinations. The same struggle was borne out in every person, over and over, from the very most beginning of time, and you could only answer for yourself which brother would win. Varina had told her later that it wasn't true, that the Bible said it plain, spelled it out in those little letters Rue couldn't read. There was Cain and there was Abel. There was black and there was white. It wasn't so much that Rue didn't believe Varina, but she kept hold of what her mama said, applied it to others, held up that story to folks' faces and tried to decide which brother they had ruling them.

Varina could be good, Rue said to herself that day, as giving as Abel. They met in the clearing before the fete. Varina was lovely in her blue gown, the one she'd demanded for herself and won. Rue's dress was new also, new to her anyway, a bit of calico repurposed in a different pattern, so it almost wasn't that old rough stuff anymore. She thought it fit her fine. She thought they both were pretty.

"You can't work it," Varina said first. Not a hello or a nice thing about Rue's new dress, or her own, or even a good word about the neat coils Rue had managed to twist her own hair into with the help of some pilfered pomade — not one of her mama's ground-up oils neither, but that real patent pomade. Varina's hair blazed red as ever. "I asked for you. But Daddy's only wantin' the light girls inside servin'."

Rue could have cried, might've, she could feel the sorrow screwing up the back of her throat like a rising sickness.

"Don't you worry." Varina cupped Rue's cheek lovingly. "I've got us a solution."

The air buzzed with nightfall gnats as they walked toward the back of the House. Already they could hear the hired-out fiddler playing, little snippets of nothing that began with a flourish then scratched away to frustrated silence, then burst out again, louder. They could hear him crick his strings, 'til they whined like cats. He began anew.

Varina led Rue through the servants' entrance to an ill-lit hallway with an oilcloth floor that worked its way like a snake through the House. It was well-trod by

Varina's mama's maid, Fannie, who most often had to appear in rooms throughout the House, serve a visiting guest, and then melt away again like she never even was. Rue hadn't ever quite got the lay of this trick, had never needed to.

She knew they'd come close when she could hear the fiddler again. He played a song she knew but could not place the words to. A jaunty tune that deserved a whistle. The corridor they crept through opened into the parlor, only just. The hidden door was only a parting in the heavy flower pattern of the wallpaper — the painted flowers were of a type that did not exist in any stretch of nature Rue had ever known — and the door's outward swing was hidden by a screen and hindered by a large wooden trunk set deliberately in the path of the disused servant's door.

Just beyond the screen and the trunk in the stretch of the parlor she could see the fiddler, but at this angle he could not see them. She knew he couldn't see them because he cussed at a broken string, a thing he'd never do if he knew a white woman was in his hearing.

"Only, you have to trust me," Varina whispered.

There was a little padlock on the trunk to

which Varina produced a little key. With some effort she pulled the trunk open, careful not to ask too much at once of its old rusted hinges.

The inside was near empty but for a pile of old yellowed papers dotted black with little markings Rue knew signified music.

"If you hold tight to your knees," Varina suggested, kindly. "You'll fit inside just."

Rue's stomach dropped at the thought.

"Go ahead." Varina cocked her head; her curls danced.

Beyond the screen, farther into the room, someone out of sight had joined the fiddle player. Black or white? There was no way to tell from hushed, unclear conversation and it didn't matter much. If anybody caught them there'd be hell to pay no doubt. Rue pulled up her skirt and stepped into the box. She sat as Varina had suggested, pulled her knees into her chest, tried to be smaller than small. The papers beneath her cut into her thigh, and she had to bite down on a sneeze from the dust they'd roused. Varina began to shut the lid.

"What you doin'?" Rue hardly remembered to whisper.

"Can't leave it open, can I? It'll draw folks' attentions. They find you and we'll both of us be whupped bloody."

"Maybe I ought to just go home."

"And miss all this?" Varina shook her head, her eyes gleaming. "No, Rue, I want you to be here. To see."

Here in this box like a coffin? It was too horrible, too much like her mama's punishment in the church. Three days, three nights, in the cold and the dark. No food. No water but what leaked in when it rained. Why should Rue ever trust Varina? But there had been her mama's warning, a cruel thing tossed away that stuck and rang in Rue's memory: "You couldn't never survive that place."

Rue made to stand. Varina laid a laced hand on her shoulder, pushed her back down. "You can't miss this, Rue."

The lid yawned as it closed down over her head. With her back rounded she could fit into the domed roof, she found. Everything went black. She worried too late about biting spiders and tried again to stand. She heard the latch of the lock click shut, an impossibly loud doom. Then light crept back in. Varina's fingers snuck in the gap no more than two inches wide.

"If you sit up straight, you'll be able to push it open a li'l for yourself," Varina said, peering in at her. "You'll be able to see the show. Me dancin' and all the pretty folks.

Go on now. Try it."

If Rue turned her head just so she could, in fact, lift the lid open for herself as far as the stretch of the lock would allow. Up close was the corner of Varina's gap-toothed smile, and beyond was the lofted stage, set up for the minstrel show. Varina raised her finger to her lip, and she was so close that Rue could make out only her knuckles and the leftmost side of her nose, but she knew what the gesture meant and already the first of the white folks were crowding in.

Rue uncraned her neck and let the box fall lightly shut. Chatter grew in a buzz about the room, and the scuffing footfalls echoed louder. Bereft of sight, Rue made her ears keen, and though she could pull no voices in particular out of the din, she did mark the high, crinkling sound of white women laughing and the deeper rumble of white men pontificating and, beneath, the hush of black folks servanting, the clink of silver, and then the first trill of a flute being played with a scattering of heavy notes on a piano, joined in artful earnest by the strings. She didn't dare peek out for much of the first few songs, but by the third, a fast, roiling tune that had the wood floor shaking with the force of it, she dared to push up the lid with her head and look awhile.

There the white folks bent their knees to each other as though in greeting, and at some command of the music that Rue could not figure they began working themselves into knots, here and there turning at sharp angles beneath each other's arms like lines of ants after some flour, and how they did not smash into one another she couldn't say. The women and girls swished past her corner in whirls of solid color. Every time she picked out a flash of blue she wondered if it was Varina, but she could not see enough of them to tell, as their skirts quivered up and down with their frantic, senseless bobbing. And here a man's pant legs and tails would come sweeping in and swing the woman away, and another flash of skirt would come and bob in the same fashion as the last. By the time she'd worked out which way the dancing ought to go, the song had come to an end and they were about the bowing again and she knew she must retreat back to her closed position like a tortoise drawn in on its own self.

The only indication she had of the time was the growing crick in her neck and the changes in the music, and she'd already lost the sense of how many songs had come and gone. The applause caught her attention, but it was when the strains of a harmonica reached her, muffled through the box, that her curiosity got to her again. She pushed open the lid and looked.

The white folks had stopped dancing, had made an audience of themselves, and though Rue could not see quite over their heads she could see their legs, the backs of which strained in their desire to watch something that was happening in the very corner of her sight on the far edge of the stage. She saw the first man that came out, an old black man she did not recognize. He walked out on the stage to the strain of the small metal mouth organ he played, his hand working, his wrist flicking as he set the notes to ripple. As he moved across the stage she quickly lost sight of him but his music remained, and she gave her sore neck a rest and let the lid fall down.

Darkness, 'til she heard a curious spring of laughter. Though she knew she shouldn't, she pushed her way up again so that she could just see who next crossed the stage. They were, she understood right off, meant to be black men. What they were instead were white men with their faces soot-smeared to a shining solid black. Their lips were reddened out to huge false smiles as gleaming and ugly as bleeding wounds. As one they skipped and tapped their way from

373

the makeshift wings, propelling themselves out from behind the heavy red curtains like they'd been given a swift boot to the behind by some unseen foot.

The last man in that line lingered in Rue's sights as he paused to raise his white gloved hand in an enthusiastic wave. He reached up and tipped his tall black hat to reveal a crop of black wool beneath that stuck up in wild tufts. The crowd shook as one with laughter at the mottled wig. Between the pristine white gloves and the sleeve of his threadbare overcoat, Rue saw the true pink skin of his bony wrist before it disappeared again beneath the fold of cloth and he too moved on, obscured to her by the nodding heads of his captive audience. They jerked in time to the swelling music of the black fiddle player starting up again.

If she shifted her weight she could see clear only the last man, the one who'd so delighted the crowd with the unruly kink of his false black curls. He'd taken up a seat on the edge of the stage, and he sat with his legs comically wide. He leaned in now and then to watch his fellow performers or to react to their clowning by slapping his hand at his knees in an overdone imitation of mirth.

They introduced themselves with a comic

374

lack of humility as the world-renowned Ethiop Choir, promising the crowd the most authentic Negro melodies they'd ever had occasion to hear. At this, the one on the end jumped up, stomped his foot as if a thought had hopped on him like a flea.

"Whee," he began with a low whistle through his front teeth. "Why, y'all ever hear how it came to be that us black folks gotsta be so black?"

His fellow players moaned like they'd heard this one before, but the audience chuckled, shook their heads. Some amused themselves by baldly calling out their own punch lines: Tar. Paint. Falling asleep during sunup.

"I tell you it goes back to when the good Lawd was handin' out colors." His accent was overthick. Sludgy. "The good Lawd says one day to all his peoples, 'A'ight now I'mma start handin' out colors tomorrow and y'all better come through on time if y'all want 'em, ya hear? So's the next day folks is lined up and the Lawd, he say, 'You there, y'all Chinamans? Y'all folks be yellow. And, y'all Injuns, y'all folks be red. And you there, you fine folks, you will be white.'

"And then the Lawd, he look round hisself and find one of the groups of his people is missin'. He draw out his pocket-y watch"

375

— a dim laugh rose from the audience at his overdone pantomime — " 'Di'n't I tell y'all folks to be on time if you wantin' yo' colors?' "

Rue had heard this joke before. It was one her mama liked to tell, berating the lateness of this or that person. Miss May Belle did it better, didn't belabor the telling as a long walk for a small drink of water. God was never angry in her version, just benignly amused at the way things were.

"So's finally the last group come runnin' up from Africa to get they colors and they so greedy and wantin', climbin' over each other like that, and the Lawd say to 'em 'Get back, get back.' But so fevered was they, all they heard was 'Get black, get black' — and that's the truth!"

The trumpet blasted as the crowd clapped and laughed and the end man dipped a bow so low his nose touched the waxed-up floor of the stage. They drew further cheers as they trotted in high-stepped kicks switching places and hats and jackets in a comedic whirl. They plumped up their collars pretending to be black folks who were pretending to be white dandies and, that done, they plunked down in their original seats in slovenly postures of exhaustion.

"Lawdy," said one of them, "it sure is tiresome bein' white folk."

Rue thought to sink low again but then the raucous crowd turned soberer as they waited on the next act, and lo the man on the end began, without the aid of music, to sing.

He drew his cap from his head and held it over his heart. "If you want to find God, go in de wilderness, de wilderness."

He was good, there was no denying. He sang it so sweet that Rue wanted to take his advice. She thought if only she could rear up that she would run away right into that wilderness he promised, but her neck and legs stayed cramped; she shifted and the box she was in fell shut. She listened as the other men joined him, lending him their voices in four blending parts. She found she could pick them apart better there in the darkness.

Hours might have passed in which Rue grew drowsy the longer she remained in that damned box breathing in her own stale air. She itched, she needed to relieve herself. The revelers took their time in leaving and she heard them go one by one, asking their black footmen to bring about their carriages or going away reluctantly on foot themselves or begging a spare room in the House, stumbling away drunk and ecstatic.

Varina appeared so suddenly in the gap Rue would have jumped if she'd had the space to do so. The girl was grinning, and her curls were flattened-down ringlets matted to the sweat on her forehead. Her cheeks were rosy beneath false rouge.

"Can't you let me out now?" Rue found her voice gritty with disuse.

Varina lifted a bare finger to her lip to sign for silence again. She'd lost a glove it seemed.

"In a moment," she said in whisper. "Shh. He's coming."

"Who?" The lid slipped shut again.

Varina was giggling, Rue heard that plainly — a high, sweet giggle nothing like her usual laugh. Rue could not make out the man's words, but she did hear the deep baritone vibration in his voice, which seemed much too loud, which bounced and echoed in the suddenly emptied room. At first she made him for Marse Charles, but no, Rue knew her master's voice in her sleep and this man's voice was much too deep to match it. Varina laughed again. Rue's legs ached something awful.

The man was fixing to ask a question, Rue could tell that much in the pitch of his voice, and she strained to hear Varina's side of the conversation. There was no response, laughter or otherwise. Rue didn't quite dare peek, not with the strange man there and liable to beat her if he realized she'd been there all along. She figured him for white he sounded so sure of himself, the way he kept demanding. His voice came back in the same low rumble it had before, like he was disciplining an ill-behaved child by asking it to explain exactly what it had done. Again, there was the long, strange stretch of Varina's silence. Rue edged open the top of the chest, just the barest amount.

They were across the room from her, nearer to the stage, and all she could make out was the tight cinched waist of Varina's new dress and the man's middle in a fine suit. He wore a white glove, she saw, and he took Varina's bare hand in his, squeezed her roughly at the wrist. Varina tried to pull away but at the last minute faltered like she didn't know what to do, did not want to offend. The center of their bodies glowed in the orange of kerosene lamps, the only light left lit, and they stood there in their awkward tableau like dancers primed for the music to start.

The man's question came again, and Rue caught the very ends of it. "Wartime," he'd said.

Varina was not giggling now. The center

of her body was so strangely tight and still and she said then, quite harshly, "Please." At that he twisted, reached out his other hand. He yanked up the good blue fabric of her dress as if it had offended him. He pushed her against the wall and tilted her body wholly back like a swinging bell, her thin, pale fighting legs for the clapper. There was the sharp sound of ripping fabric, of seams collapsing. Something skittered, a button perhaps, then a sharp intake of breath, and now Rue could see Varina's pink bared thighs. Rue balled herself up and disappeared.

But the image of Varina's pale hand, tensed and gripped by the pristine white glove, seemed to imprint itself wholly in Rue's dark hiding place, and she couldn't tell if her eyes were open or whether they were shut. She listened to the thudding of her blood in her ears and told herself if Miss Varina wanted to reveal her she need only call across the room. Rue reasoned there was nothing to be done, nothing she could do; she herself was still bound by the lock.

Rue began then to hum, not aloud but in her head, trying to put right the words the minstrels had sung: *the wilderness, the wilderness.* It had been lovely music, no matter the color their faces were painted. She heard Varina scream out loud just the once and thought of the wilderness, a place to run for both of them.

The abrupt turning of the lock seemed like violence, the lid cracking full open was like a trigger pulled. The dim of the room felt like too much bright and Rue squinted and there was Varina, alone, with tracks of tears ruining her rouged face.

"Varina." She reached out her hand. Varina smacked it immediately away.

With her head bowed and her legs jellied Rue stepped out of the box at Varina's command. She straightened Varina's pretty blue dress so it fell down again in the perfect circle it had held before.

"We ought to get to sleep," Varina was saying. "It's very late, isn't it?"

Rue shrugged, she didn't know. She looked around the room, suspicious of its dark corners, of what lay behind the minstrels' curtains, even suspicious of the box she'd just come out from.

"He gone?" Rue asked quietly.

Varina sniffed, choked on a sob and stifled another back. "Who?"

This time when Rue put out her hand Varina took it, and Rue was shocked with how cold Varina's hand was, and clammy. Was this the hand the man had held? Now she could not remember which it had been. It felt like the memory was slipping away from her, like she'd just sat up from sleep and tried to grasp at the tendrils of a nightmare. Who would want to remember this?

"I'm very tired." Varina did not look tired. Her eyes were red-rimmed and more aware than Rue had ever seen them, like someone had forced them open, peeled back the lids. "Take me to bed."

Rue did, if *taking* was the word for it. She followed behind Varina through the still, sleeping house, a white girl and her shadow. They moved like they were walking through a graveyard, afeared of raising the dead. Every movement felt too loud underfoot to Rue, the night seemed so fragile, the air made all of glass.

THE RAVAGING

In grief, the town chose to sit up with their dead. Rue did not altogether care for the idea that had rose amongst the people, that they ought to hold a town-wide wake in respect of the children that had died. Wakes were for the living, she figured. Their grief, no matter how good, would not bring the dead babies back. It would not bring Bean back.

They had chosen just three boys to serve as the symbols for all the other babies they'd lost since the sickness took hold. "The Ravaging" they called it amongst themselves, as though the illness was a swarm of locusts, a collective doom fallen on a mutual harvest, a force so great it could not be attributed to one man, or one woman neither. Give Him the glory, Rue thought darkly as she gathered death's flowers. She was careful what ones she picked, steering wholly clear of the type that grew in the graveyard, particularly wary of the pot marigolds that grew thick as head hair around her mama's stone. She didn't wish to call up the spirit of Miss May Belle, not on this occasion, as she made to decorate Bean's small body with no more special favor than she paid the other two child bodies she had been charged with. Preparing them in her cabin, she set Bean out as the one on the far left instead of the one in the center for that same reason; he was not a Christ, just some third criminal hung on a lesser cross.

Rue wept. Hard and heavy 'til she thought her body would be wrung completely dry of all its water. She was glad folks had let her alone in her work preparing the bodies so she could afford the right to cry. She was glad especially that Bruh Abel was scarce. If he suspected that she had made him her vessel, he did not show it. He did not slow down, but moved from house to house, ministering to folks, praying.

What did Bruh Abel ask for, Rue wondered, when he talked to that God of his? And did He ever give a good answer back?

Bean's body was small and waxen and fully white. With his eyes closed he was just as harmless as any child could be in sleep. His russet hair grew in tight at the root of his head, but the longer locks weighed themselves down into fine loose ringlets. Rue cut them neat and short with the thought that she'd give a piece to Sarah. But she wouldn't, for Sarah could not be trusted to weep on it as well as Rue would. No, Rue would keep the lock for herself, in the depths of her pockets.

Set in the corner was her small metal tub and she tugged it out to the center of the room in three sharp pulls, the bottom scraping at her floor in sickening squeals. When she lifted him Bean was light. She set him down inside the empty tub like a baby into a crib.

She covered him waist to knees with a washcloth but she left his face clear, didn't mask him as she sometimes did with bodies she feared might stare back at her. No, she wanted to look on him, to look upon what she had done.

She poured cold water from out of clay pots, cascaded it over the still planes of his body. First the right then the left. He'd once screamed when water touched him. It'd woken him once before. She turned him slightly to clean along his legs, his behind. Rue's hands shook through the whole of the scrubbing.

She added camphor to the water. The deliberate perfume, that flavor of hidden death, left her choking. She had to stop and gasp in acrid breaths that made her weak, cracked inhales that cut straight through her. She was sick in her guilt. There was a sharp pain in the bottom of her stomach that grew and had her suddenly bent double, spitting up yellow-tinged sorrow right there on the floor. She thought of how her mama had used to rub her back when she was a sick child, a strange rhythmic motion she didn't know the point of. Rue felt it then in the small of her back, that up-and-down love rubbing, even though she was alone with only the dead for companions.

"Bean?" His hands hung limp from the tub.

Rue stood. She wiped at her mouth and her eyes. Dried Bean's body and drew him up again in her arms. She finished all the preparations, washed the body of the middle boy, arranged the flowers in a neat wreath around the head of that boy's casket, and started in on the third. There was always something more to do, and had that not been what she'd wanted? To be needed just like this?

By the time the wake came, Rue was already a full day sleepless. Sitting up with the dead had always brought haints to the back of her tired eyes. She'd not seen so many bodies buried as others had on the plantation during slavery times. She was young then, and those last years before the war had been a relatively robust time if not an easy one. Black folks young and old still died, sure, died in numbers — of overwork and over-tiring, of having lived too old or having been born too young, of hunger or fever, of sorrow or neglect, but just as many new healthy babies were being born at Marse Charles's behest, and if there was birthing happening or liable to happen, it was that vigil Rue and her mama were tasked to keep. Naught to do for dead bodies once they'd been cleaned, no promise there and no profit made on mourning.

Still, Rue knew how a sitting-up went as well as anyone, and she had always liked those nights in a sad kind of way for the simple honesty of them, just singing and wailing and reflecting in long stretches of impenetrable quiet 'til it was time to lay the body, and the saved up sorrow, to a final rest.

But this day it seemed none of them could raise the exuberance that had harbored them in tragedy so many times before. Their sitting-up was no sitting-up at all but a march of stations, the crowd moving in a

387

stunned roulette amongst the three houses to look in at a child for a spell and then to move on to the next with promises to come back round in an hour or so. They passed each other in the square, mourners with solemn candles, crisscrossing their lights to keen at one another's doorstep.

What singing there was came low and listless. It was orphan Sarah who'd been the loudest, strongest singer amongst them in all the time that Rue had been alive, as though the girl could be possessed by the full-limbed spirit of grief on the behalf of others. But now that little girl was a grown woman, and a mama besides, and she sat black-veiled with both her two living children in her lap, perched at the far end of the mismatched chairs they'd hastily assembled in the front room of her home. Sarah kept that single vigil for Bean, not singing or weeping or anything but just struck still, same as her dead son, there in his open coffin. Any tune her visitors took up, even those songs laden with love for the Lord and his wisdom, seemed to taper off into thin scraps of nothing without Sarah's voice.

A fine red oak casket held Bean, the brass handles of which winked yellow in the low candlelight. He wore a little white calico sleep gown, the ends sewn up like a sack. His head was lofted on a white pillow, and all around him was a hedgerow growth of flowers as though he were a doll someone had left out in the yard for weeds to grow up and around.

Folks came and went as the night darkened, but after one respectful circuit Rue stayed with Bean. The men, Rue noticed, came the latest, stayed as long as they were able, which was not long at all. It reminded Rue of the birthing rooms, the anxious daddies with no stomach for the pushing or the hollering or the waiting on the water to boil.

They'd come back to carry the casket, she knew, just as they'd show up when the babies were born, washed, and snipped.

Rue had always been quietly proud of her own endurance for suffering. Being surrounded by the mamas' grief-stained faces seemed to her to be the first in a receiving line of self-inflicted punishments she might bestow upon herself.

Bruh Abel came along to Bean's wake round midnight with some of the other men. Bean's daddy, Jonah, was mute amongst them. Certain of the men passing through smelled of liquor, but the smell was miasma on them, a vapor that couldn't be husked from the group to be better assigned to one or another in particular. Bruh Abel seemed the most sure on his feet, but Rue knew him for a drunk. He'd always had strong sea legs and could keep his mask painted on just right when he had need of it. Rue kept her eyes on him as he trailed past Bean's body.

All night she'd received compliments on how well she'd made the three boys look; she could vomit again with the bile of that poor pride. But Bruh Abel didn't look like he was fixing to pay her any sort of compliment. He walked right by her, didn't even look at her, but came to settle after a time with Jonah and Sarah. He knelt before them with one hand on their daughter's head and the other as a slow-rubbing comfort on Sarah's knee.

He leaned forward and Rue watched him whisper in Sarah's ear. Didn't need to hear it to know it. He'd asked her to sing. For the first time that evening she obliged, setting down her son and daughter and starting with no preamble or pretense on the slow steady words: "Wade in the water, children. Wade in the water."

This was the part of the song they all knew well, where her call was to earn a response, but Sarah didn't stop for it, and no voice in her small, close house joined hers. She continued singing alone, her voice straining roughly on the top notes so that every time she trilled for one Rue held her breath, afraid she wouldn't make it, but she did, every time.

"Look o'er yonder, what you see? God's gon' trouble the water. The Holy Ghost a-comin' on me. God's gon' trouble the water."

In the midst of Sarah's dirge Rue let her head bow down, dug her hands in her pockets, stroked the sprig of Bean's baby hair. She tried to call up the words of the song for herself, feeling like if only she could draw the strength, if only she could sing beside Sarah, it all would be made right, or else not have happened at all, none of it. Instead she'd be back at the river where she'd last heard the hum of this particular song from that assembled earnest crowd on the day Bruh Abel had baptized her and Bean both: "God gon' trouble the water."

But Rue couldn't sing. She couldn't speak; all she could get her messed-up mind to do was pray. She was there again, under the river, gasping out bubbles, falling headlong, and there was no one to pull her up from it this time, no one to bring up her

391

head from this dry, barren drowning on land.

"If you don't believe I've been redeemed, just follow me down to the Jordan's stream," Sarah sang. "God's gon' trouble the water."

The silence that followed that last note of hers was filled up fast with keens and claps and folks borrowing bits of her song and humming it to themselves as they wiped in vain at their tumble of tears. Sarah had sat back down heavy, like her legs had been snatched from under her, and her man and her babies crowded around her in her swoon. Bruh Abel stood aside from them as though completing some biblical picture, but soon, without saying any more, he turned from them and made to leave.

Rue took to her feet. "Wait. Bruh Abel. Wait."

Wait for what? Her senses were far ahead of her mind. Her eyes had spied something her head hadn't even put words to yet, for there in the little coffin was a small, stirring movement. A little white hand raised itself up, grabbing at the air as though falling and looking for something to catch on to.

Rue ran over so fast she clattered past chairs and stools, tripped over her own anxious feet, but she landed at the head of Bean's coffin and grabbed on to that searching hand. With her other she began tugging at the flowers, throwing them from around his stirring head same as she'd plucked them from the dirt. She tossed them over her shoulder not caring where the stems and leaves and heads landed or who they hit, not caring when one landed smack in Bruh Abel's face — he'd come to join her kneeling on the ground. Once the casket was cleared of its bouquet she could feel for the little boy's neck and yes, there, there was the slow but steady streaming thrum she'd been looking for. In the red oak casket below Bean opened wide his black eyes and looked around, blinking away the dust of death.

Bruh Abel said, "I told 'em all it was a miracle."

Rue nodded. "It was."

They were walking from Jonah and Sarah's cabin where everybody had gathered at that sitting-up that ended like none they'd ever seen before. Rue had been the one to pluck Bean wholly from his casket. When she'd buried her face into his good clean skin, he'd wriggled in her hug and said that he was very hungry. He had fallen asleep again a few moments later, clutching a heel of bread someone had fetched. It bore only a few tiny nibbles when he fell into a doze, but his sleep was light, his breathing even. He fussed when Rue handed him over to Sarah but he did not wake again as he was carried off to the bed, safely draped on his mama's shoulder. Even then folks had tried to follow after him, an unsure parade, 'til Jonah had intervened, thanked them and shooed them all from his home.

"Bean," he said, "he need his rest." It was a funny thing to say after all that time he'd spent sleeping.

No one else slept. The town was alit with curiosity, and they just about hummed with questions they couldn't give voice to other than to say how good was God and hallelujah.

How long, Rue wondered, 'til they'd get their minds around to asking other things? Eventually they'd have to close the other boys' coffins over their still faces. Those boys hadn't woken, hadn't stirred, and with morning approaching no one had moved to put them in the ground. No one could say the words.

Going through the quarter, Rue and Bruh Abel let others linger behind or go ahead of them so that they walked side by side now as if by chance.

"Is it a miracle?" Bruh Abel asked. It was

394

the first time she'd ever heard his voice ring with doubt, and she found she didn't like it.

"I wished it," she answered.

The lines on his forehead wrinkled at that.

"I prayed," she said instead.

"We ought to look after him," Bruh Abel said, and Rue could see his mind grinding down each thought. "Ain't Bean goin' to need us more now?"

"He got us," Rue said. She found she ached inside for leaving Bean with Jonah and Sarah. They never had known what to make of him. Would know even less now that he was "a miracle."

Bruh Abel was following her, she realized after a time, or else letting himself be led straight to her home at the far end of the town, past where all the good folks lived, close and huddled together.

"Come on in," she said at her door. "We can talk on it." The memory of Bean's black eyes opening up and seeking hers.

Inside they did not talk at all but stood facing each other. Bruh Abel hovered near the shut door like he was trying to build up a good reason to run through it. Rue stood tensed with her hip hitched up on her table, feeling she'd fall without the aid of something solid.

Bruh Abel chuckled at some joke that

didn't need speaking and then his laughter grew and Rue joined him in laughing, shook her head like it might loose the shock. It didn't.

The laughing made her belly hurt. Rue crossed the room to Bruh Abel, tired of their being on separate ends of the same thing.

It was some strange affirmation from somewhere that flooded through her mind then. Want, it said, and you shall receive. She put her hands on the sides of Bruh Abel's face because she wanted to. She pulled him near because she wanted to. She kissed his open, slack-jawed mouth — usually so slick-tongued but now gaping, yielding — because she wanted him.

He regained himself in a moment, kissed her back. She moaned the words of her wanting right into his mouth with the unrelenting force of her own lips, felt the rising feeling of wanting like a swell in her whole elastic body as she reached and reached and reached 'til, short of air, they pulled apart and gasped in shallow mismatched breaths, like they'd swum across a river and come out on the opposite side together.

"Jesus," Rue said.

Bruh Abel took her by the waist, so suddenly sure, and stirred her over to her own bed. There he folded her over easy like she was a sheet so that her back was on the thin mattress and her knees were so bent they near about touched her shoulders. He scratched at her when he pulled up her dress and she might've drawn blood tugging at his pants, but they worked it together in the end, got each other free.

Rue bucked. He pressed into her like a blazing fire, and the thrill of him spread wild as one too. She felt him in even the tips of her fingers, burning. He buried himself deep and his eyes grew wide and unfocused like he'd gone over to some other place, and she put her hand to his cheek, drawing him back to her in slow, careful measures.

No tricks, now, no sprung trap, just wanting.

Simple and just the thought brought her over to that cresting pleasure she'd been after, just as Bruh Abel burrowed his face into her neck and ground out, "Rue, Rue, Rue," as desperate as a man drowning that wanted rescue.

"I'm here," she said to him. Loud and clear. "I'm here."

Rue made a visit to the church, basket in hand.

"You listenin'?" She called out to Varina,

and there was no answer.

She went down the dusty aisle and up the bowing steps and, she couldn't help it, she was humming. She felt Bruh Abel's wanting in her body and Bean's rising in her heart and she would not let the shadows of the old white church despair her, even in the face of one of Varina's tempers.

"You hidin' from me, Miss Varina?"

Rue had to look up to find her. Varina sat in the bell tower, and from below Rue could only make out her legs swinging off the landing of the third floor. Rue climbed the ladder, clutching nervously on each rung, and Varina didn't reach out to help her even when Rue struggled up beside her onto the thin wood slats. The thick rope for the corpse bell hung heavy between them.

Varina had bunched her skirts round her thighs and her bare legs were pale in the moonlight, dotted with russet downy hairs. She'd put on a bonnet and wore a moth-bitten pair of evening gloves like she had someplace to be, though, of course, she did not.

"What you doin' way up here?" Rue said.

Varina did not answer, but kept on looking where she was looking, out through the arrow slit window. Rue watched her in profile, studied her harsh gaunt face. Va-

398

rina's tongue darted out to lick her lips, a nervous gesture like a troubled snake.

"I saw them comin'."

"Who you saw, Miss Varina?"

The window Varina gazed out of looked over the woods and the river and beyond, to the graveyard on the hill and to the plantation that used to be. It was the whole of the world as much as either of them ever knew it.

"Soldiers," Varina said. "They've come to kill us."

"You was only dreamin'."

How many times now had Rue quieted this same fear? How many times too had Rue stoked it? For it was fear that kept Varina locked away, and fear that kept her safe.

"I wasn't sleepin'. You don't dream if you don't sleep," Varina said. Then, "There. Rue, look." She pointed her gloved finger out the window.

Rue looked and saw, or dreamed she saw, down below on the path she'd walked and walked: one pale rider on a horse. He was all white except the black holes cut out for his eyes. But then Rue blinked, and he was gone or he never was, swallowed up by the woods, made black by the midnight.

■ ■ ■ ■

PART FOUR

■ ■ ■ ■

* * * *

Part Four

* * * *

PROMISE

1871

Have you heard about him? The boy that rose?

There was word of mouth to stretch out the news, the telling and retelling. The gossip ran upriver, so it was that people were tramping down to them from a journey of weeks, of months, from all over and kingdom come, just to come up close on a miracle.

Now a tent rose to house those multitudes. It sat on the cleared-up ruins of the old House. Gone were the broke-down balustrades of Marse Charles's plantation home, gone the ashen outlines of his grand rooms. The high, swirling stairway existed now only in memory, and who could say for sure that any of it had ever existed at all?

That tent might have been magicked, it rose up so fast. Rue could see it, just, from the one window of her cabin, its cresting top poked up higher than the tree line. She had near forgotten that the plantation had been structured around the House and not the other way around. Her home then felt like it was set in the back row of a gathering crowd, all eyes riveted on the show.

Strangers came. Rue did not like it. First they were relations of folks she knew or had known, folks dispersed to different counties, sold away or run away in slaverytime, or folks that had took their after-war freedom and fled with it.

Charlie Blacksmith was among these; he'd came on back ashamed of the money he'd stolen that had been meant to buy the town a white doctor during those dark days of the Ravaging. The money was long since spent, but Charlie's mouth was filled up with apologies like apologies were tobacco chew. They forgave him. At Bruh Abel's pious suggestion they were forgiving everybody.

The peak of the tent replicated the chimney of the fallen House. The whole tent structure, white once and quickly dust-darkened, was like a ghostly afterimage of what had been, a stain of light on closed eyes.

Bean had healed up slow, but he had healed up. The Ravaging had left them. The babies had begun being born again in earnest, and of that season two were boys, two were girls, like someone repaying a debt by giving double. Their people had given them names, not like Joseph or Mary or Charles, but like Divinity and Freeman and Jubilation and Promise.

Folks thought Bean ought to remember something about God or heaven, but he did not. He was like any five-year-old child, really; he fussed when asked too many questions, he sucked his thumb. They all came with the idea of wanting to see him, the Wonder, the Imperishable Seed, but once they saw him and got their own glimpse of his black eyes, they were sated. They came to see Bean, but they stayed for the tent, where inside Bruh Abel was known to give great, thunderous sermons so stirring they had crowds of people falling over in stunned worship. Rue sometimes sat in the back aisle and watched Bruh Abel. There was something about his strut, his absolute confidence, that she could admit now she had always hoped to learn from him.

It was on the nights of his most impassioned sermonizing that he'd come to her cabin, lie down beside her with all of his sweat and fervor still shining on him. She always let him in, kept him 'til morning.

Rue began to heal again in fits and starts, began with visits to Bean and Ma Doe, and then just carried on, unable as she'd always been to ignore a body in need. Just as, after the war, folks had returned to Miss May Belle in gradual dregs, so now they returned to Miss Rue, first for aches and pains, then for bigger things, for matters of life or death. She had to keep telling people, there was no promising she could raise their dead. Still, they kept after her, asking.

Around town administering to folks, suddenly Rue had gone and gained herself a shadow. Bean had fixed his black eyes on her upon his waking and now it was if he could not look away.

Even when she shooed him off she'd come home to find him curled up like a sow bug at her doorstep.

There was no way to wake him then but to crouch down beside him, smooth his soft brown hair. It had grown back since she'd cut it, sprang up in wilder corkscrews.

"What you doin' here?"

"I like where it's quiet, Miss Rue." The peak of the tent loomed in his sights like a mountaintop.

"Wanna know something secret?" Rue said.

"What?"

"I don't much like that tent either."

Rue let him come inside her cabin only when he promised to let her alone, not ask so many questions. He was fond of touching things, asking what's this and what's that to every stem and leaf, asking why, before she'd hardly got round to answering the last thing he'd asked.

Still, better to have him there than amongst all them strangers, or worse, wandering on the edge of the woods. One time, Bean had wandered out of the tent in the middle of one of Bruh Abel's more fervent orations, just walked on out under all the amen-ing. Rue had chased after him only to find him standing at the place where the wilderness thickened, the place where the trees grew so mightily that it was almost always night. Bean was there, at the very edge of the sunlight, squinting in at the dark.

Rue caught up to him, breathless. "What you lookin' for?"

"My friend," he said.

He'd pointed then into the shadows, at nothing.

There came a day that a knock sounded on Rue's door. She said, "I'm comin' and comin'," and she swung it open and startled. There in front of her was a white woman with a newborn baby, smallish and wrinkled and pink, drooling on the woman's shoulder. She could have been Varina, and for a long, bad moment Rue thought she was, and she couldn't say a word or hardly breathe.

The white woman's teeth were brown spokes in her gums. "You the conjure woman, ain't you?"

Well, when a white woman told you you were a thing, that's what you were. Rue nodded dumbly, and the white woman and her baby came right on in.

Rue knew poor and this woman was poor — she could see it, and smell it, on her. Still, the woman wasn't ashamed to make herself at home. Rue had but the one good chair, and the white woman dropped herself down in it, raised one mud-blackened foot, and rubbed at the heel.

"Come a long way, Missus?" Rue asked.

The white woman nodded, dislodging the pink body on her shoulder. "Heard this was a place a' healin'."

"Preacher's in the tent." Rue gestured through the window. The tent was so blaring white it was like a presence in the room with them. "He'll be preparin' for the night's sermon, but I can take you to him if you like."

The white woman shook her head. "I come lookin' for you."

Rue stood and waited, afraid to sit or even slouch in the presence of this white lady, no matter how poor she might seem.

"All my babies I ever had were taken from me before they first birthday."

"Taken?" Rue thought of Ma Doe, who'd had every last one of her children sold off.

"Taken to heaven," the white woman said. "All 'em doctors came and went each time and still 'em babies died, and I says to my husband I gotta find me somebody what knows what they about, that's got some divine correspondence what can save this here boy."

Rue could have laughed. If divinity was coming now in forms of correspondence, then she was more than illiterate to it; she was deaf and blind besides.

"I tell you, Miss Conjure, I do got a fear."

"Rue."

"Huh?"

"My name. It's jus' plain Rue, Missus."

The white woman put her baby to her knee and bounced both in agitation. The baby yawned and jiggled, unbothered. "You got a baby, don't you?"

Only a white woman could ask something so intimate so pointedly. Rue shook her

409

head. The woman leaned forward, really squinted at her through a fall of grease-stiffened hair, looked at her like she didn't quite believe it, which was fair enough. It was strange, Rue supposed, hard to think of a girl, and then a woman, who'd made her whole life and livelihood from other folks' babies never having one. Not wanting one herself. Well, Rue had never thought it would or could be. But now.

"You soon to have one," said the white woman. She sat back, satisfied like she'd won an argument. "And when you do you'll know just exactly what I'm feelin', all the fear and the baby love. Every single minute a' every single day. It'll eat you up."

She leaned forward and kissed the top of her baby's creamy head. The baby crooked its mouth in pleasure; drool dribbled from his open lips and dangled down to the woman's blue-scabbed knees. She didn't seem to feel it puddle.

"Come back on Friday," Miss Rue said. It was a thing her mama often said, because magic was meant to be best on Fridays. Probably it was just to give her space to think. Friday was in two days' time.

The woman nodded and stood. She swooped up the fussing, restless baby. Rue would've liked to hold him, but she didn't.

410

"Y'all got some place you stayin'?" Rue wasn't offering.

"We on at my uncle John's place." It took Rue longer than a moment to remember Ol' Marse John. He'd been her daddy's old master. The Marse John who had died under his wench saying, *Goddammit goddammit god—*

"You a relation to him?" Rue did not remember any living family, but a son, Jack, who had died, not in lovemaking like his daddy, but in the war. Rue thought, it seems the dead is rising.

"I'm the daughter a' his sister what married up and lived east a' here. Government man come to me and said he was tracing up white folks' properties that were deserving. A bit a' Christian charity that. Yank devils tore Uncle John's whole house asunder but no matter," the white woman said. She was talking singsong to her baby, her voice roiling as she bobbed him in her arms. "Don't matter, no it don't. We come here for the land."

Varina's expression was haunted. "I seen 'em. A white man and a white woman. A mangy black dog. A baby."

"They ain't see you?" Rue asked.

"No, no, I stay well clear of that white

man." Varina made *white man* sound like a cuss word every time she said it.

"Good." Rue walked the length of the rectory. Five steps, turned, walked the other way. It made for agitated pacing. She thought, not for the first time, how could Varina stand it here?

"They lay traps in the woods catchin' rabbits and varmint." Varina sniffed, that old plantation daughter's affectation. "They let that baby go round stark naked."

Varina still carried herself stiff with her lost wealth and station, queen of a cotton industry so mighty she could play the hostess to visiting princes and have them feel grateful to be received.

"Miss Varina," Rue said, startled. Knew then what about the room had set her so suddenly on edge. Varina had hid her bedroll, neatened her one dress, tamed down her curls. She turned her chair toward the door and there were two tea cups set out, like they were just waiting for a housegirl to run up and fill them. Sweet tea for company. "Has somebody been in here with you?"

Varina's blush rose on her pale skin like a fever tell.

" 'Course not. Whyever would you think that?"

Secrets. They had always had them.

Weren't the meek to inherit the earth? Rue felt she'd heard a preacher say that once or twice before. It was the truth. The tent near glowed in the dark as she approached it. Inside, lit lanterns and the fiery passion of all them people made the thin covering shine yellow from the outside. As Rue neared, the applause that emanated shook away the smudge of black on the tent's far side that she'd been thinking was a shadow. It was, in fact, a thick murder of crows that took flight and cawed as they did so. Such a synchronous exodus that. How'd they know? Not just to flee but to flee as one, none left behind.

Rue parted the flaps of the tent. The enthusiasm shook her, a blast of hot air. Standing before hard-hewn benches, a crowd of fifty or so folks, come from far and wide, were on their feet, praising. They needn't have bothered making the benches. This was not a place for sitting but for standing up and hollering, for rising up in ecstasy to be that much closer to the good Lord. Their hands worked in clapping and fanning and upturned exalting. They stomped and sweated, raised up whorls of

413

dust and grass into the air, audacious on the very spot that had once been the plantation House.

Rue's man hotfooted at the front of the crowd in his usual glory, and there beside him, like a miniature in white robes, was Bean, holding out a collection basket half his size, taking in the action with the full of his big black eyes.

Bruh Abel threw Rue a wink across the crowd when she came in. Didn't miss a step. Bean moved amongst the parishioners with his little wicker basket, collecting dark-colored coins and even dirty, coiling slips of paper money that he had to tamp down with his little hand, lest they get caught up by the wind. Folks gave and gave. Here Bean was, a little miracle, or the little miracle that they had made him, five years old, and he carried himself like a man. Who had taught him that? Up in the front Bruh Abel was kissing the wrinkled hands of some reed-bent old grandmama who was moved to weeping just to see him.

Folks left in an unhurried fashion. They kissed and hugged and goodbyed each other, exuberant, congratulating themselves for worship well done. They dropped money in Bean's basket, rubbed his thick brown hair, same as if he were a rabbit's foot, a disembodied thing for other folks' luck. They streamed on past her and said, "Miss Rue," if they knew her or just cast a smile in her direction if they didn't. They knew she was someone important, leastwise, because she was important to Bruh Abel.

Rue waited as the tent all but emptied. Bean, drifting, neared her, and she caught his eye. "Miss Rue," he said politely, and she liked the way he said it. He mashed the two words together like they were one. For him, there was no distinction. She was who she was.

"Bean, I brung you somethin'."

He held out the collection basket and it made her heart hurt to see that that was what he was expecting. From her apron pocket she pulled out a little bag full of marbles. Bean's eyes narrowed down to strange black stitches of delight when he smiled. He pulled the drawstring open and spilled them right out onto the grass aisle.

"I can have 'em?" he asked. His collection basket was all but forgotten now as he plopped down to play with the marbles. Rue laughed and scooped the basket up.

" 'Course you can."

"Can I take 'em to play with her?"

An ill chill ran through Rue at that. Her enthusiasm shriveled but surely he had meant Sarah, his mama. Who else?

Bruh Abel came up on her from behind and put his arm around her waist, took Bean's basket from her in the same motion.

"Y'all stayin' on to listen to the next sermon?"

Bruh Abel's services had grown so sought after, he'd lately had to double them. It was a fascinating thing to see them back-to-back. To watch the things he mirrored in himself and the words that came to him in one and not the other, the movements of his hands, the twitch of a smile in his face. It was like catching someone admiring their own reflection. "Ain't vanity one of them big sins?" she'd sometimes say to him, and sure enough he'd just grin, suck her into that sinking cheek dimple. There was no shaming him. Not there under his own big white tent, with his own Lazarus playing marbles at his feet.

"I come to speak to you in fact," Rue began. Now that she was here to say it, she didn't know quite how to put words to her urgency or the fear that was rising up inside her. "I seen a white woman."

Bruh Abel quirked his eyebrow. "What? You ain't never seen one before?"

"She come to see me about her baby."

"You help her, ain't you?"

Rue worried her lip. "I tol' her to come back. I plan to help her," she hurried to say. "But she a relation a' Ol' Marse John who owned the only other plantation near here durin' slavery times. She stayin' on at his place. Got a husband with her."

"Tell 'em to come hear some prayin'," Bruh Abel said. He busied himself adjusting the tall wood lectern he'd had made. It was where his Bible often sat, open but untouched. Already, the tent was filling up again for the second go-round.

"That ain't it," she said. She hated him a little then. How easy he was with words when she wasn't.

The last time strange white folks had come through the woods, her mama had been alive and the country had been warring. And they had come as an army.

Bruh Abel bent to start picking up Bean's marbles, ignoring the small whine of protest the little boy made. Rue couldn't understand why Bruh Abel didn't see it. That he had made Bean in his image, made him a curiosity on which the town hinged, when he'd said all along that that was what they'd been trying to avoid. For her part in it Rue felt sorry, but in a town now known for its curiosities, she had begun to fade quietly into the weave. Hadn't that fact saved both

417

of their lives — hers and Bean's?

Sarah came in at the lead of the next flood of parishioners, heading straight for her son with a sense of duty if not of ease. She laid a kiss on Bean's forehead, one he didn't seem even to feel, then straightened up slow to greet Bruh Abel and then Rue. Her expression was tight and tired. Jonah was away working at some port, here-and-gone the way only a man could be in the name of supporting his family.

"Bean, you mindin' Bruh Abel?" she asked her son. She petted his head the same way the other faithful had. No feeling in it, just a kind of reluctant awe.

"Yes'm," Bean said.

Rue wanted nothing more than to scoop him up and run. Instead she said in a hush to Bruh Abel, outside of Sarah's hearing, "I just ain't think it's a good sign. White folks wonderin' after us. After all a' this."

Bruh Abel raised his arms wide. If he could've he would've held in his palm the very idea of all-of-this. "Ain't you heard? This our time. The time that was Promised."

He kissed her, full on the lips, there in front of Sarah and Bean and those waiting on worship. Rue extracted herself quick from his arms. She was dizzy from just the sheer force of how free he thought he was.

Nothing like that could last.

"Miss Rue." "Good evening, Miss Rue." "Sister Rue." It all clattered around her brash as church bells as she forced her way out of the tent against a crowd clambering to get in.

It was never fully dark anywhere now, not with the candlelight in the tent always burning, emanating that constant soft glow of promise. The woods on the periphery were what was all dark; the distance in between stayed stuck in everlasting twilight. That's where Rue lingered, masked in shadow, with a steadying palm to her belly. She was making herself afraid, she reasoned, because it had always felt safer to her to be afraid. From the tent she heard the beginning of Bruh Abel's second sermon, thick and clear and well-rehearsed.

"Out of the land of Egypt," he was proclaiming, "out of the house of slavery. You shall have no other gods before me."

"Miss Rue," a man's voice called. There was no getting away from folks, was there? Rue stopped and put a smile on.

It was Charlie Blacksmith approaching her. His wide face was weighted down with contrition as it had been the whole time he'd been back. If anyone had killed them babies it was him, she might have said, if

419

she were to let hard devil thoughts in. He'd run off with the money meant for the white Quaker doctor who might've healed them. Rue was not a preacher, or a Quaker, or an angel besides. She didn't have to be forgiving.

He pulled his hat from his head, showing the place where his hair was thinning, the roots coming in a startling gray. She'd known him all her life. He'd known her daddy, too, 'til he'd died.

"I got a story for you, Miss Rue, if you'll oblige an ol' fool," Charlie said. "After I left here I went searchin' for word of any relations I had still livin'. Had three sisters an' four brothers that got sold away, always wondered where they got to, what they'd grown up to be like, but I couldn't find no trace of 'em. Got round to the place I myself was born to see if I could find my mama's grave at least, but that place is all gone too. The white folks stayin' there now ran me off their land with the assistance of a shotgun.

"In the end I just roamed. Got to feelin' that everybody I'd ever known was gone. But then I recalled an ol' sweetheart a' mine by the name a' Airey. Y'all remember her, don'tchya? You was only such a little thing back then."

Rue remembered her: Airey, that pretty runaway so many of them had envied when she'd stayed and envied more when she'd gone. And Rue remembered her mama's hand in it, though the miracle at the river when Airey had taken flight, just disappeared like a bird, surely was just a wish, a muddling of Rue's childhood memories and dreams. Still, didn't miracles abound?

"I remember."

Charlie grew excited. "Weren't she beautiful?"

"She was."

"Well, I went lookin' an' askin' round an' finally I found her." He paused to grin, perhaps stirred by the memory. "She made it up to the North, she did, an' once there she hired herself out as a cook like she was always wantin'. Done real well fo' herself. Got herself a lawful husband an' a whole crop a li'l 'uns, littlest of 'em favors her mama." He moved his hand over his own arms like he was sprinkling stardust, to indicate the birthmark patterns up Airey's body. "She done named that last baby May, after yo' mama's memory."

A bubbling sadness rose up in Rue but underneath was joy. "It's a good name."

"It is," said Charlie. "But Airey, she say she missin' home, this place the onlyest one

421

her family ever known, goin' back generations. Her daddy plant the first seed, that's
what folks says. I tol' her if she can scrape
together the money maybe she oughta come
back to look on it like I done. I hope that
she do.

"Anyhow, I got to askin' Airey how she
made it north when so many others didn't
or couldn't, how she escaped the patrolmen
an' the swamp an' the sickness an' the dogs.
Well, she set me down an' she cry a li'l for
all the time an' all the years an' all them
people we done lost, an' at the end a' it she
tol' me how she got over. She say, 'Charlie,
I just flew.' "

That night, Bruh Abel came to her, crawled
to her, woke her from sleep and kissed her
and worried at her chest and nipples with
his teeth ravening as only a man could. He'd
leave moons with his front teeth, bite marks
that would remain as indents on her skin
for lovely long hours after.

"Quit that," she said in the midst of her
sleep. She was trying to stay angry at him.

"Can't," he said. He was cupping her
breasts now in his hands like water he was
bringing to his mouth to drink. "These gon'
heavy. Like to break yo' back."

She hadn't quite noticed that. She hadn't

been letting herself notice a lot of things. But there it was: the tightening of the click-clack beads Miss May Belle had taught her to wear, and just earlier that white woman's telling grin. Rue's brimming senses, her full breasts teeming with promise, spreading longways and sideways across her chest, her body making ready, making room.

Rue pulled Bruh Abel's head away from her flesh-full nipples.

"That ain't for you no more."

"What?"

"Them is for the baby now."

She watched for what seemed like hours but was only one small moment as Bruh Abel caught on to her meaning, his gray eyes going just the littlest bit wide, his lips parting in wonderment. And then the whole of his face brightened with revelation, with delight, and only then was it real, because it was real for him, the whole idea, a quickening of her heart.

"You sure?"

She laughed. "I make my name on being sure when a woman's got with child."

"Yeah, you do, but it's different when it's you, ain't it?"

"Lord." It was so different.

He pulled away from her, drawing back his weight, suddenly careful. He inspected her naked body now like he'd never seen a woman before in the whole of his life. It was sort of wonderful, even just to shock him, to make Bruh Abel, of all people, care-filled and new.

On Friday, early morning, the white woman came back, and Rue had to see to her, like it or not. She had the vial ready, one of Bruh Abel's empty jars, cork stopped on whiskey and water. The white woman had made herself at home again.

"I done made you three cures," Rue told her.

Her baby looked well, Rue had to admit. He was smallish, but boys she'd found were often smallish 'til they all of a sudden grew into men. She hoped she herself would have a girl.

Rue didn't know what she would say, even as she cast a handful of emptied walnut shells across the open floor, shells upon which the white woman was singularly transfixed, believing without even being told that those cast shells had the power of divination simply because they'd been cast by Rue's black hand in the close mystical quarters of a fall-down plantation house in the woods.

Next Rue brought out the necklace she'd

424

made. It was a simple bleach-boiled bone wrapped in rough twine. The white woman tied it around her neck quick and eager. The little hooking bone sat primly on the top of her low-slung cleavage, the twine already irritating her neck, splotches of red forming.

"What is it?"

Rue struggled. "It a coon's penis, Missus."

The white woman nodded reverently, her baby cooed. "What it for?"

"Keep yo' husband virile."

" 'Course."

Lastly Rue handed her the vial, held out her hand, and waited for payment. It came, one silver coin in her palm, that simple.

"It'll work?"

"It'll work," Rue lied. "This one won't be took from you."

The white woman showed again her habit, bending over and kissing on her baby's head, breathing that scalp in greedily, like that was where all the air in the world was coming from.

"Thank you, Miss Conjure," the white woman said. Rue did not correct her.

When the woman had gone Rue went walking, past the crowds, past the tent poles, past the graveyard and the creek. The knot on the tree faced north, that was how she always found it, occluded as it was by a thick matting of moss. Making sure that no one had followed, she slipped her two coins — one coin from the easy work she'd done, the other spirited out of Bean's collection plate — into her little bag of treasure hid away in the hollow.

WARTIME

1864

The drumming was in the sky. Marse Charles had woke the whole plantation to come and hear it. It was before sunup even, that he'd sent out the trumpet player whose bellow usually started the day. Come so early, this music had not been meant to signal work time for the field hands, or to summon house slaves who felt they'd only just rested down their heads. It was to herald doom. The trumpeter played a mournful tune, like a sad, strange accompaniment to the distant syncopation of warfare.

But who did Marse Charles think he was waking? They were all already awake, braced in their beds. Was this it now — kingdom come?

"Come on now," Miss May Belle said to Rue.

They joined the sweeping crowd of black

427

folks being summoned by their master, a black cloud moving dazed in the first crack of morning light.

The mood was tense. They were shaken, like a whole mess of sleepwalkers startled awake to find themselves in the yard of the House, field workers on one side, house workers on another, and between them Marse Charles high on the top step of the porch, which reminded Rue of the stage he'd constructed and deconstructed in the space of a day for his fete. Six months had passed since the party, but it still made her dizzy just to think on it.

A loud bottomless boom echoed in the distance, and the house seemed to rock within their vision. Behind her daddy, Varina came out as if summoned by the cannon fire. She was dressed already for the day, looked small and pale and likely to break the next time the crashing sound came down. It shook through them all like they were the bunched leaves on the same branch of a tree. With no means of knowing from which way the echo was coming, they all of them instinctively turned their eyes to the North.

"Y'all hear that?" Marse Charles's voice was high and strained, harder than any of them had ever heard it. This man who had

428

whupped them and cussed them and told them he was selling them off or ripping apart their families. He who had plain said no to any bit of independent hope they'd ever thought they'd found — never in any of those times did he sound so tore up as he did now. So downright sorry.

"Those vile Yankees. Those perfidious devils. They mean to snatch y'all up in yo' sleep," he warned. "They brought this feud to blood, them Northerners. To get at y'all." He leveled a shaking finger at the assembled crowd. He was so pale there in the gloaming. Did any of them believe him? "Y'all hear that? That's the stamp of their cloven feet."

What they did hear over their master's small, reedy voice was another explosion in the night, the seams of the world coming all undone. On his whim they waited there for what seemed like hours as the twilight eased to day, waited on him to release them.

"I'm to be married."

Varina had been in front of the mirror when she said it, and Rue was behind her brushing out her red curls. Everywhere about them was the heady scent of ash blown downwind from the battlefield. The fighting was miles away and yet too close;

its smoke was pervasive as a plague and Varina, fool she was, seemed to think the smell was about her. She'd already taken two baths that day, made Rue carry bucketfuls of bathwater up the stairs each time and lug it away again after. Varina had stunk up the water with rose syrup enough to make herself gag. She hadn't allowed Rue or any of the house girls in to help her wash but had gotten into the hot bath alone, and there stewed herself for what seemed like hours before she'd let anyone in to dote on her. Now her hair was taking up an agitated frizz from all the washing and it wouldn't obey Rue's ministrations as she tried to gather it in a low braid. Rue never had liked white folks' hair, the way it clung wet and stringy, the way it slipped and slid and would not hold.

"Did you hear me, Rue? I said I'm to be married at last."

They caught eyes in the glass, neither one of them looking glad. It seemed to Rue that they were waiting, watching for the drama of these two people to play out before them. Who were these strange, tired little women they'd turned into? They'd lost the children they'd been — now they were grown and picking bits of war-flung ash out of their hair. The mirror told of the years, but there

430

were things the mirror couldn't tell. The time-flattened scars from a tree branch on Rue's back, the price of a friendship she couldn't let go — and for Varina, were there marks from the minstrel show six months back? Hurts of the kind that left no earthly scar, showed no reflection?

They never spoke on it, that awful night. It was meant to have been Varina's coming out, but instead Rue felt she'd collapsed in on herself. Like a promised harvest that never came, Varina had wilted before she'd ever come to bloom.

The misery that had lately plagued Varina had little to do with her brothers turned to soldiers, brother against brother at war, or a world made suddenly bereft of men, eligible husbands slim for the picking. It seemed to Rue that there was a corruption now growing in Varina that had never quite been there before. Just because you couldn't see it or hold it or heal it didn't mean it didn't exist. The Rue of the mirror eased her face into passable excitement and said, "I heard you, Miss Varina, and I am happy for you."

"Do you want to see him?" Varina pulled herself and her hair out of Rue's grasp, pawed through her belongings. Ribbons and pins and nets and combs tumbled from in front of the mirror, and in it Rue watched

herself watching Varina, watched herself trying to stay small and out of her mistress's
way, lest she become just another bit of clutter to be knocked to the floor and trampled
on.

"Here it is."

It was a little nothing bit of tin that Varina
could hold in her two hands, and at the
insistence of her fingernails it peeled open
like a storybook might. It revealed no
stories, only the one little picture: a man,
his uniform, his gun.

"Henry is his name."

Henry peered up at Rue, and Rue had to
push back on that self-saving instinct to look
away from the probing eyes of a white man,
real or no. He was young and thin-lipped,
and someone had rosed up his cheeks in
the image like they thought it would give
him life. It hadn't done anything but made
him look sterner. Beneath the dark shadow
of his heavy brow and the flat brim of his
soldier's hat, his colorless eyes seemed like
empty places where something had been left
out.

"Handsome Henry," Varina sung out. She
wasn't even looking at his hard-tin face. She
was instead waiting on Rue's expression like
it held some soothsaying, reading for tea

leaves in her squinting eyes and wrinkled brow.

"Handsome," Rue agreed.

Varina shut the tintype like it was a sprung trap.

Sarah and Rue were summoned to the parlor. Just them two. Led there by Ma Doe, who would tell them nothing of what they were about to hear.

All that week they had been in preparations, flushing the house of every single sign of mourning, searching out every inch of black and removing it in preparation for Miss Varina to receive her suitor, who, visiting temporarily from the somber northern battle lines, would not want to come to his future wife's home and find death clinging there also.

"Sit," Ma Doe told them. Neither of them moved. They'd never been asked to sit in a white person's living room a single moment of their lives. Their knees wouldn't bend that way.

Ma Doe said, "He's in a gracious mood so you best keep him that way and do as he say."

Ma Doe left and the both of them sat on the very edge of two wooden chairs like they thought comfort would lick at them from behind. Marse Charles didn't come in for nearly half an hour. That whole length of time Rue and Sarah did not speak. The sun-dense parlor grew hot from the daylight streaming in through the wide bay window. The light played tricks with the pattern of the floral lace curtain hung from the win-dowsill, sent an illusion of black roses across the floor to pass the time.

When Marse Charles did come, he was wearing a soldier's uniform and was trailed by a reluctant-looking Varina, her eyes downcast. There was a large desk there in front of the wide window and he sat behind it, seeming to struggle to bend at the middle in the uniform. It was not like the one Varina's beau was wearing in his little photograph. It bore no buckles or spangles. It was a ragged moth-eaten thing in a river-bottom brown. Rue thought she could make out old blood on its hem before he sat. Where did he think he was marching to in that?

Marse Charles drew out a piece of paper from the drawer. Peeped out his tongue in a pink point and wet the nib of a pen. Began writing. To Rue the scratching sounded vio-lent.

"I'm making a gift of them to you and your future husband," he said. "To round out your household."

"Thank you, Daddy," Varina said.

Rue didn't understand. She didn't catch on that he was referring to the two of them, to Sarah and herself, to the facts of their bodies, not 'til Sarah began suddenly to cry. It was a silent crying, just the hitch of her chest and one slow track of hushed wet down her jaw and neck. Rue doubted that Marse Charles and Varina at the other end of the room had even noticed. Sarah curled her head down so the light wouldn't catch on her tears. If he saw, Marse Charles would certainly smack her face dry.

"What this one's name. May Belle's girl?" He sighted his pen at her.

"That's Rue, Daddy."

"How many years?"

Rue didn't know if she was meant to answer or if Varina was, but no one spoke. Marse Charles grunted and scribbled something down for himself.

"And Sarah. Quadroon. Sixteen years," he added with a pen flourish. "Belongin' to you and yo' husband now."

Varina kissed her daddy dutifully on the cheek.

Miss May Belle cackled when Rue came home and asked her what it all meant. The

435

sound wasn't laughing. It was the brittle cracking of something, some illusion Miss May Belle had let Rue have, maintained the way someone lovingly raises a pig knowing full well they plan to plate it and make a feast.

"It mean" — Miss May Belle leaned in, pausing to look around their one-room cabin like she thought that someone might be there to overhear — "that yo' new Marse Henry is gettin' hisself quite the dowry along with his new wife. Sarah's the dish, sure. But you the seasoning."

"Mama — ?"

Miss May Belle wouldn't let her finish, in fact couldn't seem to stop herself. "It mean too that Marse Charles don't want Sarah round no more. Can't have her round no more. Not growin' so pretty like she's doin'. Even he won't let that kinda sin tempt him. Though Lord know he wouldn't be the first, would he? To take a drink from his own stream?

"And it mean most, Rue-baby, that they gon' take you away from me like I always knew that they would."

When Rue shut her eyes at night she'd be cast back in the darkness of the box that Varina had locked her in, like maybe she

436

had never left it. Like maybe this Marse Henry would be the one to open up the trunk this time instead of Varina. Lay her open like she was a gift-wrapped present from one master to another. Varina had allowed it. Asked for it even.

In Rue's mind, Varina had laid for her a curse. But Rue knew well the way that curses worked, for Miss May Belle often warned against them, saying, you can tell who's got a mind to curse you by who you done wrong. A curse was a problem that could be countered. Rue would need a piece of him to do it, a lock of hair, a toenail clipping. An image to direct her curse toward.

In the midday empty, the air in Varina's bedroom was a stale outline of the mistress — it smelled of rose hip and burning hair and sweat, all a uniquely Varina scent that Rue had never been able to put words to 'til she smelled it in the air of the room without her there. It gave Rue pause, that smell — made her feel that Varina was right behind her, ghosting in her steps. She persisted despite it. Began searching under and behind things just as Varina had. She'd have secreted the photograph of her sweetheart away, no doubt.

When Rue couldn't find the photograph, she turned to the dolls, like they might hold

437

the answer. All in a row, gorgeous doll babies that had been handmade in far distant places Rue could not even cobble up enough imagination to dream about. They were the only acceptable gifts of Varina's childhood, Rue knew, and the only real education. Varina had been taught to want to be a wife and a mama from the very day that she was born.

Rue unscrewed their heads. Ignored the plaintive squeaks their hinges made. Inside their hollow was cobwebs and disused fly parts some spider hadn't thought to eat. Nothing.

She thought about smashing them, Varina's porcelain babies, even took one by the head and raised her arm high and willed herself to do it, waiting on the satisfying crash and crunch, the sound of the porcelain skittering across the hardwood she'd just scrubbed clean. In the end she didn't do it. Couldn't. She set the doll down back in its outline of dust on the shelf, even smoothed down its hair like it was a child she was putting to sleep.

There was no use in fighting Marse Charles's commandment. Varina and Rue, they were bound to their roles, and always had been, Rue figured, by something stronger than curse and conjure — simply, they'd been raised to be the women they had become.

PROMISE

Ma Doe had lost her words. She had always had that slow, stately way of speaking, the deliberateness of a schoolteacher, every breath of hers a lesson. But by the summer that the tent swelled, Ma Doe's speech had slowly turned into a slurry. Worse than this — and Rue cussed herself for thinking there could be worse — Ma Doe could not write.

The pen trembled violently in her hands whenever she took it up, as if some fear of her own failure started even before she could lay the nib to paper.

It had begun when Bean had died, Rue recollected; the grief of it had sunk Ma so low. Even when he rose again, Ma Doe, who had been battered by so much loss the whole length of slaverytime and after, could not herself be resurrected to her former buoyant majesty.

The letters from the North piled up and Rue hardly knew what to make of it. She

440

lied to Ma Doe, told her not to fret over it, but Rue fretted enough for the both of them. Varina's auntie in Boston would have to note the silence soon, and rather than take it as her due, she was liable to be sparked to action, of what type Rue dared not think on. She'd never known a white lady to leave well enough alone, and the scribbles of words on all them unanswered letters began to follow Rue everywhere she went, shading her as black clouds on the horizon.

They'd devised together a plan, Rue and Ma Doe had, but it was slow going. Every evening they'd sit at the back of the emptied classroom, and Rue would lay her hand atop Ma Doe's and together they would write. They wrote 'til their candle burned low and still only got to a sentence a night if that, had yet to finish even one letter, but they kept on.

"What's that word?" Rue asked. They'd taken a break, exhausted at the bottom of a page. Rue pointed to a word they'd just finished. It was short but she liked well the loops and swirls of it, recognized the tiny *V* in the center.

"That one?" Ma Doe's voice trembled, also. "That one says 'love.' "

"It's so small." Rue's hand, which ached

441

from holding Ma's still, went straight to her belly in wonder. " 'Love.' "

There were a thousand different ways to love somebody. But Rue still hadn't settled on which was the one Bruh Abel was needing. They'd never made promises. She did not know where he slept when he did not sleep with her, and she did not want to know. But with her stomach growing fat he'd been lured into her bed every night, and despite herself she made room for him.

After their lovemaking he was bound for his tent. He climbed up and out from their bed, put on his suit with quick, well-practiced movements, always did it the same way, dressed himself pants first, regimented, like if the day called for it he could go just like that, running at a moment's notice.

"You comin' to hear the sermon?"

Still naked, sheet tangled, Rue thought about saying no. She hadn't grown used to the tent, probably never would like it, and liked less the fervor that folks felt for Bruh Abel. The way Bean paraded down the aisle at the end of each service like some kind of finale.

"You comin', Rue?"

Rubbing at the small, hard peak of her belly, she said, "If you want me."

Sarah had set herself up singing, formed a little choir who wound their music around the shape of Bruh Abel's sermonizing. Charlie Blacksmith was forging horseshoes by the dozen for weary travelers come at the end of their long journey from there to here. Dinah made big quilts stuffed thick with Spanish moss, a dollar a piece for any one of her woven stories. Li'l Sylvia sold ashcakes, honey sweet, a secret recipe passed down from her mama. Ma Doe had spread her schoolhouse between two cabins, employed the knowledge of newcomer women with Northern book-learning, and everywhere the children were beginning to scratch out their letters and numbers too, easy as if they'd always known them. They had all grown prosperous, as Bruh Abel had always said they would. Sarah's choir sung on the subject of prosperity this day. They stood on three-tiered risers, wore long gowns in baptism white. They bellowed it — Sarah, as always chief among them and tallest, proclaiming "This is the day the Lord has made."

Bruh Abel strutted over to the choir in step to the enabling *mhmm*-ing of his audience. Rue watched as he caught eyes with Sarah, the choirmaster of her own creation. Was there a wink passed there that Sarah

caught and received as a signal to start singing? He looked up at her on the riser like
she was the only one he was talking to, a
whisper for her ear: "What y'all go out to
the wilderness to see? This here a prophet."

The choir burst into praising ol' John the
Divine. It was a good old-fashioned, foot-
stomping tune, like to get you picking
cotton faster. But just as Bruh Abel stepped
away from her, Sarah's knees began to
buckle and sway, and the choir, thinking
she'd been took by the spirit, sang louder.
Rue watched as Sarah drew in breath but
no sound came out. She crumpled and fell,
hitting against each tier on the way down.

Sarah was pregnant.

"You needa rest up," Rue told her. In the
new world that they'd made, maybe a black
woman could afford a little rest for her own
sake. "Stay in bed."

Bruh Abel carried Sarah all the way to that
bed and laid her down in it.

"When's Jonah due back?" he asked and
propped her pillow. Rue looked on, wary.

Sarah, still faint, could barely shake her
head without making herself dizzy. "Inside
a month or so. But just as soon as that he'll
be off again."

"He's a good man," Bruh Abel offered.

"You go on back, tell 'em Sarah's just fine," Rue told him. Bruh Abel turned to her, seemed to see her and her belly for the first time.

"You right. I oughta leave womenfolk to womenfolk."

Bruh Abel kissed Rue's hand and took himself out. She could see in the set of his retreating shoulders that he was already reforming himself, shape-shifting back into the preacher returning to his tent to talk of a miracle. "Let us pray for Sister Sarah," Rue could already hear him saying.

"You pregnant," Sarah said.

Her warm brown eyes looked on Rue, sharper than they had cause to be. Womenfolk to womenfolk indeed. Rue laid her hand on the slight stretch beneath her own oversized dress.

"Folks talkin'," Sarah explained.

"They always do." She sat herself down on the edge of Sarah's bed, her legs already aching. "I ain't even as far along as you is. How come you ain't say nothin'?"

"How come you ain't?"

They were both of them just passing through that strange twilight where the new feeling stirring in their bodies was pushing past simple sickness and weakness and aches and pains into being a real idea, a person, a possibility. But to say so aloud seemed over-proud, like fate itself might wend in, overhear, and intervene.

Sarah sighed. "You'd think I'd know by now, how to go about bein' with child. It don't get no easier."

"You just havin' a rough go is all. Some babies is just more difficult than others. You take it slow, like I say, you be alright."

"You too," Sarah said, easy. "Think ours will come at round the same season. Like twins. What you think?"

"That'd be nice." Rue almost meant it too.

Bean had disappeared again. They'd forgotten him in the confusion and by the time Rue got herself back to the tent no one could say where the little wonder had got to, only that he'd vanished. *Into thin air,* they were saying. *Like he Raptured.*

"Now, now." Even Bruh Abel wouldn't allow that type of gossip to start up. "Most likely the boy just wander off."

"He upset about his mama," Rue said, though she didn't think that was altogether true. She had the notion Sarah and Bean would never warm to each other, as mama and son ought to. Rue recalled what Sarah had told her the night of Bean's short death: *He don't belong to me.*

To whom did he belong then? They got up a search party. Folks went through cabins, looked in outhouses and amongst the tall, prosperous wheat in the field, but Rue went straight into the thick of the black woods, not knowing why, but just *knowing*.

It was coming on dusk, but Rue's eyes were sharp. She was just beyond the sickle-bend of the river when she first saw it, black and shining amongst the roots of a hedge of thorns: one black marble. The next one was blue and not so far from the first. Then a green marble led Rue away from the river and brought her to a grouping of three more scattered along a disused footpath.

Now Rue had strayed so far that she could no longer hear folks' cries of "Bean!" — could hear only her own urgent footfalls and the insistent hum of sunset insects. The night was their time but hers also. One more marble, there, at the end of the path.

Rue turned on her heel when she heard the low growl behind her. Slinking, the gray fox stepped out from behind a tree, its eyes glowing. Something was grasped in the fox's jaw, caught in its pointed teeth. It looked to be a bit of black and green fabric.

Her stomach lurched. She'd never known a fox to attack a human child, only livestock, hens and rabbits and smaller prey. But a

447

mama fox might do anything to defend her babies, and Bean was only such a little boy, so naïve and curious.

The sound of a gunshot came, so close and so loud that Rue thought the bullet must've tore through her own body. But before her the fox jerked and fell in a splash of blood. The shot was true, so neatly through the spine it had near severed the fox's head.

Stunned but unhurt, Rue shivered. She shrunk down to her knees beside the fox, and from the trees a white man stepped down, heavy-footed over twigs and leaves. His shotgun still bloomed smoke and he whistled as he approached, impressed.

"Damn," he said, delighted. "That thing near got you."

Rue wouldn't look up or meet his eyes, not even when he crouched down to inspect his kill.

"Foxes is wild in this part a' the country," he was saying. "Like I ain't never seen. Distemper most like."

"Please, suh." Rue's voice came out in a warble, child-thin, like it had been in slaverytime when every white man was *sir*. "I'm lookin' for a li'l boy. He lost."

The man stood and Rue took it as permission to do the same. Her stomach ached.

The dead fox lay between their feet and Rue couldn't stop watching the man's cooling gun.

"Figured somebody done run him off," he grunted. "That boy sick or somethin'? Eyes ain't right."

Rue didn't know how to answer so she didn't. The man whistled again, this time like he was calling a dog.

At the sound a white woman waddled down from the same direction he'd come. She was less sure on her feet over the vines, for she had a drooling baby on her hip. And she led Bean by the hand. Rue knew her at once.

"Miss Conjure, ain't it?" the white woman asked.

Rue was surprised when Bean ran straight over to her, hugged at her waist. He smiled up at Rue, didn't seem bothered at all by the white folks or the gun or the dead fox's unhinged neck.

"Found him wanderin' the woods," the woman said. "He belong to yer missus?"

Rue blinked. So they thought Bean was white? And Rue his good nurse? She felt something rise in her throat, maybe bile or bitter laughter.

"Yes. Thank you fo' findin' him," she said and scooped him up in her arms. Bean was

449

heavy in a pleasant way, and his warmth calmed the thud of her heart. "I best take him on home before his mama get to missin' him."

"You oughta keep better care a' him, girl," the white man said.

Rue wondered if under his bloodstained overalls the white man was wearing the coon penis charm she'd made for his wife.

With Bean in her arms, she walked backward a ways before she felt safe turning away from them: the man, his wife, their thriving baby, the lifeless fox. Rue broke into near a run, best she could with Bean cuddled over her shoulder.

When they came close to home Rue stirred the boy, set him down to walk on his own.

"Where was you runnin' to?" she asked him.

"Wasn't runnin'. Wantin' to see my friend."

"Which friend is that?" But at the bottom of her belly Rue felt she already knew.

"The lady" — he yawned — "that lives in the woods."

"The lady what found you?"

"Not her." Bean squeezed Rue's hand. "The other lady. With the pretty red hair."

"How you come to know her? You follow me?"

Bean shrugged. Of course. He followed Rue everywhere 'til she'd shoo him off, tell him to find somewhere else to play. The other children were averse to his strangeness, all the things that made him different. Or was it that they remembered the Ravaging, when they had sickened and some had died and Bean had lived and died and lived on? Who would want to play with a miracle?

"Her name is Auntie V. I go there when I don't wanna be seen."

He told it like a riddle and Rue might've hoped he was speaking on an imaginary friend as children sometimes did, made real enough because they believed in them. But Rue knew he knew her, Varina. Easy as he'd told Rue about it, he might tell somebody else.

The tent still glowed as Rue and Bean neared it. There were voices within, joyous. Had they given up their search for Bean as soon as that? Or rather had they given up searching in favor of praying? Rue could've spat.

She took him home, or leastwise, to the place where he was born, to the very bed in fact, and there was Sarah, wide awake. Her eyes were rheumy; the weakness that had caused her swoon had only worsened while Rue had been gone, and Sarah didn't seem even to know her boy had been missing the whole of the evening.

"Don't worry," Rue said, touching Sarah's fever-warm skin. "I'll keep watch over Bean 'til you get yo' strength up."

And she would, if only to keep him from telling things better kept hidden.

Rue did as she promised, kept Bean close after the day he'd disappeared as a god-mama might. Black women always had been good for caring on each other's children, even since slaverytime, a point of pride that. As Sarah's condition worsened, Rue took on Bean, especially as it became clear that even the most reverently charitable of the newly come folks would not keep him long in their houses. There was something eerie, they whispered, about his eyes. Not even the color but just the way he stared like he could see past things and through things and into things that weren't quite there.

Did he see his mama's sickness? Seven months along now and Sarah could hardly walk the length of her own room without some hand-holding. Persistent, Rue made her walk the little bit that she could. Sarah's growing baby sat low like a stone at the bottom of her belly and seemed just as strange and still. When Rue would check on Sarah, Bean insisted on following. The whole visit he'd stare at his bedbound mama, not at all upset, but like her sickness, her decline fascinated him.

"What's doin'?"

Rue steeped mint leaves in the bottom of a cup, the water still bubbling at the boil. Bean followed close, nearly underfoot as Rue brought the drink over to his mama.

"She weak is all. Carryin' the new baby."

Bean wrapped an arm around Rue's leg. Birth, sickness, death, and resurrection, it had all happened in those two slim, dark rooms of the cabin, Rue reminded herself. Was it a wonder that Bean saw things in the shadows, when all over, every cabin in that plantation, there were so many shadows to see?

"It's a girl this time, I'm thinkin'." Sarah's voice showed the weakness Rue had warned against. She wasn't doing enough eating. Holding nothing down.

"What make you say so?"

Sarah shook her head just a little. No answer then, just a feeling. "What you think fo' yours?"

Rue hid her grin by blowing the steam off Sarah's tea. She was supposed to say she just wanted one come healthy, fingers and toes. Ain't that what the mamas always said? "Girl maybe? Tryna think up good names."

Sarah breathed a laugh. "Bruh Abel's liable to pick a page out the Bible."

Rue shook her head. "Think I'll pick somethin' I ain't heard no one have before. What you thinkin' for yours?"

"S'pose I'll 'llow you to tell me when she comes out."

It was the closest they'd ever come to talking on it, the way Black-Eyed Bean had got named. No other thing had stuck to him. In the beginning Sarah had tried. Called him by his true name, Jordan. But folks that saw him had whispered in horror "Black-Eyed Bean" around him so often he'd got to thinking that was what he was called. He would answer to no other thing but Bean. Would just sit in the same mute fascination that froze his face now.

Was it meant to be a slight, what Sarah had said about Rue naming her baby? A curse? Rue could not say. Sarah had shut her eyes, grown tired maybe from that little bit of jawing, her tea gone untouched. From the other side of his mama's chair Bean was watching her sleeping, examining the rise and fall of her chest, unaware or uncaring that they'd been speaking on his origins.

■ ■ ■ ■

Bruh Abel dreamed of other tents, a sky-wide spread of tents as lofty as a field of clouds. "Can't you just see it?"

Rue shrugged. "Not really."

"Girl, you ain't got no imagination."

It tired her out just to watch him moving through the wide, empty space inside his tent. The area seemed so much larger without all the worshipping bodies who'd just left it, and Bruh Abel moved like a little boy at play in it, going from stillness to sudden motion in unpredictable bursts like summer rain.

"When the baby come," he said, "we can go south first. Follow the warm in winter."

The life Bruh Abel dreamed of sounded to Rue like the exhausting up-and-down movement of migrating birds. In search of what? Everything he said lately began with *When the baby come* and ended in a kingdom of revival tents stretched the whole way from north to south. Rue couldn't begin to see how they might get from here to there, what sacrifices might hammock in between. There was Bean to think of. And Ma Doe's health. There was Varina most of all, whose existence was every day threatened by Bruh

Abel's growing flock. Their trepidation about the wilderness beyond the revival tent could only so long be fueled by secondhand stories of haints.

Bruh Abel wanted to preach, he said. He wanted her to heal. Lately Rue had no stomach for healing. There was growing a sudden fear in her, a distaste of touching other folks' sickness. When the baby came, her sweet little girl as she'd lately been thinking of her, Rue didn't wish to lay hands on any skin but hers.

Still, something was coming. There was no denying that same something that had Bruh Abel spreading his wings hawk-wide and her doing the exact opposite, pulling up twigs around herself for a nest. Was it always like this? she wondered. Being with child had sent her into a hoarding up of love, like she'd got word that a hard frost was coming to befall everything, love being nourishment. Love being hope.

Bruh Abel jumped up onto the bench in front of her. Stood on it straddled and carefree like it were a log he was balancing down a creek.

"When we get down there," Bruh Abel was saying, from above. "When the baby come, we'll get ourselves good and married. What y'all think a' that?"

She made him no answer, for in the corner of her vision a ghost flickered. "Get down," she said.

Behind him through the thick of the tent she saw the black outline of the people on the other side, running. The sound of their panic came through the tent skin in muffled singular chaos. Outside someone had let out a high, feral scream. Bruh Abel jumped down from his perch. Came to wrap his arms around her, protecting her. Them.

The shadows of the crowd loomed long and large as their outlines came across the tent. They were coming closer, a few startled sweating men, Red Jack and Charlie amongst them, a few others Rue didn't know. Bruh Abel hid her behind him.

"What's happened?"

"We need yo' help," Charlie said, and Rue saw that he carried a curled-up body on his back, something as still as a carcass. He laid it down gentle in the grassy aisle and the men stepped back as if afraid to approach it. It looked like an overgrown black crow, spilling everywhere its feathers. It was only as it unfurled itself in a slow jerking fit that Rue realized what it was they'd brought her. It was a woman, and one she knew: Airey.

Oil wouldn't budge it, water neither. When

457

Rue put either to Airey's sore, ruined skin, the woman would begin to wail and thrash. They couldn't even move her but left her down in the center of the church tent where Charlie had placed her, and as Rue worked she had amassed an audience of disturbed onlookers, all of them whispering about the haints in the woods.

"Who done this?"

"You seen 'em?"

"White faces."

"Monstrous."

"Come to kill us all."

Rue found she couldn't focus with their chittering. Her fingers kept sticking in the tar that covered Airey head to foot. It was still warm. Rue tried to get at the root of a black feather and instead set Airey to caterwauling.

"What you need?" Bruh Abel asked, kneeling beside Rue. He secreted a hand at her back and rubbed where he knew it often ached her when she was bent working like this.

"A clean new knife."

Bruh Abel asked Charlie to fetch it, but Charlie refused to leave Airey's side, kept pacing and smacking at his chest and saying, "I'm the one that done this to her. Told her to come down here. Told her her home was safe again."

Airey's home was not safe. In halting fevered confusion, she'd whispered about the monsters she'd encountered as she'd approached the town, a woman traveling foolishly alone on the road to a fabled land of Promise. She'd made the long journey back from the North, the reverse of the one she'd fled through, this one in leisure on a train and then a steamboat, but after that there was no sure way to get to their isolated strip of land except on foot, so that's what she had done, with a little money in her pocket and a lot of determination. She had wanted to come and see where her folks were buried, maybe buy them up a headstone so that no one would forget their names.

The ill spirits had come up on her from behind she said, and by the time she'd heard their horses' hoofbeats, their mangy vicious dogs barking, there was no point in running, no safe place anywhere, and she'd crumpled to the ground.

"Who was they?"

"Devils," Airey kept saying, writhing in the dirt. "They must have been devils."

They were masked. Airey could identify only the grim black of their cut-out eyeholes, bearing down on her from the white of their full-body robes. Hid beneath those sheets was surely something much more horrible, something so heinous it couldn't even be bared. Still, Airey fought as their cold, white hands had ripped off her clothes. As they poured the hot tar. As they dumped the feathers. She was still fighting.

Bean was the one that brought Rue the knife. He came quick, his chest still panting from the run he'd taken to her cabin and back, swift on his little stick legs. He'd picked just the type she needed, one good and sharp.

"What you mean to do?" Bruh Abel asked.

"Ain't no way I can see but to cut it from her. Just slice as close as I can, try not to get too much of her own skin." Rue whispered to him. "But dammit, she won't be still."

"I can help," Bruh Abel said. He got down on his knees beside Airey, careless of his own white robe, which straight away picked up mud and grass and tar and some of Airey's blood as he drew close to her and clutched her fighting hands.

Airey had never met him but she stilled and looked right at him, like she knew him and was trying to puzzle out where from.

"You ain't alone in them woods anymore, Sister Airey," he said. "And I got to tell you,

you weren't never alone."

"They hurt me so bad," Airey croaked out. "They say they only gon' leave me alive to be a message to the rest a y'all."

Bruh Abel drew nearer to her, his expression placid but determined. Rue placed the knife a hair breadth shy of skin, beginning at Airey's arm, which beneath the black tar was white-speckled still, just as it had been long ago, with the force of Miss May Belle's curse.

"Oh, you a message, alright," Bruh Abel said. "One heard loud and clear."

Airey's whole body tensed like she was about to bolt.

"You a message, sister, that any devil can be fled from, can be survived no matter how pervasive. You beautiful as an angel, girl. You just sprout wings of faith and fly."

She relaxed, breathed in his words, kissed his hands to her mouth, and began to cry. And hearing his words, seeing through his eyes to his vision in the clouds, Rue, slowly, carefully, was able to make the first slice, and the first of the feathers came free.

461

WARTIME

Miss Varina's betrothed was soon to arrive. They waited. Every one of Marse Charles's colored slaves stood in the yard of the House, assembled in the same manner they'd listened to the exploding cannonballs in the distance weeks earlier, a gathered awkward collection of black folks and their two white owners. But unlike that war-torn morning, this noontime was hot and quiet, a stillness punctuated now and then by heat-drunk flies and one or the other of the slaves fidgeting, quelling the urge to swat.

Varina waited on the veranda, which offered no shade at this time of day. Rue stood beside her holding up a white lace parasol, her arms aching. Varina was not satisfied. Halfway through their waiting she'd sent Sarah into the house to run and bring to her a small white hand fan. Now Varina was working herself into a sweaty anxiousness with that fan, flapping it about her flushed face, her madness burning hotter than the sun could. Marse Charles hovered in the doorway, looked like he'd like to snatch that fan straight out of his daughter's hand.

Because of their gathered stillness they heard the carriage rumbling up through the gravel road from a great distance, but they could not see it at all through the thick of the trees, and so they were left to stand there in anticipation, listening to the horses' hooves beating the ground and the strain of the wagon rolling over craggy land. The assembled slaves had long, strange minutes to imagine their new master inside, perhaps sitting with his head in his hand and his hat in his lap and his leg across his knee, his foot tapping in nervous but eager anticipation, deep in thoughts of his new bride. Would she look like her photograph, hair tugged back tight, and center parted, cheeks pinked? Would her voice be soft and sweet when they sang at the piano at night? Would she make him lots of children, boys preferably but a girl too that they might name after his mama? Would she love him for all the rest of her God-given days, and his?

When the wagon turned the corner, it was obvious it was empty. There was only a sad, thin-looking black man at its helm, old as creation, with a straw hat and a bad limp.

He said nothing but disembarked and hobbled his way over to them, looking sorry about the time it took him to cross those few yards.

"Got a letter here for the mistress a' this house?"

Varina stepped forward through the crowd of her slaves and took the letter as if the paper alone was a badge of shame that ought not see the light of day. She unfolded the letter at its crisp lines. The envelope bore an emblem of the Confederate army, and after she'd read the letter, her lips moving furiously, her gloved finger slipping and shaking over the handwritten lines, she dropped it to the ground and let the wind take it and none of them knew whether to go after it — so they didn't, just watched the emblem swirl away. The old negro messenger was watching even with his eyes downcast. Perhaps he'd been told to report back on her reaction; perhaps he was only waiting to have his pass marked, his old bones being unsure of how and where to move without being dismissed.

Varina's low keening was explanation enough. It was a sound like a sick cow might make. She turned and fled into the house, and Marse Charles did not follow her but sighed as though this was an eventuality

464

he'd been wise enough to see coming.

"Go and see to her."

Rue didn't know if he had meant her. She was the only slave on the veranda. She tried to look out at the crowd for her mama, but if Miss May Belle was there she was just another black sweating body, waiting and tense.

"Go on," Marse Charles hollered and Rue went, taking the stairs through the house two at a time with the aid of the folded-up parasol as a cane, all the faster to propel her.

She found Varina in her room, panting and yowling and ripping off her clothes like she couldn't get them away from herself fast enough.

"Miss?" Rue didn't know how to calm her. "Is he died in the war?"

"Better he was dead," Varina moaned. "Better we all were dead."

Rue tried to approach her, but she cussed and swung away. Varina rampaged to her vanity table and swiped at the contents on top; her perfumes and hair things and jewelry all clattered to the ground. She raised her gloved hand and slapped at the mirror, and Rue braced herself for a shattering that didn't come. The mirror held and, enraged even further by that futile

465

gesture, Varina stumbled back into the center of the room, headed, it seemed, for her doll collection. They were looking on her calmly with their rictus smiles.

Rue didn't know why she moved to defend them. They were only dolls. But it flashed in her mind that she had always loathed the stupid things and if anyone was going to destroy them it ought to be her. She stepped in front of Varina's path and tried to soothe her.

"I don't understand what's happened."

"He ain't comin'. Ain't never comin'. Only sent the letter as a courtesy." Varina cracked out a sharp laugh. "A courtesy to tell me the engagement's broken. He's found himself a better girl. One who ain't touched. Ain't ruined."

At that one word, *ruined,* Varina ripped the parasol from Rue's hands and swung it once and hard across Rue's face.

Rue felt the angry welt already rising in a perfect line across her face and she tasted blood boiling up in her mouth.

"I don't understand," Rue said.

"Oh, don't you see?" Varina kept saying. "Don't you see? Don't you see?"

Varina backed away. She was throwing down her clothes, all her pretty things. The net she'd put her hair up in snapped in its

466

stretch and her curls came raining down on her bare freckled shoulders. She was tugging at her gloves, angry at each individual finger as she pulled. Varina was all come undone as the world around her was, and Rue, always behind, it seemed, always foolish, didn't put it all together until Varina was all but naked in front of her save a thin white slip, see-through and gossamer. Still bent, cowering, Rue looked up and saw Varina's belt, the one she'd made for the courses that had never come — just as the husband had never come — and in that instant of seeing it and remembering it, Rue watched it snap, all the little beads of nutmeg scattered across the floor like marbles, and some broke in half and spread their dust, and Varina began, again, to cry.

Oh, Rue understood what she was seeing then and how right Miss May Belle had been, as she always was, for the belt had served its purpose and sent its message as good as any letter: Varina's little belly was protruding, the skin already rounded out in a stretch of six months.

PROMISE

Miss Rue had been, all her life, a liar. Over the years, in slaverytime, wartime, in freedomtime, she'd lied and said, *I know.*

When the mamas told her something was going wrong below, something they could not explain, *I know,* she'd say, to shush them. But she had never got to understand wrong from inside herself. She realized she had spent her life in kneeling, in peering in, in parting legs, touching skin, squeezing hands. In wiping brows and blood and bits of birth. In interpreting moans and sighs and vague descriptions of other folks' pain.

Ooh, Miss Rue, it's like a fire, like a stabbing, like a burning, like a gunshot, like a tearing, feels like I'm dying.

She always wanted to ask them, how you know what dying feel like if you never done it?

I ain't know nothin'.

The thought rang through her as she woke

468

in the middle of the night to the feeling from the inside that she didn't have a name for other than wrong. The feeling persisted, grew, in the place at the bottom of her stomach, the warm round place she had been sending love feelings to for months now.

Bruh Abel was asleep beside her and she hesitated one lonely second before waking him because waking him meant that the wrong was real.

She shook him. He looked at her like he didn't know her, and she understood then that she did not know him, she could not gasp out his name or make sense of his shape in her bed. She could only keep saying, "Something's wrong." He touched her hot, flushed skin and he looked angry, spitting mad, and that's how she knew it was so much worse than wrong. Bruh Abel was never angry unless he was worried, and he was never worried unless the world was tore up, all hope come undone.

"What am I s'posed to do?" he said as he climbed up out of bed. "You the one that's s'posed to know."

He didn't say what he'd decided when he decided it; he only scooped her up in his arms, cradle style. He lifted her from the bed. The sudden, hysterical thought came to her that he meant to baptize her again and certainly it hadn't taken the first time, so why would it now?

She hid her face in the hard-pulsing hollow of his neck and his shoulder. She could feel his shifting panicked muscles with her lips, taste his salty sweat. It did not calm her to know him scared for the first time.

They walked awhile, him clutching her and her clutching herself. If she thought too hard she knew she'd break; if she thought too hard she'd lose what she was holding on to. She had to hold on.

She had her face still buried and hid and she only knew they'd gone outside by the sudden cool whip of night air. He was carrying her fast, running near as best he could with the burden of her, and each step gave a bounce and each bounce disrupted the wrong that had worked its way up from her stomach and blossomed now in her chest.

"Feels like I'm dyin'," she told Bruh Abel's neck. "We dyin'."

"Hush, girl."

Now she knew they were in Ma Doe's house by the warm, by the smell. She'd made the old woman a new gris-gris charm only days before, stuffed with all her favorite stinks. Ma Doe, for all that she was a learned woman, had always believed in asafetida as a way of warding off haints and hate alike. Miss May Belle had made them for her, and Miss Rue did the same after. And lately Rue had been making them for everybody in town, a little faith to clutch at if they glimpsed whiteness in the woods. The smell when she'd packed the bags had nearly sickened her, but now, stretched out in the empty cabin, it seemed dull, a pathetic stink.

"What's this?" she heard Ma Doe saying.

Bruh Abel's chest thumped with his every word. "The baby's comin'."

"It isn't yet time for the baby to come."

"Well, it's comin'," he said.

The wrong unfurled in Ma Doe's long silence.

"You'd best find her help then."

Bruh Abel roared, swung them round so fast she thought he meant to throw her.

"Don't know of anybody here that can safely bring an early child but Miss Rue," Ma Doe called after them.

It jarred her to hear her own name, as if Miss Rue were some other person than the one there hanging in Bruh Abel's arms and if that other person would only come, she could save them. Well, it didn't look as if she were coming.

There was that shock of the cold again

471

and she opened her eyes to see the stars above her, swimming in trails of silver. Dizzy. She shut her eyes and the next thing she knew was the hay.

It clung to her, that hay, in her hair and nightdress, on her fever-damp skin, stuck to her fingers when she tried, weak, to pick it off. Through the wooden grates of the borrowed merchant cart she could see the world rushing by her, blending all its colors. Up ahead was the broad stretch of Bruh Abel's back. She squinted at a sweat stain on his nightshirt, a senseless expansive pattern that grew as he whipped the one tawny horse pulling them, urging it to go faster and faster, though there was everywhere the sound of its hooves beating the ground with a fury and the cart creaking after. She was all ashiver, felt the way lips felt with a hum passing through them.

Finally the wagon stopped. Bruh Abel jumped down. He came round and plucked her from the hay. She wanted to scream when he gripped her waist. He didn't know how to touch her with her stomach in the way, with the wrong big between them. Bruh Abel settled on clutching her in something like a hug.

"It's just a li'l ways down the road," he said. She felt him pointing, his fingers bending against her back. "You gotta help me, girl."

She tried to walk but her legs felt as though they'd been replaced by double-pointed needles. They stuck to the ground, they stabbed up her hips.

"Where we goin'?"

"He's gotta help you," Bruh Abel said.

She knew it was a white person's home by the size of it, though she'd never before seen it in her life, never ventured out so far in all her days. It was opulent and it was devastated. Taller than Marse Charles's House that she'd known in her youth, this one shared the familiar white balustrades but the whole thing was covered in creeping green, as if the land itself was tempted to consume it, a slow, methodical swallow.

She saw right off why Bruh Abel had left the horse and cart at the path. As he led her closer, the grass of the grounds gave way to mud that gave way to swamp. The world sank as they moved forward; the house, the trees seemed to sit on the brackish water before them, floating. Bruh Abel drew her forward as best he could, saying sweet things, saying she'd be alright, they'd be alright. He was saying it too convincingly for it to be true. Below them the ground made sucking sounds, and they stepped barefoot

473

through the yard, bound together like some hideous four-legged creature, damned to struggle lifelong against itself.

It was strange to enter through the front of a white person's home without permission. Inside, the house was the kind of dark too tar black to see through, and Bruh Abel set her down on the floor. She rested her head on his calf, gripped the cracked wood beneath her hands as a particularly strong pang of wrongness ran through her. The bottom of her dress clung to her legs with wet and she could not think what that wet was but hoped that it was all swamp water. Above her, Bruh Abel fiddled with a book of matches and cussed, his hands too clumsy, cold and shriveled by damp.

It gave Rue a queer kind of comfort to imagine that the house was like the one she'd known in her girlhood, and in the uneasy dark she could just see the entry to the parlor, the fine furnishings, the stairs swirling up to heaven, Varina descending the steps two at a time, as unladylike as she wanted to be when she thought no one was looking.

Bruh Abel's match caught, illuminated the truth as he stretched away from her for a candle set by the door. The flame took and bobbed bigger on the wick of the wasting-

474

away stub of wax and before them a stretch of empty beds was revealed. This was no ordinary home then. This was something like she'd never seen. The rows of beds stretched as far as her eyes would let her see, blocks of white packed even closer together than the tightest of slave quarters, tattered curtains hung on rods between them, made a meal of by moths. There was no one in those beds, though they were made up like they were waiting for someone. Me, she thought. Us, she thought again. Bruh Abel lifted her, laid her on the first bed they came to, where she let herself curl up around the pain.

The rough mattress gave up a sigh of dust, and it was with just the barest of strength that she managed to move her head away from a stiff dark stain that she only recognized as old, old blood after long minutes of staring.

There were hurried steps and then a voice that echoed. "No flame," it said, harried. "Please, no flame."

Bruh Abel put out the candle he had lit just as Rue strained to see who'd spoke. She could only make out the glaring white of his face, the anxious flapping of his mouth surrounded by a mass of dark hair, a beard that shaped the hollows of his face into something like a skull. "No flame," he kept saying, and when the dark blanketed them again she had to imagine the rest of him. His manner of speaking called to her memory the marching-up-north army that had tramped through their woods years back, as disorganized and forceful as locusts.

Bruh Abel, all dark save for the pale linen of his nightshirt, stepped between her and the white man. He matched the whisper tone of his words, and she could not make out what was passing between them any more than she could make out their expressions. They were making a deal she feared, an arrangement, perhaps a sale.

Bruh Abel stepped away and she saw the white man's hand coming at her in the dark. She feared she would die if he touched her. She reared back from him fast and slammed herself backward into the metal head of the bed. It rained down rust on her face. His hand when he reached her only settled around her wrist. His fingers, shifting along her skin, were cool and coarse.

"Help me hold her now."

She did not want to be held, not even by Bruh Abel, maybe especially not by him, not then when it seemed like it was all going wrong, inside and out. He laid his hands on her shoulders and she tried to shrug him away. She fought him to the rhythm of her pain, like the wrong was music and her fists beat the drums.

The white man brought back with him a sweet smell so weighty she thought she'd be crushed by it. She tried to draw away. Bruh Abel wouldn't let her and then her body wouldn't let her. She could only lie there, gasping, as the white man laid a sheet, white as a cloud, over her mouth and nose, over her eyes completely. It was the softest thing she'd ever felt, that sheet, and he pressed it to her face and she figured he meant to kill her with it. Her eyes searched but all she saw was the white, and the scent it bore coiled down into her, and she knew it had to be true that something so sweet must mask something full evil. Surely beneath it there was brimstone. The white cloud scudded across Rue's eyes, spread across her sky, disintegrated. In another place, another time, back when she was a child at play, she might have looked up into the wide-open sky and dreamed.

In that memory place, the trees dripped down water, though Rue couldn't remember the last time it had rained. The bed of grass beneath her was weighted with dew. It drenched her back, it greened her dress, but she didn't mind because she was the mama. And Varina was the conjure woman.

"Rue," said the cheeky little redheaded child, "it's time."

Varina was on her knees above her, smiling. Her hair was falling loose of the careful braid Ma Doe had put it in that morning, the red ribbon unspooling slow, without Varina even noticing.

"Look here, Rue."

Varina held up a knife, something like a saw with jagged teeth, the sharpness of each tooth inconsistent with the next, as if it had been used to cut something irregular and never sharpened after. It was the wood handle that made Rue's stomach buckle. It was varnished dark and looked strange in Varina's hands, which were delicately covered in her lady lace gloves, so dainty her pink skin shone through the gaps of white. The knife's wood varnish was dark, Rue knew, so the blood wouldn't tell.

"Won't it hurt?"

"This time, yes," Varina conceded. The knife bit down. "But I know better'n anybody. These'll harden so the next time and the next time it won't hurt quite so bad."

"Ain't gonna be no next time. This here's my last."

Varina gave her a knowing smile.

The cut was more a pressure than a pain, and Rue sat up a little to watch the flourishing of the pen in Varina's hand. She held it delicately by its dark varnish hilt and wrote something Rue of course could not read. She recognized the *V* though, it was the one letter that Varina had ever taught her, over and over, again and again, in the dirt of their childhood.

"Now," Varina said when the cutting was done, "we got the same birthmark." The baby inside of Rue was cradled in her flesh and blood. It drew up its arms through the wound propelled by instinct, its small fists grabbing already, climbing already, as though it were drawing itself up through the branches of a tree.

Varina pulled the baby out of Rue's belly. It was so small its body fit entirely on the length of her two hands. She sawed through the cord, back and forth with quick tree-felling motions. All the while the baby cried, and Rue felt she knew the sound so well it was as if she'd made it herself. Her Posy, finally come.

Varina held out the little loving thing, and Rue brought her daughter to her chest.

"I wanna show Bruh Abel what we done."

Varina looked over her shoulder into the woods. "He's a-comin'. I hear him." Rue heard nothing except for the crying of her own baby girl, a heaven-sent sound. How simple and strange it was, to ache and love at once.

"What we gonna do with all of this?" Varina asked. She puzzled over the gash she'd made in Rue's belly, the spew of her innards, the bag that had held her baby and the shriveling snakelike cord that had nourished it. Varina had her thumb in her mouth, sucked at the filigreed tip of her glove, heedless of the blood darkening the lace.

Rue didn't much care about what Varina meant to do. She wanted to touch her skin to Posy's skin, how perfect and dark it was. She was secretly pleased that it was more like hers than Bruh Abel's. If only he'd come along and see what they'd made.

Varina drew the ribbon out from her hair, carefully pulling it through the more menacing snarls in her curls. When it was fully free she set to work stitching Rue closed with it, building an intricate series of knots end over end through the loose pools of Rue's skin. "There now," Varina kept saying, pleased with herself. "There now."

Posy's cries had quieted to a self-comforting whimper. She had big brown eyes that took an interest in Rue's face. She knows me, Rue thrilled herself in thinking.

"There now."

The drape of moth-eaten leaves parted like double doors and Rue, fool she was, expecting Bruh Abel and expecting him to be pleased, held up her Posy. Presented her. But it was the fox that came.

"Varina?"

Varina was too busy making her knots.

"Not me," Rue said. "Don't be worryin' about me. Help Posy."

The fox drew forward slow with the leisure of a predator. Hungry but not hungered. It trained its eyes on them. If she ran, it would run after. She could not run, she was still weak, she was laid open, she had her baby girl in her arms and Varina had tied her down with her wealth of red ribbon. Still she tried, Lord how she tried and tried, to run from this, to break free.

Rue saw the bunching muscles of the fox's hind legs, felt the coiling of time before the pounce. She waited 'til the very last moment to shut her eyes. She held Posy close as long as they would let her. And even when she could no longer feel her, she listened for her. As long as she could. She cradled her baby's cry 'til the very end. Such lovely, lovely crying.

WARTIME

Varina's pregnancy was a blight. She wished it gone. Had wished it gone for months and months before anyone had even noticed — her widening or her wishing.

"How long this been goin' on?"

She could not name the precise moment she knew that it had happened, that it was happening. Only that after her daddy's jubilee, every day her nightmares thickened, and her sleep thinned, and she woke one morning to find her mouth filling up with a volley of saliva like a flood so acrid and awful that she spat it out in her bare hands. Outside a cock crowed the morning into being and she, frantic, disentangled her legs from the covers that stuck to her like fetters, and there in the dipping valley in her mattress, between her legs, was a spot of red followed after by a darker, browner line, the whole stain fine and thin as a scripted point of exclamation. Her body heaved. She was sick onto herself and she called, high and shrill, for the housegirl Sarah, who did not come for long horrid minutes in which she shivered in the wet of her own vomit. Her body had betrayed her.

"You still bleedin', Miss?" Sarah had asked.

Varina sighed, sunk deeper. The water in the tub scalded at her shoulders. She bade her house girl to make it hotter and hotter still. It was not enough.

"No. The bleedin's stopped."

"It's like that for me too sometimes." The mulatta had dipped her voice low, sharing a secret as if she thought it was something Varina needed. "Like it don't want to get started. But it always comes."

Varina knew it wasn't going to come, not for her. This was not the start of her monthly courses. This was an end. Varina kept her expression steady, though inside she rocked with shame, with horror. Was that the moment she'd known? She had wished for more blood, known it wasn't enough somehow. Knew that it meant one way or the other that something was wrong. She was wrong. She'd skipped something important in her life. Gone from child to woman, violently.

"Ain't the water too hot, Miss?" Sarah

483

warned.

In the tub Varina let her body slip down and down. Slowly. Inch by boiling inch, then she let her face sink down too and watched the strange quivering way her curls floated up above her, stretched in their effort to stay at the surface. She watched bubbles flutter from her nose and mouth. They called to her dimming mind a memory of the moths she'd chased through the yard sometime in those endless dragging days of her youth. She'd never caught a single one, had she?

Sarah yanked her upward by the arms so forcefully that half the water gushed out to splatter on the wood floor. Varina drew in air in desperate clumps and the mulatta hissed at her and Varina watched Sarah's big pretty brown eyes go wide with panic as their two hearts pounded, and then go wider still when she realized she was still gripping onto a white woman's arms with enough desperation to bruise. She let go.

"What's the matter with you?"

"I don't know," Varina had said. But she did know.

They both seemed to recall themselves in the same moment. Varina wicked the wet from her eyes. Sarah began to clean the puddles on the floor. When she was done, she stood and stared down at Varina, which was a thing she should have known better than to do, and Varina would have told her so. Would have scolded her and screamed. But Varina couldn't draw the breath.

"Can I help you outta there now, Miss Varina?" Sarah spoke like she was bargaining with a stubborn child.

"No," Varina said, the one word harsh and terrible. She couldn't bear the thought of being touched again.

Her daddy took to wearing that old dusty uniform, relic of another war, marched around the house planning a one-man campaign against the Yankees, saying how the youngbloods nowadays didn't know how to fight, had no pride in the things they were fighting for, and that was why they were losing. He'd told her of the offer of marriage as an afterthought, not even looking at her. Not even seeing.

Varina hadn't cared. Not about her daddy's hurt that he was too old to fight at the front line. Not about pride, or tradition, or ways of life. She cared about her one life and tried to ignore the new one gurgling inside her. The sooner the husband came the better. Maybe she could tell of it then. Maybe she could love it. Take pride in it.

Give it a name.

She couldn't say when she first felt it move, only that it felt like moth's wings in the dip of her stomach, a sensation so strange and small it seemed like something she'd made happen by half-wishing that it would. There was so much half-wishing then when her daddy had showed her the tin countenance of the man she was to marry. A man she'd danced with only once. Hard and fast and rough and alone, a dance to no music or at least no type that she had ever imagined to hear in her life. No time for courting in wartime, he'd told her, and no time to be so shy. Varina had never been shy a moment in her life 'til then, 'til a man, a supposed-to-be-beau, had ripped up her dress and made her shy of everything, shy of her own reflection in the glass, shy of a flutter in the bottom of her stomach that should have been a good thing. Her life should have been a good thing, but there was a war to the north and there were explosions in the sky and the first time she felt it kick, really kick, it had been a musket shot come from her insides so hot and hard, she'd half-wished she were dead.

Varina asked for them for comfort, her two little nigras. She'd take them with her right

486

to her marriage bed if she could, like a beloved childhood blanket to stick between her and her new husband, a moth-eaten shield. But Varina wasn't stupid; in fact, she felt smarter as she grew fatter, like she was filling up with a sharper, keener knowledge.

Varina knew what she saw when she looked at that mulatta girl, Sarah, and it was something like seeing her own face looking back up at her, distorted only by a ripple in the pond. Sarah was darker than Varina; that mark of Cain left by a dead black mother made them only half sisters, but if not for that they might have been twins.

Her daddy, Varina realized, was a dirty man. The fact did not surprise her like it ought to. She'd lately been introduced to the dirtiness of men, was growing heavy with it. And if she were to pack up Sarah and take her as her double, it would be all the sweeter that she might send Sarah out to her husband, a soldier for proxy.

"How long this been goin' on?" Rue asked.

Varina had stripped herself down to next to nothing. Had ruined her room. Had smacked Rue across the face with a parasol handle. Dully Varina marveled at the red raising up on the nigra's cheek even through the black, a perfect line of the parasol.

The beads off of Varina's broken belt were still rolling. She could hear them reaching the far corners of her bedroom. Spinning. Under her bed and vanity, bouncing off the walls and edges and corners and still spinning. What would it take to make them come to rest? Varina didn't have an answer to Rue's question. To her it had felt like a lifetime that she had been nursing her shameful secret.

PROMISE

His word. It was all Rue had. Bruh Abel kept saying, *Girl, you have my word.* She did not want his word or anything his.

"The baby come dead," he said. He said it slow each time, careful, like this was the first time she was hearing it.

Spat on the floor and said to him, "I don't believe you."

He cut her nails for her because he thought he was being kind.

"Used to do this for Queenie," he said of his mama, trying to make Rue smile. "Toes too."

She did not want to think of Bruh Abel's mama, she did not want to think of him as coming from a mama who was real, and anyway Queenie did not feel real. She waxed and waned in each story, first kind then cruel, first brilliant then flawed. Rue had it hard enough trying to believe him.

So why did he keep trying to pile on more lies?

She wanted to take herself to the field, told Bruh Abel she was going to go look for some sort of quiet and he ought not to follow her. He didn't want to let her go off alone, that much she could tell from the way his eyes roved over her. He was trying to figure if she could be trusted by herself.

"Stay here," he said.

He blamed it on the danger that was thrumming through the town, the fear of the newly come whites lurking around, scheming to take their Promised Land, looking vengeful of it. But Rue knew what Bruh Abel was fearing. Rue's worst threats had always come from within her own self. She could find death in the weeds. It had always impressed her how many things could harm you just by being eaten wrongly. How many things could kill.

"It's the plant's defense against predators," Miss May Belle had explained once. That answer didn't satisfy.

"It's too late to be poison," Rue had argued. "If you already bein' eaten."

Miss May Belle had laughed at that and said no more.

Rue was not even shamed by the thought that occurred to her, which was to put Bruh

490

Abel to sleep so she could slip free of him. She could give him something she could trust in. Lavender or valerian or lemon balm; she mixed a poison for him in her head. In the end he did it to himself. He placed the bottle of label-less liquor on the table between them as though it were a solution.

"Drink," he said. Maybe his mind was working the same way hers was. Thinking near fondly on the time he'd first wiled his way into her home. She had meant to slip free of him then in much the same way but couldn't work it. She had tried to trick him and he had tried to trick her and the two of them had known each other for what they were. Liars. She could've almost felt nostalgic after it, if it hadn't all ended up so bitter.

Rue got up from the table. Fetched two cups and ignored the pull of the stitches on her stomach as she moved. The ache of the healing wound centered from the deep cut where Bruh Abel had told her they'd taken her baby out. She didn't like to think on it, being laid open by the Quaker doctor. It didn't bear thinking about.

Rue set the cups down hard on the table in front of Bruh Abel.

Miss May Belle had used to say that you

491

ought to pour in drink if you wanted to pour out truth. So, his cup she filled to near the brim and did the same to her own.

He took a sip and she watched to see that he swallowed it. She sipped, and he did the same. They watched each other, wary as any two creatures that knew they were well matched.

"Queenie lost her last child," he said.

It wasn't like Bruh Abel to start one of his tales in such an unfanciful way, to lay down the bare bones of a thing without a careful, purposeful arrangement of false skin to dress it up. No preamble here, no magic.

"I thought you was her last."

He shook his head. Rue took a sip and listened.

"Was after me. I was little then. I watched, though I wasn't supposed to. No men in the birthin' room was what folks used to say back then."

"Bad luck." Rue touched her stomach. Sipped. That wasn't true. It was just something folks said. Something Miss May Belle had used to say: "Where d'you think Adam was when Eve brung out Cain and Abel?"

"I was scared," Bruh Abel said.

She blinked at him. For a moment she forgot what time he was speaking on. She was all mixed up; the present was the past

492

come again.

"I hear my mama screamin'," Bruh Abel said. "I loved her more than anythin' then. I didn't understand it. I thought they was killin' her, them strange doctorin' grand-mamas that come. Them two crones who'd rid themselves of their menfolk and lived together in a one-bed cabin. Folks whispered about 'em as much as they relied on 'em.

"Queenie, laborin', was hollerin' somethin' awful when they laid her down. Me, a child, I thought, 'I'm the only one that can stop it. I'm the only one.' "

Bruh Abel could weave a tale, Rue knew, and she shut her eyes to see it, this birth, unremarkable as all the ones any woman had ever suffered before and after. But Bruh Abel transfigured it, made it sound so terrifying, his mama there sat up in bed and a pair of old prune-black women at either of her fat ankles, her dress shucked up to her thighs, her toes writhing round the ends of the metal bedpost — all that Abel could see from his vantage point.

He paused in the telling to take a long sip, like he was pushing something down. "I don't know how y'all women do it."

"I don't know either."

He was deep in his drink by now, drooping across the table already. He'd fall asleep soon, like she'd been after. Now the story wanted finishing.

"What happened to her baby?"

"Come dead." She held back on hitting him. For telling this story of all stories. But she felt too sluggish and too sick and too defeated.

"I seen him, though." Bruh Abel's voice grew thin. "Before they named him a lost cause. The baby. He was as strange a li'l thing as ever there was. Blue all over. So pale he was, it seemed strange to think he'd come from my mama, who was big and dark. But she was his mama alright."

" 'Course she was." Rue was growing fed up. "He come out a' her. Ain't no question a' origin to be had there."

"What it was, though, was his skin," he ventured quietly.

"They had the same colorin'?" It always seemed to come down to a matter of coloring.

Bruh Abel scoffed, polished his glass to empty. "Not hardly. Queenie was dark as the night is. This baby boy was lighter even than me."

Rue tried to remember what she knew of Queenie, could recall only that she'd been the figurehead on her master's boat, every

494

detail of her fecund body chiseled out as a mahogany mermaid, the whole of the boat patterned as her flipper tail.

"So what then?" Rue asked.

"The baby was light enough to be white; that's why it looked so vivid on him and was nothin' on her." He touched his own smooth arm. "A birthmark maybe. All up the body."

"What it look like?"

"Looked something," Bruh Abel said, "like scales."

There were so many sights in the world that Rue hadn't ever seen. But what she had seen, once, was the birth of a shock-white baby with ochre black eyes. Sarah's baby, born in a caul and covered all in a birthmark that looked like scales. Just like Queenie's lost boy.

Bruh Abel had no birthmark that Rue had ever seen, but she understood now that that was how it worked sometimes. The past revealed itself in mysterious ways, and Bruh Abel it seemed had passed his mama's brand onto his own son. Bean.

Maybe Rue's girl would have had the same birthmark had she lived.

Posy, half-born and half-remembered. Rue could almost see her baby. The new dark skin, still wet. The wanting O of her little mouth, suckling at the empty air. If Posy had not been real, then nothing was.

Rue's body remembered. Inside, her muscles still ached, caught in a suspended spasm, still pushing. Her arms and fingers remembered that soft feel of baby, rich and butter smooth as flower petals. Did all babies feel that sweet, and she had never known it? She didn't wish to touch another to find out.

What was it she thought she'd find out there in that wilderness besides singed earth and bark, same as ever? The clearing in which she'd held Posy was one from her memory, lusher, greener probably than it had been even before the war. Fertile, the way only the land in wistful memory could be. Fool she was, did she think she'd see Varina there waiting? Proud of the predictable childish trick she'd pulled — *Here's your doll baby, Rue.*

Rue had loved that stretch of empty green once, for how solitary it was. Now she felt that she'd never be alone again, that she'd be alone all her life. The shed still stood with that usual crooked perseverance at the river's edge. It was in that place that she'd found Bruh Abel, hiding from the Ravaging, the scores of dead babies. She had told him then to come into town, give the mamas balm in the form of lies.

"My baby come dead," Rue tried saying it aloud.

She was bleeding. Down below and from the neat gash in her stomach. The liquor she'd shared with Bruh Abel had made her blood rush. There was one more place still to look. Rue could have walked through those woods with her eyes closed, might have sleepwalked there, for before she knew what was what, she was tumbling through the church's double doors, expecting to be scolded by white parishioners. It was empty as always, the ground torn up, the grass poking through the old wood floor a harsh reminder of time. The woods were trying to take the space back, chew up the bricks and spit them out crooked.

Rue came to a rest on a bench in the old white folks' section, cleared a cobweb off with her hands and laid herself down across it. The high white ceiling of the church was going dim on its edges. She put pressure to her bleeding. She could feel her heart beating under her hand.

"You listenin'?" Rue screamed or whispered. It was the way she knew to summon her haint.

"What's happened to you?"

Rue could taste blood in her mouth, metallic and tangy. There was no way of knowing if she'd bit her tongue or brought it up hot from her stomach.

"Did you take her?" Rue asked.

Varina swam into her vision. She looked pale and troubled. Not at all like she'd been in Rue's dream.

Here, alive, she was a grown woman made small by the cavern of the church. Her hair was turning muted at the roots. She looked more like her daddy than she ever had. Varina sat down on the bench beside her, and Rue felt the wood shift beneath her back for the added weight. Varina's hands hesitated over her, unsure how to help but twitching with the urge to, little birds hovering, looking to perch.

"Rue. You're bleedin'."

"Did you take her?"

"Take who?" The worry lines lately etched in her forehead deepened. "Rue, you ain't makin' a lick of sense. Here, let me help you."

Varina fussed at her, tried to make her sit, but the incision at her stomach set Rue screaming.

"Where's my baby?"

"That li'l boy with the eyes?" Varina

frowned. "I only meant to watch over him."

Varina made to get up but Rue caught her arm, sunk her jagged clipped nails into the thin flesh, felt the bone roll beneath the skin as Varina struggled to move away from her.

"Posy." The name came rusted out of Rue's throat. She hadn't ever got to name her girl out loud.

"I don't know who that is. Rue, you're not well. Please, let me get you help."

Varina's arm slipped from her hand and Rue let her go, let strength leave her too, let herself lie on the cool hard bench, imagined it to be a burial slab welcome against her cheek. This had been her last hope, her last place to look for Posy. But the church was, as she was, hollowed out and empty. Gutted of its value. Sealed.

"She'll be alright now." That voice was a woman's. Far away.

"You sure?" That voice was a man's. Close up.

There was no more sound from either of them, and in the stretched-out silence Rue opened up her eyes.

Jonah. Rue almost didn't recognize him, couldn't reconcile his work-darkened skin, his shorn-short hair, or the new scar that wormed its way down from his brow line to the corner of his eye, looking like a fishing hook beneath the skin. He couldn't be real. He didn't belong inside the dank, dust-thick church that no one was meant to recollect existed.

"Easy, easy," he said. He didn't want her getting up, but she couldn't think on her back. Her head stewed and swirled. Far behind him Varina stood stock-still in a different aisle of the pews.

"What you doin' here, Jonah?"

"Just come through now. Back from workin'." He hefted up a haversack at his feet to prove it, half-filled with his traveling possessions. He handed Rue a canteen from its depth, but she felt too ill to drink. He wouldn't say more 'til she did. Rue took a few sputtering sips that made her feel sicker.

"Ran into Miss" — Jonah glanced back at her — "Varina at the side a' the river."

"I couldn't find my way to the quarters with the river up. Isn't that silly?" Varina's voice had gone high and tight in a way Rue hadn't heard in years. Her company voice.

"She said you was in need a' help. So I come runnin'," Jonah finished.

"I'm alright," Rue said, but she didn't feel alright.

"Take yo' time," Jonah said. Whether he

meant in moving or explaining she couldn't figure.

Varina, never good at silences, moved to fill it. She walked around one whole bench only to settle in the next aisle, eyeing Jonah, skittish the whole time.

"Is it alright, Rue? I didn't know what to do. I thought you'd died and if you died —" She cut herself short at some horror.

"It alright, Miss Varina. Thank you."

But now that Varina had got going she couldn't seem to stop. "I knew it wasn't safe for me to be seen. But he said he ain't a soldier. I wasn't sure. Don't the North have nigger soldiers?"

Jonah seemed to flinch. "I ain't a soldier, no ma'am," he said. He wouldn't look at Varina, knew more than well enough not to, but he did stare goggle-eyed at Rue. "I let her know that I'm on the side a' the South."

"Thank you." Rue could only get herself to whisper it.

Jonah walked her back like he was escorting her on a promenade, a firm hand on her arm, another on her back. Maybe he feared she'd fall, but to Rue it felt like he feared she'd take off running. He was wanting answers.

"Miss Varina ain't even recognize you,"

Rue said, tried to make a joke of it. Jonah wasn't laughing.

"We wasn't long acquainted," he said. "When she come runnin' up to me I ain't know what to think. When I figured who she was, though, I did wonder if I hadn't lost all my senses, seein' for myself a woman what's supposed to be dead. Then I remembered Ol' Joel, all 'em crazy mutterin's he made through the town."

"Folks that have glimpsed her, they tell themselves she a haint."

The hand Jonah had on her back swatted dismissively, resettled at her hip. "I ain't believe in all that. I saw her, first thing I thought was she just a white woman run mad. We walked back to the church an' she kept on askin' after news from the war. Wasn't 'til she say her name that I recollect that she was Marse Charles's daughter, aged over five years since last I knew her. If there is haints in this world, they don't grow old."

Did Varina look so old? Rue couldn't tell. For her the five-odd years had passed on Varina's face gradually. To catch her aging, to really see her youth lost, it was like trying to catch the moon moving across the sky at night.

A mile on, the tent reared its white head up over the treetops. "I heard about this here tent, but I ain't half believe it," Jonah said. "All that for Bean?"

"It's grown bigger than Bean," Rue said.

The way was a steep upward struggle, and it would have been faster by half to cut straight through the woods as Rue often did. But she could sense Jonah's nervousness as a twitching hand at her side. He kept peering into the thick knit of gathered trees, double-checking every shadow he saw. Likely the white woman had given him a fright. He hadn't had any way of being sure of where she meant to lead him. Jonah'd followed her anyway, for Rue's sake.

"She went away north and come back? Miss Varina?"

Rue shook her head, no.

"Don't say she been among us all this time."

"Since the House burned," Rue admitted. "That ol' church was meant to house a minister. She got all the things she need."

Jonah let go of her hand. His face crinkled up in wonderment. "Ol' Joel. He done saw it all clear."

"Not all clear," Rue said quick. "Ain't no hoodoo involved."

"Just lies."

She shrugged. Jonah should have long ago lost the ability to make her feel the fool.

503

She had kept him safe all these years, and everybody else too.

"You feed Miss Varina?" Jonah asked. "Clothe her? All this time? Like a li'l child?"

Rue nodded.

"What if she fell sick?"

"She was sick for a long while," Rue said, and in saying she could almost smell again the acrid stink of laudanum, hear the clink of the syrup-sticky vials that Varina had sucked from the way she had used to suck at her thumb as a girl.

"She near-about died. But she come back to life." Rue looked to Jonah, but she was thinking of Bean. "And now she's wantin' after things again. It makes her bold."

"How'd you keep her hid this long?" Jonah wanted to know.

"She believed when I tol' her it wasn't safe to go out. She believed when I tol' her she'd get out of there soon. She believed in me," Rue said. "Everybody did."

Now Jonah fell dumb silent and Rue asked a question of her own, one that had been pounding at her. "Jonah. You ain't tell her the war was done when you met her?"

"No, I did not."

"Why didn't you?"

"I ain't in the business of tellin' white women they wrong," he said. "Why didn't

504

you never tell her? Now or all them years ago?"

Rue had thought on an answer to that question for years. Chewed on the question and tossed and turned on it, sleepless at night, coming up with kindness as an answer on some days and rage as an answer on others. She could have said to Jonah that Varina didn't have any living relations save a spinster aunt up north that she'd never known. She could have said that Varina, opium-blind, had been too fragile to accept the South's surrender 'til the lie told to comfort her was too old to alter. Rue could have said that the world would not be kind to a disgraced belle who'd never been expected to even bathe herself. She could have said that Varina would have reclaimed her home, or what was left of it, would have turned her slaves into her workers, paid them in scraps and promises like nothing had ever changed, a different name for the same thing. She could have said that Varina deserved it, deserved only to see the light of day in small gasps, to prowl the woods only safely unseen at night, that Varina deserved to still have nightmares of her brothers dead on battlefields and of exploding cannonballs and of Yankee devils with cloven feet. That Varina deserved it all, deserved to be locked up, left to stay waiting and praying after a glory that wasn't ever going to come.

All of those things were true but what Rue did say to Jonah was true most of all: "I just didn't want her to leave."

■ ■ ■ ■

PART FIVE

■ ■ ■ ■

PART FIVE

EXODUS

1872

Rue had herself some nightmares. Haunted dreams in which her dead baby was a part of a collection. A pickled curiosity on a white man's shelf, floating and ill-fitting inside a jar, preserved with whiskey, posed and primed to raise her thumb to her mouth in an aborted suck. She woke from these dreams screaming, hollering, clawing. Beside her Bruh Abel was a man she didn't know. He tried to kiss her and hold her, and she wouldn't let him. He swore to her the dreams weren't real. Swore he'd paid the white Quaker doctor, and not the other way around, to see to it that the baby got buried proper. When she got well they could go up and see the place, if she liked.

Rue wouldn't believe him, wouldn't go anywhere with him, wouldn't make love to him ever again, she swore, even though his hands were loving and soft and gentle. What was the point? He said they could start again, make another, but she knew it wouldn't take. The place inside her where she'd held Posy was gone all arid now, an earth of dry, cracked clay.

"You can't know that," he said, kissing at her neck.

"Yes, I can know."

She knew now the secret of Bean's origin, from Queenie to Bruh Abel. The secret had been as plain to see as a mark of Cain, but she had not been looking. Now she could not look away.

In her nightmares Rue would walk on over to that white man's shelf and stare. She would pick up the specimen jar in her two hands and hold up her Posy in repose and spin round the liquid in it to get a closer look. She would inspect her baby's skin and see that it was dark like hers, but with all this dream time in which to look and ponder, she could see things she hadn't had the chance to see before. Or hadn't wanted to see. Posy's skin was like Bean's. Bean's skin was like Queenie's, patterned all over with little scales.

Inside the dream, Rue threw the jar to the ground where it splintered and shattered, all the liquid gushing away like a foretold flood. But what came out was not her baby

Posy. It was Black-Eyed Bean, no longer Sarah and Bruh Abel's baby, but Bean grown and freed.

When Rue woke, her eyeballs were like packed mounds of mud in their sockets, as if she'd stared into the sun unblinking and let them bake. She could see then what it was that needed doing.

As she crept up on Sarah and Jonah's house, slow going still with the pain in her gut, Rue thought she saw a baby. No, that weren't it. It wasn't a baby but a child, but still the sight made her heart gallop. When she drew closer she saw clear that it was Bean, and he held in his hands a corn-husk doll, surely one his sister had used to carry around everywhere when she herself was his age. It was a sad thing dressed in a green sack with its face muddied to make it seem black, and Rue recollected one time that she'd humored Sarah's daughter by looking over the corn-husk baby and pronounced it as thriving.

Bean stood there on the porch with the doll propped up on his shoulder the way he'd probably seen his daddy transporting wood. He'd watched Rue coming down the path and seemed to want to be noticed in that way that children sometimes did and sometimes did not. Rue thought about picking him up, to what end she could not rightly say. She edged closer, not knowing if she meant to love on him or turn him over. Did he look like Bruh Abel in other ways? Ways she'd never known or didn't let herself know?

It was the doll baby that made Rue stop. It was not, after all, the one that had belonged to Sarah's daughter as she'd first guessed. This was far older, blacker. One made lovingly with red bow lips and a green dress and wild hair in a bramble of yarn, and there in the dead center of its head, as she had done with all her hoodooing dolls, Miss May Belle had likely put in a tuft of Rue's baby hairs. Her own signature.

Slung over Bean's shoulder just so, the doll's skirts turned and tousled and showed the black baby's underside, where the white doll ought've been, the one that Miss May Belle had made to look like Varina. But there was nothing. Only a hollow, loose fabric, and a trail of straw stuffing, come undone.

"Where'd you get that?"

Miss May Belle had made those two halves, those two dolls tied together like one soul. Conjure to keep Varina from being sent away. But Rue had misunderstood from the start, supposed Miss May Belle had made Varina tied to the land, when all along it was Rue that Varina was tied to. The two of them bundled up together and trapped for it. No feet, or knees, or thighs. No legs to run with.

"Bean. What you done with the other half a' the doll baby?" Rue knew her voice was too harsh but she couldn't temper it. Bean's eyes filled up with tears. He backed away from her, for the first time, frightened.

"I done a surgery," Bean said.

Rue stilled.

They both heard the ring of Sarah's voice coming from inside, and though Rue couldn't make out what she'd said, Bean responded to his mama's call and disappeared into the house in a hurry, like he was being pulled away from Rue on the end of a string.

Rue thought to chase after him, to snatch away the doll and make certain she had seen what she'd thought she'd seen. But from down the road a group of men ambled along slow, bearing an injured body between them, and they were coming straight at her the way folks always seemed to with their hurts. It was Jonah, she saw, who hobbled between them. He had to be supported on either side by others, but at least he was moving himself.

Rue sighed. "Take him on to my cabin," she said before they could even tell her the full story.

Way they told it, the black men in the town had grown ashamed of their own fear, and in their shame they grew belligerent. They refused to wait out the perceived white demons squatting in the woods. Would not be haunted by haints in white robes.

They'd gathered themselves into a party of the bravest amongst them to ride out and stand their ground. Jonah was a natural leader, just as he had been during slavery times when he'd been entrusted to protect the women of the plantation, the closest he'd ever been to being viewed by his white master as a man.

Bruh Abel had told them that they shouldn't go into the woods, but they'd done it anyway. They had only the one sad-sack mare between them on which Jonah rode out. Before they had even got halfway to where the danger was, the horse had sensed something it felt it had no business going near.

From deep in the darkness a black mangy dog had appeared and began to bark. The horse had run off in a spook, dragging its rider along, trampling on his leg in its haste to get away.

So with a leg badly sprained, if not all the way broken, here was Jonah at last, who Rue had wanted for so long. She had learned to want by the lines of him, his broad shoulders, yes, and the strong prominence of his brow and, yes, his dark dark skin, shining. But more than that it was his hands that had always fascinated her, marked as they were from his work by a motley pattern, a deep intersection of scars from reeling fish bare-handed, flesh healed and broken and healed over. His hands reminded Rue of her daddy's scarred back, a smaller history all in a similar brutal constellation.

"Horse drug me far," Jonah said. "Foolish I know."

Rue shook her head. "Mighta saved you. Them white folks out for blood and worse."

Now was the best chance Rue had to talk to Jonah, what with him lying across her supper table hissing softly at his hurts, and there was a lot that wanted saying. He'd kept secret his discovery of Varina; as far as Rue could tell no one else was any the wiser that their old mistress had been living amongst them hidden, trapped away thinking the war still raged. For that Rue was thankful, but now she had a favor to ask.

She started off light, asked him about where he'd been when he'd been away, the things he'd seen and the money he'd made. Jonah talked between gasps as she looked him over, giving her the bare bones of a scheme he'd heard tell of in a Northern city.

"I'm of a mind to go back and take it up, permanent-like," Jonah said. "That's what I heard from the other men too. That it ain't safe here and ain't gon' never be. You right, Miss Rue, they won't never let us rest. Now more than ever."

Rue didn't disagree with him. Men were not trees, she knew, black men especially; it had always been dangerous for them to take root.

"Sarah's too far along to travel safely," Rue said.

In truth Rue had been neglecting Sarah, who had not had an easy time the whole length of this pregnancy. But even with the mama's suffering, the baby in her still thrived and Rue couldn't help thinking it was the most unfair thing she'd ever seen. That woman's big, proud high-yellow belly. To have another baby when Sarah had never claimed her last baby rightly, had wanted to cast Bean out if it came to it.

Would this baby have skin like scales too? As Bean did. As Posy might've.

"I'll send for Sarah after," Jonah said. He hadn't quite said it in a way that Rue believed. But Jonah had always been the good kind. She had to hope, and this was her chance.

She said, "When you leave you oughta take Bean with you."

"I can't do that." His answer came calm as a windless sea. "As I see it they ain't mine to take."

Rue was bracing to tell him, figuring how to put into words what she knew about Sarah and Bruh Abel. It was the same truth that she'd had such a difficult time telling for herself. Because beneath the shock of their hoodwink was the low-down hurt of an infidelity. It was base and it made Rue angrier to think on. That she had expected any different when she had named Bruh Abel as a liar with lies in her mouth also. And laid down with him just the same. It was the least original of all sinning.

But Jonah was leaning toward Rue, straining across the table, coming so close she thought he meant to kiss her. He said in her ear, "Miss Rue. You know ain't none of 'em mine." She pulled away from him like he'd scorched her. Busied herself on the other side of the room pretending she was gathering up healing things. More so she was

517

gathering up her wits. None of them children were his?

Rue tried to figure the times that Jonah had traveled away, count up the years that Bruh Abel had been amongst their town, and came up empty. There was no way of knowing, was there, for Bruh Abel had come like a thief in the night and made a fool of them, and of Rue most of all for thinking that her trickery was the only trickery that mattered.

"Cold hands," Jonah murmured when Rue brought herself back to him. He was smiling even with his teeth gritted and there was a fond haziness to his eyes. Dark eyes, she reminded herself, dark as any she'd seen, true black African eyes. But Jonah's eyes had never been as dark as Bean's.

She'd heated a knife 'til it glowed the hot red she liked. She undid Jonah's belt without asking him, pulled it free of his belt loops in a fluid tug and handed it back to him, said, "Bite down."

He looked like a warhorse with a bridle. She surveyed the wound again on his leg, like a general taking in the land and how it lay. She eyed his pant leg and didn't hesitate.

"I'll be needing to cut the fabric away."

He didn't hesitate either. "Go 'head," he said and he didn't even remove the belt from his mouth but balanced it on his thick bottom lip. She began cutting the pants up their damaged seam.

The weak chambray pants tore away easy, worn-down as they already were. Next were his drawers, and she pulled them off fast to get over the pain of where they stuck to him in stitches of dried-up blood. He didn't even wince as she ripped them full open.

Rue couldn't help herself, she looked away. Had to. Because there in his lap she saw the real horror. The real wound.

Jonah's thighs bore the same dark skin as the rest of his body, but as they crawled higher there was the menacing singular black of old burnt skin. And the horrid snaking pink where the skin had broken clear open, like looking into tore-up earth. Above his thighs there was nothing but that black puckering made darker here and there by flashes of more horrific white boils, nothing at all there to make him a man but a few curling dark hairs that had somehow had the audacity to grow in the landscape of pink angry scar tissue, of the black cracking pattern not even worth calling skin and the strange empty nothing between his legs. He was a ruin. Jonah was ruined.

"Apologies, Miss Rue," Jonah said in that same soft, gentle way he'd sometimes say good morning or good afternoon or remark on the coolness of the day. "Only I thought you knew a' it."

Questions bubbled up with bile. "When this happen?"

"Years and years," he said but he didn't need to answer, she could tell that. Of course she knew what a fresh scar looked like and this, some distant part of her mind impressed, had healed long ago and healed quite nicely despite itself.

She still held up the knife, high up like she meant to stab him with it if he moved too sudden, and the gruesome thought came to her mind that maybe she ought to, the poor wretched man, not a man at all, and then she recalled when she'd had a similar thought, held a similar weapon aloft. She'd thought to snip away the life of little Bean when first she'd discovered the horror of him wrapped up beneath the black veil. Jonah's son. No, not Jonah's son at all.

"Miss Rue?"

"Why would I know a' it?" She put the knife down. "How could I?"

" 'Cause Miss May Belle knew."

Rue took up the whiskey and sipped it and then gave it to him. He shook his head no but she pressed.

"Yo' mama knew," he qualified, like she'd

forgotten who Miss May Belle was, and, well, maybe she had. Her mama been dead and gone over five years.

Then it must have happened years back in slaverytime. And Bean was soon to turn six, had been born into freedom. Into peace.

"How'd she know?"

"Well, 'course she knew." His eyes looked past her like he was trying to remember it. "Miss May Belle was the one that done it."

WARTIME

May 1864

I know the real story, Miss May Belle says.

"The fox didn't kill 'em chickens" is what I told Marse Charles, but he too fool to listen.

"You don't know a damned thing, May Belle," he tells me.

The slaughter of the chickens on the edge of Marse Charles's property is the first crime of the promised war that I have seen with my own two eyes. A small bit of violence done by some scheming soldier-boys, picking at the edges of King Cotton.

Marse'll shrug it off as a nothing crime, blame it on a fox at best, or a colored at worst. He don't know what I know.

A wise mouth nibbles before it bites down whole. Ain't the worst still yet to come?

I only knew of them dead chickens because I went to see my man, to meet him behind the shed, to kiss his lips in secret.

He got there before me, like he do. I seen him standing in the clearing and it made my belly do that wishful thing, that mournful tumble. I just about ran to him, 'cause walking wouldn't've got me to him fast enough.

"May." He said my name when I got near, said it like it was a warning, and that's when I knew there was something awful to know.

First thing I did was look him over. Can't help habit. Awful, in my mind, is always borne by the body. I was looking for a new lashing scar, a cut, a burn, a bruise. A loss. He caught on to what I was after and shook his head. Not the body then. The head?

He took up my hand and pulled me over the whole way to the shed by the creek. We had to step out of the safe thick of the wood to cut through the clearing, and I felt like we were stark naked there, like anyone could see us and know what we were about. He stopped me at the door and pushed it open and so I looked in.

I couldn't see rightly 'til my eyes could catch up, but it didn't matter — my nose got to it first. There's no mistaking the smell of dead things, not when you've known it as often as I have, like a oft-worn cologne. When I could see right I put it together fast.

There were all the chickens, and they'd been slaughtered. Splayed-out innards and feathers made all red. Their heads were gone. Their clutch of eggs had all been smashed, the fertilized and unfertilized alike so's that the dead headless hens lay in a mess with all the possible outcomes of their purpose. Blood and yolk and blood and chicks not yet chicks, pink and small and all dead too.

"Marse Charles'll be sore," I said first.

My man shook his head. There was something I was not getting at quick enough, but he wasn't going to say it for me. That's his way. He don't ever press a thing. He lead you where you need to go then let you make up your own mind, horse to water.

"It's a message," I said, building up the thought as I spoke it. "Somebody got somethin' to say and this is how they sayin' it."

"More'n that."

"Yes, it's a message and it's punishment also."

We've heard tell of the abolitionist folks, Northerners who ain't just angry for their own sake, but on behalf of colored folk. If not heard them straight out then heard echoes of theirs, reverberating. But they'd spoken for themselves now, here, and spoken right out loud.

"More'n that too," my man had to say. He was leading me away from the shed, but I still had my eye on it, and even when I couldn't rightly see into it I still saw the no-sense slaughter behind the blink of my eye. That little meaningless massacre, them headless chickens, they had me shaken as much as any violence I've ever seen, and I seen just about every kind. Only what was the point of it?

"Tell me plain." In the shade of the trees I touched his face. He leaned his long body up against a tree and looked at me in his way, considering.

"Them Northerner soldiers ain't saints. They ain't want nothin' more than to be right. This their way of winnin'. They wanna make you hurt. Yo' marse and li'l mistress and slavefolk too. They wanna make you go hungry."

I laughed, looked up at the fecund green of the wood, yonder, persimmon and mul-berry and Chickasaw plum in blossom. The eucalyptus hanging down and tickling at the top of my man's head. He swat at it like it was a bother.

"We hardly livin' on chicken offal alone out here," I said. "Why you suddenly got so

525

much hate for some Blues you ain't even met?"

He shook loose my searching hand. Is it so wrong that I was wanting him right there? Not even a stone's throw away from the awful stink of death and I was still wanting him, wanting him more because of it. The whole length of his body was warm and alive, so broad and strong he was making the tree trunk behind him seem weak. As I snaked my arms around him, my fingers touched the wretched grouping of scars on his back. Can he even feel me there anymore? That I don't know.

"May." He undid the knot of my hands. "Marse John takin' me with him when he go to enlist. Said doin' so will make me free."

Now something in me come loose. I sat myself down hard. I beat at the earth. I pulled up grass in rough fistfuls like there was some answer to be found buried underneath if only I could get at it. My man took me in his arms and shushed me with kisses come too late to be comfort.

We sat together in the grass longer than we should have. We were watching the creek babble. That thin offshoot of the river was what divided Marse Charles's land of plenty from Marse John's small lot, and in the high heat of noon when everything was lazy, a smart slave might steal away for a quarter of an hour. That quarter hour was ours for lovemaking, but instead he let me weep softly and we let the chickens fester. He'd be wanted back there soon to take up his toil in the field. He's Marse John's favorite, a workhorse he call him.

"When he joinin' up?" I stirred up the strength to finally ask it. Marse Charles and Marse John had been jawing on it but we never thought they'd really go, old as they were. But the war's been growing desperate, running low on bodies.

"Soon" is all my man could give.

I nodded, knowing neither of us was deserving of knowing what time we had left.

"Marse John, he say the day we leave he will see rightly to give me my freedom."

"Marse John been danglin' freedom so long, sayin' it easy as passin' wind to him."

"Stinks as bad too."

I had to laugh through my melancholy at the surprise of something so wicked coming from his careful mouth. But there's a loyalty there, beneath the toil and the sweat and beneath the scars growing ever outward. My man ever as sweet as a kicked dog, returning and returning 'til that last kick kill him. Marse John is God to him, and how could he not be? I never seen the face of the Lord but I have seen a white master decide who suffers and who don't. I've seen that every goddamn day.

We could run. I thought of it while looking at the creek then, though I've thought of it so many times it's as constant as a heartbeat. But we don't. We never do. I thought of my girl and I can't say what my man thought of that kept him from running, but I'm sure there's something of that too.

I done a cruel thing to him by having Rue, I know it. I could've stopped her coming, like I'd done before and done since, every time I feel a stirring in my stomach or a pausing to my courses. But that was some years ago and now I don't have that worry. Now I'm a woman where nothing's gonna grow, perhaps before my time, but who can say how many years I've got really? Enough.

I can only say something came over me like loneliness and when I first felt my girl, when she was nothing to me but a corn seed, I knew her even then and a sudden thought come to me: I swear in the shape of my long dead mama, that he and I could die and leave nothing of our love. So I done it without asking. I let one baby grow warm in my belly. And now I can't ever leave her.

"I mean to have my freedom on paper."

My man's promise cut off my thoughts. "And when I do," he said, "I'll come back and make you somethin' you ain't never been."

"And what's that?"

"A wife."

I'm struck altogether silent by the thought of that.

When our time was done we both felt it in our bones. We retreated from each other, him going his way me going mine. No goodbye. Every word, all the time, might as well be goodbye.

"Promise me somethin'?" I asked.

My man nodded. He don't even know what I'm fixing to say, but already he nodded.

"Promise me if ever they let you get a musket in yo' hand you shoot yo' Marse John. That's freedom."

I could deserve to die just for saying it. I expected my man to cuss at me for being so foolish. But he didn't. He nodded just once, then he disappeared into the woods like he was part of it, so easy that even I couldn't keep track of him.

White folks won't say they scared in our hearing but they show it in their actions. Marse Charles one day gets himself three new slaves just like that. We been as we were for so long I forget what it's like to change. See, Marse Charles proud that he don't need to buy new when he got me to make sure all his nigras putting out babies every season and that all his old black folks stay living and living and living whether they want to or not.

The new souls come to me in a wagon from somewhere, fit with hay for easy cleaning and chains for binding. A woman, a girl, and a boy about to be a man, and I'm bid to look them over for sickness and for louse bites or for some reason why Marse Charles might be able to barter after the price of them even though the sale is already done, the goods delivered this one hot day with nary any word of the bodies to be added to the expanding plantation.

The woman and girl are ordinary, two sisters, dark and heavy and good for the field. I take them inside, bid the boy to wait a spell. Up close they smell sweet, almost sickeningly so, and I guess rightly that their used-to-be master had them work at sugar kettles making molasses. I try to smile at them because I know they scared, and as I feel through their hair looking for nits I tell them to come to me if they find themselves bothered by a man, any man, if they need a remedy. Next I inspect the full of their bodies, my hands moving on Marse Charles's behalf, seeking out defects, roaming gentle but persistent inside the slick wet of their low-down fear. The older one I can tell has the kind of chest that's known a child, that's grown engorged by wasted milk. I don't ask her where the baby gone. They both clean and worth their price, and I'm glad at least they have one another, that rare threadbare gift you might pass off as benevolence.

I send them on their ways. Their new home is a cabin of single women, three to a bed, and I don't feel guilty that I don't offer them a place in my own bed. I've earned the whole of my greed.

Next the boy. The boy is near a man, and as men and boys often do he's thinking how to look at me, mama or whore or both, and when I meet his eyes he holds on to my gaze a moment then looks down and that's how it's going to be between us. I cross to him and feel the strength of his arms. I do it not like a master but like a mama. Lifelong hunger's done battle with years of hard work on his body, and I can tell he's just escaped thin by growing into lean.

"What they call you?"

He don't answer me at first and I think,

Lord, don't tell me he slow. But finally he look up and give me his name, and you can see the smart in his eyes. Nah, he ain't slow. He too smart for his own good, and I don't have to wonder too long what Marse Charles was thinking when he brought this young cock to our hen house. I only have to think — why now?

"Y'all come from the same place?"

"Yes'm. We from Marse Avis Payne's place," he say. "Out west a ways. 'Bout five days' ride it took us."

He was paying attention then. And he know his directions.

"How'd Marse Charles come to get you?"

"Marse Payne dead in the war. We parcel of a forfeiture."

A good deal then. Marse Charles lucky, always has been, rubbing on me for luck.

I ask the boy, "You got people back there?"

Now he's turning his face back into that fool-stone and I suppose I can't blame him for it. He don't know me; far as he's concerned I could be the master's right hand. I hope fiercely that I ain't.

"Mama?" It's my girl at the door.

When my girl come in I have it figured all out, just from her look. This boy was bought for breeding. See, she's eyeing him like she someone who ain't never tasted food and he's the dish being brought into a feast. But my girl is shy and given over to thinking on things too hard. That child is so like her daddy and she don't even know it.

"Rue-baby," I say to her. "This Jonah."

After I sent Jonah on his way to the men's cabin Rue takes me aside and says to me that thing that all mamas long to hear and horror after, too: "Mama, I need yo' help."

I done forgot the way to the old white folks' church. I ain't been there in so long and the last time I was took there it was through nightfall and I was being dragged, clawing and grasping at the root of trees as I went. I don't wanna go out that way, not at all, but Rue says there's something I need to see, something she can't speak aloud no how, so I bundle up my fear like a sack of spikes and sling it over my shoulder and follow her through them miles.

When we get there the double doors are slight-ways open, like someone just went through them, and it makes me so nervous I stop and shy like a wary dog that's sniffed up trouble on ahead of itself. I nearly whine in fear from down in the thick of my throat. My girl Rue beckons me forward. What can she be thinkin'? What could be so urgent? I have a bone-deep feeling that this might be my very worst fear come real, that they finally turnt her against me, that she's the one that's gon' drag me back there, put me in that jail, that hole in the ground. She's gon' turn the key for them.

"Please hurry, Mama." So I do.

Little Miss Varina is sat up by the pew looking anxious in a dress too flimsy for propriety, and I don't have to go all the way up to her to see it. Her big round pregnant belly.

"No."

"But, Mama."

"I said no."

I turn right around and drag my daughter after me saying no no no.

Varina's hefted herself to her feet and she's yelling stop but I don't have to listen. Not as if she can chase me down in that state. Let them kill me later, but I'm leaving with my girl right now.

"Mama, she need you," Rue says, chasing after me as I clatter through the grass and around the trees, wheeling so fast I almost can't remember which way home is. "She ain't got a husband now. She can't have that baby."

I grab Rue by the hair and drag her after me the same way Marse Charles done to me so many times. No no no.

"We will not. I won't and you won't. That's death you talkin' about. Killin' a white woman's baby for her."

I smack at her back. Stupid soft-hearted darling. Push her further into the woods 'til we're far from there.

"But she need our help," Rue is saying and stumbling. She wants to turn back. After how far we come, she's still trying to turn back.

"I'll kill you myself first."

She stops. She looks at me and knows I'm speaking the truth. Rue don't argue after that.

I'm dreaming pure mad and I know it. I burnt up a leaf meant to give me sweet-nothing sleep but breathed too deep it seems, came up on the other side of silence, where the nightmares gallop. In this dream I am the headless chickens and I am the fox snapping their necks. That's all wrong. That weren't how it happened. There's a *tap tap tap* that I wake to and my girl Rue's in my arms, thank the Lord, sleeping undisturbed. She ain't forgive me for leaving Varina, and I don't care if she never do.

"Who there?"

I hear the *tap tap tap* again and I know who it is right off. It's Ol' Joel and his goddamn cane. The one Marse Charles give him. The one he think as good as Moses's own staff. He's rapping it at my door, impatient.

I open the door to him, not caring I'm in my nightclothes, and the old filthy man has a long, slow look from my bare feet on up, before he finally gets to the reason he's woke me up while the moon is still shining.

"It's the new 'un," he says.

And I say, "Which?" fearing it's one of them sisters.

"Jonah," he say and I bristle at it. Surprised he's even bothered to get the boy's name.

I throw on a shawl against the cold night air and Ol' Joel looks disappointed at the loss of my pricked-up chest.

"He hurt?"

"Bleedin' bad."

I grab the healing things, ones good for when there's no forewarning what the danger might be: yarrow and oak bark and comfrey root come to hand. I have one tallow candle left to light, and I can see Ol' Joel looking at it with envy as I draw it out and set the wick afire. The shadows writhe something sinister. I all of a sudden want to stop and kiss my girl, but there's no time for that. She doesn't stir even as I draw the light from the room. Outside, Ol' Joel moves slow with his cane and I'm too frustrated to wait on him to lead.

"Where's the boy?"

"By the creek," he say and I run off in the direction of his crooked, pointed finger. The night's set in too deep to see the water, which runs black as ink in the thicker parts of the wood. I follow its lapping sound awhile and I feel it the moment I've left the bounds of Marse Charles's lands, though I can't say how. Still, Jonah ain't too far from home when I do find him and I gotta wonder who put the whisper in Ol' Joel's ear that this would be the place the boy would be.

The nighttime screeching of wild hogs is a strange, awful thing, for they ain't nighttime animals and they know it, but the poor starved creatures ain't stupid neither. They know a feast when they see it, and this boy is the feast, doused as he is in bacon grease. Somebody's tied him to a tree by his wrists, covered him in hog fat and offal. Them wild beasts is eating the remains of their captive cousins with feral glee and eating up Jonah along with it. He struggled I can see by the deep red gashes the rope made on his wrists, rubbed raw down to the bone. Now he's suffered so long, he ain't even making a sound no more. He dead?

I swing my candle at the hogs — it's the only weapon I've got — and they scream and grunt and hiss at me awhile and I worry that they're so ravenous they'll turn on me next but they don't. They trudge back into the wood as my flame swings near, and they take their awful grunting with them so that finally I can hear the low whimper coming from the boy.

"Jonah." I speak to him to keep him hearing sense. "Jonah. Boy. Jonah."

He chatters his teeth and looks at me like I'm hollow, like he's seeing through me to some other place. "Stay here now, Jonah."

It seems like forever 'til Ol' Joel catch up, like he took his time. He's brought with him two other sturdy men and I suspect the delay was in waking the overseer, in asking permission. They pick up Jonah like he's nothing at all and I'm left to trail by his side, to hold his hand, to say his name over and over. I make them take him to the House, as it's nearest. We go in the back hall through the servants' quarters, and Fannie, our dead mistress's housemaid, is up, looking scared, her arms crossed over her breasts. How dare she have time for propriety?

They lay Jonah down right on the ground

on a threadbare bit of rug. There's nowhere else left to put him. I go down with him, afraid to pull my hand out of his firm grip, the only thing about him holding on.

"Mama?" he ask me, like to make my heart break.

"Yes, baby," I say. Lying comes easy. "I'm with you now."

I'm looking round the kitchen and in my meager basket thinking, what can I use? How can I save him? I can barely catch my breath, never mind my thoughts. The men are watching, the housemaid is watching; I can see the horror lilting off their faces as shadows in the night. That's when I remember my candle, the single flame, all mine. Yeah, I know what needs doing to close up those wounds.

"I'll be needin' somebody to hold down his arms," I tell the room. "And someone to hold closed his mouth. Mind he don't bite his tongue, now. Muffle him. He will scream. And we don't need to wake no more white folks."

When it's over I am weary. I walk to my cabin slow because I have to drag all my gathered sorrow along with me. I push open the door, wanting only my sleeping girl, wanting only to rest my head. But I can't

539

'cause I'm not alone. I walk in and sniff the air and know that he's been waiting on me and that he's been waiting awhile. I always know him by his smoke, white-man smoke too thick and fine for the likes of us. It's in my clean air, still curling.

I ignore him. Sit on the bed by my sleeping girl, watch the breath come in and out of her easy, like he must have been doing this long while. She sleeps so deep, my baby. She don't know how cruel real life is. My own fault. I want so bad to touch her but my hands are stained. I look at my palms in what little light the moon gives out.

"You know you too pale to hide in the shadows, don't you?" I whisper-speak.

He chuckles out a breath of that smoke. "You take care of that boy?"

"Jonah."

"Yeah, him," he say. "Y'all fix him up?"

"He'll survive it. Can't take no drink 'til it heals. Can't pass no water. If the thirst don't kill him, he'll survive it."

"Good," he say. "Knew you'd save him. It's a waste but we'll have to make a good use of him elsewise now that he's a eunuch."

When he says "we" I don't know if he means me and him, but there's a thrill in his voice like maybe that's what he'd intended for Jonah all along from the moment

540

he bought him, his mind on how he'd keep his henhouse safe when he gallops off to war.

It's a greedy shame, but I can't help but touch Rue's thick dark hair. So much thicker than mine too, resilient. She's been sticking flowers in her hair again and I pick out the petals. Fool girl. Wasteful little sweetheart.

"Belle," he says from behind me. I keep my eyes on my girl just a little while longer. Now, where did she get that warm, dark skin so much like her daddy's? I gave her everything else but that's all his doing.

"Come along now, Belle," he says and I know my defiance has gotta run short sometime. I kiss her, my girl. Not her face but the air above it and I'm so sure that she feels it, even through his smoke. She smiles in her sleep.

I go outside with Marse Charles but I don't have to go where he's wanting to take me. He's a fool, doesn't even know what's happening to his own daughter, to his own land.

I'm always free to leave, you see, to run away in my mind. And every time Marse Charles touches me, in my head I am gone. I go and meet my man by the river. In my freedom, I make it daytime 'cause I love to see his body in that light with no fear of being seen or found out or stolen back again. We can love in the daytime, take every moment the sun has to give, pull off all our clothes, no sinful shucking up of dresses here, Lord no, we can know each other like man and wife do, stretched out beneath the trees. And I can touch every inch of my man, claim him, even the sweat behind his kneecaps is mine, the small seashell curve of his ear or the field of his back, timber brown and rippling with muscle but here in my mind, and here only, he is unblemished, unscarred, unhurt. I can howl at the thrill of loving him and him me, and when we're done we can wash each other clean in the river, safe with the feeling that the rocks under our toes are as steady as the shore.

"Belle," he say and I flinch away because my man doesn't never call me that, not here, not anywhere.

"Shh," I say to him. I press my finger on his lips. The water moves around my waist and his arms snake up around my neck. I can feel the slow, steady lacing of his fingers against my spine, slipping against the wet. North is the way the river flows here and it could sweep us away if I let it.

"I love you, Belle," he say.

And I say, "Hush, hush," because in my

542

mind I'm only May. And my man's hands break free of my neck and different hands appear.

Marse Charles's voice breaks into my mind, says, "Do what I tol' you now, Belle," and he grabs roughly onto my face, his fingers dig deep into my cheekbones like as if they wish to rip them out. And he has me again, there in the moonlight and the worst of it, the very worst of it is, beneath all of it is the stench of his white fingers that smell so hotly of bacon grease. Even my spring-time river can't wash that stink away.

Marse Charles goes his way and I go mine.

In the bed my girl is safe, hasn't even rolled over. I love her so, love how dark she is like her daddy. I lay down beside her hardly rippling her sleep. I shouldn't have had her, but I did. Kept her hid no matter how big she grew in my belly, and when it was time for her to come on out I stole away to a clearing in the woods and birthed her all by my lonesome.

I tell that tale all the time, about how I brung my own baby out into the world alone. But I ain't never tell it true. For if my Rue-baby had been born into this cruel life half-black, half–Marse Charles's child, I would have dashed her head in on the rocks myself.

"Rue-baby," I say to my sweet dozing child. Almost a woman grown. "Rue. You listenin'?"

Sleepy and slow her voice comes out like it had far to travel.

"Yes, Mama?" she say.

EXODUS

"It's almost time," Sarah said.

Over the top of her pregnant belly, she stared blearily as Rue looked her over.

"Oh, we got a while yet."

In the front room of Sarah's cabin Rue settled in, Bean right beside her. She looked around regretfully at the empty house. Jonah had took up his things and left, chasing prosperity up north, and there were empty places on the walls where a man's belongings used to hang. His hat. His axe. The painted walls had not faded even, left outlines of what wasn't there.

She sat herself down at the table where she saw there were leaves spread in orderly lines like they were marching in. She recognized their various patterns.

"What's all this?"

"I got 'em for Mama," Bean said.

Rue looked closer. She saw what Bean had gathered, leaves and stems of various uses,

545

heaped together by type and color and shape, things he'd seen her bring to Sarah over the months. He'd gone and got them himself.

"Let me see you." She pulled him into her lap and he didn't squirm but let her look him over, his hands down to his legs. She had a fear that he'd troubled into some poison while he foraged. He didn't know what to avoid. But as Rue looked at the uneven crag of his skin she saw that there was not a scratch on him.

"How'd you do all that?"

He shrugged, a warm easy weight in her arms.

"I watch you," he said.

What else did he know? What else had he seen but every little thing they'd all done up to now, every lie and hid truth? Every sickness and every worship. Bean with his big, smart watchful eyes.

He let himself be cuddled closer and Rue rubbed her face in the thread of his hair. An oiled-leather brown, so much like Bruh Abel's. Why hadn't she seen it? She'd never bothered to look past his eyes.

"And she helped me some," Bean admitted, like he wasn't really wanting to share the credit. "Auntie V. She nice."

"You friendly with her, ain't you?"

"Sure. I like her plenty. She look like Mama."

Rue squeezed him in her arms like to say sorry with her squeezing. It was folly to think that she was the only one that had ever had any secrets.

Bean told her of the woman who'd let him call her "Auntie V," how she'd been kind to him and spoke to him and kept him safe from the white demons riding through, and as he told it Rue settled it all in her mind, muddled together a bittersweet solution but a solution all the same.

"Yo' mama gon' be alright," she said to Bean.

"How you know?"

" 'Cause I'm gon' stay here. I'm gon' watch for you."

"Miss Rue? Where am I goin'?" he had the sense to ask.

Rue told Bean a story to remember her by. It was what Miss May Belle would have done, she reckoned.

This is a story, she said, of how Bruh Rabbit done fooled God. He went up to the sky, straight up to God, and said, God, I'mma bring you one hundred slaves and all you need give me to do it is one kernel of corn. God laughed. Said, you can't make one hundred slaves out of a kernel, but he gave the seed to Bruh Rabbit anyway just to see what would happen.

Well, Bruh Rabbit took that seed and he planted it and it did grow up into a mighty cornstalk, and when it had grown tall he picked the ear and traveled on to the next town over. There Bruh Rabbit begged a room, told the innkeeper, this here corn is special. This is God's corn. Don't let no harm come to it. But Bruh Rabbit was clever. In the middle of the night he hopped out to where he'd left the corn and he plucked every kernel from it and, unseen, took himself back to bed.

Come the morning he pretended like he didn't know nothin' 'bout it. Screamed to the townspeople, some chicken must've ate God's corn. You best replace it or you'll be sorry. Afeared of God's wrath the townsfolk gave to him the chicken they thought must have done the eating.

Now he took the chicken on to the next town. Told the folks there, this here is God's chicken. Don't let no harm come to it. But in the night he crept to it and killed that chicken also. And when morning come he hollered at the people, said, that's God chicken. You best replace it. Just then some workers passed by carting after them dead bodies fresh from the war. So Bruh Rabbit took himself the littlest amongst them as payment and went on to the next town.

There he dressed up the body like a child and he moved him and spoke for him and told the folks there, this here's God's child. Don't let no harm come to him. But come mornin' Bruh Rabbit cried at what he'd found. Somebody done killed God's child. Now the townsfolk were aggrieved and didn't know what all they could do but to replace the child one hundredfold with their finest, strongest men of good stock.

Bruh Rabbit marched those men to heaven, right up to God's veranda, and proclaimed, here I have done it. From one corn kernel to one hundred slaves.

And God did have to admit that Bruh Rabbit was the most cunning of all creatures.

WARTIME

Varina sucked her thumb. She hadn't done it in years, but there she was, sixteen, her body worming with pain, and she put her thumb in her mouth because it was the only thing she had at hand to keep herself from screaming. She sucked hard at it 'til it was red and sore, the nail down to the quick, the skin puckered and wrinkled and raw. When she put it in her mouth she tasted only the acrid lye-white bubbles that she had held in her hands when she'd prepared the flush of soapy water to do what needed doing. To clean out her baby, root and stem.

Now she curled around her aching middle like someone had put a sawed-off shotgun to her belly button and pulled the trigger. She rolled on the varnished wood floor of her bedroom, her body sliding and twitching. Stuck her thumb in her mouth as the pain rose and rose, bit down on her thumb to try to hold in the mounting scream, because she knew if anybody came upon her, if they came too soon, their first thought would be to save the baby.

But the scream broke loose and came out jagged, tearing at her insides as it carved its way up and out of her throat, a mournful cry against her will.

Miss May Belle rolled back her sleeves. Didn't know truly where to begin. It was a poor sight to see Varina as she was, shaking and screaming, foam coming from her lips like she'd swallowed the soap instead of the truth, which was that she'd stuck it between her lily-white legs. Marse Charles had sent for Miss May Belle reluctantly but it was better than the alternative, which was to send for the doctor, who, miles and miles off, might not come in time and upon seeing Varina would know instantly the nature of the shame she'd brought down on them, on her own good name — once for conceiving and again for committing such a foul, twisted act as trying to end that conception.

Well, the girl was paying for it now. She might not make it to sunup. And there was a part of Miss May Belle that thought, now maybe that would be the better ending for all of their stories to say she'd tried her damnedest but there was no saving neither of them, mama nor child.

Miss May Belle kneeled and held her hands in a rictus of uncertainty, and beneath her Varina curled and cried, looking like a salted-over slug. Miss May Belle had brought with her everything she had, every type of healing she knew of. It wasn't the first time she'd seen a woman in such a state, though the slaves down there on the plantation had different ways and different reasons. Varina had chosen a hard-chemical death for her baby and to that end Miss May Belle brought with her harder medicines, tinctures in bottles saved up from Varina's mama's sickness that had come too late to be used.

"Calm her with the laudanum," Marse Charles had told Miss May Belle. "Don't give my daughter any a' yo' shit black grass."

The bottle held enough, Miss May Belle knew, to put Varina to a dreamless forever sleep, and she did think on serving it to her for a long dark while. In the end, Miss May Belle administered Varina only a taste, decided soul-deep that she simply didn't have it in her to let any woman die, especially not for the mere sake of taking her fate into her own two hands after the world of men had shackled those hands behind her.

Rue ran. Out through the slave quarters of the House, a labyrinth of tight dank corners, underground rooms, not hardly fit for habitation but lived in all the same, and she came up gasping on the other side of the slaves' entrance with the little bundle in her arms wrapped and wrapped and wrapped in cloth. If she encountered anybody she was meant to lie, tell them what she held was a bundle of kindling or a sack of root medicine or a collection of rusty bloodied knives, whatever lie needed telling to get her fast away because the baby needed to be buried and it needed to be buried quick.

Don't even think on it as a baby, Miss May Belle had said when she'd passed off the little strange bundle, already swathed and hid from Rue's curious eyes. It ain't a baby really. It's just a shame.

Rue took Varina's shame to the river, as far as she could go without being thought of as running away, the very edge of Marse Charles's vast territory so large he probably had never even strolled the half of it. There she dug deep with use of little more than a piece of slanted rock that cut and bruised her palms, but the mud was yielding, softened by a slow-falling rain.

She laid the shame down in the hole, and there she could just make out the baby's figure through the dried blood on the thin blanket. There, his little arms and his little legs, his twisted-up chest and sunken stomach. There the outline of his shock white face. She looked on him so long that the rain collected in the hollow of his skull, pooled on the blanket in black, where his eyes should have been. All black.

Rue plugged up the hole with mud, packed it in deep. She buried him and prayed the whole while. That the shame would stay hid. That the creek wouldn't ever rise and bring the dead baby back again.

Varina wouldn't speak. When her daddy came to see her, his fellow want-to-be soldiers were in his company, bedraggled and obviously drunk. Ruddy and heavy with it, they'd called her down to the parlor because her bedroom, the whole upper floor of the House it seemed, was a tainted place in Marse Charles's estimation. She had stained it all over with a womanly sin.

Her legs would barely take her down the stairs, her head rocked and flipped and did not settle. On the long walk she saw ghosts of women, translucent spirits, all of them with babies to their bared breasts, laughing. She was lost in her own home and it took two slave girls to find her and lead her back, and when she did finally reach the parlor she lay shriveled and pale on a stiff-backed chaise. The men were automatic and polite in her presence, but they were ready. They had their dogs and their guns and their whiskey and their rope. All they needed was the name, they kept saying, and the hungry dogs kept barking, and the ghost women with their babies stood over Varina and let themselves be sucked dry. A name. A name.

"May Belle," she said to quiet them. "May Belle, she ought to have helped me."

"May Belle?" Marse Charles said. "May Belle's man? He's the beast that attacked you?"

The question echoed. Above her the ghost women leered. A name.

EXODUS

Rue had smacked Bruh Abel. Once and hard and across the face. Named him a cheat and a liar and told him to get gone. She had never hit anybody before, let alone a man, let alone one she might have loved.

Bruh Abel had still been grinning, even when blood bloomed from his split lip, but there was sorrow in that grin. It had been there awhile, Rue knew, since her baby died. Their baby.

"Guess I was deserving that," Bruh Abel said and rubbed his swollen cheek.

She'd made him a poultice to soothe the red mark her hand had left on his fair skin.

Deserving? What did she herself deserve? She thought on it now as she sat on a pew in the white church as though it were the subject of a sermon.

Across from Rue, Varina held Bean in her lap.

"How long?" Varina bit out.

She'd already asked. Rue answered again. "Comin' up on seven years that the war's been over."

"We lost?" Varina said.

Rue didn't know if she counted as "we," but she nodded.

"You never told me. You never said."

"I thought I was helpin'," Rue said and that much had been true at the start.

That first year Varina had been delirious, her body half-poisoned from the lye, half-poisoned from the laudanum she'd sipped and sipped.

Rue hadn't known what to use to cure Varina of the addiction. She'd never had to counter white medicine with her own, and Varina seemed so content to die in her dreams. By the second year, if Varina had cared enough about the war to ask after it, it was easy for Ma Doe to arm Rue with scraps of old newspaper. Varina'd lost her sense of dates, quickly lost her appetite for news entirely. After that she'd simply waited and trusted and believed.

She'd believed that the South's glory and the life she'd been promised would rise up from the war ash resurrected and reconstructed, as if by magic. Faith in magic was far more potent than magic itself — hadn't Miss May Belle said that all along?

Rue held out her hands like she meant to give Varina something, but her hands were empty and her right palm stung. "I thought you were safe here."

"Safe? When was I ever safe here?" Varina moaned, and it echoed off the church walls. In her arms Bean snuggled close to her, unaware of what they were speaking on but keen to hurt just the same.

Rue figured Varina would rail against her, would scream, would haul off and hit her, same as Rue herself had hit Bruh Abel. Or worse, Varina would drag her off to the middle of the used-to-be plantation and whip Rue raw.

But Varina was not the girl she had been or the mistress she might have become.

She was a woman like a flower that had lived in a dark, dark place and tried her best, if not to flourish, then to survive — and that sort of thing made a body grateful, Rue well knew.

"So it's over?" Varina asked again. "I can go?"

"Yes."

Varina kissed Bean's head, then looked up to the church rafters. She said, "Thank God."

IN THE BEGINNING . . .

There was the ship hold. The early swirling motion of the sea, sickening. The heat of fever, the heat of fear, the only thing cold the new chains, and even those warmed quick and rusted over with rubbing with sores, with blood, with futile struggle. The darkness, the void of that black ship bottom, the darkness on the face of the deep, and then someone said unto them let there be light, piercing light, did you know light could hurt so bad? On the deck above they were made to dance under that brightness. So much light — the light of the heavens, and also the light of the heavens reflected on the sea, and then a few black bodies that got somehow free of the dance went jumping into that sea, blind, perhaps confusing the sea they'd never seen before for heaven, God's face in the waters. Waste that. False profits. The rest of them were sent back to the dark void 'til the ship reached firmament.

She had no words for then; they hadn't given them to her yet. But if she thought back and tried to give words to the memories of the ship and after, there was the one that had rung out when they'd stood her up before the curious white faces and made her hold out her arms and then hold open her mouth and then hold open her legs. Sold.

And was a mama the warm body that made you in a time and a place and a land you couldn't remember? Or was a mama what you made for yourself — the good warm body, the first kind memory of the older woman who slept beside you in the hayloft, who let you fold into her warmth that first evening that you were owned? And she hummed to you because she couldn't speak what you spoke. And that first sense of love, the earth still for the first time beneath your back, and for the first time, through an opening in the roof, the evening sky. You can make due with unspoken kindness and the stars also.

There were signs and seasons and days and years. After a time she was called Dorothea, named in the mistress's own image. They whupped the name into her, but it couldn't stick right. "No," she could say. And then "Doe" for the rhyme. In the end, they tied the two together, called her Doe — and it was good.

EXODUS

If anyone had ever loved Varina, Ma Doe had. Rue knew that. Had sometimes envied that, but now she made good on it, or as good as good might ever get leastwise.

Rue walked slowly between her two prizes like she was the juncture between the beginning and the end of time — Ma Doe on her right, Bean on her left, a march for penance.

The new school building wasn't all the way erected but it had four walls. In Rue's estimation that was enough to make a room or a home, a permanence, that one could start to feel safe with for a time, never mind that the roof was not quite finished and the rain came blustering in.

"It's dangerous," Ma Doe kept warning. She knew as well as anyone the danger the night could hold.

"I want you to see her 'fore she goes."

Inside Varina had made a seat for herself

out of a fat leather case, crafted for her special some years ago for a trip she'd never taken. She sat in the corner as nervous and hair-raised as a wet cat, but she was alert. Ready. She troubled on the finer details of Rue's plan, seemed to not understand at times the things Rue was asking forgiveness after, but she was not angry to learn that blacks were freed, was only relieved to hear that no hurt was coming after her. Varina was ever fierce after her own survival and she was fierce after the things she loved and now Bean had become one of them.

Ma Doe broke into a shudder when she saw the little baby girl she'd raised from birth. All these years and Ma Doe had been protecting Varina like a jewel in a box she could not open, for there was hardly any safe time that they could meet where others mightn't discover the secret. Rue hadn't ever understood how you could love something you couldn't have and hold, not 'til she'd loved and lost her own baby, loved hard on empty air and an idea.

Ma Doe moved faster than Rue had ever known her to and wrapped her ancient arms around Varina. They hugged and whispered to each other, ignoring the hard-falling rain. Rue looked on, her hands tight on Bean's little shoulders, rubbing to keep him warm, keep his spirits up. He didn't seem afraid, though, only curious to see Ma Doe, who he'd known all his small life as a fine marbled rock of a woman, moved to such tears.

Every other bosom baby of hers was gone to meet their maker by various hard means. Marse Charles's boys had marched away, had not even sent her a letter before the war ended them, she who had taught them their first stumbling words. Marse Charles had followed after, gone out to fight in the last pathetic dredging battles and had gotten not much farther than the next county before he'd surveyed all they'd lost and put a pistol to his mouth, frowned on the metallic taste, and drunk down a bottle of strychnine instead, or so the story went.

At least they had stories. Ma Doe's true-born baby boys all had been torn from her arms, not one word to say what had become of them. Rue could, in some ways, sympathize, could understand the way a losing and not knowing was the only thing in the world worse than simple out and out losing. This was the gift she could give before Varina and Bean's departure. Knowing.

Rue had done the same for Sarah, had asked the bedbound woman permission to disappear her son away.

563

"A mama'll suffer just about any heart-break," Sarah had said, through sweat and sorrow. "If it means her child is someplace safe."

When Ma Doe and Varina had finally pulled apart, Varina turned to look on the boy that was Black-Eyed Bean, Sarah's baby and, Rue supposed, Varina's nephew if the tangle of rumors surrounding Sarah's origins was finally to be named true. Marse Charles had prided himself on his sons, but here were his two daughters, Sarah and Varina, planted in the same season, and like to overgrow the world if the world would only let them.

In the little schoolhouse, Varina and Bean took the measure of each other, and then Varina crouched down to match his height.

"I like your hair," she said, easy and familiar.

"Me too."

He'd fidgeted and fussed when Rue had spread the calendula and carrot juice mixture through his hair to lighten it. All it took, a simple change of coloring, of wording, russet to redheaded, and there he was, a white boy before her like she'd laid magic on his head. The color had come out just right, that was clear to see with the two of them face-to-face, close as kin.

Bean looked to Rue and rubbed his big black eyes with both fists in the loving little way of his. "Miss Rue say Mama gon' be alright."

"Yes," Varina said. "Miss Rue has the care of everybody in hand."

Rue only waited out the rain. There were things that wanted doing and night was coming on with the intention of blackening out the sky, though the sun still had the edges.

She walked Ma Doe halfway back 'til she knew she was safe in the center of the old plantation where folks were still milling about in a hurry to finish what needed finishing before the threat of nightfall. There was something hanging in the air around them, call it foretelling, call it inevitability. Rue kissed Ma Doe's cheek and said goodbye.

"Where you off to?"

"Goin' to grab a li'l magic."

Ma Doe frowned, not catching her meaning, and Rue rubbed her fingers together to indicate coin.

"Thought you gave 'em what they needed." Ma Doe turned her head in the direction they'd left Varina and Bean, like she could see them going. Between them they carried the satchel of letters that had turned brittle waiting all those years in Ma Doe's locked desk. The correspondence to the Northern auntie to whom they now were headed had been taken up in two thick bundles: letters received, and, in Ma Doe's meticulous hand, copies of the letters sent. Two sides of the story. Varina'd read up on the facts of her life. She was like to add embellishments. Hadn't that always been her way?

"They'll do just fine," Rue told Ma Doe.

No dark back roads for a white lady and her white son. Bean with his shock-white skin and his new orange hair would pass as easy as folks had always told Bruh Abel that he could. Why the man had never chose to do so Rue couldn't rightly say. There were so many things about loving him she'd formed whole cloth in her mind and wouldn't now ever get the chance to turn over and examine proper in the light.

"This money ain't for Varina. It's for someone else."

Ma Doe *mhmm*ed a smart rolling sound from the back of her throat, like to say she'd lived so long, she'd heard everything before. "And what are you fixin' to tell him when you give it?"

"Don't know, Ma," Rue said. "Maybe somethin' like goodbye?"

SURRENDER

1865

They hanged Rue's daddy from a tree. He'd been named the cause of Varina's shame. That was all it took to enact Varina's curse upon Miss May Belle, revenge for her refusal to heal her of the baby she did not want. Lily-white conjure. Simple as pointing a finger.

Rue hadn't been there when they'd done it but she could see how it went. It was an oft-enough told tale. They'd come upon him up the road, on his way to join up with the Rebs. Hadn't his marse freed him after all and everything? So there he was when Death came upon him, a black man with the flimsy protection of freedom papers.

Maybe they'd been brutal and rough, beat him to bloodied before they'd done it, though Lord knew they didn't have to. They could just have easily bade him string himself up.

Fetch the rope, nigger.

Miss May Belle had not been witness, either, when they'd killed her man. But she knew what they'd done the moment they'd done it. Sat in their cabin, Rue watched her mama's body twitch and bend like she was bearing an assault of unseen hands. Then she went all-over rigid, her neck overextended, her head tilted too far back. Inside her skull her eyes rolled to all white and a gasp shuddered out of her mouth with such force as to be her last. Just like that it was over, and Miss May Belle was herself again, sullen but dry-eyed. *He ain't gone,* she kept saying like saying could make it so.

They'd left him to swing. Said the darkie-loving Northerners could cut him down if they felt so inclined. But the truth of it was his slow-spinning body, big and strong and heavy enough to bow the branch he dangled from, was meant to serve as a reminder in the master's absence. That they would be back once the war was won.

Marse Charles had left Jonah in charge. Who better than a clipped cock to guard a henhouse? With Ol' Joel beside him, overseeing, things didn't hardly change. Miss Varina was like a ghost watching from her bedroom window, searching outward. From that height she could just see the tree they'd hanged Rue's daddy from. She told them the next day to cut him down.

Folks said the Union army was creeping closer. They'd taken Marse John's plantation for themselves, eaten up all the goods left in the stores, drank and sang their Northern songs, trampled on the fledgling crops, smashed things in Marse John's parlor that weren't worth the trouble to steal. Did they have horns, hoofed feet, like they'd all been hearing? They'd disappeared away with the slaves left there, it was said, marched them away not as free but as contraband. Better maybe the devil you know.

By then Miss May Belle had took to her bed with something worse than grief, which was denial. Said, *He ain't gone,* of her man and Rue knew she'd find no help from her mama, maybe never would again.

Time was drawing to a close, it felt like, and there was a bristled-up anticipation amongst the people they couldn't name, precisely, because it was tinged in fear. They'd led their whole slave lives waiting on *someday,* singing *a day will come,* promising *on that day* that they would be ready. Rue never had been good at singing along. She had decided not to wait on the Day but to act in the Night.

The moon lit the way for her, and Rue took herself right on in through the front door of the House, straight up the spinning stairs and down the gilded hall to Varina's door, went in without knocking, without seeking permission or needing it.

Varina was deep asleep. One of her slave girls had tucked her neatly in her bed like a body laid out for burial, and all her earthly belongings surrounded her. Rue watched Varina for a moment in her repose knowing the moment she woke everything would change.

Rue shook the girl by the shoulders like to snap her neck. What had come over her, Rue could not say, only she knew it needed doing. Had to happen now.

The white girl shocked awake, saw Rue wild in her bed, and seemed to think it was her judgment day, started confessing.

"I didn't know they meant to kill him," Varina hollered.

Rue didn't follow her meaning at first.

"Your daddy," Varina said. She clutched her bedsheets close and shook. "I swear I didn't know what they were asking when they asked it. I didn't know."

Maybe it was so. But the trouble was that Varina had never had to know anything up

571

there in the House; she could close the blinds if she didn't like what she was seeing, could turn away in her featherbed.

"It alright." Rue began with a lie. "Come with me now. It ain't safe for you. The army is a-comin'."

Varina grabbed at Rue. Hid her face in Rue's little chest, and Rue could feel Varina's tears and snot and sorrow soaking through her own muslin dress.

"I can't bear it," Varina said.

Rue knew that for all her life the little white mistress had been told the bedtime stories where the black man was the brute, the creature to fear in the darkness. Now the world was all turned over and at Rue's suggestion Varina could just hear the boot stomps of a hundred Northern men, none of them a savior, every one of them like the gentleman Rue had glimpsed defiling Varina's innocence the day of the Dead Man's Jubilee. A white-gloved monster. Rue never had been good at comfort, but she comforted Varina's fears then, laid a kiss on her forehead, said, "Ain't I gon' keep you safe?"

It was likely when the Blues came through that they'd be kind to Varina, send her on to wherever disgraced women went to be hid away from the fighting with others of their station, to write letters and sing songs and wait out the new dawn. But it was just as possible that those Northern soldiers, hungry and vengeful, would swoop in and see her as part of what her opulent house stood tall for, just another room in which to plunder. And Varina still had Rue's name and Sarah's name on a spirited away bit of paper that promised her ownership of her nigras should she ever take a husband. Any day now the world might right itself and the old laws would hold. Rue had never seen that thing the Yankees were promising — freedom — and she did not trust in what she could not see.

There'd always been rumors of what lay beneath the white church, and in the end the rumors held true. The little locked room under root and earth was not a room at all but a pit, a grave, and Miss Varina, mistress-made, had the key.

"But, Rue," Varina kept on saying, even as she eased her way into the dark. When her feet landed in the mud down below there was the sound of it sucking, the earth swallowing. Looking up at Rue from down below, Varina shivered.

"It's the only way." Lie two. How quick they grew and strengthened and tangled.

"You'll come back for me, won't you?

Please?"

Rue slid closed the lid. Turned the key hard in the lock.

Day started dawning, and Rue met it. Everybody on the plantation was sleeping still, dredging the last of their resting hours, for normal folks toiled all day, slept at night. Not Rue, never Rue. She was all opposite, a nighttime creature. She could see through the darkness and she had seen what was coming from way off.

Rue stood on the porch of the House alone, little, thin and nothing to her. When they came she faced them down, an army. She had her hand on the pillar for strength, laced her fingers in the etched grooves and rubbed so hard, feeling like it was the only thing left that was real. If she didn't hold on here she would float away — that was her thinking, as she drew her breath on the next lie.

The leader of them walked up, no uniform on him, but just an air of command. He talked to her slow like he thought maybe she wouldn't understand.

"Step away from there now, girl." Already he was snapping orders at one of his men to come and grab her away.

She held, gripped. Spoke: "Only I need to

tell you, suh. Miss Varina, our mistress, is dead. Died of the pox just late last night."

It was the best lie to tell. She saw the effect it had, the way the men shivered and stepped back afeared of the House as if she'd painted a curse on it, and in a way she had, the conjure of contagion. The only course they had was fire, that one true final cure.

The crackling, popping, hissing of the House going up in flames seemed to speak to the slavefolk in a forgotten language they hadn't known they'd lost. When they heard it talking they came out of their quarters, out from by the river, out from the cotton fields, to hear what the fire had to say, to watch it devour all they'd known, turn that white House black, sunder it all to a thin windswept ash. When it had eaten up all it could, the fire, still hungry, went after the trees.

Miss May Belle came out amongst the gathered people, strange and stumbling in the light, like somebody just drawn out from the depths of a cave. Rue ran to her, wanted to whisper to only her mama the truth of what she'd done. Let the rest of them mourn after Miss Varina or dance on her grave if they liked. Rue held the truth of her trick to her like treasure. The key was in her pocket.

But when Rue reached her mama the woman was not smiling; instead she was collapsing, falling like her knees were where the fire was, all her bones popping and snapping.

Rue held her mama, hugged at her, tried to understand where her grief came from. Miss May Belle was pointing at the trees, to one in particular, a tall white birch where the flames had caught the very top, blazed all orange like a new type of leaf.

"My man," Miss May Belle cried. "My man. Lord, Rue, what you done? Ain't you know I made him safe? Ain't you know I turnt him to a tree?"

EXODUS

"You wanna see her 'fore you go?"

"You think there's time?"

Rue did not.

"You think she mine?" Bruh Abel said "she" because Rue had said "she." There was really no telling what a baby meant to be 'til it had come.

"Don't you know?"

"Even Adam wasn't sure a' Eve an' they was the only two in the garden."

Save the snake. Rue shrugged. "Won't know 'til she come out. An' even then." Even then.

Bruh Abel smelled of his faith, the bold, beautiful kerosene lights that illuminated his church's tent like a lone star in the night sky. Did the moon see it and envy? Most likely, and if it did not, he'd only go on and build that light bigger. The scent of the burning oil clung to his clothes, traveling clothes of a type Rue'd never seen him in.

Unadorned and ordinary, they fit close to his lithe body like extra skin. Running clothes.

"It was done with long ago, me an' Sarah was. Rue, I swear it."

Rue had never asked him to swear. And maybe that had been her failing. She didn't know how to ask. Or how to believe.

They were in the front room of Sarah's house, looking on water boiling in a pot. When it was time to go Bruh Abel had nothing with him but the tied-up bundle of his suit wrapped around his Bible and whatever he could hold in its smaller pockets, as if he'd accumulated nothing in all those years. That couldn't at all be true. Rue kissed him while the water bubbled and popped and hissed.

Their plan, like all the plans they'd ever formed together in the rut of their shared bed, between the optimism of flesh to flesh, was simple. Bruh Abel would lead his people out in the early threads of morning light, march sure through the gathered dew, wind up northward, away from the legacy of danger, all of them that wanted gone, going together. Those that would stay would stay, the old, the infirm, those tied to the land they found too beloved to leave, it being theirs by bitter rights, a home where they'd sweated and bled and lost as much as it was a place they'd planted seeds and watched things flourish. Miss Rue was among those staying. She felt rooted here.

"What if folks change they mind, if things get too bad?" Rue asked. "Wanna follow after you?"

From inside his bundled suit, from inside the fluttering pages of his Bible, Bruh Abel conjured. Paper. Pen. He wetted the pen on his tongue. With a swirl of ease and grace he began to write. The words blossomed black out of his pen like fast, elegant little miracles, and Rue was astonished to see his agility — and with his left hand no less.

"You can write," she said.

He smiled.

"You can read."

"The two things go together nicely I'm told."

She was too shocked to slap his smart mouth. "I didn't know you could read."

"When did I ever say I couldn't? 'sides, some knowledge is better kept hid."

Rue would keep that. It was the truest thing he'd ever told her.

Ma Doe would read it, tell the others the direction they'd run if they were wanting to know it. Rue herself found she didn't want to know. Rue had told Bruh Abel that Bean

579

was gone but safe, spirited off to a trusted location, though she did not tell Bruh Abel the color of his son's escape. The gift of one last lie.

"You sure you gon' be safe here?" he asked.

"They was always after you," Rue told him, "yo' faith and yo' freedom. The power you and Bean had made here. Them white men, they ain't heard tell a' me."

Bruh Abel grinned for her a final time and went.

Rue sang when Sarah sang as they made their way in a slow march around her bedroom waiting on the baby, that last leaving of Bruh Abel's, to come on out and greet the world. The song was a simple sweet appeal to God, and when the pain got so great that Sarah could not grind out the words, Rue hummed with her too, felt the squeezing of her hand and squeezed back.

When the hooves beat in the distance, when the dogs barked, when they heard the gunshots and the whooping and the hollering, all the telling signs that the white demons had come down from the trees, Sarah and Rue quieted.

Sarah labored in terrified silence as they listened to the night fall all around them.

Rue laid her down, not in the bed but on the ground, where they were as well hid as they could be, far from the windows, the white robed men, and the malevolent light they bore, a skittering glow from their passing torches. Rue told Sarah to be brave, to close her eyes and pray. To bear down close in her crouch, push all she could toward the ground.

"Easy, easy," Rue whispered. She stroked Sarah's face, tried to pass comfort through the tips of her fingers.

When she looked up she spied him, the white man in the window. He stared down at them, watched Sarah push and twist and scream all from inside the hollow of his draped white disguise, no expression painted there, just the crooked point of his hood, the deep pool black where he'd cut for eyes.

Rue said one, small word. "Please."

Just like that, the man was swallowed back up by the night.

An hour or an eternity had passed by the time the baby came on out in three forceful pushes and Rue was there to catch her, to pull her into her arms and to hear that first powerful cry, afraid that cry would call back the demons, but loving it too much to ever quiet it.

"Sarah," Rue told her. "You got yo'self a baby girl."

The baby blinked up at Rue, gray-eyed as Bruh Abel was, and perfect, as promising as any fresh day.

In the quiet of the morning Rue woke. Sarah was beside her, watching her. In her arms the baby suckled with delight. The dawn was still. The air smelled of smoke. Rue rose from the ground where they'd survived the night and made her way to the door.

"You ain't tell me what her name is, Miss Rue."

She turned to look back at Sarah, who stood and pulled herself and her baby into the bed. Mama and child settled in, looked safe and small.

"I think her name is Posy."

"Posy," Sarah said.

Outside, the town was a mess of toppled houses, of scorched grass and bitter smells, the work of the white-hooded demons.

"Miss Rue," folks said as she passed. Their voices were rough from smoke and from grief. "Them that left with Bruh Abel? You think they got away safe?"

" 'Course," Miss Rue told folks, and they were appeased. "I gave them a charm, best

582

that I got, to see them safely north. Root a'
High John the Conqueror."

She walked on, through the town square,
out from what had used to be the plantation up to the clearing where the House had
stood and fallen, where the tent had stood
and fallen also. Now there was nothing there
to mark either, no words on a grave, just
the lone thing the white devils had left
standing to say that they had come and
gone, burning itself out to black: two planks
of tall wood formed perfect in the shape of
a cross.

GILEAD

1929

Rue walks. If she doesn't keep walking the pain catches up on her, settles round the low of her stomach and burns. The thing is, there isn't much place to walk in the hospital room. She amuses herself by fitting her bare feet full in the tiles, avoiding the sharp black lines delineating the edges. The tile is cold beneath her feet, unyielding beneath her uncut toenails, and it takes only ten of those tile steps lengthwise to take her from one side of the room to the other, and then she has to turn round and start back again. But it takes only these next ten steps for her to grow nearly so weary that she can't stand. And she has a notion that soon it will take less, and less still.

One day, today, whatever day it may be, a doctor comes. He is not the first doctor, let's say he is the third, who seeks to cure what can't be cured. Now the first doctor said, "Miss Rue, we will try to cut it from you, to cut your body clear of it." And he took her to a place he called a theater where they watched from above what was done to her. That doctor, a small mustached man who spoke in a voice like her old master, made an incision where an incision had been already made, tried to take something out of her that had been put in long ago, a curse, she liked to think of it. A bitter taste in her mouth. But it grew again and bigger. The affliction would not leave her.

Then came the second doctor, big and ruddy and from the North, though the country was one borderless place now, or so they told her. That doctor came and said to her, "Miss Rue, we will try a course of poisoning." But her sin-sick soul worsened while the affliction fed on the poison they put to her and multiplied.

Now the third doctor comes to her. There's no door to her room but he knocks politely at her doorframe.

"Miss Rue," says he.

She stops in her walking, paused on the sixth and seventh tile, turns to him and squints to see him better. She is twice forty now and failing. He is a white blur at her threshold.

"Come in," she gets to say, and there's

585

power in that at least.

Up close he's as handsome as any doctor she's seen. The freckles on his nose make him appear boyish; the slicked-back brown of his hair suggests a root that would coil if it had half the chance. He's carrying a chart he doesn't need to read from, but he puts on thick-paned glasses anyway and it's through that glass that she notices his eyes, big and all glossy black as spilt oil. He looks at Rue then like he knows her. Looks at her like he knows.

But quickly he fiddles with the heavy folio in his hands, flutters open the pages to their well-worn center, and the moment's broken. He clears his throat to speak. He has a lovely voice, she notices, like music to be heard. "Miss Rue, how are you feelin' this mornin'?"

They always start off that way, the doctors, like someone has told them they ought to. Rue nods to him politely, the way she'd nod to any white man asking her something. But inside she does wonder.

"Alright, thank you," says she.

"Any advanced discomfort? Any pain?"

There is always pain, but you don't tell a man that nor a white man besides. "No, suh."

He sighs, shuts his papers. "I think we'll

try a different course today if you don't mind, Miss Rue."

She does mind, very much, their cold metal and their bright lights in her eyes, their nods and their note-taking. She can't figure why they don't know what she knows. There is no help for it. She's dying.

"What course is that, suh?"

He smiles, as bright a smile as any balm.

"Well, Miss Rue," says he, "I thought we'd go walkin'."

AUTHOR'S NOTE

Immeasurable recognition is owed to the people whose real histories informed the fictional stories that make up *Conjure Women.* I drew largely from *Slave Narratives: A Folk History of Slavery in the United States from Interviews,* as conducted in the 1930s by the Work Projects Administration, to find voice and flavor, curses and cures. So, too, is great recognition owed to Lucy Zimmerman, Anarcha Westcott, and Betsey Harris, as well as countless unnamed, unknown women whose indignities and suffering under the medical "care" of J. Marion Sims were detailed in his own *The Story of My Life.* I offer gratitude to the African American men and women who, through their own written narratives, through interview or amanuensis, willingly and at times unwillingly, shared their experiences within

the horrors of the transatlantic slave trade
and its long-lasting aftermath.

ACKNOWLEDGMENTS

Raising *Conjure Women* was a village-wide undertaking. I am immensely grateful to all those who aided in ways great and small in this novel's conception, labor, and birth. Thank you:

To my mother, Diana Okyere Atakora, who offered great insight into matters pertaining to medicine and motherhood and everything in between — who taught me, always, that I could do anything, and then helped me to do it.

And to my grandmother Dora Akua Akomaah, "Ma Doe," who relayed a hundred years' worth of memories, stories, and proverbs all the way from Ghana and did not let the language barrier, the Atlantic Ocean, or her dwindling cellphone battery keep her from inspiring her granddaughter.

To all those at ICM who advocated both at home and abroad. Most especially to the amazing Amelia Atlas, who saw this novel's potential long, long before I did and who tirelessly guided me in every step of the journey.

To the incomparable Kate Medina, who is in possession of that singular skill of extraordinary editors (and midwives) to ask for one more push and one push more, and under whose immeasurable guidance this story thrived.

In the United States, to the team at Penguin Random House — most especially Erica Gonzalez, who warmly read and reread, and in so doing re-sparked my enthusiasm at every turn.

And in the United Kingdom, to the team at Fourth Estate, HarperCollins — most especially Helen Garnons-Williams, who believed early on that the magic of *Conjure Women* could cross all borders.

I am indebted to the many teachers, mentors, and friends who supported early drafts. At the Tin House workshop: to Elissa Schappell, Dana Spiotta, and the lifelong cohort I formed there over one wild week. And at Columbia University: to Binnie Kirshenbaum, Chinelo Okparanta, Rebecca Godfrey, and the group of daring, witchy women writers who studied and conjured alongside me. Heartfelt thanks to Joni Marie Iraci, who offered wisdom and wit in equal measure.

Thank you to my beloved literary sisters Janet Matthews-Derrico and Rosemary Santarelli, who read every crazy incarnation and only ever asked for more crazy.

And to the "biddies," my best friends and chosen family, for celebrating the successes and celebrating the failures, for making celebrating a lifelong pursuit.

Lastly, thank you to my husband, Sean, my best friend and partner in every way, who kept me fed and watered, who heard me say a million times, "I'm going to do the thing," and answered, every single time, "I know you will."

ABOUT THE AUTHOR

Afia Atakora was born in the United Kingdom and raised in New Jersey. She graduated from New York University and has an MFA from Columbia University, where she was the recipient of the De Alba Fellowship. Her fiction has been nominated for a Pushcart Prize and she was a finalist for the Hurston/Wright Award for college writers. *Conjure Women* is her first novel.

The employees of Thorndike Press hope you have enjoyed this Large Print book. All our Thorndike, Wheeler, and Kennebec Large Print titles are designed for easy reading, and all our books are made to last. Other Thorndike Press Large Print books are available at your library, through selected bookstores, or directly from us.

For information about titles, please call:
(800) 223-1244

or visit our website at:
gale.com/thorndike

To share your comments, please write:
Publisher
Thorndike Press
10 Water St., Suite 310
Waterville, ME 04901

Striking a Balance

Striking a Balance

Making National
Economic Policy

*

ALBERT REES

THE UNIVERSITY OF CHICAGO PRESS

Chicago and London

ALBERT REES is president of the Alfred P. Sloan Foundation and has been professor of economics at Princeton University and the University of Chicago. He is a former director of the Council on Wage and Price Stability and a former staff member of the Council of Economic Advisers.

THE UNIVERSITY OF CHICAGO PRESS, CHICAGO 60637
THE UNIVERSITY OF CHICAGO PRESS, LTD., LONDON

91 90 89 88 87 86 85 84   1 2 3 4 5

Library of Congress Cataloging in Publication Data

Rees, Albert, 1921–
   Striking a balance.

   Includes index.
   1. Economic policy.   2. United States—Economic policy.   I. Title.
HD75.R43   1983   338.973   83-17881
ISBN 0-226-70707-5

* CONTENTS *

Preface

SOME PARTS of this book reflect my experience in Washington as a staff member at the Council of Economic Advisers (1954–55), a public member of the Construction Industry Stabilization Committee (1971–73), and director of the Council on Wage and Price Stability (1974–75), as well as membership on several panels to review federal economic statistics. The book was written while I was president of the Alfred P. Sloan Foundation. The views expressed, however, are my own and not those of the staff or trustees of the foundation.

I am indebted to Dr. Sharon Smith, Dean Harry Weiner, and three readers for the University of Chicago Press for helpful suggestions, and to Mrs. Evelyn Hunt for her careful typing of the manuscript.

✳
Introduction

MAKING NATIONAL ECONOMIC POLICY means facing a never-ending procession of hard choices among conflicting objectives. Unlike military policy, where the only goal is to win, or business policy, where the overriding goal of the firm is to increase profits, economic policy involves much more than finding the best path to a clear objective. There are many important objectives of policy, including full employment, stable prices, the growth of output, and greater equality in the distribution of income. These diverse goals are related to one another by a complicated and largely unknown system of trade-offs, such that one can advance toward one objective only by sacrificing progress toward others. Many people would like to understand how choices are made among these policy goals and what instruments are available for attaining them, but they are not prepared to master the intricacies of economic theory in order to do so.

I believe that the key issues of economic policy can be understood without the need for elaborate theory, higher mathematics, or sophisticated statistics. This book seeks to contribute to an understanding of these issues. Economic theory underlies it all, but the book has been structured around policies rather than theory and the theory is kept as unobtrusive as possible. The first part of the book sets forth the major objectives of national economic policy in the United States since World War II, the second part deals with the major policy instruments used to pursue these objectives, and the third discusses how policy is (or is not) coordinated.

Not all aspects of economic policy will be considered. Little attention will be devoted to policies concerned with particular industries or localities. The focus is on the economic policies of the federal government, though state and local economic policy are discussed where they are most relevant. In economists' jargon, the main concern of this book is macroeconomic policy, or policy influencing the general level of prices, employment, and economic activity. The term "macroeconomic policy" is used in contrast to "microeconomic policy," which refers to policies affecting particular markets, such as agricultural price supports or minimum wages. The policymaker, however, is not concerned with the neat textbook distinction between macro and micro—the whole and its parts. To him economic policy is a seamless web. Trying to influence the broad aggregates of prices or employment always has intended or unintended consequences for particular smaller activities, and policies designed to affect particular markets have consequences for the aggregates. In tracing these consequences, we shall not hesitate to cross the textbook boundaries between macro- and microeconomics, nor to cross the larger boundary between economics and politics.

For that reason, this is a book about political economy. The term "political economy" was once the name of the discipline now called economics, the adjective serving to distinguish it from "domestic economy," or the management of the household. Today, the old term connotes the borderland between economics and public affairs, and it is this borderland we seek to map.

I
The Goals of Policy
*

* ONE *
Full Employment

THE UNITED STATES EMERGED from World War II still bearing
the fresh scars of the Great Depression. Every adult had vivid
memories of soup kitchens and breadlines, of shantytowns in the
parks, and of the unemployed selling apples on street corners.
The economic policy of the postwar years was shaped by the bitter
experiences of the 1930s.

It is estimated that in 1933 almost 13 million workers were
unemployed—one of every four members of the labor force. In
the early years of the depression, the unemployed had no regular
means of support. There was no unemployment insurance, no
welfare, no food stamps—only savings, which were soon exhausted, and the meager resources of private charity, which were
soon overwhelmed. Many workers fortunate enough to keep
their jobs had their hours cut or their wages reduced.

Unemployment was only one aspect of a much wider distress.
The prices of farm products fell sharply. The price of wheat, for
example, fell from $1.04 a bushel in 1929 to $.38 a bushel in 1932.
Farmers could not meet their mortgage payments; many mortgages were foreclosed and some farmers were dispossessed.
Small businesses went bankrupt. Banks failed, with heavy losses
to their depositors, who had no deposit insurance. Factories stood
idle or worked at far less than capacity. The real Gross National
Product, the nation's total output of goods and services measured
in constant 1972 dollars, dropped from $315 billion in 1929 to
$222 billion in 1933, a drop of almost one-third.

After Franklin D. Roosevelt took office in 1933, the programs
of the New Deal began to grapple with some of the problems
created by the Depression. Federal deposit insurance restored
faith in banks. Unemployment insurance, old-age assistance, and
emergency public employment programs provided income for
some of the unemployed and the poor. The Social Security system was initiated. Public works programs constructed new post
offices, libraries, and dams for power and irrigation.

Despite the bold programs of the New Deal, only the outbreak
of war in Europe sufficed to bring the unemployment rate down
to more reasonable levels as the United States rearmed and supplied the Allies. The first year in which the unemployment rate

3

fell below 10 percent was 1941. By 1944, with the United States at war, the unemployment rate was only 1.2 percent.

Since only war had reduced unemployment, there were widespread fears that a severe new depression would start as soon as the war ended. These fears, shared by economists and politicians, proved of course to be unfounded. The first postwar recession did not come until 1949 and was very mild.

In the anxious and uncertain atmosphere that prevailed just after the end of the war, maintaining full employment was the overriding objective of national economic policy. This objective was embodied in the Employment Act of 1946, legislation that set forth postwar economic goals and created the Council of Economic Advisers and the Joint Economic Committee of the Congress.

The concept of full employment was brand new in 1946. It had first received wide attention in 1945 with the publication of Sir William H. Beveridge's *Full Employment in a Free Society*.[1] Beveridge, a distinguished British economist, defined full employment as "having always more vacant jobs than unemployed men." This definition alarmed conservatives. It implied that wages would always be bid up in the market by employers who were short of labor, and that union negotiators would always bargain in an atmosphere favorable to their claims for more pay. Rising pay would lead in turn to rising prices, that is, inflation. For these reasons, Congress avoided the term "full employment" in the 1946 legislation. Instead, the policy objective stated in the law was "to promote maximum employment, production, and purchasing power" and to create "conditions under which there will be afforded useful employment opportunities, including self-employment, for those able, willing, and seeking work."[2]

DEFINING FULL EMPLOYMENT

The Employment Act of 1946 made "maximum employment" an objective of national economic policy without defining it. The precise goal was to remain undefined for many years. In practice, people thought of trying to keep the unemployment rate at a minimum, and it was generally recognized that this minimum could not be zero. Even under Beveridge's definition of always having more vacant jobs than unemployed workers, some work-

1. New York: W. W. Norton and Co.
2. Public Law 79-304, declaration of policy, section 2.

4

ers would be looking for work at any given time because they had just lost a job and had not yet found a new one, or because they had just entered the labor force. The unemployment associated with job turnover and labor force entry is known as "frictional unemployment." It is far easier, however, to state the concept of frictional unemployment than it is to measure it.

During the Great Depression, the United States had no current system of measuring unemployment. Various unofficial measures were devised by manipulating data from the 1930 census, demographic statistics, and the movement of payroll employment, but these unofficial estimates diverged widely depending on the methods of estimation and the viewpoint of the estimator.

In 1940, a new system of measurement called the Monthly Survey of the Labor Force (now the Current Population Survey) was put in place by the Bureau of the Census. This survey measured employment and unemployment through monthly interviews with a carefully constructed national sample of households. A person was counted as unemployed if he did not work at all in the reference week of the survey and was looking for work, or if he was on an indefinite layoff.[3] The methods and definitions of this survey have now been used for more than forty years with only modest changes, though with substantial expansion of the sample of households. Chart 1 shows the movement of unemployment as a percentage of the civilian labor force for the years 1947–82.

The household survey made it possible for the news media to report the unemployment rate each month. Substantial changes in the unemployment rate (especially increases) became front page news and attracted wide attention. Unlike Great Britain, the United States has never had regular national statistics on unfilled job vacancies. Because the American measurement system did not indicate the balance between jobseekers and job openings, it did not make clear whether the current level of unemployment was merely frictional or represented a net shortage of jobs—a condition that economists call "demand deficiency" unemployment.

As the new unemployment measure continued in use, one could begin to look back on the statistical series and see how the current unemployment rate compared with those of past periods. A rate well above past minima was taken as evidence of a reces-

3. For further explanation of the definitions used, see the Appendix to this chapter.

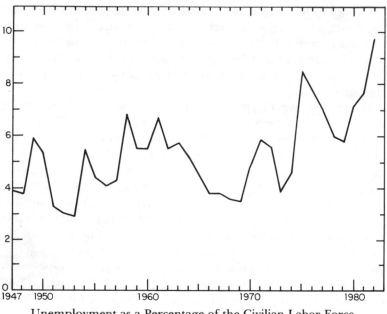

Unemployment as a Percentage of the Civilian Labor Force,
1947–1982

sion, or a lapse from full employment. High unemployment and other signs of recession usually led the government to adopt policies that would stimulate employment, such as tax cuts or new expenditure programs.

In 1962 the federal government gave its first quasi-official definition of full employment. The Economic Report of the President for January 1962 (the first report of the Kennedy administration) set an unemployment rate of 4 percent as a "reasonable and prudent full employment target for stabilization policy." The target rate of 4 percent was not the lowest rate recorded from 1946 to 1961; unemployment had been in the neighborhood of 3 percent for three years, 1951–53, during the Korean War. The Council of Economic Advisers argued from the historical record that 4 percent was the lowest rate at which product and labor markets would not be excessively tight, producing upward pressure on wages and prices.

In 1978, a numerical full-employment target was enacted into law with the passage of the Humphrey-Hawkins Full Employment and Balanced Growth Act. Its interim target was the same 4 percent rate first set administratively in 1962. This act also set an interim target for the inflation rate of 3 percent. Both targets now seem very difficult to achieve, and almost impossible to achieve simultaneously. The unrealistic goals embodied in the Humphrey-Hawkins Act have had little or no practical effect on policy.

As can be seen on chart 1, there has been a pronounced upward trend in the unemployment rate during the period since World War II. Rates below 4 percent, first reached during the Korean War, were reached again during the Vietnam War (1965–68) and for the year 1973. In the most recent economic recovery (1975–79), the lowest unemployment rate reached was 5.8 percent. The peak annual rate during the recession of 1975 was 8.5 percent, and in 1982 the rate was 9.7 percent. Both figures set new highs for the postwar period. Some of the factors contributing to the upward trend of unemployment are discussed below.

WHAT DETERMINES THE FULL EMPLOYMENT LEVEL?

In setting its target unemployment rate in 1962, the Council of Economic Advisers was careful to choose one at which, in its judgment, the number of workers employers wanted to employ would not exceed the number willing to work, thus departing from the concept of full employment originally advanced by Beveridge. The implicit aim of the council was to have a rough balance between these numbers. But the frictional rate of unemployment represented by such a balance does not stay constant through time. Although 4 percent may have represented a rough balance in 1962 as the Kennedy administration believed, it did not necessarily still represent one in 1978, when the Humphrey-Hawkins Act was passed.

Two factors determine the level of frictional unemployment. The first is the number of people who enter the labor force or quit their jobs to seek new ones in a given period. The second is the average length of time it takes these workers to find acceptable new jobs, that is, the duration of job search. As business conditions improve during an economic recovery and as labor markets tighten, voluntary quit rates rise and the size of the labor force increases. In other words, there are more job seekers in good times than in bad. This effect, however, is more than offset by a drop in the average duration of job search. In good times, many job changers and new entrants to the labor force find a job with no period of unemployment at all. They already have jobs lined up when they enter the labor force or when they quit their previous jobs.

Apart from business conditions, some less transient factors influence the frictional unemployment rate. One is the demographic composition of the labor force. In general, women and teenagers enter and leave employment more frequently and characteristically have higher unemployment rates than adult men. Teenagers are especially prone to quit jobs. Some leave when they return to school from vacations, but even those no longer in school change jobs frequently because they are still exploring different kinds of work and are not yet responsible for supporting a family.

Some effects of demographic shifts in the composition of the labor force can be seen by examining historical unemployment statistics. The unemployment rate for all workers was almost the same in 1963 and in 1979: 5.7 percent in the earlier year and 5.8 percent in the later. Yet the unemployment rate for men twenty years of age and over was 4.5 percent in 1963 and 4.1 percent in 1979—a larger difference in the opposite direction. The rate for teenagers had also fallen. Markets for two major types of labor were somewhat tighter in 1979 than they had been in 1963, yet the rising proportion of women and teenagers in the labor force meant a slightly higher overall unemployment rate.

The second major determinant of the level of frictional unemployment, as suggested earlier, is how long an unemployed worker looks for work before he accepts a new job. Even in bad times, there are always some jobs available. Many demand specialized training or experience that most job seekers do not have. Others are unskilled jobs that may stay vacant because of low wages, disagreeable working conditions, remote location, or undesirable hours of work. Whether an experienced job seeker will accept a job less desirable than his previous one depends in part on his alternative sources of income. One earner in a two-earner family will be more selective if the other earner is still employed, for the family still has a regular income. Adequate unemployment insurance and the availability of welfare payments or food stamps will also prolong the search process. Indeed, one of the original purposes of unemployment insurance was to permit the unemployed to look for work that utilized their skills, rather than being compelled by need to take the first job of any kind that came along. In short, the more humane a society, and the more adequately it provides for the welfare of those without work, the higher its frictional unemployment rate is likely to be. When new income-support programs, such as food stamps, are introduced or existing programs are liberalized, some rise in the unemployment rate will probably result.

This leads us to ask whether full employment is really a goal in its own right. On one hand, if jobs are merely a means of earning pay, providing income from other sources meets the same goal. If, on the other hand, income earned by the sweat of one's brow or the exercise of one's skills is more meaningful and more rewarding than income from transfer payments, the two goals are not the same. Moreover, employed workers produce output and unemployed workers do not. Money paid in such transfer payments as unemployment insurance or food stamps comes from taxes on workers and employers, and these taxes tend to diminish the incentives of taxpayers to produce. This reasoning suggests that full employment is indeed a meaningful goal, distinct from maintaining incomes.

Both the rise over time in the proportion of women and teenagers in the labor force and the increase in transfer payments to the unemployed have tended to raise the frictional unemployment rate. Some recent statistical studies suggest that the level of unemployment at which labor markets are in balance was about 6 percent in 1982. If this is correct, the old target of 4 percent unemployment now represents a situation in which there are substantially more job vacancies than job seekers, and reaching this target would cause substantial upward pressure on wages and prices.

FULL EMPLOYMENT AND THE PRICE LEVEL

If reaching full employment did not involve the sacrifice of other policy objectives, how we defined full employment would not matter. One could safely err in the direction of setting the target rate of unemployment very low and nevertheless pursue this goal vigorously. But this is not the case. Let us examine the trade-offs involved in more detail.

Setting and reaching a full-employment target so low that employers want to use more labor than workers want to supply—that is, creating excess demand for labor—will make wages rise more rapidly than usual. Employers will bid wages up as they seek to recruit new workers, and unions will be encouraged to take a tougher stance in collective bargaining, which leads to higher negotiated wage rates. But this is not the end of the matter. If wages rise faster than average productivity (output per worker hour), labor costs per unit of output will rise. Since labor costs are a large part of total costs (about three-fourths of all costs for the American economy as a whole), total costs per unit of output will also rise, putting upward pressure on prices. This process is often called "the wage-price spiral," a term that suggests that the higher prices in turn may encourage higher wage demands. Nor is this the only route by which prices are affected. Because labor is hired to produce products and services, an excess demand for labor (a labor shortage) also creates an excess demand for some final products and services. Shortages of products at current prices encourage producers to increase their prices even faster than their costs are rising. Profit margins will thus widen as buyers compete for their share of products in short supply.

Beveridge's work on full employment was part of the "Keynesian revolution" that followed the publication of John Maynard Keynes's *General Theory*.[4] The early expositors of Keynes thought of full employment as a sharp boundary between two possible states of the economy. When the economy was in the first state, less than full employment, increasing aggregate demand (the total demand for all goods and services) would put unemployment workers back to work without raising prices. When the economy was in the second state, in which demand exceeded the full-employment level, further increases in aggregate demand would make prices rise rapidly, but employment could not increase because labor was already fully used. If policymakers could define the full-employment target properly and regulate their policies well enough to stay precisely at it, they would attain two policy goals at once. Unemployment would be at an irreducible minimum, but the price level would nevertheless be stable.

It was soon realized that this view is much too simple. An economy moving from depression toward full employment would not reach its capacity simultaneously in all sectors. Shortages of plant capacity or labor might appear in some industries or geographical areas in which demand was especially strong while there was still excess capacity and unemployment in other industries or areas. Because of such bottlenecks, as they were called, the prices of some products would start to rise while unemployment in the

---

4. *The General Theory of Employment, Interest, and Money* (London: Macmillan, 1936).

aggregate was still above frictional levels. In short, the full-employment target was not a sharp boundary, but a broader region. Where in this region the policymaker wanted the economy to be depended on his own preferences—the relative priorities he attached to the conflicting goals of reducing unemployment and minimizing inflation.

Some years later, the relationship between wage increases and unemployment was estimated by A. W. Phillips and became known as the Phillips curve.[5] Phillips's work suggested that the relationship was a stable function over long periods. Others were quick to point out that this implied a stable policy trade-off between unemployment and inflation in the long run. This view has always been controversial and no longer has much support because it has been undermined by recent evidence. There is little dispute, however, over the proposition that in the short run, policies that create very low rates of unemployment contribute to inflation and policies that tolerate higher rates of unemployment will tend to restrain inflation. Whether the policies that restrain inflation by reducing aggregate demand do so at an acceptable social cost is a question of what are appropriate social values.

GAINERS FROM FULL EMPLOYMENT

Reaching any policy objective is usually more important to some groups in society than to others, and this is certainly true of reaching full employment. In one sense, full employment benefits everyone, since it makes possible a larger total output than is produced during depressions or recessions. There are particular groups, however, whose gains are largest and who are the strongest advocates of vigorous full-employment policies.

The demand-deficiency unemployment associated with depressions and recessions falls most heavily on blue-collar workers in construction, mining, transportation, and industries manufacturing durable goods such as steel and automobiles. These are the industries most affected by cyclical fluctuations in demand. Although some white-collar workers in these industries are also laid off when demand slackens, the layoffs are much larger relative to employment for blue-collar workers. Blue-collar workers in cycli-

5. A. W. Phillips, "The Relation between Unemployment and the Rate of Change of Wages in the United Kingdom, 1861–1957," *Economica*, n.s. 25 (November 1958).

cal industries are heavily unionized, and unions are strong advocates of full employment policies. Black and Hispanic workers are heavily represented in the occupations and industries that experience the most demand-deficiency unemployment, and leaders of the black and Hispanic communities have also been vigorous advocates of full employment.

Most layoffs are made in reverse order of seniority, so that young workers and new entrants to the labor force are particularly vulnerable to increases in the unemployment rate, while senior workers have a greater measure of job protection. Young workers, however, do not have political organizations that represent their special interests. It should also be noted that when older workers do lose their jobs, it often takes them a very long time to find new ones.

The managers and stockholders of companies in industries sensitive to the business cycle, such as steel and automobiles, are also substantial losers from recessions. Management salaries and bonuses may be cut, and dividends may be reduced or eliminated. Nevertheless, business support for full-employment policies has been far weaker than that of unions. The business community is seriously concerned about inflation, and this tempers the expansionist views of business leaders, even those with the most to lose from recessions.

As the inflation rate climbed during the 1970s, the primacy of full employment as a policy objective receded. It is still an important goal, but many more political leaders and a much wider segment of the public would now argue that fighting inflation is more important. Some policymakers look harder for new ways to pursue both goals at the same time and offer ingenious schemes designed to do so.

Appendix MEASURING UNEMPLOYMENT

The monthly Current Population Survey surveys 56,000 occupied dwelling units every month and obtains interviews (in person or by phone) with respondents from about 53,500 households. The units surveyed come from a large number of geographical areas chosen to be representative of the entire United States.

The interviews obtain information on the labor force status of all members of the household sixteen years of age and over. This information refers to a particular week (the reference week), which is the week including the twelfth day of the month.

A person is counted as employed if he did any work at all as a paid employee during the reference week, or if he worked fifteen hours or more as an unpaid worker in a business or on a farm owned by a member of his family. Hours of work are collected for those employed. A person is counted as unemployed if he did not work during the reference week, was available for work, and had made specific efforts to find work during the preceding four weeks. People on layoff from jobs or waiting to report to a new job within thirty days are also counted as unemployed. The sum of the employed and the unemployed is the civilian labor force. Those who are neither employed or unemployed are counted as out of the labor force.

The people counted in the Current Population Survey are classified by age, sex, race, and relationship to other members of the household. Employment, unemployment, and labor-force data are therefore available by age, sex, race, and marital status.

The definitions used to measure employment and unemployment can be criticized from various perspectives. Critics who believe that unemployment is underestimated point out that someone who works only a few hours during the survey week may want to work more, but cannot find more work, and may therefore be partially unemployed. They also point out that some of those counted as out of the labor force would like to work, but have not been actively seeking work because they believe that none is available. (Such attitudes are much more difficult to measure without bias than actual activity.) People who hold such beliefs are counted in a separate measure called "discouraged workers."

Critics who believe that unemployment is overcounted point out that "making specific efforts to find work" as the term is used in the Current Population Survey includes being registered with the public employment service. Such registration is a condition of receiving unemployment insurance and some other kinds of transfer payments. Some of those registered may be doing nothing else to find work, and in this sense, they are not actively seeking employment.

Changes in the definition of unemployment can have substantial effects on the measured level. The measures generated by different definitions, however, tend to move in parallel over the course of an economic cycle and thus give much the same signals to policymakers about changes in the state of the economy.

Before 1983, the unemployment rate was reported as a percentage of the civilian labor force, excluding the armed forces. Beginning in 1983, it is also reported as a percentage of the total labor force, which includes the resident armed forces (those not stationed outside the United States). This larger base lowers the reported unemployment rate by 0.1 or 0.2 percent.

Unemployment data are also available from the administrative records of the unemployment insurance system. These are less widely used than the household survey data because more than half of the unemployed do not receive unemployment insurance. The data can nevertheless be useful in providing early warning of changes in unemployment because some of them are reported weekly.

Data on employment in nonagricultural industries are also collected by the Bureau of Labor Statistics from employer payroll records. These data provide industry and geographical detail not available from the household sample and enable policymakers to see just where in the economy employment is expanding and contracting.

* TWO *
Stable Prices

IN A FREE MARKET ECONOMY, the prices of individual products and services change frequently. The prices of some products, such as computers, fall because rapid technological progress reduces the cost of making them. The price of wheat or soybeans may fall because there is a bumper crop. Some prices rise because of increases in the demand for the product,[1] or because of rising costs of labor and materials that cannot be offset by technological progress. These fluctuations or trends in individual prices serve an important social purpose: they direct scarce resources to their most important uses by encouraging producers to furnish the products and services that consumers value most and by inducing consumers to conserve the products that are in short supply. The stability of particular prices has never in itself been an objective of national economic policy.

Serious problems arise when the upward and downward movements of individual prices are not roughly offsetting and the general level of prices rises or falls persistently. The general level of prices is measured by changes in a broad index of prices of final goods and services, such as the Consumer Price Index or the Gross National Product deflator.[2] A sustained rise in the general level of prices is, of course, inflation; a sustained fall is deflation. Deflation was a serious policy problem in the last third of the nineteenth century (the distress it caused to farmers and workers gave rise to the free-silver movement and William Jennings Bryan's famous "Cross of Gold" speech). It has seldom been a problem in the twentieth century, although consumer prices fell almost 25 percent from 1929 to 1933. Inflation, as we all know, has become a major problem since World War II.

Charts 2 and 3 show the movement of the Consumer Price Index (CPI) since 1947.[3] Chart 2 presents annual averages of the

1. Street vendors in New York City raise the price of umbrellas when it starts to rain hard.
2. We specify an index of prices of *final* goods and services because rises in the prices of raw materials and in manufacturers or wholesale prices are sometimes offset by decreases in the cost of further processing or distribution.
3. For further explanation of the construction of the Consumer Price Index, see the Appendix to this chapter.

15

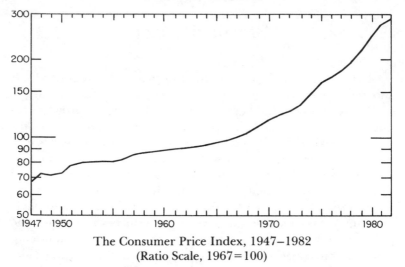

The Consumer Price Index, 1947–1982
(Ratio Scale, 1967=100)

absolute level of the index; chart 3, the percentage changes in each year (December to December).

The charts demonstrate clearly the acceleration of inflation. The two years in which prices fell, 1949 and 1954, both came early in the period and were both recession years. The CPI rose by more than 5 percent in only two of the years before 1968: 1950 and 1951, at the start of the Korean War. In contrast, the index has risen by less than 5 percent in only three of the years since 1968; in three years (1974, 1979, and 1980) it rose by more than 12 percent.

WHY INFLATION IS A PROBLEM

It is immediately apparent why unemployment is a problem—the waste of resources and hardship it creates require no explanation. It is not quite so apparent why inflation is a problem.

If all prices in the economy doubled overnight, nothing of consequence would be changed. Everything would go on exactly as before, except that all prices would now be multiplied by two. There would be some minor costs of printing new menus and remarking price tags, but these costs would not have a substantial or lasting effect on the economy.

The key word in the preceding paragraph is "all". If this word is not taken in the most literal possible sense, then the conclusions

16

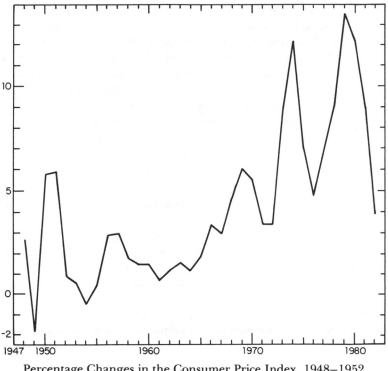

Percentage Changes in the Consumer Price Index, 1948–1952
(December to December)

of the paragraph are wrong. "All prices" in this context must include wages, salaries, and all other income payments. Among the prices that must double are the payments specified in all contracts to pay future amounts of money, such as leases and loans; all dollar amounts stated in tax laws, such as exemptions and tax rate brackets; and the amounts of all pension and social security benefits. If these stringent conditions are not met, then doubling the prices of products and services currently produced wỏuld have very grave consequences indeed. Of course, these conditions are *not* met in real world inflations.

The classic case of gains and losses created by inflation or deflation involves the relation between debtors and creditors. Suppose that Jones borrows $100 from Smith, which he agrees to repay in ten years. If over those ten years the price level doubles, then the $100 Smith receives when the loan is repaid has only as much purchasing power as $50 had when the loan was made. The *real* value of the repayment (its value in dollars of constant purchasing power) has been cut in half. Moreover, if the loan called for periodic interest payments, the real value of the interest Smith received would also have been declining over the life of the loan.

Many loans, especially mortgage loans, are made by thrift institutions such as savings and loan associations from savings deposited with them. This has been the traditional channel through which people of modest income invest their savings, because they know little or nothing about investing in real estate or other physical assets, and the amounts they save are too small for such investments. If the value of savings in thrift institutions is eroded by inflation, moderate-income households will have less incentive to save. The country may then consume a larger fraction of its total income, and invest less in real capital to provide for the future.

The ultimate borrower of these savings is the homeowner who gets a fixed-interest mortgage. His real debt burden is reduced by inflation because he pays back interest and principal in depreciated dollars. Such gains to borrowers induce additional investment in housing.

By 1981, inflation had forced many savings and loan associations and mutual savings banks to pay savers more interest on their deposits than the associations were earning on old mortgages. A number of thrift institutions became insolvent and had to be merged with other institutions. Mortgage lenders also began to change the form of their loans to eliminate fixed interest rates and provide for rate changes during the life of the loan.

Rental payments under long-term leases and payments of pension benefits stated in dollar amounts decline in real value with inflation in just the same way that interest payments do. The effect on private pensions can be especially severe. A pensioner who retired at sixty-five in 1960 on what appeared to be an adequate pension would, if he lived to 1980, have found the purchasing power of his pension to be less than half what it was when he retired. This might be wholly inadequate to meet his needs.

Inflation also moves taxpayers who pay personal income taxes into higher tax brackets even when their real income has not increased. Inflation therefore raises the real tax revenues of the government and correspondingly lowers the real after-tax income of taxpayers. This so-called bracket creep can reduce the incentives of taxpayers to work and to invest or can induce them not to report their full or true income. From time to time, Congress has corrected this bracket creep through tax reductions.

18

Most of the adverse consequences of inflation would disappear if inflation could be perfectly anticipated. For example, if a potential lender knew for certain when he made a loan that prices were going to rise at 10 percent per year over the period of the loan, he would adjust the terms of the loan accordingly. Specifically, he would demand higher interest rates that would compensate him for the loss of real value of the payments he was to receive. This means that it is *unanticipated* inflation, rather than simply inflation itself, that causes windfall gains and losses to borrowers and lenders and distorts incentives.

Interest rates that are not regulated by the government do indeed fluctuate with anticipations of inflation, rising when the rate of inflation is expected to rise and declining when inflation is expected to subside. Neither borrowers nor lenders, however, can generally anticipate inflation accurately, so that deviations of actual from expected inflation still cause windfall gains and losses despite the adjustments in market interest rates.

The argument that only unanticipated inflation is harmful suggests that any steady rate of change in the general level of prices would be as good a target for economic policy as price stability. So long as the rate of change of prices did not fluctuate, all expectations and long-term contracts would eventually adjust to it. But it is not quite true that any perfectly steady rate of change will do as well as no change at all. A positive rate of inflation, even a steady one, erodes the real value of money (currency and noninterest-bearing bank deposits) held by the public and is therefore a hidden tax on the holders of money. Steady inflation also erodes the value of interest-bearing deposits if the rate of interest that can be paid by banks is limited by law to a rate below the rate of inflation. This erosion of the real value of money will induce people to hold less money than they would hold with stable prices, and to hold less convenient assets instead.

It can also be argued that zero is inherently a very special number, and that it therefore has special appeal as a policy target. A target rate of inflation of, say, 3 percent seems arbitrary by comparison. A less mystical argument for a zero inflation target points out that not all participants in the economy are equally sophisticated. On one hand, the terms of large transactions extending over several years, such as mortgages and leases made by knowledgeable borrowers and lenders or lessors and lessees, could reasonably be expected to adjust to any long-standing steady rate of inflation. On the other hand, the terms of many

19

smaller transactions involving future payments, to which less sophisticated savers or tenants were a party, might not take even a
perfectly steady rate of inflation properly into account.

INDEXATION

If the rate of inflation cannot be anticipated, it is still possible to
write long-term contracts that protect the parties against it. These
contracts provide for payments whose amount is adjusted peri-
odically according to changes in some specified price index. This
procedure in its most general form is called "indexation."

The most familiar kind of indexation in the United States is the
use of cost-of-living-adjustment clauses (COLAs), also known as
escalator clauses, in collective bargaining agreements between
unions and employers extending over more than one year. Such
clauses provide for periodic changes in wages in response to
changes in the Consumer Price Index. Social Security payments
and federal government pensions are also indexed to the CPI.

Canada has indexed the exemptions and brackets in its personal income tax to its Consumer Price Index. In the tax legislation of
1981, the United States provided for indexation of personal income taxes beginning in 1985. Some countries experiencing
rapid inflation have issued index bonds, which use a price index
to adjust the amount of interest payments and the value of the
bond at redemption.

If indexation can mitigate most of the harmful effects of inflation, then price stability need not be an important policy objective. However, the relief provided by indexation is never complete in scope; only some long-term agreements are indexed. The
administrative costs may be excessive for agreements that have
short lives or that do not involve substantial sums. The risks of
indexing to one party to a long-term agreement may also be
considered excessive. For example, private employers have seldom agreed to index their pension obligations, since to do so
would expose them to an open-ended liability.

Some opponents of indexation argue against it on the more
general grounds that if the costs of inflation are reduced, there
will be less political resistance to policies that permit or cause
inflation. Without such resistance, the rate of inflation could accelerate without limit. When inflation becomes very rapid, even
indexation may be insufficient to prevent windfall gains and
losses. Because the adjustments provided for in indexed agree-

ments take place only at predetermined times and lag behind actual price changes, they would not fully compensate the receivers of payments for very rapid rises in the price level.

LOSERS FROM INFLATION

We have already suggested who some of the losers from unanticipated inflation are—creditors, pensioners, and landlords with long-term leases. These are perhaps the most obvious cases, but there are others. Salaried workers, whose salaries are usually adjusted only once a year, may be more likely to lose real income than wage earners, more of whom receive cost-of-living adjustments or other more frequent wage changes. The size of annual salary increases, however, can be made larger to anticipate inflation during the year. Companies that cannot adjust prices without the permission of regulatory authorities (for example, telephone companies or electric utilities) suffer greatly from the combination of inflation and regulatory lag.

A more difficult question concerns the effect of inflation on unregulated business. American tax law bases depreciation allowances on the historical cost of depreciable assets. When inflation raises the prices of new plant and equipment, the accumulated depreciation allowances charged as expense against gross income will be insufficient to pay for the replacement of existing plant and equipment when it wears out. For this reason, business argues that in time of inflation it is reporting too little depreciation expense in its tax returns, and correspondingly, it is reporting fictitious profits. Since these fictitious profits are taxed under present tax laws, inflation transfers resources from business to government.

The preceding argument is sound as far as it goes, but incomplete. Businesses in general are net debtors to the rest of the economy. Like other debtors, they gain from unanticipated inflation because the real value of their debts and of the interest paid on these debts declines when prices rise more than expected. Since the depreciable assets of most businesses are larger than their long-term debts, it seems probable that their inflation losses through inadequate depreciation allowances exceed their inflation gains from reduced real debt, and that therefore most businesses are indeed net losers from inflation; but the loss is substantially smaller than the depreciation argument alone would suggest.

ACCELERATING INFLATION

The last case we shall consider for making price stability a major goal of economic policy argues that inflation, once accepted, tends to accelerate. We have seen that in the short run there is a trade-off between full employment and inflation. Policies that increase aggregate demand make labor and product markets tighter and therefore raise wages and prices. If prices are already rising even when unemployment is high, as has been true in recent recessions, then the use of vigorous policies to reach full employment could raise the rate of inflation despite unused capacity.

What may be needed to restore full employment, it is argued, is not merely inflation, but accelerating inflation. An increase in the rate of inflation would temporarily raise final prices faster than costs, widening profit margins and inducing employers to expand output and employment. A sudden injection of aggregate demand by the government could produce this outcome. The restraining influence of excess capacity in moderating price increases might be offset by the expectation that stimulatory policy would continue into the later stages of an economic recovery.

Those who advance this argument sometimes make the analogy to an addictive drug, where larger and larger dosages are needed to produce the same effect. The analogy may be overdrawn, but it is not without support from the historical record. The peak rates of inflation at times of full employment have tended to rise throughout the postwar period, and the record thus reinforces the case for a goal of total abstinence. The argument against pursuing this goal is that we simply do not yet know how to get to a state of zero inflation, starting from a position of rapidly rising prices, without passing through a long period of less than full employment. Some policymakers are not prepared to pay this cost.

Appendix MEASURING PRICE CHANGES

The most widely used measure of price changes in the American economy is the Consumer Price Index compiled by the Bureau of Labor Statistics. In the preparation of this index, information is collected on rents from 18,000 tenants, on property taxes from 18,000 housing units, and on the prices of other goods and services from 24,000 retail establishments. The data are collected in eighty-five urban areas.

The price series are weighted according to the expenditure patterns of a sample of urban families in 1972–73. As of December 1981, 46 percent of the total weight was for housing, including fuel, utilities, home furnishing, taxes, financing, and insurance. Transportation accounted for 19 percent of the weight, food and beverages for almost 18 percent, apparel and its upkeep for about 5 percent, and medical care for 5 percent. The great strength of the Consumer Price Index is that it is based on the prices of a large number of items from a large sample of retail outlets. The items are carefully specified to maintain comparability through time.

Until 1983 criticism of the Consumer Price Index focused primarily on its treatment of the cost of owner-occupied housing, which was questioned for two reasons. First, housing was heavily weighted in part because the purchase of a new house was treated in the expenditure survey as a consumption outlay. Critics argued that it should be considered for the most part as an investment, which would substantially lower the weight of home ownership in the index. Second, the price of mortgage interest was defined as the prevailing interest rate for new mortgages, not the average rate being paid under existing mortgages. This was unlike the treatment of rent, which was priced as the average rent paid under existing leases. This treatment of mortgage interest made the CPI highly sensitive to changes in long-term interest rates. A treatment parallel to that of rents, measuring the average amount paid on existing contracts, is more appropriate for an index used to escalate wage payments and social security benefits. Beginning in 1983, the Consumer Price Index treats changes in the price of owner-occupied housing by the movement of rents for similar rental housing.

In addition to the Consumer Price Index, several other general price indexes can be used as measures of inflation. One of these is the Producers Price Index (PPI), formerly known as the Wholesale Price Index. This measures the prices of commodities before they reach retail outlets. Separate indexes are available for raw materials, intermediate goods, and finished goods. The movement of the Producers Price Index is sometimes said to lead or predict the movement of the CPI, but it does so only imperfectly. Unlike the CPI, the PPI includes the prices of investment goods and excludes the prices of consumer services.

A third broad price index is the Gross National Product deflator, which is used to convert the measure of total output (GNP) from current to constant dollars. It is composed largely of components of the CPI and PPI but is weighted by current weights instead of fixed weights. Until 1983 another major difference between the GNP deflator and the CPI was that the deflator has always priced the services of owner-occupied housing by the movements of rents for similar rental housing. For this reason, the portion of the GNP deflator that covers consumer expenditures (the Personal Consumption Expenditure deflator) was considered by many economists to be a better measure of consumer prices than the CPI. The general public, however, is not familiar with this measure.

There is a general tendency in periods of inflation for the PPI to rise more than the CPI at first, although the CPI may catch up later. The GNP deflator is generally the most sluggish of the three measures.

* THREE *
Growth and Efficiency

SINCE WORKERS ARE EMPLOYED to produce output, the policy goals of reaching full employment and increasing output might seem at first glance to be the same. In fact, they are quite different, as the following example shows. Imagine an isolated society with a constant population where all workers are fully employed producing consumer goods and services such as food, clothing, and medical care, and just enough capital goods (plant and equipment) to replace the existing capital stock with identical capital goods as it wears out.[1] No workers are employed in adding to the capital stock or improving its quality, nor in adding to the stock of useful scientific and technical knowledge. In this imaginary economy whose capital stock and methods of production are constant, real output per worker would not grow and the standard of living would never improve. One would have full employment without progress.

Such a stagnant economy would be unsatisfactory. People want to be a little better off tomorrow than they are today and want their children to be better off than they are. The growth of real output per worker also permits a society to help its least fortunate members improve their standard of living without having to make the more fortunate worse off. Economic progress thus allows us to achieve greater equality of real income among families and groups with a minimum of social conflict. Moreover, if the average productivity of labor (output per hour of work) is growing, workers can produce more output and still work fewer hours, so that each generation can enjoy more leisure than the last in the form of shorter work weeks, longer vacations, more holidays, or earlier retirement. Finally, from the point of view of a single country, economic growth makes it easier to strengthen national defense. In a stagnant economy, more guns mean less

---

1. Economists distinguish between stocks, which are quantities, and flows, which are quantities per period of time. Wealth, measured in dollars, is a stock, while income and output, measured in dollars per year, are flows. A bathtub provides a useful analogy. The amount of water in the tub, measured in gallons, is a stock. The amount coming into the tub from the faucet, measured in gallons per minute, is obviously a flow.

butter. In a growing economy, one can have both more guns and more butter.

In the United States, economic growth is generally measured by the growth of real Gross National Product. This is a measure of the total output of goods and services of the economy, including both the private and public sectors and both consumption and investment goods. The term "real," as always, indicates that the measure is expressed in dollars of constant purchasing power. The term "gross" indicates that no deduction is made for the depreciation of capital stock or for the depletion of natural resources. Thus when the production of machine tools is measured as part of GNP, no distinction is made between the machine tools that are net additions to the stock of equipment and those that replace obsolete or worn-out machine tools. Gross National Product, as distinguished from Gross Domestic Product (GDP), includes the earnings of American-owned assets located abroad. Most other countries use real GDP as their basic measure of output and growth, and the United States may eventually adopt this practice.

To measure the growth of labor productivity (output per hour of work), a somewhat different measure is used.[2] It is a ratio whose numerator is the Gross Domestic Product originating in the business sector, and whose denominator is the total hours of work done by all workers in this sector, including the self-employed and unpaid family workers. Government and nonprofit institutions are excluded because their output as measured in the national accounts is by definition equal to their labor input, so that measured productivity in these sectors cannot change. The output of services of owner-occupied dwelling units is also excluded from the productivity ratio because there is no measure of the labor input in this sector of the economy.

Chart 4 shows the percentage change in output per hour of work in the business sector from 1948 to 1982. The trend, although somewhat obscured by cyclical fluctuation, is clearly downward. Before 1968, output per hour grew between 2 and 4 percent in most years, and its growth was never negative. After 1968, the fluctuations are larger, but the growth is seldom above 2 percent and is negative in three years. This marked decelera-

---

2. For some purposes, economists use a broader measure of productivity that relates output to both labor and capital inputs. This is called "total factor productivity."

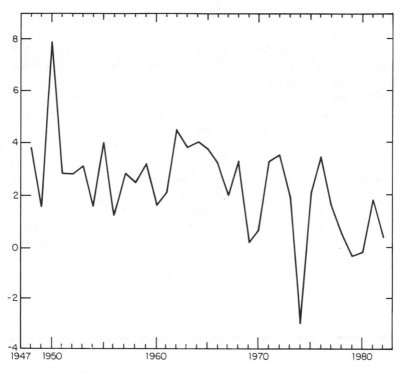

Percentage Change in Output per Hour, Business Sector, 1948-1952

tion in productivity growth has been of major concern to policymakers.

THE COSTS OF GROWTH

Until recently, it was taken for granted that growth and progress
were important goals for the economy. In the 1970s, however,
the legitimacy of these goals began to be questioned. Part of the
concern is over population growth—whether the United States
and the world are becoming overcrowded. Population policy,
including immigration policy, involves thorny questions that lie
outside economics; we shall not try to deal with them here. Rather
we take population growth as given and define the goal of economic policy as increasing the growth of output per person.

The growth of output per person, though it does not create
overcrowding, can also have adverse consequences. As we are
now painfully aware, uncontrolled economic activity (public or

27

private) can create noxious wastes, some of which are toxic or carcinogenic. The pollution of streams and ground water by sewage or chemical discharges kills aquatic life and makes water unfit to drink. Air pollution from motor vehicles and smoke-stacks creates damaging smog and acid rain. Uncontrolled log-ging, mining, and recreational activities can destroy our re-maining wilderness areas and wipe out endangered species of wildlife. Although such problems occur in static economies as well as growing ones, many environmentalists believe that they are exacerbated by economic growth. Economic growth also de-pletes our finite resources of fossil fuels and other minerals more rapidly. For such reasons, the goal of rising output per person could be rejected even in a country with no population growth.

The proponents of growth argue that the problems associated with past economic development can themselves be solved only by future growth, and particularly by the application of appropri-ate new technology. Examples come readily to mind of the possi-ble use of technical progress to improve rather than damage the environment and the quality of life. Improved modes of mass transit could relieve the congestion of city streets by automobiles. Investment in facilities for treating discharges of gaseous and liquid wastes can reduce air and water pollution to acceptable levels. Other kinds of innovation can save nonrenewable re-sources. For example, the use of communications satellites and glass optical fibers conserves copper that would be used in tele-phone cables. New technology in automobiles, such as the use of microprocessors to control the combustion process, promises to reduce both fuel consumption and air pollution.

These examples suggest that it is not economic growth or tech-nical change as such that have degraded the environment and depleted scarce resources, but rather our past failure to guide growth in the optimal directions. New mechanisms for control-ling industrial activity, such as the air and water pollution regula-tions of the Environmental Protection Agency are now in place. Some of these present serious problems of their own, but they have the potential to make economic growth compatible with other social goals.

It is very hard to specify how much growth an economy should try to achieve. If the undesirable by-products of growth, such as pollution, can be controlled, one is tempted to say the more growth the better. But economists point out that growth, like other goals, is achieved only at a cost, and the basic cost is present consumption. Growth can be accelerated by investing more in research and development, in the training of scientists and engineers, and in the construction of new plant and equipment that embodies the latest technology, but the resources used in these activities are then no longer available to produce goods and services to be consumed now. The question of how much growth to seek depends fundamentally on the willingness of the society to forego present consumption in order to permit higher living standards in future years.

Private investment in plant and equipment increases when the rate of return on such investment exceeds the cost to the investing company of acquiring new capital. This cost of capital ultimately represents the return needed to induce individual savers to use some of their income, not for consumption, but for investment in private securities that finance productive facilities.[3] In principle, the desirability of expanding public investment in such facilities as roads or harbors can be judged by similar rate-of-return criteria.

The problems of setting goals for investment and growth are complicated by the fact that the future return on any investment, and especially on investment in radically new technology, is unpredictable. Some very large investments in new technology, such as the development of supersonic civilian aircraft, have never recovered their costs.[4] Even in areas of technology where the rate of return on investment is generally high, there is enormous dispersion in the returns to individual projects and enterprises. This means that investors in these projects must be compensated not only for postponing consumption, but also for taking the risk of losing their investment.

Because it is so hard to know how much growth is possible, policymakers tend to set growth targets based on simple comparisons. They might seek to restore in the 1980s the rate of economic growth that was reached in the 1960s, or to have the rate of growth of output in the United States match that of West Ger-

3. The investor who saves $10,000 to invest in the common stock of a corporation that is expanding or re-equipping its plants could instead have spent this income on immediate consumption (say a vacation trip to Europe) or on investment in durable consumer goods for his own use, such as a new car. His inducement to buy common stock instead is that he hopes it will pay large dividends, or rise in value, or both.

4. The Concorde supersonic aircraft is a technical success because it transports passengers much faster than any subsonic aircraft. It is as economic failure because its high operating cost and small passenger capacity make it lose money even at premium fares.

many or Japan. It is unfortunately far easier to set such targets than to know how to reach them.

EFFICIENCY

Efficiency, or the elimination of waste, is often considered to be a goal in itself. It can also be viewed as one way of improving economic growth. A one-time increase in output is made possible whenever resources are used more effectively, and further growth can then proceed from a higher base.

Inefficiency takes many forms. The simplest is using more of a resource than one needs to do the job. Thus efficiency is increased if one can produce more machine parts and less scrap from the same quantity of metal stock, or if by modifying a production process one can reduce the proportion of defective parts produced.

More complicated forms of inefficiency arise when resources are not used in the most effective way because they are not allocated properly among different possible uses. This kind of allocative inefficiency can arise from distortions in pricing that warp the incentives of producers and consumers. Suppose, for example, that the market price of butter is $1.00 a pound. Dairy farmers complain that they are not getting a fair return on their efforts and investment and persuade the government to set the price of butter at $1.50 a pound. At the higher price, more butter will be produced and less consumed as dairy farmers increase their herds and more consumers switch to margarine. The government will have to add the excess output of butter to inventories or perhaps give it away.[5] In this example, each pound of butter is being produced as efficiently as possible, but the resources used to produce the extra butter could, if they were used to produce something else, produce output of greater value to consumers.

If the only goal of economic policy were efficiency, governments would never adopt such policies, yet most of them do.[6]

5. The example is not a fanciful one. In 1982, high price supports for dairy products resulted in large surpluses of government-owned butter and cheese kept in cold storage at high storage costs. These surpluses were only slightly reduced by a program that gave free cheese to the poor.

6. The *Wall Street Journal* for 8 July 1981 reported that to avoid the high prices set by the European Common Market, German and Dutch consumers were buying butter and meat from floating grocery stores anchored in the North Sea outside the twelve-mile limit.

Perhaps they do so simply because the producers of subsidized products or services are politically powerful, although both governments and subsidized producers try to cloak this motive in some other rhetoric. Often some producers of the subsidized product are poor, and the subsidy is a way to achieve greater equality in income distribution. Less costly ways of helping these poor producers and thus increasing the equality of income are always available, but they may not be politically acceptable.

Controlling Monopoly

In competitive markets, competition between many independent producers keeps the price of output close to the costs of production, including as part of these costs the normal rate of return on invested capital. The output of a competitive industry will therefore be the largest output whose costs customers are willing to pay.

Where there is only one producer or supplier in a market (the situation called monopoly), the monopolist can restrict output. Customers will be willing to pay more than the costs of production for this smaller output, and the producer will earn a monopoly profit in excess of the normal return on the capital he uses. A small group of producers acting in overt or tacit collusion to restrict output (an oligopoly) would have the same effects.

From another perspective, we can view the effect of monopoly as being in the first instance to raise prices above the competitive level. Customers will be willing to buy only smaller quantities at the higher price. The result is the same from either perspective. The monopolist can control quantity, in which case the market determines the price, or he can control price, in which case the market determines the quantity. He cannot control both price and quantity independently because he cannot force people to buy more of his product at any price than they choose to.

An excellent illustration of this point is provided by the experience of the OPEC oil cartel. The member countries of OPEC set high prices for their oil, which caused users of oil to restrict their purchases by conserving energy and using other energy sources. In 1981 the cartel prices came under severe downward pressure because at the high price that had prevailed OPEC members wanted to produce more oil than their customers were willing to buy.

Breaking up, preventing, or limiting monopolies has been an

important proximate goal of American economic policy since the Sherman Antitrust Act of 1890. Most people think of the purpose of antitrust legislation as preventing excessive prices. Viewed this way, breaking up a monopoly results in a one-time lowering of some prices and thus contributes in the short run to controlling inflation (although inflation can still proceed from this lower base). It is equally valid, and perhaps more fundamentally correct, to view the result of breaking up a monopoly as increased output and efficiency. The formerly monopolized industry will produce more output under competition. Higher wages and input prices will attract the resources needed to produce this added output into the industry from other parts of the economy where they were producing output that consumers valued less.

In some industries, such as the telephone and electric utility industries, it is inefficient for technical reasons to have more than one supplier service the same service area. To do so would require duplicating the distribution system. Such industries are often called natural monopolies. Both the federal and state governments regulate natural monopolies for the stated purpose of keeping rates low and output high, though this has not always been the actual result. Regulatory bodies sometimes set high rates to protect the financial interest of the firms already in the industry. The operation of such regulatory agencies will be discussed further in part 2. The point to be made here is that laws and government agencies established to pursue one objective of economic policy may gradually change over the years so that they eventually serve quite different purposes.

A government that wanted to stimulate economic growth would try to promote investment in plant and equipment, research and development, and the education of a skilled work force. It would seek to eliminate waste and inefficiency, prevent monopoly where possible, and regulate monopoly wisely where it cannot be prevented. Not all of this involves having the government do something. Substantial parts of this agenda may best be followed if the government allows the private sector to pursue its own ends with neither special incentives nor burdensome regulations.

Appendix MEASURING THE GROWTH OF OUTPUT

The Gross National Product is one of the measures that make up the system of national income and product accounts maintained by the Bureau of Economic Analysis of the U.S. Department of Commerce. The GNP measures the total value of the nation's output of final goods and services. When deflated by the Gross National Product deflator, a price index on the base 1972 = 100, the measure becomes real Gross National Product, or Gross National Product in 1972 dollars, a measure of the physical volume of output.

The final goods and services included in GNP are both those sold or provided to consumers and those used in investment, including additions to inventories of raw materials, work in process, and finished goods. Raw materials and intermediate goods such as wheat or steel enter directly into GNP only if they are added to inventories. Otherwise they appear as components of final products such as bread or automobiles.

For goods and services produced by businesses and sold at a price, the basic method of measuring real output is first to measure the value of total output at current prices, next to subtract the inputs of goods purchased from others at current prices, and finally to deflate each of these values by an appropriate price index to put them both in constant dollars. This method will not work, however, for government output that is provided to the public without charge, nor for the output of nonprofit institutions, such as private colleges and universities, that charge less than cost for their services. In the general government and nonprofit sectors, the Bureau of Economic Analysis uses the convention that the value of output is equal by definition to the cost of labor input. Thus no output is imputed to the capital used in these sectors. Government enterprises, such as the Post Office, that charge for their services are treated like private businesses.

The imputed value of the services of owner-occupied dwelling units (houses and condominiums) is included in GNP and valued as equal to the rent of similar rental units.

Some of the economic activities included in GNP do not represent additions to economic welfare. For example, if an increase in crime causes local governments to hire more police and private businesses to hire more guards and watchmen, the increased employment of these security forces would cause a rise in measured GNP, although the welfare of the society as a whole was decreased by the crime wave.

The value of the work done in the home by members of the household is not included in GNP, which gives rise to the famous anomaly that GNP decreases when a man marries his paid housekeeper. There is also a portion of the output of the market sector that is missed in the measured GNP. This portion arises in what is called the unobserved or underground economy. It consists of market transactions that are not reported to the government, or whose full value is not reported, so that one or both transactors can evade taxes. Many such transactions are made in cash rather than by check. Some economists have suggested that the unobserved economy has been growing faster than the measured economy in recent years and that this explains part of the rise in measured unemployment and the lag in measured productivity growth.

There have been many proposals to alter the GNP measure to make it a more complete or accurate measure of economic welfare. Because of severe conceptual and measurement problems, none of these proposals has been adopted and the concept of GNP has remained basically unchanged since the 1940s.

* FOUR *
Equality

EQUALITY HAS BEEN a major goal of democratic governments since the American and French revolutions. Originally equality was more a political than an economic concept, expressed first in such terms as equal justice under law and later in universal male suffrage. The concept was gradually extended to include equal educational opportunity as embodied in free public schools and later in government support of higher education.

It was long believed that providing equal opportunity was as far as egalitarian policy should go, and some conservative thinkers still hold this view. If all people have equal opportunity they argue, the more intelligent and energetic will get ahead, the less able and industrious will fall behind, and the distribution of income will reflect differences in people's worth or merit. More recently, the prevailing view has held that many people are poor through no fault of their own, for example, those who have learned and worked hard at a trade made obsolete by economic or technical change. Such arguments suggest policies that go beyond providing equal opportunity and seek to achieve more equal economic outcomes. These are sought by helping the least fortunate and imposing heavier burdens on the more fortunate. Modern economic policy does a great deal of both.

HELPING THE POOR

It has always seemed unjust to compassionate observers of the human condition that some people should live in dire poverty while others could afford to indulge their most costly appetites. For centuries, moral philosophers and religious leaders have sought to temper this injustice by teaching that the rich have an obligation to help the poor through private charity. The tradition of private charity is old and deep in the United States. Some public assistance to the poor has also existed for many years, though at first it was limited and perhaps grudging.

The Great Depression of the 1930s was a watershed in the assumption of government responsibility for relieving poverty. As unemployment rose and the number of people in need multiplied, private charity could not find the resources to meet even their most pressing needs. In the administration of Franklin D. Roosevelt, the federal government stepped into the breach, first with work relief and public assistance, and later with unemployment insurance and old-age insurance. Other public programs were developed to give the poor assistance in kind, such as public housing and free school lunches.

By the 1960s, the obligation the government had assumed to help the poor had grown, and it continued to grow rapidly as the war on poverty became the major domestic policy objective of Lyndon Johnson's administration. Old programs were expanded and new ones were added, such as Medicare (medical insurance for the elderly), Medicaid (medical assistance for the needy), and food stamps. By the late 1970s, transfer payments to individuals through assistance and insurance programs had become the largest category of federal government expenditures. In fiscal year 1982, the federal government spent $248 billion on income security, as compared with $187 billion on the next largest budget category, national defense.

The nature of poverty was also changing. Fewer poor families were headed by unemployed men in their working years. More poor families were headed by women or headed by men past working age. As population moved from farms to cities, rural poverty became less important relative to urban poverty.

In 1959, the federal government adopted an official definition of poverty based on the concept that a family is poor if its income does not exceed three times the amount required for a minimum adequate food budget as established by the Department of Agriculture. Using this definition, the percentage of all families who were poor declined from 18.5 percent of the total in 1959 to 9.1 percent in 1978. The percentage of black families below the poverty line is much higher than that of white families (27.5 percent compared with 6.9 percent in 1978).

When measured as the percentage of people, rather than of families, the figures are somewhat higher. This measure includes individuals living alone and reflects the fact that many poor families are large. In 1978, it is estimated that 11.4 percent of the population lived below the poverty line: 30.6 percent of blacks and 8.7 percent of whites.

Since 1978, the Census Bureau estimates indicate that inflation and recession have raised the percentage of people living in poverty. For 1981 the figure was 14.0 percent for the whole population: 34.2 percent for blacks and 11.1 percent for whites.

36

The concept of income used in the official measure of poverty excludes transfer payments not made in money, such as food stamps and medical care. The number of people who are poor after all transfers, including transfers in kind, may therefore be substantially below the official estimates. Many poor families, however, do not participate in these programs.[1]

Reducing the number of people below a constant real poverty threshold is by no means the same thing as increasing the equality of income distribution, which is a much harder task. As average real incomes grow, aspirations grow with them, and people consider themselves poor at higher absolute standards of living. One typically judges how well off one is relative to others in the surrounding society, not by some abstract standard. A measure of equality that captures this concept of relative poverty is the fraction of all personal income received by the lowest 20 percent of families in the income distribution. Such measures of relative poverty have changed very little over the period since World War II.

Table 1 shows the percentage shares of total family income received by each fifth of families in the distribution, and by the top 5 percent, for the years 1947, 1957, 1967, and 1977. The source of the data is the same household survey used to measure unemployment. The stability of the income shares over a period of 30 years is striking, despite the slight decline in the share of the two highest groups in the decade 1947–57. In each of the years

TABLE 1

The Distribution of Income among Families in Four Years, 1947–1977
(percentage shares)

	1947	1957	1967	1977
Lowest fifth	5.0	5.1	5.5	5.2
Second fifth	11.9	12.7	12.4	11.6
Third fifth	17.0	18.1	17.9	17.5
Fourth fifth	23.1	23.8	23.9	24.2
Highest fifth	43.0	40.4	40.4	41.5
Top 5 percent	17.5	15.6	15.2	15.7

Source: *Current Population Reports*, Series P-60, no. 118, table 13.

1. A Census Bureau study indicates that one household in six received food stamps, Medicare, housing subsidies, or low-price school lunches in 1981, but that 41.5 percent of families below the poverty line did not receive benefits under any of the four programs (*New York Times*, 13 September 1982).

shown, a typical family in the highest fifth of the distribution received roughly eight times the income of a typical family in the lowest fifth. The lowest fifth no doubt includes a larger proportion than the others of small (two-person) families. Adding transfers in kind (food stamps and medical care) would also raise the share of the lowest fifth slightly by 1977 (from about 5 percent to about 7 percent of total income including transfers in kind).

It should be noted that this stability of relative income occurred despite the rapid growth of money income-transfer programs. In the absence of such programs, relative inequality would have increased during the postwar years.

Taxing the Affluent

A government that assumes heavy burdens of helping its needy citizens must somehow raise the revenues with which to do so. It also needs revenues to provide for national defense, pay interest on its debt, and cover the ordinary costs of running the government. Throughout the nineteenth century, most of the revenues of the federal government came from tariffs on imports and from excise taxes on a few domestic commodities. Early in the twentieth century, it was argued that an income tax would be a more equitable source of revenue, since it could be based on the taxpayer's ability to pay. In 1913 the Sixteenth Amendment to the Constitution was adopted, giving the federal government the authority to levy income taxes.

At first, the individual income tax had low rates and very large exemptions. The 1913 act set tax rates ranging from 1 percent on the first $20,000 of taxable income to a maximum of 7 percent on taxable incomes in excess of $500,000. In the 1920s and 1930s, only 4 to 5 percent of the population was covered by the individual income tax, but this figure shot above 50 percent during World War II and has continued to rise since.

The individual income tax is now the largest single source of revenue of the federal government. In fiscal year 1982, it accounted for revenues of $298 billion out of total federal revenues of $618 billion. The rate schedule is progressive, meaning that a larger fraction of a high taxable income than of a low one is paid in taxes. People with very low incomes pay no income tax. In 1980, the rates for others ranged from a minimum of 14 percent in the lowest tax bracket to a maximum of 70 percent, though income from wages, salaries, and other labor earnings was not taxed at more than 50 percent.

The Tax Act of 1981 reduced tax rates for all taxpayers in a series of steps to be completed in 1984. At that time the lowest rate will be reduced to 11 percent. The highest rate was reduced to 50 percent in 1982.

The federal personal income tax is in fact a good deal less progressive than it seems to be because of the presence of numerous exemptions. For example, income from interest on state and local bonds is not taxed at all, and deductions are allowed for interest payments, charitable contributions, and some medical expenses. Such provisions make it possible for some taxpayers with high incomes to pay rather low taxes.

Some states also have progressive income taxes, but because state and local governments rely heavily on sales, excise, and property taxes, the total incidence of state and local taxes is regressive (falls most heavily on those low incomes) through much of the income range. The combination of taxes at all levels of government is only mildly progressive.[2] As a result of the combined effects of transfer payments and taxes, however, the distribution of income among households after all taxes and transfers is substantially more equal than the original distribution.

REDISTRIBUTION AND INCENTIVES

The intuitive case for income redistribution argues that when one takes away a little bit of the income of someone who has a lot, he will not miss it much, and that when one adds a small amount to the income of someone who has very little, even the small increment will be important to him. This proposition seems plausible to most people, but there is no way to prove that it is true. If, for example, everyone soon became fully accustomed to whatever standard of living he enjoyed, reductions in income would be painful even to the rich.

In traditional societies with well-established social classes, the

---

2. A careful study by Joseph A. Pechman and Benjamin A. Okner of the Brookings Institution estimates that for 1966, combined federal, state and local taxes were roughly constant in the general range of 20 to 25 percent of family income for incomes up to $50,000 a year but were as high as 49 percent for incomes over $1,000,000. The exact figures depend on particular assumptions about the incidence of various taxes. See their *Who Bears the Tax Burden,* (Washington, D.C.: Brookings Institution, 1974).

poor may be resigned to their lot and expect no more. The United States, however, does not have a strong tradition of social classes. Even those very near the top of the income distribution think of themselves as middle class rather than rich, and the poor aspire to the kind of middle-class life they see around them or depicted on television. One seldom hears a truly aristocratic argument in defense of inequality—for example, that the rich have more cultivated tastes and therefore greater capacity to enjoy their income, or that the poor deserve to be poor because of laziness or low intelligence.

The limiting factor in redistributive policies is not that the resulting income distribution would be unacceptable, but that it would be reached at a high economic cost. The cost arises from the effect of taxes and transfers on incentives to work and to invest. In principle these costs are obvious, yet it is very hard to measure them.

Someone already in a high tax bracket has substantially reduced incentives to earn more taxable income. He therefore makes most of his new investments not in productive assets, such as shares of corporate stock that pay taxable dividends, but in such tangible assets as gold, coins, works of art, or real estate. These are held for appreciation or capital gains, on which the tax is lower and long deferred. For similar reasons, a high-bracket taxpayer may reduce his work effort. A highly successful doctor or lawyer may refuse to take new patients or clients, preferring somewhat more leisure to more taxable income. Because wages and salaries are taxed, but many fringe benefits and perquisites of employment are not, employers pay less of the compensation of their employees in money and more in fringe benefits than they otherwise would. Some economic activity is driven out of the legitimate economy, where income is reported to the Internal Revenue Service and taxes are paid, and into the unobserved or underground economy, where people work for cash they never report.

As tax rates rise, they must eventually reach a point at which raising them further would discourage so much economic activity and drive so much underground that the higher tax rate would not raise any more revenue.[3] This point, however, is not some

3. The proposition that at some point raising tax rates will lower tax revenues has recently been popularized by Professor Arthur Laffer of the University of Southern California and is referred to as the Laffer curve. The curve depicts tax

single constant number. It must vary depending on the efficiency of tax enforcement, the details of tax law, the attitudes of the public toward government, and people's preferences for income and leisure. Although it seems unlikely that the United States has reached the point at which raising taxes produces no added revenue, that is not really the issue. Long before one reaches this point, higher taxes may reduce output and efficiency enough to restrain legislators from increasing taxes further or from making them still more progressive.

Just as taxes affect incentives, so do transfer payments. For example, the existence of the Social Security system has been a strong inducement to earlier retirement. In the 1930s, when unemployment was high and Social Security payroll taxes were low, this was of little concern. As the costs of the Social Security system have risen and longevity has increased, early retirement has become a less affordable result of public policy.

Some public assistance programs, such as public housing or food stamps, are open only to people with incomes below a certain limit. If such a person gets a chance to earn a little more, he may turn it down because the loss of benefits from the assistance program would exceed the income earned.

Free medical care is a boon to those who are needy and ill. The availability of free care, however, leads some patients to visit the doctor more often than necessary, and government reimbursement induces some doctors to prescribe marginally needed treatment that they would not prescribe for a fee-paying patient with low income. In the process, scarce medical resources can be diverted from patients whose medical needs are more urgent.

Recognition of the disincentive effects of taxes and transfer payments is not in itself an argument against the goal of greater economic equality. It does remind us that programs to achieve this goal must be carefully designed and cautiously introduced, and that they should not be extended so far that the benefits to some are greatly outweighed by the costs to others. Designing programs that meet these tests is a difficult task.

---

revenue as a function of tax rates rising from zero at a zero tax rate to some maximum, and falling to zero again where no income is reported at a tax rate of 100 percent. The logic is irrefutable. Professor Laffer suggests that the United States is now past the maximum point, so that tax-rate reductions will in fact increase tax revenues. There is little or no evidence to support this contention. The Laffer curve is part of the set of ideas now called "supply side" economics, in contrast to the demand management emphasis of Keynes.

LUXURIES AND NECESSITIES

Through taxes, subsidies, regulations, and tariffs, governments pursue many policies that encourage or discourage the production or consumption of particular commodities or services. One might think that a government committed to greater economic equality should encourage the consumption of necessities and discourage the consumption of luxuries through its tax system, and indeed some governments do. The terms just used, however, are tricky ones.

One thinks of luxuries as goods consumed largely by the rich, say caviar or champagne, and necessities as goods consumed in larger quantities by the poor, say potatoes or bread. But necessity also has the meaning of being needed to sustain life. In this biological sense, cigarettes, beer, and coffee are not necessities, yet they are consumed at all income levels. Despite their frequent use by people with low incomes, cigarettes and beer are heavily taxed. From the point of view of governments, the best source of revenue is a tax that does not discourage consumption very much, and taxes on addictive products meet this test.

Income redistribution is one argument for subsidizing mass transit, which is most heavily used by low-income groups. The affluent, however, are more likely than the poor to attend operas and concerts and to visit art museums or national parks. Yet governments subsidize such activities to sustain a cultural or natural heritage despite the antiegalitarian implication of these subsidies for the distribution of real income. The goal of greater economic equality is highly relevant to the broad thrust of taxation and the provision of social services, but it can be made ludicrous if it becomes the touchstone by which every detail of economic policy is judged.

* FIVE *
Maintaining the Balance of Payments

MOST COUNTRIES would like to determine their economic policies solely in terms of domestic priorities, but they are not free to do so. International trade and international monetary flows are too important. Rising imports can reduce employment in domestic industries, changes in foreign exchange rates can raise the rate of inflation, and changes in export growth can raise or lower the growth rate of the whole economy. To understand these influences, we must examine a set of accounts called the balance of international payments.

The balance of international payments is the balance between the payments the United States receives from other countries and the payments it makes to them. When all transactions are included, these amounts must be the same by definition. If, however, we exclude the transactions undertaken by the United States monetary authorities, (the Federal Reserve system and the Treasury), the balance on other transactions can be either positive or negative. It is positive (receipts exceed payments) when people abroad want more dollars, which they use to pay for American goods or services or to buy American assets, than are being made available by American purchases of foreign goods, services, and assets. This positive balance will raise the value of the dollar in foreign exchange markets unless the monetary authorities sell dollars (for other currencies) to meet the excess demand. In other words, a dollar will be worth more yen, lire, or francs than before. Conversely, when the balance before official transactions is negative, the value of the dollar in terms of other currencies will fall unless the monetary authorities buy dollars with other currencies. If the monetary authorities stand aside, the private accounts will eventually be brought into balance because the new relative values of currencies will affect the volume of imports and exports and of purchases and sales of assets. When the value of the dollar is high, American exports become more expensive to foreign buyers, and imports become cheaper to American buyers. In what follows, the term "balance of payments" is understood to exclude the transactions of the monetary authorities, so that a temporary imbalance is possible.

Maintaining a favorable balance of international payments is not a fundamental goal of economic policy in the same sense as

TABLE 2
United States Current Account International Transactions, 1981
(Billions of Dollars)

Merchandise		
Exports	236.3	
Imports	−264.1	
Net balance		−27.9
Investment income		
Receipts	85.9	
Payments	−52.9	
Net		33.0
Net military transactions		−1.5
Net travel and transportation		−0.2
Other services (net)		7.7
Balance on goods and services		11.1
Remittances, pensions, and other unilateral transfers		−6.6
Balance on current account		4.5

Source: U.S. Department of Commerce, Bureau of Economic Affairs. Detail may not add to totals because of rounding.
+ Credits
− Debits

the goals we have already discussed. Rather, in the last analysis, it is a way of achieving the more basic goals. In the short run, however, it can become a proximate goal of policy so compelling that more fundamental goals are sacrificed for it, and for this reason it cannot be ignored. In small countries, where foreign transactions are larger relative to the size of the domestic economy, maintaining the balance of international payments is even more important than in the United States.

The balance of payments is made up of several parts, the first of which is the balance of merchandise trade, or imports and exports. From 1946 to 1970, the balance on merchandise trade was always positive, that is, the United States was a net exporter of physical goods. Since 1970, however, the balance of merchandise trade has frequently been negative by large amounts. This situation reflects the heavy dependence of the United States on imported oil, as well as substantial imports of such manufactured goods as clothing, shoes, steel, and automobiles. On the other hand, the United States has become a major net exporter of agricultural products and coal, and continues to be a net exporter of some high-technology manufactured products such as computers and aircraft.

The second major part of the balance of payments is the balance on services. The largest item in this is investment income, where the United States has had a large positive balance since World War II. American income from investment abroad substantially exceeds foreign income from investment in the United States. When remittances, pensions, and U.S. government grants to other governments are added to the balance on goods and services, one obtains the balance on current account. Remittances and pensions are a net outflow because many American residents retire abroad or help to support foreign relatives. The balance on current account has been negative in some recent years (1977–79) but by less than the balance on merchandise trade. United States international transactions on current account for 1981 are shown in table 2. The balance was a positive $4.5 billion.

The final component of the balance of payments is the balance on capital account, which includes both changes in financial assets, such as foreign purchases of American securities, and changes in nonfinancial assets. Among the latter are the construction of facilities abroad by American-based multinational corporations and foreign investments in land and facilities in the United States.

An adverse or negative balance on current account indicates that foreigners are providing us with more goods and services than we furnish them, accepting our money or securities in return for the difference. Economists usually argue that this situation makes Americans better off, since we have the extra goods now, and the other countries have extra dollars that may decline in value. Clearly, an adverse balance benefits American consumers. As the word "adverse" suggests, however, the opposite view generally prevails. An adverse balance on current account hurts American producers because they are selling less abroad and facing more competition from imports. The usual goal of international economic policy is to promote exports and to restrict imports and to keep the balance on current account positive. Political pressures strongly reinforce this traditional view. Automobile manufacturers and automobile workers and their union, who would like to restrict the imports of Toyotas or Datsuns, are a far better-organized political force than the buyers who want to buy foreign cars at the lowest price. More generally, positive net exports of goods and services raise the GNP, while negative net exports would lower it.

THE END OF THE GOLD EXCHANGE STANDARD

Before August 1971, the United States always stood ready to buy or sell gold to or from foreign monetary authorities (treasuries or central banks) at a fixed price. From 1933 to 1971, this price was $35 per ounce. Most other major non-communist countries followed the same general system, which is known as a gold exchange standard. The domestic gold standard, under which American citizens could redeem paper currency for gold at a fixed price, ended in 1933.

Under the gold exchange standard, the relative value of national currencies was fixed for long periods. It changed only at intervals when a country revalued or devalued its currency by changing the price at which it agreed to buy and sell gold. The United States dollar was seriously overvalued under this system in the years just before 1971. The resulting deficit in the private balance of payments was closed by gold outflows or other decreases in U.S. official reserve assets. During this period, American goods were overpriced in world markets so that exports grew slowly and imports became cheap and made new inroads into domestic markets. The balance on merchandise trade turned negative in 1971 for the first time in the postwar period.

In August 1971, the United States suspended the convertibility of the dollar into gold for foreign official holders. Agreements between the United States and the other major non-communist countries soon established the new international monetary regime that still prevails. In this regime, the relative values of national currencies fluctuate in the market from day to day, although such fluctuations are often moderated by the transactions of the various national monetary authorities. Under this system, major currencies are much less likely to be over or undervalued for long periods.

Gold remains a monetary asset under the new system, but its market price fluctuates. The price of gold in dollars a decade after the end of the gold exchange standard was more than ten times the price before 1971, and at times had been almost twenty times this price.

The system of flexible exchange rates has worked well in that it has permitted international financial markets to deal with substantial shocks, such as several enormous increases in the price of oil, without the imposition of new restrictions on the convertibility of one national currency into another. However, critics of the system argue that it has facilitated the worldwide inflation of the 1970s, which might have been checked by a gold standard. A gold standard severely restrains the creation of money because the monetary authorities must maintain the redeemability of the currency and prevent the dissipation of their gold and foreign exchange reserves. Of course, substantial changes in the price level took place in the days of the gold standard, but they were not as consistently upward as the price changes of the past decade.

In response to such arguments, the Congress in 1981 created a distinguished commission (the Gold Commission) to look into a possible new monetary role for gold. The majority report of this commission did not recommend a return to the gold standard. It recommended that the United States resume minting gold coins, but these would not be exchangeable for other currency at a fixed rate. Such a domestic substitute for the South African Kruger-rand would have no important impact on domestic or international monetary policy.

The Relation between the Balance of Payments and Other Goals

Countries usually want to have strong currencies, and the United States usually seeks to have the value of the dollar high in terms of other currencies. Countries may seek to maintain strong currencies as a matter of national prestige or to attract short-term investment from abroad. There are, however, two more fundamental advantages in a strong dollar. The first is that it makes foreign goods and services cheaper for American consumers, so that fewer dollars are needed to pay for a trip abroad or to buy Swiss chocolate, Dutch cheese, or a Japanese car. The second, which flows from the first, is that a strong dollar, by keeping down the dollar price of imports, restrains price increases by American producers whose goods compete with imports. Both effects tend to lower the rate of inflation, at least in the short run. For our trading partners, however, the effect is reversed. The increase in their exports and decrease in their imports caused by a strong dollar could raise their rate of inflation.

The obvious disadvantage of a strong currency is that by reducing exports and encouraging imports, it tends to reduce domestic output and employment. Firms and workers (or their unions) in the industries affected by declining export sales or increased competition from imported goods will either seek a cheaper currency or, more probably, will advocate higher tariffs and other trade barriers, such as import quotas to protect their industries against foreign competition.

The problem of the monetary authorities in seeking to regulate the value of the dollar is greatly complicated by the fact that the exchange value of the dollar can be high even when the balance on current account is adverse, because exchange values are so sensitive to interest rates. If the Federal Reserve, in order to control inflation, restricts the money supply and allows short-term interest rates to rise above the levels in other countries, this makes investment in short-term American financial assets (such as treasury bills) more attractive to residents of other countries.[1] The resulting demand for dollars bids up the foreign exchange value of the dollar. Although this further helps restrain inflation, it makes American exports more expensive to foreigners and makes imports cheaper in this country. This change in exchange rates may substantially reduce employment and output in export industries or industries facing import competition, even though its effects on the level of employment in the economy as a whole are much smaller.

The policy of maintaining a strong dollar to fight inflation has a logical counterpart during severe recessions. The monetary authorities could seek to increase employment in a recession by lowering the foreign exchange value of the dollar, either by maintaining interest rates below those of other countries or, more directly, by selling dollars for other currencies. This policy would encourage exports and restrain imports. Because it tends to export the unemployment, John Maynard Keynes called it a "beggar-my-neighbor" policy.[2] It would probably be ineffective because it would invite retaliation by the countries with which we trade.

1. The foreign countries most affected by high American interest rates may find it necessary to keep their own interest rates high to check outflows of short-term funds. This policy, however, will have adverse effects on their own output and employment. For such reasons, the very high American interest rates of 1981 and 1982 were severely criticized by some of our European allies.

2. The policy of using a strong dollar to fight inflation, which tends to export inflation, can also be considered a "beggar-my-neighbor" policy in the same sense.

* SIX *
Balancing the Goals

> And thus it is seen in all human affairs, upon careful
> examination, that you cannot avoid one inconvenience
> without incurring another.
>
> Niccolo Machiavelli, *The Discourses*

EACH OF THE GOALS of economic policy, if it could be pursued without regard for the others, could be reached without too much difficulty. Even when there is a trade-off between two goals, as is so often the case, there might be some agreement on the best balance between any pair of objectives. But there are in fact more than two goals, and there are interrelations among them all.

Most discussions of economic policymaking suggest that policymakers face trade-offs along two principal dimensions. The first of these is the trade-off between full employment and stable prices; the second is the trade-off between equality and efficiency. This view correctly identifies two of the main axes of policy choice. The actual process of making policy, however, is even more complex than the tradition suggests. Movement along one of the main axes of choice usually has implications for the other. An example will illustrate the problem.

In January 1981, the new Reagan administration took office committed to reducing the rate of growth of taxes and government expenditures. This policy was intended both to reduce the rate of inflation and to promote savings, investment, and economic growth. The administration was also committed to increasing military spending substantially, which made the task of reducing the growth of total government spending far more difficult. The area of government expenditure that offered the greatest promise for budget cutting was transfer payments to individuals, and some substantial cuts were proposed in this area. But here the administration was constrained by promises to keep a "safety net" protecting those who were truly poor and to maintaining Social Security benefits. To reduce the growth of total spending subject to these constraints, the Reagan administration proposed cuts across a broad spectrum of nonmilitary programs. These included some, such as science education, that might be expected to contribute to economic growth. Finally, the new administra-

49

tion was committed to a balanced federal budget within its first term.

Reagan's opponents in the Republican primaries and the general election of 1980 had suggested that all these goals could not be reached at once, and George Bush (later Reagan's vice-president) labeled the plan "voodoo economics." Two years later, the critics had been proved right. The objective that had to be sacrificed was the balanced budget. The deficit grew from $59.6 billion in fiscal 1981 (the last budget of the Carter administration) to an estimated $208 billion for fiscal 1983 (January 1983 official estimate).[1]

On the tax side of its economic program, the Reagan administration originally proposed a 30 percent reduction over three years in individual income tax rates for all taxpayers (later changed to 25 percent). This proposal was strongly attacked by Democrats as inequitable because it would give much larger absolute tax reductions to taxpayers with high incomes than to those with low ones and thus would increase the inequality of income after taxes. Major cuts in corporate income taxes were also made by the 1981 tax legislation.

By July 1982, the Reagan administration was enough concerned about the growing budget deficit to support vigorously a bill increasing tax revenues (though by substantially less than they had been cut the year before). In a speech in Billings, Montana, on 11 August 1982, President Reagan told a crowd of twelve thousand that failing to raise taxes and reduce the deficit would cause higher interest rates and higher unemployment. The bill he supported was passed soon afterward. What is remarkable about his statement is not that the president had changed his economic policy. Many presidents have been forced by circumstances to do that. It is rather that his argument sees *higher* taxes as reducing unemployment. The traditional view has been that cutting taxes, by raising consumer spending, would lower unemployment. President Reagan took the view that raising taxes (which would result in smaller deficits, less government borrowing, lower interest rates, and therefore increased private investment) was a policy more likely to stimulate employment, despite

---

1. In 1982 and 1983, the deficit will set a new high not only in dollar amount, but as a percentage of Gross National Product. This percentage was 1.5 for the average of 1960–82, and 4.8 for 1982 (calendar years). It seems certain to go even higher in 1983, perhaps as high as 6.5 percent.

its adverse direct impact on consumption. He was generally supported in this view by moderate Republicans and attacked by the right wing of his own party.

Thus we have reached a point where disagreements over economic policy go far beyond the different weights given to different goals. We also have profound disagreement among able people, economists and elected officials alike, as to which policies promote which goals. Macroeconomic policy is in a state of disarray that will take years to repair.

Making economic policy choices is hard because economists do not always agree what the effects of proposed policies will be. It is also hard politically because of the strong constituencies that support and oppose the various options. A policymaker who favors controlling inflation at the cost of higher unemployment alienates unions, minorities, and blue-collar workers. A policymaker who favors reducing unemployment at the cost of more inflation alienates salaried workers, pensioners, and lenders. There is therefore a strong incentive to devise policies, such as wage and price controls, that are (or seem to be) compatible with attaining both goals at once. But such policies, will, on careful examination, be found to have costs of their own and will alienate still other constituencies. Wage and price controls, for example, reduce economic efficiency and alienate both business and organized labor. No wonder policymakers are tempted at times to do nothing at all. But as readers of *Winnie-the-Pooh* will recall, unwillingness to make any choices can get one into tight places. Pooh, visiting friend Rabbit in his burrow, was asked whether he would like honey or condensed milk with his bread. He replied "Both," and proceeded to eat so much that he got stuck for a week in Rabbit's front door. In the somewhat analagous situation in economic policy, refusing to make a hard choice when a problem first arises usually forces one to make a still harder choice later. The Reagan administration has followed some economic policies that have not worked as well as it expected, but the preceding Carter administration got into severe difficulties, and may have been turned out of office, because in the face of economic problems it often seemed unwilling to make any decisions.

The next part of this book will examine the instruments available to economic policymakers and will pay particular attention to the costs of using each of these instruments.

II
The Instruments of Policy
*

* SEVEN *
Taxing and Spending

THE TAXES AND EXPENDITURES of the federal government are powerful instruments of national economic policy. In political debate, attention is sometimes focused only on the difference between the two—that is, on whether the federal budget is in deficit, in balance, or in surplus. For most purposes, this is too narrow a focus. The level and composition of the expenditures and revenues matter a great deal, as well as the difference between the totals. Taxes and expenditures are discussed in this chapter; the deficit is discussed in the next, after consideration of federal borrowing and lending.

COUNTERCYCLICAL TAX POLICY

The federal government has a long-established structure of taxes that generate revenues covering most of its ongoing expenditures. Policymakers almost never re-examine the whole tax structure at once; it would be too formidable a task. Tax policy consists of re-examining selected aspects of tax level or structure for particular purposes or at particular times.

Raising the general level of taxes is considered when there is a large and unexpected increase in the level of federal expenditures, such as took place during the Korean and Vietnam wars. If taxes are raised promptly under such circumstances so that the added revenue covers the new government outlays, taxpayers will be forced to reduce their private spending for consumption and investment. This reduction in private spending will offset most of the increase in federal spending and there will be little inflationary increase in aggregate demand. Some increase in aggregate demand will occur because the private sector will try to maintain expenditures by curtailing saving. Moreover, the shift in the composition of total expenditures, public and private, will create bottlenecks and raise prices in certain industries.

If, on the other hand, a large increase in federal expenditures takes place without an increase in taxes, or with only a small increase, the total of government and private expenditures will increase correspondingly. Unless the economy starts from an initial position well below full employment, this increase in total

55

expenditures will increase the rate of inflation by augmenting an already adequate demand for goods and services. Higher prices will curtail some private demand for goods and services, allowing the government to buy a larger share of the available supply. In this sense, inflation acts as a tax on the private sector, which is competing with the government for a limited real output.

The contrast between the financing of the Korean and Vietnam wars illustrates the difference between the two approaches to financing an expenditure increase. During the Korean War in the early 1950s, Congress raised taxes promptly to cover the increase in military outlays. The price level rose sharply at the outbreak of the war, but soon stabilized. In contrast, in the late 1960s, the Vietnam War produced a large increase in military outlays two years before taxes were raised. Prices began to rise during this period and continued to rise even after taxes had been increased.

Reducing the general level of taxes is usually considered when the economy is in a recession and unemployment has been rising. Cutting taxes in these circumstances, by raising private spending, increases the total demand for goods and services and thus helps to arrest the recession or strengthen the recovery. The income tax reductions of 1964 are the best example of such a policy. At 1964 levels of income, personal income tax liabilities were reduced in 1964–65 by $11 billion and corporate income taxes by $3 billion. The cut for individuals amounted to almost one-fourth of the receipts from the individual income tax. These tax reductions were enacted after several years of sluggish economic growth and (by the standards of that time) high unemployment. They began the process of reducing unemployment that was later accelerated by the war in Vietnam. The unemployment rate had been 5.7 percent in 1963; it fell to 5.2 percent in 1964 and 4.5 percent in 1965.

A tax reduction act was also passed in 1975 during the sharp recession that began late in 1974. It probably helped to make the recession of 1974–75 a short one.

The tax reductions of 1981, however, were enacted for a different purpose. They were a response to the effect of inflation in forcing taxpayers into higher tax brackets and thus raising taxes as a share of before-tax income. Since the tax cuts were supposed to be balanced by expenditure cuts, the purpose was not to expand aggregate demand, but to lower marginal tax rates (the tax on an additional dollar of income) so as to improve the incentives to work and to invest. The proponents of the 1981 tax reduction call this "supply side" economics, in contrast to the "demand side" economics of 1964. How strongly investment and labor supply will respond to the lower tax rates remains to be seen.[1]

In principle, discretionary tax policy is simple; in practice, it is not. First, there are important problems of timing to be dealt with. A change in tax rates, unlike most changes in expenditures, takes effect promptly when enacted; it can even be made retroactive to a somewhat earlier date. It takes time, however, for policymakers to recognize that economic conditions have changed, and when this has been recognized, it takes a long time to enact tax changes. Even when new taxes are in effect, it takes time for taxpayers to adjust their expenditures to their new disposable income. These lags in developing and implementing policy create a danger that a tax cut proposed to combat a sharp but short recession might not have its full effect until the recession was already over and might add to the inflationary pressures during the subsequent recovery.

The principal reason it takes so long to enact a tax change is the difficulty of disentangling the tax level from tax structure. If taxes are to be raised or cut, whose taxes and by how much? As we noted in part 1, the widespread desire to have government economic policy, including tax policy, reduce the inequality of the income distribution is always a major consideration in any debate over tax change.

There have been a few attempts to deal with the problem of timing through temporary rather than permanent tax changes. In 1975, Congress enacted a 10 percent rebate of 1974 taxes up to a maximum of $200. Early in his administration, in 1977, Jimmy Carter proposed to stimulate the economy by giving each taxpayer a one-time rebate of $50 on 1976 taxes. This proposal, which was later withdrawn, was a way of providing the economy with a single large infusion of purchasing power. Since taxes would thereafter remain at their original levels, the proposed rebate would not have contributed to possible excess demand during the subsequent recovery.

Temporary tax changes, however, are likely to have only small effects on private spending. Taxpayers know that they have not

---

1. A year after the passage of the 1981 act, business was cutting planned capital spending in real terms—4.4 percent for 1982, according to a Commerce Department report. The secretary of commerce said, however, that without the tax cuts, the recession would have caused an even larger decline (*New York Times,* 10 September 1982).

been made substantially better off in the long run, and will therefore be reluctant to spend their tax rebate. If the rebate is received when the economic outlook is still threatening, many taxpayers will save it toward the expected rainy day or will use it to reduce debts. The demand for goods and services would then be increased very little.

COUNTERCYCLICAL EXPENDITURE POLICY

In times of less than full employment, government policy can stimulate demand not only by reducing taxes, but also by increasing expenditures.[2] Because the level of federal taxes was very low in the 1930s, this was the principal weapon used by the Roosevelt administration to combat the Great Depression. The new expenditure programs included work relief (the WPA) and large-scale public works, such as dams for power and irrigation.

The use of public works expenditures to counteract a recession involves more serious problems of timing than do tax changes. Many years may be needed to plan public works projects, select sites, let contracts, and carry out the construction. By the time the project is in full swing, the recession could be long over, and the expenditures could add to inflationary pressures in a period of high employment.

When this timing problem was first recognized, advocates of public works proposed to deal with it by accelerating the planning phase of public projects. A "shelf" of preplanned projects would be designed, and in a recession policymakers would select certain projects from the shelf and rush them into construction. Advance planning, however, might not be enough to guarantee a countercyclical effect. For a large project, the construction period alone may last far longer than one phase of the economic cycle.

For this reason, expenditure policy in recent recessions has not emphasized constructing public works, but has moved strongly toward employment and training programs. The employment programs create additional federally funded jobs in local government and private nonprofit organizations. Even employment and training programs take time to design, staff, and get into

2. The federal government can make expenditures directly through its own programs, or it can make transfer payments to states and localities for programs they administer. For the purposes of this discussion, the two kinds of expenditure have similar effects.

operation. If the basic employment and training programs are already in place, however, they can be expanded quickly in response to a decline in aggregate demand.

Just as enlarging government expenditures is a way of increasing aggregate demand, reducing government expenditures is a way of decreasing excessive aggregate demand, but it is a hard way. Expenditure programs develop strong constituencies that fight to keep the programs in existence and maintain their funding. These constituencies include both the ultimate beneficiaries of the programs and the staff that administers them. Although individual programs are sometimes eliminated or cut back despite this, general expenditure reduction has not been frequently used as a tool in fighting inflation. The first substantial cut in expenditures across a broad spectrum of nonmilitary government activity was made by the Reagan administration in 1981.

The choice between using increased expenditures or reduced taxes to help combat a recession does not rest entirely on practical grounds. It also involves a philosophical view on whether government is already large enough. Some observers of American society, including economist John Kenneth Galbraith, see it as a society characterized by private affluence and public squalor. They therefore oppose tax cuts—even during a recession—that increase private consumption and argue instead for new expenditure programs that provide more public goods such as parks or mass transit systems. More conservative observers find the government sector of the economy less innovative and productive than the private sector. In the same circumstances, they would advocate tax cuts that would increase demand by increasing private consumption and investment.

BUILT-IN STABILIZERS

The role of federal taxes and expenditures in stabilizing the economy for the most part does not depend on deliberate policy decisions. A major stabilizing function of the fiscal system is performed automatically.

During a recession, tax receipts fall without any changes in tax rates. Workers on short work weeks pay less payroll or income tax, and those who are laid off pay nothing. Corporate profits fall sharply and so therefore do revenues from corporate income taxes. Sales and excise tax receipts fall as purchases of taxed goods and services decline.

Similar automatic changes take place on the expenditure side of the fiscal system during a recession. Without any changes in benefit levels or program eligibility rules, outlays rise for unemployment insurance benefits, food stamps, and public assistance. Some unemployed workers decide to retire early, and outlays for the Social Security retirement program therefore rise more than usual. A previously balanced federal budget can be thrown into substantial deficit by the onset of a recession without any changes in tax rates or expenditure programs. Since this happens without any need to propose, debate, and enact new laws or start up new programs, it happens with no appreciable lag behind the course of economic events.

In a recovery, the automatic stabilizers operate in reverse. Expenditures on unemployment insurance, welfare benefits, and food stamps decline; tax receipts rise. If there is inflation during the recovery, the rise in receipts from individual income taxes will be more rapid. Inflation will erode the real value of personal exemptions and move taxpayers into higher tax brackets. But this automatic counterinflationary tendency of a nonindexed tax system can easily be negated if policymakers succumb to the temptation to spend all of the increased revenue on expanding government programs.

The importance of built-in stabilizers can be seen in the behavior of the federal budget in the sharp recession of 1974–75. Fiscal year 1975, ending 30 June 1975, coincided roughly with the first year of the recession. Federal outlays rose from $270 billion in fiscal year 1974 to $326 billion in fiscal year 1975. Only a small part of this rise was the result of deliberate policy action, and nearly half the total was in outlays for income security. Since the rise in outlays far exceeded that in revenues, the budget deficit rose from $5 billion in fiscal year 1974 to $45 billion in fiscal year 1975.

Policymakers can increase the importance of built-in stabilizers by expanding programs that have cyclical sensitivity (for example, by increasing benefits or broadening eligibility for unemployment insurance) or by relying more heavily on income rather than excise taxes. Such policies may, of course, be undesirable for other reasons.

TAX STRUCTURE

In fiscal year 1982 (the twelve months ended 30 September), the federal government collected $618 billion in taxes and other receipts. The four largest tax sources were individual income taxes ($298 billion), social insurance taxes and contributions ($201 billion), corporation income taxes ($49 billion), and excise taxes ($36 billion). Social insurance taxes and contributions are taxes on payrolls and the earnings of the self-employed used to finance social insurance programs, including unemployment insurance and Social Security.

The principal federal excise taxes are on tobacco, gasoline, and alcoholic beverages, all of which are kept in place for special reasons. Tobacco and liquor taxes discourage the consumption of substances that can harm their users, and gasoline taxes help to pay for federal expenditures on highways.[3] Excise taxes, unlike income and payroll taxes, enter into the Consumer Price Index as part of the prices of the goods on which they are levied. An increase in excise taxes therefore raises the measured price level and a reduction in excise taxes lowers it. These changes in the measured price level in turn cause changes in wages and transfer payments through the operation of cost-of-living adjustment clauses in collective bargaining agreements and income support programs.

General sales taxes also enter the measured price level in the same way. However, the federal government has never levied a general sales tax. Sales taxes and property taxes have been left to state and local governments as their largest sources of revenue, although state and local income taxes have been used increasingly in recent years.

In principle, it would be possible to pursue economic policy objectives by altering the tax structure without changing its total yield; that is, by reducing one type of tax and at the same time increasing another. For example, it would increase employment and the equality of after-tax income, and might help to lower the price level, if payroll taxes were reduced and some portion of the costs of social insurance programs was paid instead from general revenues, that is, from individual and corporation income taxes.[4] Such changes in the tax structure have been often proposed, but seldom enacted.

3. Because the federal tax on gasoline remained at 4 cents a gallon from 1959 to 1982, by 1982 it financed only half of federal highway expenditures. Nevertheless, proposals to raise the tax had no success in Congress until it was raised by 5 cents a gallon early in 1983. Previously, the combined opposition of automobile owners and the producers of autos and gasoline was more than members of Congress wanted to tackle.

4. Payroll taxes take a larger percentage of low- than of high-wage and salary

Taxes within any one category can also be modified to further various objectives of national economic policy. Increases in personal exemptions in the individual income tax that exceed the rate of inflation will increase the equality of the distribution of real after-tax income. The investment tax credit, which reduces corporate income taxes for corporations investing in new plant and equipment, was adopted in the Kennedy administration as an effort to increase the rate of economic growth. The so-called windfall profits tax, an excise tax on some domestically produced petroleum, was enacted in 1980 to prevent oil producers from deriving excessive benefits from the decontrol of domestic petroleum prices, which permitted these prices to rise to much higher world levels. The decontrol of petroleum prices promoted efficiency in production, while the tax was designed to prevent greater inequality in the distribution of income. Such tax changes, however, sometimes fail to achieve the objectives for which they were designed and may have unintended consequence in other directions.

EXPENDITURE STRUCTURE

The structure of expenditures is also related to the objectives of economic policy. Some expenditures, such as those for national defense and the administration of justice, have noneconomic goals. Transfer payments to individuals for social insurance and public assistance are clearly directed toward greater economic equality. A much more diverse set of expenditures contributes to economic growth. These include most federal expenditures on education and civilian research, and expenditures on such economic infrastructure as highways and waterways.[5] Recent concern about lagging productivity has engendered proposals for increased federal spending on research and education in science, mathematics, and engineering. Thus changes in expenditure structure could in principle reflect changes in the relative importance of policy goals.

Like tax changes, changes in expenditure programs do not always achieve their stated purpose. For example, proposals for

---

incomes, since they are imposed on annual earnings only up to a fixed ceiling.

5. Federal aid to college students also contributes to economic equality by giving low-income students access to higher education and thus raising their subsequent earnings.

the federal government to build new dams or waterways are usually advanced as increasing the growth of an affected region, and hence of the whole economy. They will in fact help the whole economy only if their benefits substantially exceed their direct costs. If the rate of return on investment in a government waterway project is only 5 percent at a time when investment in the private sector is yielding 10 percent, then devoting resources to this project by taxing the private sector will retard national economic growth rather than accelerate it. Some such projects never produce enough benefits to cover their direct costs, an outcome that could often have been anticipated. But adverse probable outcomes will not quench the enthusiasm of local advocates of the projects and their representatives in Congress because the costs are paid by taxpayers throughout the nation while the benefits accrue largely to particular localities.

All federal expenditure programs contribute in some degree to the pursuit of full employment, but the same number of jobs is not created for each dollar spent. Expenditures in subsidizing jobs or in building public works contribute more directly and visibly to employment goals than expenditures for welfare or education. To be sure, recipients of welfare payments or scholarships will spend their federal checks and, in so doing, will put other people to work, but it will not be possible to identify the workers who found jobs for this reason. The aggregate amount of expenditure nevertheless matters more in restoring high employment than the nature of the particular programs in which the spending takes place.

* EIGHT *
Borrowing and Lending

THE FLOW OF MONEY to the federal government is only partly composed of tax receipts, and the outflow from the federal government is only partly composed of expenditures on goods, services, and transfer payments. Besides taxing and spending, the government also borrows and lends enormous sums. By spending and lending more than it has received in taxes, the government over the years has built up a large public debt. At the end of fiscal year 1982, the total federal debt was $1,147 billion, of which $795 billion was held by the public, and the rest by government agencies and the Federal Reserve system. Borrowing and lending, like taxing and spending, have important effects on the state of the economy.

BORROWING

Federal borrowing from individuals or nonbank businesses induces the private sector to curtail its own expenditures on consumption and investment and makes the funds thus released available for government expenditures. If we assume that the level of government expenditures has already been determined, financing them by borrowing from the nonbank public is less inflationary than financing them by borrowing from banks, but more inflationary than financing them entirely through taxes.

When funds are raised through taxes, the taxpayer is poorer by the amount of the tax and must therefore curtail his outlays. If instead of paying a tax, he buys a government bond for the same amount, he again has less money, but in this case he has another asset (the bond) to replace his money. This change in the composition of his asset holdings reduces his liquidity, which could induce him to lower his expenditures, but by far less than a tax of the same amount. Because borrowing from individuals is less inflationary than borrowing from banks, the government tries through advertising to persuade small savers to buy United States Savings Bonds. The interest paid on savings bonds, however, has almost always been lower than the interest available on other assets of comparable safety, which makes the advertising less persuasive.

Most government borrowing is done by selling Treasury securities on the open market. The buyer may be the Federal Reserve system, in which case the borrowing is inflationary because it increases the money supply (by processes to be discussed in chapter 9). When the government has needed funds urgently, however, it has never been willing to borrow them on terms that would attract large amounts from nonbank sources.

The government can also influence the private economy to some extent by varying the maturity of the debt securities it issues. By issuing long-term bonds rather than shorter term notes or bills, it reduces the liquidity of the debt holders, who might therefore curtail their spending. Since the Treasury usually must pay higher interest rates to borrow for long periods, the average maturity of the debt has usually been quite low. Varying debt maturity is a relatively weak policy instrument on which little reliance is placed.

LENDING

The federal government lends for a wide variety of purposes through many federal agencies. It lends to finance the college education of students; to finance American exports on terms favorable to foreign buyers; to assist small businesses; to relieve the victims of floods, tornados, and other natural disasters; to expand rural electrification; to help homeowners get low-cost mortgages; to build low- and moderate-income rental housing; and for many other purposes. In addition to its direct lending, the government also guarantees some loans made by banks to borrowers with limited ability to repay, thereby making the loans much more attractive to the lender. In recent years this device has been used to assist a large city and a large corporation (New York City and Chrysler) that were in serious financial difficulty.

According to the Office of Management and Budget, during fiscal year 1981 the federal government had outstanding $26.1 billion in direct loans and in addition had guaranteed another $28.0 billion of loans. The government almost never has a budget surplus from which to lend. Therefore, the more it lends the more it must borrow itself and the higher the interest rates it must pay to attract all the funds it needs.

Because government loans are usually made at lower interest rates and with longer repayment schedules than the borrower could obtain from private lenders, they expand the kinds of economic activity eligible for such financing at the expense of other kinds of economic activity.[1] An expansion of federal lending can also contribute to a general increase in the aggregate demand for goods and services, which could increase output and employment in a recession. When employment is already high, however, expanding federal lending contributes to inflationary pressures.

THE DEFICIT

If the federal government's expenditures were fully covered by taxes, it would need to borrow only to cover its own lending. It would then be substituting its own strong credit, backed by its unlimited powers to tax and its power to create money, for the weaker credit of those who borrow from it.

In most years, however (in all but two of the twenty-three fiscal years from 1960 through 1982), the federal government's receipts have not covered its expenditures. The difference is a deficit financed by borrowing; and the cumulative total of such deficits, plus the government's own lending, make up the federal debt. Congress limits the size of the federal debt by law, but this debt limit has always been raised reasonably promptly whenever it has been reached. If it were not raised, the federal government could not pay its bills or the salaries of its employees.

Deficits and the public debt have long been the subject of serious concern to many people. Some of these concerns are valid; others are not. The problem of public debt is not that it must be repaid. Treasury securities (bills, notes, and bonds) mature frequently. Ordinarily they are "rolled over," that is, repaid out of the proceeds of new securities issued. In times of inflation, the Treasury may have to pay high interest rates to sell its securities, but there is never a lack of willing buyers at interest rates slightly below those paid by the private borrowers with the best credit ratings.[2] This preferred position of the government as a borrower arises from its unlimited power to tax to repay its debts and its

1. The degree of subsidy varies substantially between loan programs. In fiscal year 1981, Veterans Administration housing loans were made at 14.6 percent interest, which was very close to the market rate, but rural housing loans were made at only 3.6 percent interest.

2. For example, in 1982, the average yield on ten-year treasury bonds was 13.00 percent. In the same year, the yield on Aaa corporate bonds (the highest rating) was 13.79 percent.

power to create money. No private corporation has comparable power to raise funds.

Because the public debt can always be refinanced, it is not true that it must be redeemed or repaid by future generations. The debt is in fact a claim by one set of people in the present generation (the bondholders) against another set (the taxpayers). Of course, the two sets overlap.

The real problem caused by federal deficits and the debt they generate is that they represent private savings that are being used for the most part in a way that does not add to productive capacity, that is, to finance public dissaving. Not much federal expenditure goes to finance productive assets. Except during recessions, heavy federal borrowing tends to drive up the interest rates paid by private borrowers, including businesses that use borrowed funds to finance such productive assets as plant, equipment, and inventories. When heavy federal borrowing raises interest rates, some private borrowers will decide not to borrow at these rates and will curtail their investment in tangible assets. This phenomenon is known as "crowding out." Crowding out private investment is likely to have adverse effects on productivity and economic growth.

If the government (including the Federal Reserve system) wanted to stimulate economic activity without having budget deficits, it could do so through an easier monetary policy. This would reduce interest rates and stimulate private investment. In contrast, stimulating the economy by reducing taxes on individuals would increase private consumption, while increasing public expenditures would enlarge public consumption and investment in public facilities. Any of the three routes, if pursued vigorously, could restore high employment. The choice among them depends on the secondary objectives—whether to encourage investment or consumption and whether to expand the public or the private sector.

The kinds of issues we have been discussing do not figure in most popular discussions of deficits and the balanced budget. The public has a more visceral feeling that deficits are bad, derived by analogy to the budget of an individual or a family. Families that spend more than they earn go into debt; if they cannot pay their debts, they are bankrupt, a situation that has traditionally been viewed as a disgrace. But national governments do not declare bankruptcy over internal debts. Instead they raise taxes or create money, courses not open to individuals. Deficits may indeed be bad both for individuals and for national governments, but for quite different reasons.

As deficits grew in the 1970s, there was increased support for a constitutional amendment to require a balanced federal budget. In 1982, President Reagan came out in support of such an amendment, and on 4 August 1982, a balanced budget amendment passed the Senate. It would require Congress to adopt a balanced budget each year except in time of war, or when set aside by a three-fifths vote of the whole of both houses.

Opposition to the amendment has been expressed on several grounds. Among these is that it would prohibit the use of deficits to help achieve full employment during a recession, even if the deficit arose solely through the operation of the built-in stabilizers. To conform with the proposed amendment, Congress might have to raise taxes and reduce expenditures in a recession, which on most analyses would make the recession more severe.

* NINE *
Monetary Policy

MODERN SOCIETIES use money rather than barter (the direct exchange of goods and services) to carry out most transactions. Money developed thousands of years ago to avoid the difficulties of barter, which requires that each party to a transaction want precisely what the other has to offer. This can be a hard condition to fulfill.

Money once consisted entirely of currency (coins and paper currency), but now consists largely of bank deposits, including some deposits that pay interest. According to the narrowest usual definition of the money stock, called M_1, the total stock at the end of 1982 was $478 billion, of which $133 billion was currency and the rest was bank deposits against which checks can be written. Broader definitions of the money stock include time and savings deposits in banks and savings and loan associations, and balances in money market mutual funds. By the broadest of these measures, M_3, the total money stock at the end of 1982 was $2,404 billion.

THE DEMAND FOR MONEY

People hold money to make anticipated payments and to serve as a ready reserve against contingencies that require unanticipated payments. Holding currency or checking deposits involves the sacrifice of the yields available from holding other assets such as stocks or bonds, a sacrifice that is greatest when interest rates are high. In times of inflation, holding money involves an additional loss arising from the depreciating real value of money. (This loss is also incurred in holding bonds or any other asset denominated in dollars). Because of the high costs of holding money, corporations and individuals have become skillful at keeping their money balances down to the minimum needed to carry out transactions.

If the supply of money increases so that the real value of the money stock exceeds the amount people want to hold, the excess money will be spent to buy other assets and consumption goods. This spending bids up the prices of goods and other assets and thus reduces the real value of the money stock. Conversely, if people feel that their money balances are too small, they will increase them by curtailing expenditures or selling other assets. This process cannot increase the total money stock in nominal units, but by reducing the prices of alternative assets and of some goods, it can raise the real value of the existing money stock. The monetary authorities, who are the issuers of money, thus control the nominal size of the money stock; the holders by their spending behavior determine its real value. In the process of trying to draw down or build up their real money balances, people augment or reduce the aggregate demand for goods and services.

THE SUPPLY OF MONEY

National governments through their central banks have a monopoly on issuing currency and thus would seem to control the size of this component of the money supply. Holders of bank deposits, however, can always convert their deposits into currency on demand or deposit their currency in banks, so that the division of the money supply between currency and deposits is fully controlled by the holders. What really matters is not the supply of currency but the size of the total money supply, including bank deposits.

Deposits are created when banks make loans. The lending bank opens a new account for the borrower (or adds to an existing account), crediting him with money that did not previously exist. To be sure, the borrower can pay this money out by drawing checks against his account, but these will be deposited in other banks. After the loan, there will be more deposits in the banking system as a whole until some depositor chooses to hold more currency or to repay a bank loan.

In the United States, the limits to the ability of banks to create new money are set by the rules of the Federal Reserve system, particularly by the rules requiring banks to hold reserves against deposits. These reserves consist of noninterest-bearing deposits by the banks in the Federal Reserve system. Because reserves do not bear interest, reserve requirements are in a sense a tax on bank deposits.

THE FEDERAL RESERVE SYSTEM

The Federal Reserve system consists of the Board of Governors and twelve regional Federal Reserve banks. The Board of Governors is an agency of the federal government whose seven members are appointed by the president with the advice and consent of the Senate for terms of fourteen years. The regional banks, owned by their private member banks, are nominally in the private sector, but they are not operated for profit and their basic policies are set by the Board of Governors.

Within rough limits, the Federal Reserve system can determine the total amount of deposits, and thus the size of the total money stock, by using three powerful policy instruments: reserve requirements, the discount rate, and open market policy. Reserve requirements specify the amounts banks must hold in accounts with their Federal Reserve bank as reserves against various classes of deposits. Raising reserve requirements restricts the ability of banks to make new loans; lowering them allows banks to expand their loans.

The discount rate is the interest rate at which member banks can borrow from their Federal Reserve bank when they need additional reserves. Raising the discount rate tends to restrict the expansion of bank deposits, and lowering it relaxes this restriction. The discount rate is often below the interest rate on short-term securities. For example, in June 1981, the discount rate was 14 percent and the rate on three-month treasury bills averaged 14.6 percent. For this reason, banks are discouraged from borrowing as much as they might like to from the Federal Reserve. The Federal Reserve has nevertheless traditionally been viewed as a "lender of last resort," meaning that it will provide funds to a sound bank that needs liquidity and cannot get funds quickly from other sources.

Open market operations consist of the purchase or sale of U.S. government securities by the Federal Reserve system. When the Federal Reserve buys securities, it pays for them by creating deposits for the sellers in the Federal Reserve banks; these deposits serve as additions to reserves for commercial banks. The added reserves permit commercial banks as a group to expand their loans and deposits by a multiple of the new reserves; this multiple is the inverse of the reserve ratio. For example, if reserves of 10 percent are required against all deposits, an additional dollar of reserves could ultimately support $10 of additional deposits.

When the Federal Reserve sells government securities, the buyers' payments are charged against commercial bank reserve accounts, reducing them and requiring banks to contract deposits by a multiple of the amount of the purchase. This multiple again depends on the reserve ratio. The banks contract their deposits by selling financial assets such as bonds or by making fewer new loans.

Open market policy is determined by the Federal Open Market Committee, which consists of the seven members of the Board of Governors and five of the twelve presidents of the Federal Reserve banks. All open market operations are carried out for the Federal Reserve system by the Federal Reserve Bank of New York.

Of the three main policy instruments of the Federal Reserve, the discount rate may seem the least important, because borrowed reserves are relatively small. At the end of 1982, member bank borrowings were $0.7 billion, while total reserves were $42 billion. Nevertheless, changes in the discount rate are important as signals of the Federal Reserve's intentions. For this reason, a rise or fall in the discount rate is frequently followed by a corresponding rise or fall in the interest rates that banks charge their borrowers.

Changes in reserve requirements are a very powerful instrument of monetary policy. An increase in reserve requirements restricts the lending ability of all banks, including those with no borrowed reserves. Because changes in reserve requirements have large effects, they are made infrequently.

The most flexible of the three policy instruments is open market operations. From day to day the Federal Reserve can vary the size and direction of its purchases or sales of government securities in response to changing conditions in financial markets. It can and does make sales and purchases in very large amounts.

The Target of Monetary Policy

The ultimate goals of monetary policy are price stability and full employment. When there is a conflict between these goals, the Federal Reserve is more concerned with price stability, while Congress is often more concerned with full employment. Nevertheless, the Federal Reserve has usually appeared to ease monetary policy during a recession, even when the price level was rising. In the short, sharp recession of early 1980, during which the price level was still rising rapidly, the Federal Reserve cut the discount rate from 13 percent to 10 percent and allowed the treasury-bill rate to fall as low as 7 percent from a peak above 15 percent.

There has been sharp controversy over how the Federal Reserve system should set its proximate target in order to reach its ultimate objectives. Traditionally, it has sought to control interest rates, especially those on short-term securities such as treasury bills. An easy money policy lowers interest rates, which encourages increased investment by business in plant, equipment, and inventories. This new investment spending creates employment. Conversely, a tight money policy raises interest rates, helping to choke off investment, to restrain aggregate demand, and thus to restrain price increases.

The influence of high interest rates on the rate of inflation is complicated by the fact that interest rates enter directly into some measures of the price level, especially the Consumer Price Index. Through this channel, higher interest rates are a source of higher prices. Most economists believe that this direct effect, except in the very short run, is smaller than the indirect effect through aggregate demand by which high interest rates reduce inflation. Much of the general public, however, holds the opposite view.

A second important difficulty is that participants in securities markets form expectations about Federal Reserve policy. A move that on its face is a tightening of policy should raise interest rates. But if the move is smaller than expected, or is regarded as too small, it could lead to expectations of further inflation. Bond-holders would then sell bonds, which lowers their price and raises some long-term interest rates (the yield on bonds). Such market reactions greatly complicate the task of the Federal Reserve system.

For many years a group of economists known as monetarists, led by Milton Friedman, have opposed the idea that monetary policy should focus on interest rates. In their view, the proximate target of monetary policy should be to achieve a steady rate of growth of the money supply. Ultimately, this growth rate would be the same as that of real output, with some allowance for technical changes in the rate at which moneyholders turn over their balances (the "velocity" of money use). The congruence of growth rates between money supply and output would ensure price stability. Because the money supply tends to fall in recessions when borrowers cut back their borrowing and banks contract their loans, maintaining a steady money supply would require the Federal Reserve to create additional money during recessions. In this way, the steady growth of the money supply would also promote high employment.

In late 1979, the newly stated policy and operating procedures of the Federal Reserve system seemed to move toward the monetarist view. The Federal Reserve now places great emphasis on meeting official annual targets for money growth, which are required by the Full Employment and Balanced Growth Act of 1978 (the Humphrey-Hawkins Act). The policies announced on 6 October 1979 gave priority to these targets by permitting greater short-term variation in interest rates. Nevertheless, rates of monetary growth have fluctuated widely since this announcement. When the Federal Reserve misses its targets, as it sometimes does, it starts again the next year with new growth targets from the new base.

The Federal Reserve targets for 1982 are shown in table 3. The details of the composition of the three money supply measures need not concern us. What is noteworthy first is that there are three different targets, and we do not know the importance attached to reaching each. Second, the range of the targets is rather large (3 percentage points), leaving the Federal Reserve much discretion on where within the range to operate. Finally, as happened in 1981 but not in 1982, it is possible for some of the targets to be met and others not, so that there may be ambiguity about whether the policy has met its objectives. In 1982, the actual growth of all three measures was above the upper limit of the target range. Perhaps the worst difficulty of all is the continued development of new money market instruments and new types of bank accounts and the constant shift of funds among them, which means that a given money supply measure does not have a constant significance from year to year.

There are even more reasons why it is hard to tell what proximate targets the Federal Reserve is actually pursuing. First, changes in interest rates need not be caused by any action of the

TABLE 3
Federal Reserve Monetary Targets, 1982

Money Supply Measure*	Target Range (percent)	Actual Growth (percent)
M1	2.5 to 5.5	8.5
M2	6 to 9	9.2
M3	6.5 to 9.5	10.1

*M1 = the sum of currency, demand deposits, travelers checks, and other checkable deposits. M2 = M1 plus overnight repurchase agreements, Eurodollars, money market mutual fund balances, and savings and small time deposits. M3 = M2 plus large time deposits, term repurchase agreements, and institution-only mutual money market fund balances.

central bank. When a recession causes a decline in the demand for funds, interest rates will fall even if policy is unchanged and the money supply remains constant in the first instance or falls less rapidly than loan demand. Monetarists would deny that such a downward movement of interest rates in itself constituted an easy money policy, since it arises solely from a shift in demand.

Another constraint on policy is that the Federal Reserve system is concerned with the relative level of interest rates in the United States and in other major countries, since this pattern of rates is a major determinant of the value of the dollar in terms of other currencies. This concern about relative interest rates across national economies may conflict with domestic policy objectives. For example, the Federal Reserve might be reluctant to lower interest rates during a recession if this would cause the value of the dollar to fall.

Defenders of the Federal Reserve argue that it has not had enough power to achieve its proximate goals fully or promptly. Monetarist critics of the system reply that the problem has been lack of will, not lack of power. The defenders point out that there have been important slippages between the Federal Reserve's actions to expand or contract bank reserves and the ultimate size of total bank deposits. In particular, until 1980 only member banks of the Federal Reserve system were required to keep reserves with the system, and by no means all banks were members. New legislation passed in 1980 requires all banks to keep reserves with the Federal Reserve, a measure that should improve its control of the money supply when it becomes fully effective. In any event, the monetarists urge the Federal Reserve to maintain tight control of the growth of the unborrowed reserves of banks, which it can control precisely and which serve as the base for the rest of the monetary system.

While monetarists have regarded Federal Reserve policy as too erratic and sometimes too loose, a host of other critics have assailed it as too tight. These include some Keynesian economists, home builders, labor unions, and Democratic members of Congress. Some of these critics have proposed to make the Federal Reserve more responsible to the administration or to the Congress.[1]

---

1. Two such bills were introduced in 1982. A House bill would require the Federal Reserve to set targets for long-term interest rates and report any changes in its targets to Congress. A Senate bill would require the Federal Reserve to set "yearly targets for positive real short-term interest rates consistent

THE INSTRUMENTS OF POLICY

Politically, such proposals are a mixed blessing to elected officials. At present, candidates for reelection can blame an independent Fed for inflation or unemployment. The less independent the Federal Reserve, the more elected officials must accept responsibility for what it does.

THE EFFECTS OF MONETARY POLICY

The traditional view of a tight money policy holds that it works because borrowers eventually become unwilling or unable to pay higher interest rates. In practice, it has more often been true that when money was tight, many borrowers were unable to get loans at any rate. This credit rationing resulted from a phenomenon known as "disintermediation."

Savings and loan associations, the principal source of home mortgages, have been (and to some extent still are) limited by law in the maximum interest rates they could pay to savers. When market rates rose much above the rates the associations were permitted to pay, many savers withdrew their deposits from savings and loan associations and similar thrift institutions, such as savings banks and credit unions, and invested instead in treasury bills or money market funds. The thrift institutions could not make new mortgage loans, and the result was a sharp drop in home building. In the years 1973 to 1975, for example, the number of new housing units started fell from 2.0 million to 1.2 million, largely for this reason. In short, the principal effect of tight money policy was to limit housing construction. Similar effects were felt in the automobile industry, whose sales depend heavily on installment credit.

In the tight money period that began in the autumn of 1979, disintermediation was largely avoided by allowing financial intermediaries to pay high interest rates on long-term deposits. As a result, the efforts of the Federal Reserve to check inflation through restrictive monetary policy seemed largely ineffective. In the spring of 1980, monetary policy was supplemented with some direct controls of consumer credit, and interest rates rose to unprecedented heights, (the highest since the Civil War). The effect again was to restrict the demand for housing and auto-

---

with historic levels." A Federal Reserve analysis of the bills expressed the fear that they would erode the independence and credibility of the Reserve and be interpreted as an effort to speed up growth of the money supply (*Wall Street Journal*, 10 September 1982).

mobiles. Allowing thrift institutions to compete for funds by paying high rates has also had serious consequences for the institutions. In 1981 and 1982, many were paying more for deposits than they were earning on portfolios of old, low-rate mortgages and losing instead of gaining on their entire operations as a result. Several large thrift institutions became insolvent and had to be merged with other institutions.

It is perhaps inevitable in an affluent and reasonably compassionate society that the effects of restrictive economic policy will be felt largely in the sales of durable goods, whose purchase can easily be postponed. People will buy food and pay the rent as long as they have any income with which to do so, but the old car can be made to run another year, or the purchase of a larger house can wait until times are better or interest rates come down. New families can rent or double up with parents.

The effects of an easy money policy are the reverse of those of a tight money policy. As interest rates fall and mortgages become readily available, home building revives. Better terms and less selectivity of borrowers for automobile loans help to boost auto sales. Lower interest rates also permit businesses to maintain or build their inventories rather than reduce them. To some extent, these effects of monetary policy on aggregate demand work not through interest rates alone, but directly through the level of money balances that consumers and businesses hold. People are more likely to spend freely when they have money in the bank than when their cash balances are low and need to be rebuilt. The relative size of these effects, however, has largely eluded measurement and has been the subject of much debate.

As a result of its effect on the level of economic activity, monetary policy also influences the rate of inflation, though with a lag.[2] The tight money policy of 1974 and the resulting recession helped to lower the rate of increase in the Consumer Price Index from 12.2 percent in 1974 to 4.8 percent in 1976 (December to December). What has been disappointing about recent experience is that prices have continued to rise even during recessions and have accelerated quickly when the recovery was under way. A monetary policy that produces short, sharp recessions has proved to be of limited value in combatting persistent inflation. The inflationary process now seems to have a life of its own, in which

---

2. Monetarists would say that monetary policy determines the rate of inflation.

higher prices produce higher wages, which contribute to higher labor costs, and in turn to a new round of higher prices. This price-wage spiral is continued even in the face of substantial unemployment. Increasingly, it seems that the monetary authorities will need to maintain some slack in the economy for a protracted period if the rate of inflation is to be reduced and kept low through control of aggregate demand.

* TEN *
Wage and Price Controls and Related Policies

As WE HAVE SEEN, controlling inflation through restrictive monetary and fiscal policy involves, at least in the short run, heavy costs of lower output and employment. Policymakers have often been unwilling to pay these costs. To avoid them, they have turned to direct restraints on prices, including wage and price controls and milder policies of the same general sort, such as wage-price guidelines. This whole set of possible direct policies to restrain wage and price increases is often known by the British term "incomes policies."

Incomes policies attempt to deal directly with the self-reinforcing process by which higher prices lead to higher wages, and these in turn lead to higher costs and still higher prices. Direct restraint of the wage-price spiral does not reduce employment appreciably, but it does reduce efficiency.

WAGE AND PRICE CONTROLS

Wage and price controls were used during World War II, during the Korean War, and by the Nixon administration during the period from August 1971 through April 1974. Controls begin with a wage-price freeze, under which any wage or price increases are illegal. After a brief freeze period of perhaps sixty or ninety days, various formulas are devised that permit prices to be raised to cover increased costs and permit wages to be raised by limited amounts. The amounts of these allowable wage and price increases are determined by government agencies established for this purpose, such as the Office of Price Administration in World War II or the Cost-of-Living Council, the Pay Board, and the Price Commission in the early 1970s. Price or wage increases larger than those permitted by the rules or regulations of the control agency are violations of the law punishable by fines or, in principle, by imprisonment, although prison sentences have seldom been imposed.

While they are in effect, wage and price controls do work—that is, they slow the rise of such official price indexes as the Consumer Price Index. There is, however, a strong tendency for these price indexes to spring upward sharply when the controls are eventually lifted. Statistical evidence indicates that this subsequent rise in prices has sometimes been larger than the original effect of controls in holding prices down.

Price controls are often used when there is strong aggregate demand. In such circumstances, there will be many products for which the quantities demanded at the controlled price will exceed the amount available at that price. This creates a shortage in which stores have empty shelves or suppliers refuse to fill orders in whole or in part. Some shortages arise from natural causes, such as the effect of drought on the size of crops. In wartime, shortages are caused by the diversion of civilian output to military purposes. Finally, price controls themselves may make it unprofitable for producers to make certain items in the usual quantities and may induce them to divert their resources to making other items whose controlled prices allow a better margin of profit. For example, a clothing manufacturer might shift production from dress shirts to sports shirts if the ceiling prices allow him a better margin over costs on sports shirts. In such cases, controls do not let prices play their usual role of rationing scarce supplies among buyers, and another form of rationing is needed.

During World War II, many scarce consumer goods were rationed by coupons issued by the government. To buy meat, one needed not only money, but red stamps. Since red stamps were distributed equally to all people, this form of rationing brought about much greater equality in the distribution of rationed goods than is present in the normal peacetime distribution of income. This policy can be justified as "fair shares," or equality of sacrifice, during a national emergency. Not all scarce consumer goods, however, were rationed during World War II, and no formal government rationing was used in either of the more recent episodes of price control. Producer goods, such as steel and aluminum, were allocated during wartime according to priorities determined by the government and based on military needs.

When goods are scarce at controlled prices and there is no formal rationing scheme, sellers distribute the scarce items on the basis of past patronage. For example, if there is a shortage of cigarettes, they will be kept under the counter and saved for regular customers. Such a system of allocation to "regulars" penalizes transients and newcomers to a neighborhood.

Somewhat similar systems operate for producer goods. Under price controls without government-determined priorities, steel producers allocate output to their customers according to purchases in some base period. A steel fabricator who opens a new plant during price controls might not be able to get enough steel to maintain his operation.

Economywide wage and price controls require a large administrative apparatus and many detailed rules and regulations. These become more and more complex the longer controls continue because administrators try to alleviate shortages of particular goods or services through amendments and exceptions to the basic rules.

Under controls that create excess demand at ceiling prices, black markets appear in which scarce goods are sold above the controlled price. Such markets may take complicated forms. For example, if onions are scarce at their controlled price but potatoes are plentiful, the grocer who wants onions may be required by his supplier to buy potatoes he does not need, which he must sell at a loss.

The presence of black markets, where actual prices are not reported to statistical agencies, means that the official price indexes can substantially understate the true price increases during periods of control. This makes controls seem more effective in the statistics than they really are.

The most recent use of peacetime wage and price controls has a curious history. Early in his administration, President Nixon announced his opposition to wage and price controls. In 1970, Congress gave him sweeping control powers he had not asked for in an effort to shift the blame for inflation to the administration. In August 1971, controls were unexpectedly imposed in connection with the end of the gold convertability of the dollar. This served to make the de facto devaluation of the dollar more acceptable both domestically and abroad.

When the 1971 controls were instituted, they were extremely popular. As they remained in effect, however, they proved less successful than anticipated in curbing inflation, which had been accelerated by crop failures abroad and by large sales of American grain to the Soviet Union. The costs and difficulties of coping with the administrative machinery of controls were highly irritating to business and labor unions.

Public irritation with controls was increased in the summer of 1973 when the price of red meat was first controlled and then decontrolled again. The decontrol was announced some weeks before its effective date. During this period, cattle were held on feed lots putting on unwanted fat, while meat counters were bare and consumers ate fish, poultry, or pasta. By early 1974, public opinion had turned against controls and Congress refused to renew them. Proponents of controls argue that this experience reflects an inept or halfhearted effort to use controls and that a more forceful administration might have avoided this outcome.[1]

Opponents believe that controls inherently lose their effectiveness and can never succeed for long in peacetime.

WAGE-PRICE GUIDELINES

The costs and inefficiencies created by legal wage and price controls have led to several experiments with milder forms of incomes policies. The Kennedy and Johnson administrations used wage-price guideposts from 1962 to 1967, and the Carter administration used wage-price guidelines from late 1978 through 1980.

The wage-price guideposts of the 1960s were implemented by exhortation and by occasional ad hoc intervention by the White House in major wage and price decisions. The wage-price guidelines of 1978–80 were much more like formal controls, although they lacked legal sanctions. Detailed rules and regulations for acceptable wage and price behavior were developed by a federal agency (the Council on Wage and Price Stability), and companies that violated these rules were threatened with the loss of government contracts.[2]

Although the economic costs of guidelines are far lower than those of full-blown controls, guidelines may also be less effective in restraining inflation. Prices rose only very slightly from 1962 to 1967, for which the guideposts may deserve some credit. In both 1979 and 1980, however, the Consumer Price Index rose by more than 12 percent despite the presence of wage-price guidelines.

1. It is true that some top economists in the Nixon administration were unsympathetic to controls. But the people actually engaged in administering controls generally did believe in them and worked hard to do the best job possible.

2. Similar informal sanctions had been used by the Kennedy administration. During the Carter administration, the federal courts upheld the use of the government's procurement power to enforce wage-price guidelines. To allow the executive branch to make rules, establish penalties, and punish violations without recourse to the courts nevertheless seems inconsistent with the separation of powers between the three branches of government.

On the price side, the principal difference between guidelines and controls is that guidelines never set individual prices for particular goods and services, and controls often do. Guidelines seek to prevent firms from widening their profit margins, while allowing them to pass on most or all cost increases to their customers.

On the wage side, both guidelines and controls usually set a numerical standard to which wage and salary increases should conform, whether they are set solely by employers or jointly determined by employers and unions in collective bargaining. In 1979, this wage standard was an annual increase of 7 percent for wages and fringe benefits combined. Determining the proper wage standard is not a trivial exercise. It if is set too high, it has no effect in restraining wage increases. If it is set too low, wages cannot keep up with increases in the cost of living, and the standard will therefore be unacceptable to labor unions. The general practice has been to set the basic wage standard low, but to construe it very liberally for major collective bargaining agreements. This practice has the unintended result of widening the differences between union and nonunion wages. Because of uncertainties about the ultimate costs of cost-of-living adjustments and changes in fringe benefits, the cost of collective bargaining agreements cannot be precisely estimated in advance.

TAX-BASED INCOMES POLICY

During the 1970s, a new form of incomes policy called tax-based incomes policy, or TIP, gained increased support among those economists who had previously favored controls or guidelines. These policies have not yet been applied in the United States.

The form of TIP most frequently proposed is to set a wage guideline, like the 7 percent guideline of 1979, and to impose penalty taxes on businesses whose wage increases exceed the guideline. Corporations that exceeded the wage guidelines would be required to pay corporate income taxes at a higher rate, with the size of the penalty perhaps related to the amount by which wage increases were excessive. One advantage claimed for TIP is that by using the Internal Revenue Service as the administrative agency, it would avoid the costs of a separate administrative machinery and would greatly improve compliance by employers. The labor shortages sometimes caused by wage controls would be avoided because in cases of severe shortages it would be legal to ignore the guidelines and pay the appropriate extra tax. Against these advantages must be set the substantial disadvantage that rules written into the Internal Revenue Code cannot be modified by administrative changes to meet particular problems. Special agencies administering wage controls have frequently found it necessary to modify their own rules to meet special situations arising in collective bargaining.

It is also possible to have a tax-based incomes policy that uses rewards rather than penalties. For example, tax credits or refunds could be given to employees whose wages or salaries did not rise by more than a given amount.

Tax-based incomes policies might help inflation arising from excessive wage increases. In an inflation arising from excess aggregate demand, they could allow prices to rise faster than wages. These price increases would still have to be kept in check by some kind of monetary or fiscal restraint.

RENT CONTROLS

Most price control policies have been enacted and implemented by the federal government. The principal exception is rent control, which has been adopted by some municipalities where authorized by state law. The largest rent control system, and one of the oldest, is that of the City of New York.

Rent control initially freezes the rents of unfurnished apartments at some existing level, which is maintained even when leases expire. It then generally permits limited increases from this level based on increases in the cost of operating buildings, including the cost of fuel and electricity. Very expensive apartments and apartments in newly constructed buildings are usually exempted from the law, so as not to discourage new construction. Rents in controlled apartments may be far lower than those in comparable uncontrolled apartments.

Rent control attempts to check inflation at the local level and to redistribute income more equally. The pursuit of the second of these objectives relies on the observation that, in general, landlords have higher incomes than their tenants. (They also have fewer votes.) The redistribution is inexact to the extent that some high-income tenants occupy rent-controlled apartments and that some low-income landlords own controlled buildings—for example, retired people who have invested their savings in small apartment buildings.

If there are gains achieved by rent control in limiting inflation and promoting economic equality, they must be balanced against the resulting losses in economic efficiency, which take several forms. Owners of controlled buildings may defer maintenance and repairs if they cannot get an adequate return on their investment through increased rents. Small families whose children have grown up and moved away continue to occupy large rent-controlled apartments because the rents they pay are lower than those of much smaller uncontrolled apartments. Newcomers to the city find it hard to locate affordable housing.

Rent control is often blamed for the massive abandonment of slum housing by landlords in such areas as the South Bronx. Casual evidence on this point is hard to evaluate, since landlords have also abandoned many tenement buildings in cities without rent control. Rent control encourages the conversion of rental buildings to cooperatives or condominiums, but such conversion is also promoted by the favorable treatment of owner-occupied housing in the federal personal income tax, including the deductibility of mortgage interest and property taxes.

INCOMES POLICIES AND BASIC POLICY OBJECTIVES

Incomes policies attempt to reconcile a high level of employment with a low rate of inflation, and they have had some success in doing so during wartime. This success is achieved at an appreciable cost in terms of efficiency, which is promoted by the normal operation of free markets. In peacetime, incomes policies have generally lost their effectiveness after they have been in force a few years. This has led some observers to seek to devise new forms of incomes policies, such as TIP, that might have lower costs and hence longer-lasting effects. Other observers, however, interpret past experience as demonstrating that incomes policies are inherently ineffective as a peacetime policy instrument.

* ELEVEN *
Economic Regulation and Government Ownership of Industry

THERE ARE TWO main types of economic regulation. The older type, which regulates particular industries by setting rates or prices and controlling the entry of new firms, includes federal economic regulation of railroads, airlines, trucking, and broadcasting, and state regulation of public utilities. The newer regulation, which often cuts across industry boundaries, is directed toward such social objectives as reducing air and water pollution, making workplaces safer, and preventing injuries from motor vehicle accidents. Some social regulation, for example, that protecting the wholesomeness and safety of food and drugs, has existed for many years, but most has been developed since the 1960s. Federal regulatory policy is made and administered by many agencies of the federal government pursuant to different and sometimes vague legislative mandates.

The makers of broader economic policy must be concerned with economic regulation because of the conflicts between its goals and other economic goals. Regulation can reduce economic growth and efficiency and can raise costs and prices. Whether or not the benefits of particular regulatory policies justify their costs is usually debatable, and the debate is often acrimonious.

BENEFIT-COST ANALYSIS

Economists approach a proposed regulatory policy by making quantitative estimates of both its benefits and its costs. Regulations with high ratios of benefits to costs are worth having; those with low benefit-cost ratios should be modified or discarded. Future benefits and costs must be discounted so that they weigh less heavily in the decision than those that come immediately; a dollar's worth of benefit to be realized ten years from now does not justify incurring a dollar of costs today. All this is difficult both because benefits and costs are hard to measure and because there is not general agreement on the appropriate interest rate to use in discounting future benefits. A high interest rate (say 15 percent) will give little weight to benefits realized in the distant future; a low one (say 5 percent) will give them much greater weight. Most economists would use a rate approximating market rates of return for long-term investments bearing some risk, such as corporate bonds.

Some regulations have such obvious benefits and low costs that formal analysis is unnecessary. For example, if one can prevent the needless death of infants by requiring that the slats of cribs be placed close enough together so that an infant's head cannot get caught between them, the costs are negligible relative to the benefits. Few cases, however, are this simple.

In this example, the costs are easy to measure because they are all incurred by one small industry (crib manufacturing). The risk reduced is also easily measured. In contrast, consider the regulations that require users of coal to reduce sulfur dioxide emissions from their smokestacks by installing devices called scrubbers, which are expensive to purchase and to operate. Here the damage to be prevented is not a sudden and catastrophic loss to a few, but a gradual and often unobservable damage to a large population, which is more likely to suffer from coughs, bronchitis, and other respiratory ailments as a consequence. It is hard to know how many people are helped and to calculate the value to each of them of making these ailments less frequent or severe. The costs of reducing emissions from smokestacks are incurred by several large industries, including coal mining and the railroads that carry coal, steel producers, and electric utilities. Most of these costs are passed on to customers in higher prices or are suffered by coal miners in lower employment. A drastic increase in the cost of using coal could reduce the general level of employment or, by increasing the use of imported oil, could adversely affect the balance of payments. The situation is made still more complicated because there are rules requiring scrubbing even when low-sulfur Western coal is burned. These rules were adopted to preserve employment for miners in Eastern areas producing high-sulfur coal.

In such a complex case, different analysts will emerge with widely different estimates of costs and benefits; the differences in the estimates are correlated with the missions of the organizations that perform or pay for the analysis.[1] Nevertheless, a careful attempt to quantify the costs and benefits sharpens and clarifies

1. Economic analysis of regulation often seems to conform to Rufus Miles's law of public administration, which is "Where you stand depends on where you sit."

the debate and provides a basis for the subsequent correction of errors.

Noneconomists often object to the use of benefit-cost ratios in cases involving loss of life on the grounds that life is priceless and its value cannot be quantified. This argument will not withstand careful examination. Both individually and collectively, we risk our lives every day, and our behavior reveals implicit prices. A rigorously enforced law requiring all occupants of cars to wear seat belts would save many lives, but Americans have judged that the costs in personal freedom would be excessive. (Some other countries have made the opposite judgment.) Many deaths from head-on collisions of motor vehicles could be prevented by having median strips or dividers on all highways, but the cost of doing so would be prohibitive. We therefore build median strips on only the most heavily traveled highways. In introducing regulations designed to reduce deaths and injuries from highway accidents, it makes obvious sense to take those measures first that have the lowest cost per death or injury prevented. Failing to take a measure that would save lives places an implicit value on human life that can be calculated, even though we may not like the result of the calculation.

It would be too much to expect public policy that regulates personal behavior to be completely logical. We now have strict laws prohibiting the use of artificial additives to food if they cause cancer in laboratory animals, even if only at very large dosages. We have only the mildest restrictions on the advertising of cigarettes, which are known to cause lung cancer in humans. This inconsistency may be explained by the economic losses to tobacco growers, cigarette manufacturers, advertising agencies, and publishers that would result from a ban on the sale of cigarettes. A less cynical explanation is that a ban would be unenforceable, like the prohibition of alcoholic beverages in the 1920s.

In 1981, the Supreme Court decided an important case involving the regulation of cotton dust in textile mills by the Occupational Safety and Health Administration (OSHA). Inhalation of cotton dust causes severe lung disease among textile workers. The court ruled that OSHA regulation of cotton dust did not have to meet the test of cost-benefit analysis, but could require any feasible measures to reduce dust regardless of cost. The decision turned, however, on the way in which Congress wrote the law creating OSHA. Congress remains free to require cost-benefit analysis in areas where it feels this is proper.

REGULATION, PRODUCTIVITY, AND INFLATION

The wave of new regulation that began in the 1960s is often considered to be one of the causes of the slowdown in productivity growth since that time. Careful estimates suggest that it did play a part, though not so large a one as to make it the principal cause of the problem.[2]

In a few industries, regulation has caused absolute declines in productivity. The most important of these is bituminous coal mining, where the strengthening of mine safety regulation coincided with a drop in output per hour worked.[3] A decline in productivity raises unit costs of production, and this usually causes a rise in the price of the product. The price of coal, however, would probably have risen even if costs had remained constant because of the sharp rise in the price of oil that began in 1973. This raised the demand for coal by inducing some oil users to convert to the less expensive fuel. If health and safety regulations had been the sole cause of a rise in coal prices, however, they could still be worth what they cost.

The example of mine safety can also be used to illustrate another aspect of benefit-cost analysis. An evaluation of mine safety regulation from the perspective of society as a whole might conclude that the benefits exceed the costs. The benefits of greater safety accrue in the first instance to one set of people—mineworkers and their families. The costs, however, are borne by other people—the owners of coal mines and of coal-using industries and the consumers of their products. The beneficiaries would favor regulation even if its overall benefit-cost ratio was adverse. By the same token, cost-bearers would oppose even those regulations whose overall benefit-cost ratio was favorable. The Congress, the administrative agencies, and the courts must act as the neutral arbiters of such disputes.

Regulation that raises the price of some products does not necessarily create a general inflationary process. If prices were

2. The best estimate is by Edward F. Denison in the *Survey of Current Business*, January 1978. He estimates that environmental and occupational health and safety regulation lowered productivity in the private nonfarm business sector by 0.2 percentage points per year for the period 1965–75. This is about 20 percent of the total decline in productivity growth between that period and the period 1948–65.

3. Output per labor hour in mining rose 4.3 percent a year in the period 1947–66 and fell 1.0 percent a year in the period 1966–77. Bituminous coal mining is by far the largest industry in this sector.

otherwise stable, new regulations would cause some one-time price increases, which might be offset by smaller but broader declines in prices elsewhere in the economy. This did not happen in the 1970s, when a sharp increase in social regulation coincided with a general inflationary process having more fundamental causes. The growth in regulation may have contributed to the difficulties of bringing this process under control.

OLD-STYLE REGULATION

Economic regulation of natural monopolies, such as the regulation of railroads by the Interstate Commerce Commission, was designed to reduce rates and increase output by preventing these natural monopolies from exploiting positions of economic power. In some industries, particularly the telephone and electric utility industries, the regulatory process worked reasonably well over long periods until the 1970s because technological progress reduced the costs of production faster than increases in labor and materials prices raised them. From time to time, the regulators would require rate reductions to eliminate excessive profits, but the delays inherent in the regulatory process permitted companies to earn a reasonable return on capital and to finance their expansion.

During the inflation of the 1970s, the cost of fuel and other inputs in the production process rose too fast to be offset by technological change. Telephone companies and electric utilities have therefore been compelled to file for frequent rate increases. When these are regularly denied, reduced, or long delayed, firms cannot earn an adequate return on investment, and service may deteriorate. Reluctance to raise rates or fares may be seen by regulators as a way to fight inflation or to promote more equal income distribution, though in the end, rate increases may be inevitable when costs rise.[4] Delay in providing new capacity can

---

4. Public officials often oppose utility rate increases in an effort to protect low-income consumers. For example, in August 1982, the attorney general of the state of New York in a statement to the Public Service Commission opposed a proposed increase in telephone rates, including a rise in pay phone rates from 10 cents to 25 cents a call, on the grounds that the poor could not afford home telephones and were dependent on pay phones.

The opposing argument would point out that if the rates for pay phones do not cover their costs, the telephone company will have no incentive to install and maintain them. There could then be a scarcity of operational pay phones, which would also adversely affect the poor.

eventually mean even higher prices than would have been needed if the investment had been made earlier.

Regulation of rates and entry has also been used in industries such as trucking and taxicabs where no firm has a natural monopoly. In such cases, the monopoly is actually created by the regulation itself, which prevents new firms from entering an industry where there are no natural barriers to entry. The effect is to reduce the amount of service, to raise rates, and to cause inefficiency. The beneficiaries of such regulation are the firms already licensed in the regulated industry and their employees; the losers include consumers and firms barred from entering. Such an outcome is particularly likely when the regulatory agency has been "captured" by the regulated industry. Presidents or governors often appoint former industry executives as members of regulatory commissions on the grounds that they are knowledgeable about the industry's problems and procedures. Such commissioners are often too sympathetic to the interests of existing firms and hostile to would-be entrants.

Old-style regulatory agencies have not confined themselves to regulating rates and entry. They have also made many wasteful rules governing the way in which service is provided. By requiring motor freight carriers to follow indirect routes between pairs of cities when they are not licensed to operate over the most direct route, the Interstate Commerce Commission has caused them to waste fuel. Civil Aeronautics Board regulations formerly required airlines that operated only large jet planes to provide scheduled service to small towns that did not generate nearly enough traffic to cover the costs of such service.

Regulation of railroads presents some special problems. For example, the Interstate Commerce Commission has been reluctant to permit the abandonment of branch lines whose revenues did not cover operating costs.[5] These losses had to be passed on in higher rates to shippers on more profitable lines. In several cases, failure to permit timely abandonment of low-traffic lines has contributed to the bankruptcy of large railroads.

Late in the 1970s, a process of dismantling some old-style federal regulation was begun, which has proceeded furthest in

---

5. The word "operating" is significant here. A line should not be abandoned because it fails to earn a return on invested capital. The capital costs are already "sunk" or committed, and cannot be recovered (apart from salvage value) whether or not the line operates.

airlines. Although the results of this experiment have been obscured by the sharp rise in fuel prices that began at the same time, it has apparently resulted in lower fares on the most heavily traveled long-distance routes. Small towns have lost service from major airlines, which has usually been replaced by service from companies using smaller aircraft and flying more frequent schedules. Some major airlines have done well financially under deregulation, while others that expanded too rapidly have had severe financial difficulties.[6] A number of new firms have entered markets serving major cities by offering low-cost service.

Most economists feel that the airline experiment bears out their expectation that eliminating old-style regulation increases output and lowers prices. They would expect similar results in railroads and trucking.[7]

OTHER STATE AND LOCAL REGULATION

Transportation, communication, and other public utilities are not the only regulated industries, though they are the most thoroughly studied. States and municipalities regulate or license a wide variety of other businesses and occupations, from taxicabs to bars and from medical doctors to street vendors. Such regulation was originally designed to protect the health and safety of the consumer. Most people would agree that the practice of medicine or dentistry should be restricted to doctors and dentists with proper qualifications. Where licensing or other regulation is too restrictive, however, it serves largely to protect existing businesses or practitioners and to raise prices. For example, when a state refuses to grant reciprocity to practitioners licensed in other states, it restricts geographic mobility and raises the income of its own practitioners. It seems unreasonable that in 1969 New Hampshire would only recognize dental licenses issued by itself and by Alaska. It has been estimated that having unlimited reciprocity among states in licensing dentists would raise the number of dentists in some states by as much as 25 percent.[8]

6. Braniff Airlines went bankrupt and suspended service in 1982.

7. The deregulation of airlines began after President Carter appointed two economists, Alfred Kahn and Elizabeth Bailey, as members of the Civil Aeronautics Board.

8. See Brian Boulier's paper in Simon Rottenberg, ed., *Occupational Licensure and Regulation* (Washington: American Enterprise Institute, 1980).

The resale at high prices of licenses to do business is also evidence of overly restrictive licensing. In New York City, a medallion entitling the owner to operate a taxicab is reported in newspaper stories to be worth as much as $60,000. Issuing more medallions would make more taxicabs available to the public and would provide employment to more drivers, although it would obviously lower the value of existing medallions and the earnings of the drivers already employed. It could also be argued that increasing the number of taxicabs would add to congestion in the streets, but much of the congestion is caused by other kinds of vehicles.

Although each such case must be considered on its merits, many states and municipalities seem to have pursued licensing and regulation further than health and safety require. This seems particularly true where licensing laws impose restrictions on citizenship, literacy, and residence that are not relevant to competence in the occupations being licensed.

GOVERNMENT OWNERSHIP

Other industrial countries take a different approach to the control of natural monopolies than the United States does. In most of them, telephone companies, electric utilities, railroads, and airlines are government owned.

The United States has the least government ownership of industry of any major industrial country. The Post Office, government-owned since the beginning of the republic, has a legal monopoly in the delivery of first-class mail. It is rapidly losing ground in package delivery to such private companies as United Parcel Service and Federal Express.

During the 1930s, the federal government constructed a number of large hydroelectric power plants, especially in the Columbia River Basin and the Tennessee Valley. Many of these also provided flood control and irrigation. The Tennessee Valley Authority has expanded into the generation of power from coal and atomic energy and has become a federally owned regional electric utility system. The federal power projects were supposed to be yardsticks by which to measure the performance of privately owned utilities. To the extent that they exploit unique sources of low-cost power or have access to low-cost federal capital, however, they are not well suited to this purpose.

Most recent federal ventures into public ownership have been undertaken to rescue regulated private utilities that were no longer viable, in part because of bad regulatory policy. These include the national rail passenger service (Amtrak) and the freight railroad system of the Northeast (Conrail). In creating these new federal enterprises, Congress was concerned with preserving jobs and wages as well as with maintaining essential services, and it saddled its new public corporations with commitments to high labor costs.

For the same reason that the federal government entered the rail passenger business, state and local governments now operate or subsidize most commuter rail lines and local mass transit systems. Local mass transit also receives capital and operating subsidies from the federal government.

There is no one clear answer to whether government ownership best serves the goals of economic efficiency and maintaining reasonable rates. The privately owned American telephone system is the envy of the rest of the world, providing better service than publicly owned telephone systems in many other countries that have underinvested in facilities and equipment. American airline service is both cheaper and more extensive than European airline service provided largely by state owned monopoly carriers. Rail passenger service, however, is far better in Japan and Europe than in the United States, where it was provided until recently by regulated private enterprise. The good rail passenger service of other countries is often heavily subsidized. Finally, one might note that some state-owned electric utilities such as Electricité de France provide service that is more efficient than that of many private regulated companies in the United States.

Whatever the result of such comparisons, it seems clear that in the United States, nationalization is not considered a usable tool of economic policy. It is a last resort in maintaining essential services, and is preferably enacted as a temporary measure in the hope that private ownership can be restored.

* TWELVE *
Trade Policy

COUNTRIES USE several policy instruments to control the flow of international trade, including taxes on imports and exports, quotas and other quantitative restrictions, and government lending on favorable terms to finance exports. Of these instruments, all but export taxes are used by the United States. The levying of export taxes is prohibited by article 1, section 9 of the Constitution.

Before 1971, under the gold exchange standard, a principal role of trade policy was to prevent an adverse balance of payments. Now this function is largely performed by monetary policy operating through the exchange rate. The most important remaining goals of trade policy are to increase exports and to protect domestic industry from import competition. Achieving these proximate goals promotes high employment in the United States at the cost of higher domestic prices.

TARIFFS

Before there was an income tax, import duties or tariffs were a major source of revenue for the federal government. Tariffs designed to raise revenue should be reasonably low, so that foreign goods can enter the country despite the tariff and pay duties. Today, tariffs are an insignificant source of federal revenue, and the main purpose of tariffs is to protect domestic industry against import competition.[1] For this reason, most goods not produced in the United States, such as coffee, bananas, and cocoa, enter without paying any tariff.

A protective tariff, as opposed to a revenue tariff, may be levied at a high rate and protects domestic industry best when it is so high that no foreign goods subject to the tariff are imported. It is clear that high tariffs have opposite effects on the interests of American producers and American consumers. For example, Wisconsin cheese producers are helped by the tariff on Dutch

---

1. In fiscal year 1982, receipts from customs duties provided $8.9 billion of total federal budget receipts of $618 billion.

and Swiss cheese, which makes imported cheese more expensive than domestic. Consumers are hurt because domestic producers of some kinds of cheese cannot match European quality, and because the tariff not only raises the price of imports, but permits domestic producers to raise their prices as well.

In recent years, the countries of the world have engaged in major international negotiations to reduce tariffs, conducted through GATT (the General Agreement on Tariffs and Trade), an agency of the United Nations. The resulting agreements have tended to reduce most American tariffs to relatively modest rates. New barriers to trade, however, have appeared in their place.

QUOTAS

Quotas and other quantitative restrictions on imports restrain international trade more directly than tariffs and may have even larger effects in raising domestic prices. If Japanese cars enter the United States in large numbers despite tariffs, the direct approach to the problem is to put a limit on the number of cars that may be imported. An efficient foreign producer can capture an entire American market despite a tariff if his costs are low enough, but no matter how low his costs, he cannot escape a quota.

The United States has preferred not to legislate import quotas on manufactured goods. It has accomplished the same purpose indirectly by persuading foreign countries to set quantitative limits on their exports, often with an implicit threat to impose import quotas if they do not.[2] This method has restricted imports of cars from Japan and of shoes, clothing, and textiles from several Far Eastern countries. Direct American quotas have been used to limit imports of meat from such countries as Australia, New Zealand, and Argentina.

Another long-standing legislated restriction on trade (the Jones Act) provides that only American owned-, American-built ships with American crews can transport goods between American ports. This gives the high-cost domestic maritime industry a monopoly on coastal shipping and shipping between the contiguous forty-eight states and Alaska, Hawaii, and Puerto Rico.

---

2. Such negotiations are conducted by the executive branch. The threat generally takes the form of saying that the president cannot restrain Congress from imposing quotas if the negotiations are fruitless.

Of course, our foreign trading partners also use quotas and other trade restrictions to keep American goods out of their markets. For example, American producers of cigarettes, citrus fruits, and beef complain that they are denied fair access to the Japanese market. Often, health and safety regulations can be written so as to favor domestic products over imports and thus act as a nontariff barrier to trade.

THE POLITICS OF TRADE POLICY

Trade policy not only divides producer from consumer interests, it also divides producers according to what they produce. The producers of such export products as cotton, tobacco, wheat, coal, computers, and aircraft oppose high tariffs and import quotas on other products because they want the countries to whom they sell to be able to earn dollars with which to buy American exports. Producers of products that compete with imports naturally take the opposite view.

As more and more American industries have experienced severe import competition, the desire for protectionism has grown. The shift of the trade in automobiles and steel from net exports before World War II to substantial net imports in recent years has been an important factor in the change in sentiment. In particular, the stance of organized labor, which once generally favored free trade, has become one of strong protectionism.

Most professional economists have argued for free trade since Adam Smith wrote *The Wealth of Nations* in 1776; that is, since anyone could be called a professional economist. They point out that international trade does more than provide us with goods like bananas and coffee that cannot be produced at home. It provides greater variety, higher quality, and lower prices in other goods because it permits each country to specialize in doing the things it does best. To the protectionist argument that imports destroy American jobs, the economists reply that foreign countries as a group must eventually use most of the dollars they earn through trade to buy other American goods, creating jobs in our export industries.

This eventual job creation is small comfort to the Detroit auto worker displaced by imports of Toyotas or Datsuns who does not have the skills or the inclination to become a coal miner or a wheat farmer. To help such people, Congress has provided for adjustment assistance, which gives cash compensation and training to

97

workers displaced by imports. The program has become an expensive one, and the agency administering it (the Department of Labor) has found it difficult to determine why particular workers are unemployed. Did they lose their jobs because of import competition, a recession, or a change in consumer tastes away from the products they make? Different analysts will interpret the evidence differently.

Professional economists have had less influence on trade policy than on most other areas of economic policy, despite the substantial unanimity of their views. Their advice is often disregarded because of the strength of the political forces mobilized to protect existing American jobs against foreign competition.

Trade policy can also become entangled with broader objectives of foreign policy. President Carter embargoed shipments of grain to the Soviet Union to protest the Soviet invasion of Afghanistan, and President Reagan has embargoed some industrial shipments to the Soviet Union to protest martial law in Poland. Trade policy thus involves a complicated mixture of economic policy objectives, domestic politics, and global politics.

III
The Policymaking Process

*

* THIRTEEN *
Institutional Arrangements

FEDERAL ECONOMIC POLICY is made by the executive branch, by the Congress, and by independent agencies. It involves extensive and complex interaction between these branches of government. We begin by examining the process within the executive branch.

THE EXECUTIVE BRANCH

Coordination of the economic policy of the executive branch is centered in the executive office of the president. Much of it focuses on three messages the president sends to Congress each January: the State of the Union Message, the Budget, and the Economic Report of the President. The first of these need not deal with economic policy, although it often does; the other two invariably do. Economic policies are coordinated by the staff of the White House itself, by the Office of Management and Budget, which prepares the budget, and by the Council of Economic Advisers, which prepares the economic report.

The Council of Economic Advisers, created by the Employment Act of 1946, consists of three members, including the chairman, appointed by the president and confirmed by the Senate. The members have usually been distinguished professional economists. Many have come from universities (for example, Arthur F. Burns from Columbia, James Tobin from Yale, and Walter W. Heller from Minnesota). Others have come from private business (Alan Greenspan), the Federal Reserve system (Lyle Gramley), or independent research organizations (Charles Schultze). The chairman is the key member, because he has the most access to the president. The members are supported by a small professional staff consisting of economists and statisticians and including both macroeconomists and specialists in such fields of applied economics as labor economics and industrial organization.

The only statutory duty of the council is to assist the president in preparing his economic report, which outlines in considerable detail the state of the economy and the administration's plans for economic policy. The council also provides frequent day-to-day advice to the president on a wide variety of economic policy matters, including tax policy, pending economic legislation, and proposed regulations of other government agencies.

The president also receives advice regularly on these matters from many other agencies of the executive branch. Most of these agencies, unlike the Council of Economic Advisers, have direct responsibility for administering various programs and laws. They have larger staffs than the council and greater expertise about the particular issues that most concern them. The council's advantage in the policy process is its strategic location within the executive office and its less parochial view. The council is seen by the president as representing the general interest, whereas other agencies may be seen as having interests related to their own special programs and their particular constituencies. The council has been more influential in some administrations than in others; variations in its influence depend largely on the strength and closeness of the personal rapport between a particular president and a particular chairman of the council and, to some degree, on the prestige of the chairman.[1] Some presidents have also used economists as senior presidential assistants on the staff of the White House itself. In such cases, the White House staff member has usually specialized in the most political aspects of economic policy and in tactics rather than strategy.

As mentioned above, the Office of Management and Budget (formerly the Bureau of the Budget) has as its principal responsibility the preparation of the budget. Its staff includes some economists, but many more budget examiners who review in detail the spending proposals of every federal agency. The budget submitted to Congress each January includes proposed outlays and forecasted receipts for the fiscal year beginning 1 October of that calendar year. These are prepared on the assumption that Congress will accept all of the president's proposals for expenditures and for changes in taxes. The budget must also forecast the state of the economy during the forthcoming fiscal year in order to translate any set of proposed taxes and expenditure authorizations into projected total revenues and outlays. A forecast of rapid growth or high inflation will increase revenues from a given set of tax laws. A forecast of recession will raise total expenditures under many kinds of given expenditure programs and will reduce receipts from a given set of taxes. Not surprisingly, the

1. For a number of interesting case studies relating in detail the role of the Council of Economic Advisers during the Carter administration in shaping administration positions on regulation, see Lawrence J. White, *Reforming Regulation: Processes and Problems* (Englewood Cliffs, N.J.: Prentice-Hall, 1981).

economic forecasts underlying the budget often seem to outsiders to have an optimistic bias.

The amounts by which differences in economic assumptions can affect budget estimates is startling. In the fall of 1982, the Congressional Budget Office estimated that a one percentage point drop in the annual rate of real growth beginning in January 1983 would lower revenues for fiscal 1984 by $23 billion, raise expenditures by $5 billion, and thus raise the deficit by $28 billion. Similarly, a one percentage point rise in the unemployment rate would lower revenues by $29 billion, raise expenditures by $10 billion, and thus raise the deficit by $39 billion. A one percentage point increase in the rate of inflation, however, would raise revenues for fiscal 1984 by $15 billion, raise outlays by $1 billion, and reduce the deficit by $14 billion.[2]

The Treasury's most important role in economic policy is to propose detailed changes in the tax law and to estimate how proposed changes will affect tax receipts. This work engages both economists and lawyers. The Treasury also has particular responsibility for debt management and the monetary aspects of international economic policy.

The various agencies within the executive branch involved in making economic policy must have ways of exchanging information and coordinating views. For many years, there have been regular meetings on economic policy between the secretary of the treasury, the chairman of the Council of Economic Advisers, and the director of the Office of Management and Budget (the troika), joined on occasion by the chairman of the Board of Governors of the Federal Reserve system. Members of the staff of these agencies also work together on a regular basis preparing materials for their joint use, including economic forecasts.

Some administrations have set up special bodies within the White House to coordinate economic policy. For example, the Ford administration had an Economic Policy Board, chaired by the secretary of the treasury, which met several times a week to discuss current economic policy issues. The Council of Economic Advisers, the Office of Management and Budget, and several cabinet departments in addition to the Treasury were represented. The views of the board were reported to the president through position papers and by its chairman. Other administra-

2. Congressional Budget Office, *The Economic and Budget Outlook: An Update* (September 1982), table B-1, p. 89.

tions have had similar, though sometimes less formal, arrangements for this purpose.

It should not be imagined that these bodies are decision-making bodies. In the last analysis, important policy decisions in the executive branch are made by the president. For example, the secretary of agriculture might propose to raise the level of price supports on dairy products, using discretionary authority given him by law. The other agencies notified of this intention might object that the proposed increase in price supports would be inflationary and urge the president to disapprove it. They could join in submitting a memorandum or position paper advocating this view to the president, who might nevertheless approve the proposed action, either because the Department of Agriculture successfully refuted some of the arguments advanced by other agencies or because the political considerations in the decision outweighed the economic ones.

The president's economic advisers may differ in their analyses of a problem or in their philosophical bents in ways unrelated to the positions they occupy in his administration. During the fall of 1974, when the economy was slipping into recession while the rate of inflation was still high, President Ford's economic advisers were divided on whether to recommend a tax cut. The most conservative of them argued against a tax cut because they felt that inflation was the more serious problem. The more liberal or more pragmatic favored a modest tax cut to help alleviate the recession. In such situations the president, of course, has the casting vote. In December, President Ford decided to recommend a tax cut, and early in 1975 Congress enacted a cut slightly larger than the one he had recommended.

It is also possible for a president to make economic policy without consulting his usual advisers. President Ford's ill-fated WIN program (an acronym for Whip Inflation Now) resulted from a suggestion by a newspaper columnist. It relied on exhortation to persuade consumers to reduce their expenditures. Similarly, the Ford administration became committed to persuading three major steel companies to roll back part of a steel price increase in December 1974 when the president in response to a question at a press conference said that he thought the price increase was excessive.

Since 1974, the executive office of the president has also been involved in reviewing regulations issued by regulatory agencies within cabinet departments (for example, the Environmental

Protection Agency or the National Highway Traffice Safety Administration) to make certain that the benefits from these regulations exceed their costs. Originally, this task was divided between the Council on Wage and Price Stability, the Council of Economic Advisers, and the Office of Management and Budget, with the first of these agencies having the largest professional staff. When the Council on Wage and Price Stability was abolished in 1981, this staff moved to the Office of Management and Budget, which is now the key agency in regulatory review. The review process sometimes persuades a regulatory agency to withdraw or modify a costly regulation; on other occasions the agency may successfully appeal to the president to let it ignore an adverse review.

THE CONGRESS

Many committees of the Congress are involved in different aspects of economic policy. The Joint Economic Committee consists of members of both the Senate and the House of Representatives, with the chairmanship alternating between the two houses. It holds hearings on the Economic Report of the President and prepares its own report commenting on the economic policies the president proposes. This report usually consists of separate majority and minority views.

Because it draws members from both houses of Congress, the Joint Economic Committee cannot report bills to either house. In this sense, it has a less direct role in framing economic legislation than many other committees. Nevertheless, ideas advanced first in the Joint Economic Committee may become the basis of bills referred to other committees.

Each house has a budget committee, and the Congress as a whole is served by the Congressional Budget Office. This office assists the Congress in reviewing the budget submitted by the president and makes its own analyses of general economic trends and of specific economic policy issues. These set forth the results of alternative policies without advocating policy positions.

The two budget committees and the Congressional Budget Office help Congress frame the budget resolutions in which it sets the overall expenditure and revenue targets to which detailed appropriations and tax legislation are required to conform. By law, the first budget resolution should be passed in the spring, the second in the fall. The budgets embodied in these resolutions may differ substantially from the president's budget, both because the economic climate has changed in the intervening period and because the Congress may not accept some of the president's proposals.

The first budget resolution now becomes the framework for all specific appropriation and revenue measures. It sets goals for total budget authority and outlays and specifies authority and outlay limits for each budget function (such as national defense and agriculture) over a three-year period. The principal way of implementing these goals is the process known as "reconciliation," which consists of instructions requiring committees in each house to file legislation that would achieve specific dollar savings by spending cuts or tax increases. These are followed by a reconciliation act that incorporates the responses to the instructions and is passed on a tight schedule.[3]

Tax changes usually originate in the Ways and Means Committee of the House. If passed by the full House, they go to the Senate, where they are considered first by the Finance Committee. Appropriations are considered by several subcommittees in both houses, then brought to the full committees and the floor of both houses in a number of different appropriations bills.

Although the fiscal year now begins three months later than it did before 1977, Congress has experienced increasing difficulty in passing appropriations bills before the start of the new fiscal year. When it fails to do so, it passes continuing resolutions that permit government agencies to spend for a time at the rates authorized for the previous fiscal year.

Economic policy can also be affected by congressional actions originating outside the budgetary process—in the committees that deal with such fields as tariffs, labor legislation, banking, housing, and agriculture.

THE INDEPENDENT AGENCIES

Agencies such as the Interstate Commerce Commission and the Federal Trade Commission have commissioners chosen by the president to represent both major political parties and to serve for fixed terms. Since the commissioners do not serve at the pleasure of the president, they are not part of the executive

3. In 1982, the first budget resolution was passed on 23 June, with 4 to 6 weeks given for reconciliation. There was no second resolution, so that the first budget resolution automatically became the second on 1 October.

branch in the same sense as cabinet departments. For most purposes they are answerable directly to the Congress.

For economic policy as a whole, the Board of Governors of the Federal Reserve system is by far the most important of the independent agencies. The United States is unique among major industrial countries in having an independent central bank. In other countries, monetary policy, even on a day-to-day basis, is fully under the control of the government of the day. Governors of the Federal Reserve system serve for fixed terms of fourteen years and the Federal Reserve reports directly to the Congress on its past and proposed policies.

It is possible for the views of the Federal Reserve system and the administration to diverge, and this has sometimes occurred. For much of Carter's term, the administration seemed less concerned about the rate of monetary expansion and more concerned about high interest rates than the Federal Reserve was. Nevertheless, when President Carter last had occasion to appoint a chairman of the Board of Governors, he chose Paul Volcker, then president of the Federal Reserve Bank of New York, who has been an advocate of restrictive monetary policy. In making this choice, President Carter realized that choosing a supporter of low interest rates would have alarmed the international financial community and thus could have lowered the exchange value of the dollar. Similar expectations would also have had direct effects in domestic securities markets. For such reasons, the administration and the Federal Reserve must seek an accommodation of views in the face of initial differences.

THE PRESIDENT AND CONGRESS

As we have seen, the president's major economic proposals to Congress are outlined in the State of the Union Message, the Budget, or in special messages. The details will be introduced as bills by the ranking members of the president's party in the congressional committees to which they will be referred. Members of the administration, including cabinet officers, then testify in behalf of the proposals before these committees. In so doing, they are expected to testify as members of an administration team and have limited ability to state dissenting personal views. Both the White House and other agencies of the executive branch have legislative liaison staffs who work with members of Congress and their staffs in explaining the president's economic proposals and reporting back support, opposition, and suggestions for modification. On important issues, the president himself may invite members of Congress to the White House to explain his views, or he may appeal directly to the general public for support of his position. He can use the threat of a veto to help to block the passage of programs he opposes.

At the same time that the president's economic proposals are working their way through Congress, other bills are being introduced by the leadership of the other party and by individual members of both houses. Some of these will have the support of particular economic interest groups, representing labor, business, agriculture, or particular industries or localities. Members of the administration may be asked by congressional committees for their views on these, and the agency whose views are requested will consult other interested agencies through the Office of Management and Budget before responding.

If the Congress passes economic legislation that differs from the president's position, he must decide whether or not to veto it. In making this decision he solicits, through the Office of Management and Budget, the views of the agencies in the executive branch with an interest in the legislation. The number of these agencies is often far larger than one might imagine. The decision is especially difficult when Congress passes a bill with many features that the president supports and a few that he opposes.

The process of forming policy in economic matters is not fundamentally different from that in other areas of government. What distinguishes it, if anything, is the multiplicity of agencies and constituencies involved. To the extent that economic policy is seen as responding to rapid changes in economic conditions, such as a sharp rise in unemployment or in prices, the legislative process is not well suited to quick response. For this reason, it has sometimes been proposed that the president be given discretionary authority to raise or lower taxes within limits prescribed in advance by Congress. Congress, however, has never been willing to delegate the taxing power.

The advantage of monetary policy, in contrast to fiscal policy, in responding promptly to changes in economic conditions lies in the relative freedom of the Federal Reserve from legislative constraints. The Federal Reserve reports to Congress after the fact, whereas the president needs prior approval for most of his important actions.

* FOURTEEN *
The Politics of Economic Policy

ANY AMERICAN can testify to the importance of economic issues in political campaigns. Candidates for public office routinely deplore the mess that the incumbents and their predecessors have made of the economy and promise if elected to clean it up. They deplore high unemployment, rising prices, and government deficits and pledge themselves to put people back to work, lower the rate of inflation, and balance the budget. They attack the power of particular economic groups, such as oil companies or labor unions, that put selfish interests above the general interest, and they pledge to restore economic power to the ordinary working man or to the middle class. Particular economic policies, such as tax cuts, are proposed and explained.

Four years later, it is frequently the case that the economy is no better or that it is even worse. If a new administration has been in power during this period, its political opponents will remind the voters of the economic promises made in the last campaign and point out that many of them have not been kept.

It is impossible for the average voter to judge the merits of specific economic proposals. He takes economics into account in other ways. First, particular groups in the economy are predisposed to favor one or the other of the major parties. In particular, blue-collar workers tend to favor Democrats, while managers and businessmen tend to favor Republicans. Second, dissatisfaction with economic conditions induces some members of all economic groups to vote against incumbents.

A cynical view of this process might perceive the candidates as deliberately misleading the voters, promising to lower unemployment or halt inflation while knowing that they lack the power to do so. Such a view would be too harsh. A major party candidate running against an incumbent president has well-qualified economic advisers during his campaign, who point out the mistakes in policy made by the present administration and suggest how in their judgment economic policy could be improved. These advisers would continue to advise the candidate if he were elected, either as members of his administration or as informal outside advisers. It is easy for a candidate with confidence in himself and his advisers to feel in all honesty that he could do much better than the incumbent has done.

The hopes of many new presidents for their economic policies have nevertheless been disappointed. Presidents who promised as candidates to reduce unemployment and inflation have seen them rise during their terms in office, and presidents who promised to balance the budget have experienced rising deficits. Why have their hopes been disappointed?

The first reason is that presidents have limited power to make economic policy. The programs they propose to the Congress may not be enacted or may be so modified that they do not meet their original goals. Monetary policy, controlled by the independent Federal Reserve system, may not follow the course the president prefers. Nevertheless, two presidents in the past fifty years have had great success in getting Congress to pass their economic proposals: Franklin D. Roosevelt and Ronald Reagan. Both took office in a time of deep economic trouble—Roosevelt during the Great Depression and Reagan at a time of rapid inflation. Both had unusual skills in presenting their programs to the public, and both swept into office with them large numbers of congressmen who shared their views.

A second cause of failure of economic policy is simply bad luck. Crops may fail, the costs of some imported raw materials may skyrocket, the country may become engaged in a costly military conflict in a remote place like Korea or Vietnam. Economic policies not designed to meet such contingencies are seldom modified enough to take them into account.

Some economic policies fail because they are not sound. For example, in the summer of 1973, the Nixon administration controlled the prices of raw agricultural products, a policy that was quickly reversed after it caused severe shortages of meat. It is generally believed that President Nixon adopted this policy against the advice of the senior economists in his own administration because his political advisers, seeking a quick cure for inflation, urged it on him.

The most important reason of all why policies fail is that economic policy has less force than both economists and politicians like to believe. A tax cut or a reduction in expenditures of $50 billion a year is very large by historical standards. It takes Congress many months, sometimes years, of arduous discussion and debate to make changes of this size. Yet the Gross National Product in 1982 was over $3 trillion, and $50 billion is less than 2 percent of that amount. Such a large economy has a great deal of momentum and does not respond quickly to small changes in course. To change policy even more drastically, however, might have substantial unintended effects on the particular parts of the economy where the initial impact of changes is felt most directly.

It would be good for America if proponents of economic policy of all varieties were more modest in their claims. Making economic policy is more of an art than a science. Despite the use of elaborate econometric models to predict the effects of policy changes, much still depends on fallible judgment. Even when the main effects of a new policy are correctly predicted, it usually has unanticipated and often adverse side effects, sometimes of greater importance than the intended main effect.

This is not the stuff of which campaign speeches or presidential addresses are made. One does not win applause or votes by hedging one's promises with qualifications. It would nevertheless be refreshing to hear more candidates and statesmen talk of making modest progress toward long-run economic goals rather than of performing miracles and reaching all our cherished goals simultaneously within four years.

Index

113